**Praise for *New York Times* bestselling author
Heather Graham**

"Graham is the queen of romantic suspense."
—*RT Book Reviews*

"An incredible storyteller."
—*Los Angeles Daily News*

"Intricate, fast-paced, and intense, this riveting
thriller blends romance and suspense in perfect
combination and keeps readers guessing and the
tension taut until the very end."
—*Library Journal* on *Flawless*

**Praise for *New York Times* bestselling author
B.J. Daniels**

"*Cowboy Accomplice*…is a masterful blend of humor
and suspense."
—*RT Book Reviews*

"B.J. Daniels is a sharpshooter; her books hit the
target every time."
—#1 *New York Times* bestselling author
Linda Lael Miller

New York Times and *USA TODAY* bestselling author **Heather Graham** has written more than two hundred novels. She is pleased to have been published in over twenty-five languages, with sixty million books in print. Heather is a proud recipient of the Silver Bullet from Thriller Writers and was awarded the prestigious Thriller Master Award in 2016. She is also a recipient of Lifetime Achievement Awards from RWA and *The Strand*, and is the founder of The Slush Pile Players, an author band and theatrical group. An avid scuba diver, ballroom dancer and mother of five, she still enjoys her South Florida home, but also loves to travel. Heather is grateful every day for a career she loves so very much. For more information, check out her website, theoriginalheathergraham.com, or find Heather on Facebook.

New York Times and *USA TODAY* bestselling author **B.J. Daniels** lives in Montana with her husband, Parker, and three springer spaniels. When not writing, she quilts, boats and plays tennis. Contact her at bjdaniels.com, or on Facebook or Twitter @bjdanielsauthor.

New York Times Bestselling Author

HEATHER GRAHAM

UNDERCOVER CONNECTION

**HARLEQUIN
BESTSELLING
AUTHOR
COLLECTION**

**HARLEQUIN®
BESTSELLING
AUTHOR
COLLECTION**

Recycling programs
for this product may
not exist in your area.

ISBN-13: 978-1-335-49839-7

Undercover Connection
First published in 2018. This edition published in 2023.
Copyright © 2018 by Heather Graham Pozzessere

Cowboy Accomplice
First published in 2004. This edition published in 2023.
Copyright © 2004 by Barbara Heinlein

For questions and comments about the quality of this book,
please contact us at CustomerService@Harlequin.com.

Harlequin Enterprises ULC
22 Adelaide St. West, 41st Floor
Toronto, Ontario M5H 4E3, Canada
www.Harlequin.com

Printed in U.S.A.

CONTENTS

Also by Heather Graham

MIRA

Krewe of Hunters

Dreaming Death
Deadly Touch
Seeing Darkness
The Stalking
The Seekers
The Summoning
Echoes of Evil
Pale as Death
Fade to Black
Wicked Deeds

Harlequin Intrigue

Undercover Connection
Out of the Darkness
Shadows in the Night
Law and Disorder
Tangled Threat

Visit her Author Profile page at Harlequin.com,
or theoriginalheathergraham.com, for more titles!

UNDERCOVER CONNECTION

Heather Graham

For Lorna Broussard—with love and thanks
for all the help and support for...well, many years!

Chapter One

The woman on the runway was truly one of the most stunning creatures Jacob Wolff had ever seen. Her skin was pure bronze, as sleek and as dazzling as the deepest sun ray.

When she turned, he could see—even from his distance at the club's bar—that her eyes were light. Green, he thought, and a sharp contrast to her skin. She had amazing hair, long and so shimmering that it was as close to pure black as it was possible to be; so dark it almost had a gleam of violet. She was long-legged, lean and yet exquisitely shaped as she moved in the creation she modeled—a mix of pastel colors that was perfectly enhanced by her skin—the dress was bare at the shoulder and throat with a plunging neckline, and back, and then swept to the floor.

She moved like a woman accustomed to such a haughty strut: proud, confident, arrogant and perhaps even amused by the awe of the onlookers.

"That one—she will rule the place one day."

Jacob turned.

Ivan Petrov leaned on one elbow across the bar from Jacob. Ivan bartended and—so Jacob believed thus far—ran all things that had to do with the on-the-ground-management of the Gold Sun Club. The burning-hot new establishment was having its grand opening tonight.

"I'd imagine," Jacob said. He leaned closer over the bar and smiled. "And I imagine that she might perhaps be…available?"

Ivan smiled, clearly glad that Jacob had asked him; Ivan was a proud man, appreciative that Jacob had noted his position of power within the club.

"Not…immediately," Ivan said. "She is fairly new. But all things come in good time, my friend, eh? Now you," he said, pouring a shot of vodka for Jacob, "you are fairly new, too. New to Miami Beach—new to our ways. We have our…social…rules, you know."

Jacob knew all too well.

And he knew what happened to those who didn't follow the rules—or who dared to make their own. He'd been south of I-75 that morning, off part of the highway still known as Alligator Alley, and for good reason. He'd been deep in the Everglades where a Seminole ranger had recently discovered a bizarre cache of oil drums, inside of which had been several bodies in various stages of decomposition.

"I have my reputation," Jacob said softly.

Ivan caught Jacob's meaning. Yes, Jacob would follow the rules. But he was his own man—very much a *made* man from the underbelly of New York City. Now, he'd bought a gallery on South Beach; but he'd been doing his other business for years.

At least, that was the information that had been fed to what had become known as the Deco Gang—so called because of the beautifully preserved architecture on South Beach.

Jacob was for all intents and purposes a new major player in the area. And it was important, of course, that he appear to be a team player—but a very powerful team player who respected another man's turf while also keeping a strict hold on his own.

"A man's reputation must be upheld," Ivan said, nodding approvingly.

"While, of course, he gives heed to all that belongs to another man, as well," Jacob assured him.

A loud clash of drums drew Jacob's attention for a moment. The Dissidents were playing that night; they were supposedly one of the hottest up-and-coming bands, not just in the state, but worldwide.

The grand opening to the Gold Sun Club had been invitation only; tomorrow night, others would flow in, awed by the publicity generated by this celebrity-studded evening. The rich and the beautiful—and the not-so-rich but very beautiful—were all on the ground floor, listening to the popular new band and watching the fashion show.

Jacob took in the place as a whole, noting a balcony level that ran the perimeter, with a bar above the stage. But that night all the guests were downstairs, and Ivan Petrov was manning the main bar himself.

The elegant model on the runway swirled with perfect timing, walking toward the crowd again, pausing to seductively steal a delicious-looking apple from the hands of a pretty boy—a young male model, dressed as Adonis—standing like a statue at the bottom of the steps to the runway.

"I believe," Jacob told Ivan, turning to look at him gravely again, "that my business will be an asset to your business, and that we will work in perfect harmony together."

"Yes," Ivan said. "Mr. Smirnoff invited you, right?"

Jacob nodded. "Josef brought me in."

Ivan said, "He is an important man."

"Yes, I know," Jacob assured him.

If Ivan only knew how.

JASMINE ADAIR—JASMINE ALAMEIN, as far as this group was concerned—was glad that she had managed to learn the art of walking a runway, without tripping, and observing at the same time. It wasn't as if she'd had training or gone to cotillion classes—did they still have cotillion classes?—but she'd been graced with the most wonderful parents in the world.

Her mother had been with the Peace Corps—maybe a natural course for her, having somewhat global roots. Her mom's parents had come from Jordan and Kenya, met and married in Morocco and moved to the United States. Jasmine's mom, Liliana, had been born and grown up in Miami, but had traveled the world to help people before she'd finally settled down. Liliana had been a great mom, always all about kindness to others and passionate that everyone must be careful with others. She had believed that words could make or break a person's day, and truly *seeing* people was one of the most important talents anyone could have in life.

Declan Adair, Jasmine's dad, was mostly Irish-American. He'd been a cop and had taught Jasmine what that meant to him—serving his community.

They had both taught her about absolute equality for every color, race, creed, sex and sexual orientation, and they had both taught her that good people were good people and, all in all, most of the people in the world were good, longing for the same things, especially in America—life, liberty and the pursuit of happiness.

They sounded like a sweet pair of hippies; they had been anything but. Her father had also taught her that those who appeared to be the nicest people in the world often were not—and that lip service didn't mean a hell of a lot and could hide an ocean of lies and misdeeds.

"Judging people—hardest call you'll ever make," he'd told her once. "Especially when you have to do so quickly."

He'd shaken his head in disgust over the result of a trial often enough, and her mother had always reminded him, "There are things that just aren't allowed before a jury, Declan. Things that the jury just doesn't see and doesn't know."

"Not to worry—we'll get them next time," he would assure her.

Jasmine scanned the crowd. Members of this group, the so-called Deco Gang, hadn't been gotten yet. And they needed to be—no one really knew the full extent of their crimes because they were good. Damned good at knowing how to game the justice system.

Fanatics came in all kinds—and fanatics were dangerous. Just as criminals came in all kinds, and they ruined the lives of those who wanted to live in peace, raising their children, working…enjoying their liberty and pursuing their happiness.

That's why cops were so important—something she had learned when sometimes her dad, the detective, hadn't made it to a birthday party.

Because of him, she'd always wanted to be a cop.

And she was a damned good one, if she did say so herself.

At the moment, it was her mother's training that was paying off. As a child, Jasmine had accompanied her mom to all kinds of fund-raisers—and once she was a teenager, she'd started modeling at fashion shows in order to attract large donations for her mom's various charities. She had worked with a few top designers who were equally passionate about feeding children or raising awareness when natural disasters devastated various regions in the States and around the world.

So as Jasmine strutted and played it up for the audience, she also watched.

The event had attracted the who's who of the city. She could see two television stars who were acting in current hit series. Alphonse Mangiulli—renowned Italian artist—was there, along with Cam Li, the Chinese businessman who had just built two of the largest hotels in the world, one in Dubai and one on Miami Beach. Mathilda Glen—old, old Miami society and money— had made it, along with the famed English film director, Eric Summer.

And amid this gathering of the rich and famous was also a meeting of the loosely organized group of South Beach criminals that the Miami-Dade police called the Deco Gang.

They had come together under the control of a Russian-born kingpin, Josef Smirnoff, and they were an equal-opportunity group of very dangerous criminals. They weren't connected to the Italian Mafia or Cosa Nostra, and they weren't the Asian mob or a cartel from any South American or island country. And they were hard to pin down, using legitimate business for money laundering and for their forays into drug smuggling and dealing and prostitution.

Crimes had been committed; the bodies of victims had been found, but for the most part, those who got in the way of the gang were eliminated. Because of their connections with one another, alibis were abundant, evidence disappeared, and pinning anything on any one individual had been an elusive goal for the police.

Jasmine had used every favor she had saved up to get assigned to this case. It helped that her looks gave her a good cover for infiltration.

Her captain—Mac Lorenzo—probably suspected that she had her own motives. But he didn't ask, and she didn't tell. She hadn't let Lorenzo know that her personal determination to bring down the Deco Gang had begun when Mary Ahearn had disappeared. Her old friend had vanished without a trace after working with a nightclub that was most probably a front for a very high-scale prostitution ring.

She could see Josef Smirnoff in the front of the crowd; he was smiling and looking right at her. He seemed to like what he saw. Good. He was the man in charge, and she needed access to him. She needed to be able to count his bodyguards and his henchmen and get close to him.

She wasn't working alone; Jasmine was blessed with an incredible partner, Jorge Fuentes.

Along with being a dedicated cop, Jorge was also extremely good-looking, and thanks to that, he'd been given leeway when he'd shown up at the Gold Sun Club, supposedly looking for work. Jasmine had told Natasha Volkov—manager of the models who worked these events or sat about various places looking pretty—that she'd worked with Jorge before and that he was wonderfully easygoing. Turned out the show was short a man; Jorge had been hired on for the day easily. They'd cast him as Adonis and given him a very small costume to wear.

Jorge had been trying to get a moment alone with her as preparations for the fashion show had gone on. Jasmine had been undercover for several weeks prior to the club's opening night, and briefings had been few and far between. The opportunity hadn't arisen as yet, but they'd be able to connect—as soon as the runway show part of the party was over. She was curious what updates Jorge had, but they were both savvy enough to bide their time. Neither of them dared to blow their covers with this group—such a mistake could result in instant death, with neither of them even aware or able to help the other in any way.

Her cover story was complete. She had a rented room on Miami Beach, which she took for a week before answering the ad for models. She'd been given an effective fake résumé—one that showed she'd worked but never been on the top. And might well be hungry to get there.

After a lightning-quick change of clothes backstage, she made another sweep down the runway. She noted the celebrities in attendance. South Beach clubs were like rolls of toilet paper—people used them up and discarded them without a thought. What was popular today might be deserted within a month.

But she didn't think that this enterprise would care—the showy opening was just another front for the illegal activities that kept them going.

She noted the men and women surrounding Josef Smirnoff. He was about six feet tall, big and solidly muscled. His head was immaculately bald, which made his sharp jaw even more prominent and his dark eyes stand out.

On his arm was an up-and-coming young starlet. She was in from California, a lovely blue-eyed blonde, clearly hoping that Smirnoff's connections here would allow her to rub elbows with the right people.

Jasmine hoped that worked out for her—and that she didn't become involved with the wrong people.

Natasha was with him, as well. She had modeled in her own youth, in Europe. About five-eleven and in her midfifties, Natasha had come up through the ranks. One of the girls had whispered to Jasmine that Natasha had always been smart—she had managed to sleep her way up with the right people. She was an attractive woman, keeping her shoulder-length hair a silvery-white color that enhanced her slim features. She kept tight control of the fashion show and other events, and sharp eyes on everyone and everything.

Rumor had it she was sleeping with Josef. It wasn't something she proclaimed or denied. But there were signs. Jasmine wondered if she cared for Josef—or if it was a power play.

Jasmine had to wonder how Natasha felt about the beautiful women who were always around. But she understood, for Natasha, life hadn't been easy. Power probably overrode emotion.

The men by Smirnoff were his immediate bodyguards. Jasmine thought of them as Curly, Moe and Larry. In truth, they were Alejandro Suarez, Antonio Garibaldi and Sasha Antonovich. All three were big men, broad-shouldered and spent their off-hours in the gym. One of the three was always with Smirnoff. On a day like today, they were all close to him.

Victor Kozak was there, as well. Victor was apparently the rising heir to receive control of the action. He was taller and slimmer than Josef, and he had bright blue eyes and perfectly clipped, salt-and-pepper facial hair. He was extremely pleasant to Jasmine—so pleasant that it made her feel uneasy.

She knew about them all somewhat because she had talked to Mary about what she was doing. She had warned Mary that there was suspicion about the group on South Beach that ran so many of the events that called for runway models or beautiful people just to be in a crowd. Beautiful people who, it was rumored, you could engage to spend time with privately. Mary had described many of these players before Jasmine had met them.

Before Mary had disappeared.

The club manager was behind the bar; he didn't often work that kind of labor himself. He usually oversaw what was going on there. He was like the bodyguards—solid, watching, earning his way up the ranks.

Still watching, Jasmine made another of her teasing plays with Jorge—pointing out the next model who was coming down the runway. Kari Anderson was walking along in a black caftan that accented the fairness of her skin and the platinum shimmer of her hair. Jorge stood perfectly still; only his eyes moved, drawing laughter from the crowd.

As Jasmine did her turn around, she noted a man at the bar. She did not know him, or anything about him. He was a newcomer, Kari had told her. A big man in New York City. He was taller and leaner than any of the other men, and yet Jasmine had the feeling that he was steel-muscled beneath the designer suit he was wearing. He hadn't close-cropped his hair either; it was long, shaggy around his ears, a soft brown.

He was definitely the best looking of the bunch. His face was crafted with sharp clean contours, high defined cheekbones, a nicely squared chin and wide-set, light eyes. He could have been up on the runway, playing "pretty boy" with Jorge.

But of course, newcomer though he might be, he'd be one of "them." He'd recently come to South Beach, pretending to be some kind of an artist and owning and operating a gallery.

The hair. Maybe he believed that would disguise him as an artist—rather than a murdering criminal.

When she had made another turn, after pausing to do a synchronized turn with Kari, she saw that the new guy had left the bar area, along with the bartender. They were near Josef Smirnoff now.

Allowed into the inner circle.

Just as she noticed them, a loud crack rang out. The sound was almost masked by the music.

People didn't react.

Instinct and experience told Jasmine that it was indeed a gunshot. She instantly grabbed hold of Kari and dragged her down to the platform, all but lying over her. Another shot sounded; a light exploded in a hail of sparks. Then the rat-tat-tat of bullets exploded throughout the room.

The crowd began to scream and move.

There was nothing orderly about what happened—people panicked. It was hard not to blame them. It was a fearsome world they lived in.

"Stay down!" Jasmine told Kari, rising carefully.

Jorge was already on the floor, trying to help up a woman who had fallen, in danger of being trampled.

Bodyguards and police hired for the night were trying to bring order. Jasmine jumped into the crowd, trying to fathom where the shots had been fired. It was a light at the end of the runway that had exploded; where the other shot had come from was hard to discern.

The band had panicked, as well. A guitar crashed down on the floor.

Josef Smirnoff was on the ground, too. His bodyguards were near, trying to hold off the people who were set to run over him.

It was an absolute melee.

Jasmine helped up a young man, a white-faced rising star in a new television series. He tried to thank her.

"Get out, go—walk quickly," she said.

There were no more shots. But would they begin again?

She made her way to Smirnoff, ducking beneath the distracted bodyguards. She knelt by him as people raced around her.

"Josef?" she said, reaching for his shoulder, turning him over.

Blood covered his chest. There was no hope for the man; he was already dead, his eyes open in shock. There was blood on her now, blood on the designer gown she'd been wearing, everywhere.

She looked up; Jorge had to be somewhere nearby. Instead she saw a man coming after her, reaching for her as if to attack.

She rolled quickly, avoiding him once. But as she prepared to fight back, she felt as if she had been taken down by a linebacker. She stared up into the eyes of the long-haired newcomer; bright blue eyes, startling against his face and dark hair. She felt his hands on her, felt the strength in his hold.

No. She was going to take him down.

She jackknifed her body, letting him use his own weight against himself, causing him to crash into the floor.

He was obviously surprised. It took him a second—but only a second—to spin himself. He was back on his feet in a hunched position, ready to spring at her.

Where the hell is Jorge?

She feinted as if she would dive down to the left and dived to the right instead. She caught the man with a hard chop to the abdomen that should have stolen his breath.

He didn't give. She was suddenly tackled again, down on the ground, feeling the full power of the man's strength atop her. She stared up into his blue eyes, glistening like ice at the moment.

She realized the crowd was gone; she could hear the bustle at the doorway, hear the police as they poured in at the entrance.

But right there, at that moment, Josef Smirnoff lay dead in an ungodly pool of blood—blood she wore—just feet away.

And there was this man.

And herself.

"Hey!" Thank God, Jorge had found her. He dived down beside them, as if joining the fight. But he didn't help Jasmine; he made no move against the man. He lay next to her, as if he'd just also been taken down himself.

"Stop! FBI, meet MDPD. Jasmine, he's undercover.

Jacob… Jasmine is a cop. My partner," Jorge whispered urgently.

The man couldn't have looked more surprised. Then, he made a play of socking Jorge, and Jorge lay still. The man stood and dragged Jasmine to her feet. For a long moment he looked into her eyes, and then he wrenched her elbow behind her back.

"Play it out," he said, "nothing else to do."

"Sure," Jasmine told him.

And as he led her out—toward Victor Kozak, who now stood in the front, ready to take charge, Jasmine managed to twist and deliver a hard right to his jaw.

He stared at her, rubbing his jaw with his free hand.

"Play it out," she said softly.

The Feds always thought they knew more than the locals, whether they were team people or not. He'd probably be furious. He'd want to call the shots.

But at least his presence meant that the Feds had been aware of this place. They had listened to the police, and they had sent someone in. It was probably what Jorge had been trying to tell her.

Jacob was still staring at her. Well, she did have a damned good right hook.

To her surprise, he almost seemed to smile. "Play it out," he said. And to her continued surprise, he added, "You are one hell of a player!"

Chapter Two

"Someone knew," Jorge said. "Someone knew that Smirnoff came in—that he was selling them all out."

"Maybe," Jacob Wolff said. He was sitting on the sofa in Jasmine's South Beach apartment.

She didn't know why, but it bothered her that he was there. So comfortable. So thoughtful. But it hadn't been until now, with him in her apartment, that she really understood what was going on.

Two weeks ago, Josef Smirnoff had made contact with Dean Jenkins, a special agent assigned to the Miami office. Jenkins had gone to his superiors, and from there, Jacob Wolff had been called in. Among his other talents, he was a linguist, speaking Russian, Ukrainian, Spanish, Portuguese and French, including Cajun and Haitian Creole. He also knew a smattering of Czech and Polish. And German, enough to get by.

Maybe that's why she was resenting him. No one should be that accomplished.

No, it was simply because he had taken her by surprise.

"Maybe someone knew," Wolff said. He added, "And maybe not."

"If not, why—?" Jorge asked.

Wolff leaned forward. "Because," he said softly, "I believe that Kozak set up that hit. Not because he knew about anything that Smirnoff had done, but because he's been planning on taking over. Perhaps for some time.

"Smirnoff came in to us because he was afraid—he'd been the boss forever, but he knew how that could end if a power play went down. He was afraid. He wanted out. Kozak was the one who wanted Smirnoff out. And he figured out how to do it—and make it look as if he was as pure as the driven snow in the whole thing himself. He was visible to dozens of people when Smirnoff was killed. He played his cards right. There were plenty of cops there today, in uniform. What better time to plan an execution, when he wouldn't look the least guilty? In *this* crime ring, he was definitely the next man up— vice president, if you will."

"The thing is, if Kozak figures out something is up, we're all in grave danger," Jorge pointed out. "Undercover may not work."

"Jorge, undercover work is the only thing that might bring them down," Jasmine protested.

She was leaning against the archway between the living-dining area of the apartment and the kitchen. It was late; she was tired. But it had been the first chance for the three of them to talk.

After the chaos, everyone had been interviewed by the police. Stars—the glittering rich and famous and especially the almost-famous—had done endless interviews with the press, as well. Thankfully, there had been plenty of celebrities to garner attention. Jasmine, Jorge and Jacob Wolff had all managed to avoid being seen on television, but still, maintaining their cover had meant they were there for hours.

She'd been desperate to shower, and her blood-soaked gown had gone to the evidence locker.

In the end, they'd been seen leaving together, but that had been all right. Everyone knew that Jorge was Jasmine's friend—she'd brought him into the show, after all.

And as for Jacob Wolff...

"You shouldn't have made that show of going off with us in front of Victor Kozak," she said, glaring at Wolff. She realized her tone was harsh. Too harsh. But this was her apartment—or, at least, her cover persona's apartment—and she felt like a cat on a hot tin roof while he relaxed comfortably on her rented couch.

She needed to take a deep breath; start over with the agent.

He didn't look her way, just shrugged. "I told Ivan, the bartender, I wanted to get to know you. They believe I'm an important player out of New York. Right now, they're observing me. And they believe if they respect me, I'll respect them, play by their rules. I'm supposed to be a money launderer—I'm not into many of their criminal activities, including prostitution or any form of modern slavery. My cover is that of an art dealer with dozens of foreign ties.

"Before all this went down tonight, I was trying to befriend Ivan, who apparently manages the girls. I'm trying to figure out how the women are entangled in their web. Apparently, they move slowly. Most probably, with drugs. Before all this went down tonight, I'd asked about you, Jasmine, as if taking advantage of the 'friendship' they'll offer me. He said you weren't available yet, but that all good things come in time, or something to that effect. He'll think I took advantage of the situation instead—and that I'm offering you all the comfort a man in my position can offer."

"Really?" Jasmine asked. "But I was with Jorge."

Wolff finally looked at her, waving a hand in the air. "Yes, and they all know you two are friends, and that it's normal you would have left with Jorge. But Jorge is gay."

"That's what you told them?" Jasmine asked.

"I am gay," Jorge said, shrugging.

Jasmine turned to him. "You are? You never told me."

"You never asked. Hey, we're great partners. I never asked who you were dating. Oh, wait, you never do seem to date."

Jasmine could have kicked him. "Hey!" she protested. Great. She felt like an idiot. She and Jorge were close, but…it was true. They'd been working together for a while, they were friends. Just friends. And because of that, she hadn't thought to ask—

It didn't matter. They'd both tacitly known from the beginning as partners they'd never date each other, and neither had ever thought to ask the other about their love life.

She had to draw some dignity out of this situation.

"At least we did the expected," she said. "I guarantee we were watched. Oh, and by the way, Ivan Petrov controls the venue. But Natasha really runs the models. She gives the assignments, and she's the one who hands out the paychecks."

Wolff looked at her. "You're going to have to be very careful. From all that I've been told, she's been with this enterprise from the beginning. She may be almost as powerful as Kozak himself. When Natasha got into it, she wasn't manipulated into sex work. She used sex as an investment. She came into it as a model, slept with whomever they wanted—and worked her way up to Kozak."

"I am careful," Jasmine told him. "I'm a good cop—determined, but not suicidal."

"I'm glad to hear it. So, this is all as good as it can be," Wolff said, shaking his head. "What matters most here tonight is that we've lost Smirnoff, our informant. And we've still got to somehow get into this and take them all down. We have to take Kozak down, with all the budding lieutenants, too. My position with this group is pretty solid—the Bureau does an amazing job when it comes to inventing a history. But the fashion show is over. The opening is over. The club will be closed down for a few days."

"I'll have an in, don't worry. The last words from Natasha this evening had to do with us all reporting in tomorrow—for one, to return the clothing. For another, to find out where we go from here." Jasmine hesitated.

"They haven't asked you to entertain anyone yet?" Wolff asked.

"New girls get a chance to believe they're just models. After that, they're asked to escort at certain times, and, of course, from there…"

"We'll have this wrapped up before then," Jorge assured her.

"And if not, you'll just get the hell out of it," Wolff said.

"You don't have to be protective. I've been with the Special Investigations Division for three years now, and I've dealt with some pretty heinous people," Jasmine told him.

"I've dealt with them, too," Wolff said quietly. "And I spent this afternoon up in the Everglades, a plot of god-forsaken swamp with a bunch of oil drums filled with bodies. And I've been FBI for almost a decade. That didn't make today any better."

"I'm not saying anything makes it better. I'm just saying I can take care of myself," Jasmine said.

She really hadn't meant to be argumentative. But she did know what she was doing, and throughout her career, she'd learned it was usually the people who felt the need to emphasize their competency who were the ones who weren't so sure of their competency after all. She was confident in her abilities—or, at least she had thought she was.

With this Fed, she was becoming defensive. She hated the feeling.

"Guys, guys! Time-out," Jorge said.

Wolff stood, apparently all but dismissing her. "I'm heading back to my place. Most days, I'll be hanging around a real art shop that's supposedly mine. Dolphin Galleries."

He handed Jorge a card, then turned to look at Jasmine. "Feel free to watch out for me. In my mind, no one cop can beat everything out there. We all need people watching our backs. I'm more than happy to know I have MDPD in deep with me."

His words didn't help in the least; Jasmine still felt like a chastised toddler. What made it worse was the fact he was right. They did need to look out for one another.

She wanted to apologize. They had met awkwardly. She wasn't brash, she wasn't an idiot—she was a team player. But despite his words, she had the sense that he was already doubting her.

"I'll be hanging as close as I can," he said. "The woman managing the shop, Katrina Partridge, is with us. If you need me and I'm not there, just ask her. I trust her with my life."

He didn't look back. If he had done so, Jasmine was certain, it would have been to look at Jorge with pity for having been paired with her.

When Jacob was gone, she strode to the door and slid the bolts. She had three.

"Jerk!" she said. She turned back into the room and flounced down on the sofa.

"Not really. Just bad circumstances," Jorge said, taking a seat beside her. "I, uh, actually like the guy."

She looked at him. "I don't dislike him. I don't really know him."

"Could have fooled me."

She ignored that. "Jorge, how did it happen? We were all there. The place was spilling over with cops. And someone shot and killed Smirnoff—with all of us there—and we don't know who or how."

"They were counting on the place being filled with cops, Jasmine. Detectives will be on the case and our crime scene techs will find a trajectory for the bullet that killed him. We do our part, they do theirs. Thing is, whoever killed him, they were just the working part of the bigger machine. We have to get to the major players—Kozak, whoever else. Not that the man or woman who was pulling the trigger shouldn't serve life, but... it won't matter."

"No, it won't matter," she agreed. What they needed to do was find Mary. She nodded.

He took her hand and squeezed it. "You're just thrown. We weren't expecting to take them all down tonight."

"We weren't expecting Smirnoff to get killed tonight. I—I didn't even know he'd gone to the FBI!"

"I knew but couldn't tell you. And I didn't know that Smirnoff would be killed before I had a chance to loop you in. I'm sorry—I put you and Wolff both in a bad position. At least you didn't shoot each other. You know you're resenting him because he had you down."

"He did not have me down."

"Almost had you down."

"I almost had him down."

"Ouch. Take a breath," Jorge warned.

She did, and she shook her head. "I worked with a Fed once."

"And he was okay, right? Come on, we're all going in the same direction."

"He was great. Old dude—kept telling me he had a granddaughter my age. Made me feel like I should have been in bed by ten," Jasmine said and smiled.

Jorge arched his brow at her.

"Okay, okay," she said. "I resent the fact he almost had me down. But really, I almost had him, too." She squeezed his hand in return. "How come we never have discussed our love lives and this stranger knew more about you than I did?"

"'Cause neither of us cares what our preferences are, and we work well together—and we enjoy what we're doing. And Wolff for sure had all of us checked out before agreeing to work with us. He'd need to know our backgrounds and that we're clean cops. Also, you're a workaholic and even when we're grabbing quick food or popping into a bookstore, we're still working."

"Not really," she told him. "Honestly, not until this operation."

He nodded. "Mary," he said softly.

"Jorge, I'm so afraid she's dead." She paused. "Even more now. Do you have any details about the oil drums they found today? All I've seen is what has been on the news. Captain Lorenzo was even with the cops doing the interviews at the show, but I didn't get to ask him anything. Obviously, I did my best to be a near hysterical model."

"You were terrific."

She laughed. "So were you." Jasmine tried to smile, but she was searching out his eyes.

"Mary wasn't in one of the oil drums," he said.

"You're sure?"

"Positive. The bodies discovered were all men."

"Oh, thank God. I mean… I'm not glad that anyone was dead, but—"

"It's all right," Jorge assured her. "I understand. So, tomorrow will be tense. I'm going to get out of here. Let you get some sleep." He started to rise, and then he didn't. "Never mind."

"Never mind?"

"I'm going to stay here."

"I don't need to be protected," she said. "Bolts on the door, gun next to the bed."

"You don't need to be protected?" Jorge said. "I do! Safety in numbers. Bolt the door and let's get some sleep."

She rose. "Okay, I lied, and you're right—anyone can be taken by surprise. And I have been a jerk and I don't know why."

"I do," Jorge said softly. "You really shouldn't be working this case. You have a personal involvement. And in a way, so do I. I've met Mary."

Jasmine nodded. "I don't feel that I'm really up to

speed yet, despite what we learned from Wolff. I'll get you some pillows and bedding," she told him.

"What time are we supposed to be where?" he asked her as she laid out sheets on the sofa.

"Ten o'clock, back at the club."

"I'm willing to bet half of it will still be shut down."

"We won't be going to the floor. We'll be picking up our pay in the offices, using the VIP entrance on the side to the green room and staging areas."

"You know that we can get in?"

She nodded. "I wound up with Natasha and the other girls in a little group when the police were herding people for interviews. Natasha asked the lead detective— Detective Greenberg is in charge for the City of Miami Beach—and he told her that they'd cordon off the club area until they finished with the investigation. Owners and operators were free to use the building where the police weren't investigating."

"Then go to bed. We'll begin again in the morning."

Jorge was clearly thinking something but not saying it.

"What?" she pressed.

"I didn't know until today that the FBI was in on this case—the briefing was why I arrived late. MDPD found the group operating the Gold Sun Club to be shady, as did the cops with the City of Miami Beach. But there's been no hard evidence against them and nothing that anyone could do. I know you've been talking to Captain Lorenzo about them for a while, but…we just found out today that Smirnoff was about to give evidence against the whole shebang. I'm just—"

"Just what?"

He grimaced. "I like the Feds. They have more resources than we do. They have more reach across state lines. Across international lines. And I don't know how long I'll get to be one of the models—if the big show ended in disaster, I could be out fast. And then I won't be around to help you."

"I'm willing to bet the Deco Gang will keep planning. Kozak will say that all the people who had been hired for jobs at the club will still need work. He'll go forward in Smirnoff's name—Smirnoff would not want to have been frightened off Miami Beach. We'll be in."

"You will be. I may not. So, I'm just glad that... well, that there's another law enforcement agent undercover on this case. Speaking of undercover..." Jorge grabbed his blanket and turned around, smiling as he feigned sleep.

Jasmine opened her mouth to speak. She shook her head and went to the bedroom. Ready for bed and curled up, she admitted to herself that she just might be glad for Jacob Wolff's involvement, too.

She had assumed the group was trading in prostitution, turning models into drug addicts and then trafficking them.

She hadn't known about the bodies in the barrels. And she hadn't suspected that Smirnoff was going to die.

So she was glad she would have backup if she had to continue getting close to these dangerous players. Otherwise she probably should back right out of the case.

Except she just couldn't. They had Mary. They had her somewhere.

And Jasmine had to pray her friend was still alive.

Chapter Three

Jacob could remember coming to South Beach with his parents as a child. Back then, the gentrification of the area was already underway.

His mom liked to tell him about the way it had been when she had been young, when the world had yet to realize the beauty and architectural value of the art deco hotels—and when the young and beautiful had headed north on South Beach to the fabulous Fontainebleau and other such hotels where the likes of Sinatra and others had performed. In her day, there had been tons of bagel shops, and high school kids had all come to hang out by the water with their surfboards—despite a lack of anything that resembled real surf.

It was where his parents had met. His father had once told him, not without some humor, that he'd fallen in love over a twenty-five-cent bagel.

The beach was beautiful. Jacob had opted for a little boutique hotel right on the water. Fisher House had been built in the early 1920s when a great deal around it had been nothing but scrub, brush and palms. It had been completely renovated and revamped about a decade ago and was charming, intimate and historic, filled with framed pictures of long ago. The back door opened to a vast porch—half filled with dining tables—and then a tiled path led to the pool and beyond down to the ocean.

Jacob started the morning early, out on the sand, watching the sun come up, feeling the ocean breeze and listening to the seagulls cry. The rising sun was shining down on the water, creating a sparkling scene with diamond-like bits of brilliance all around him.

It was a piece of heaven. Sand between his toes, and then a quick dip in the water—cool and yet temperate in the early-morning hour. He loved it. Home for him in the last few years had been Washington, D.C., or New York City. There were beaches to be found, yes, but nothing like this. So, for the first hour of the day, he let himself just love the feel of salt air around him, hear the lulling rush of waves and look out over the endless water.

There was nothing like seeing it like a native. By 9:00 a.m., he was heading along Ocean Drive. The city was coming alive by then; roller skaters whizzed by him and traffic was heavy. Art galleries and shops were beginning to open, and tourists were flocking out in all manner of beach apparel, some wearing scanty clothing and some not. While most American men were fond of surf shorts for dipping in the water, Europeans tended to Speedos and as little on their bodies as possible. It was a generalization; he didn't like generalizations, but in this case, he was pretty sure he was right.

A fellow with a belly that surely hid his toes from his own sight—and his Speedo—walked on by and greeted Jacob with a cheerful "good morning" that was spoken with a heavy foreign accent.

Jacob smiled. The man was happy with himself and

within the legal bounds of propriety for this section of
the beach. And that was what mattered.

He stopped into the News Café. It was a great place
to see...and be seen. Before he'd been murdered, the
famous designer Gianni Versace had lived in one of
South Beach's grand old mansions. He had also dined
many a morning at the News Café. Tourists flocked
there. So did locals.

Jacob picked up a newspaper, ordered an egg dish
and sat back and watched—and listened.

The conversation was all about the shooting of Josef
Smirnoff at what should have been one of the bright-
est moments in the pseudo-plastic environment of the
beach.

"You can bring in all the stars you want—but with
those people—"

"I heard it was a mob hit!"

"Did you know that earlier, like in the morning, three
bodies were found in oil drums out in the Everglades?"

"Yeah. I don't think anyone had even reported them
missing. No ID's as of yet, but hey...like we don't have
enough problems down here."

People were talking. Naturally.

"Told you we shouldn't have come to Miami."

"Hey, mobsters kill mobsters. No one else was injured. Bunch of shots, from what I read, but only the
mobster was killed."

Someone who was apparently a local spoke up.

"Actually, honestly, we're not that bad a city. I mean,
my dad says that most of our bad crimes are committed
by out-of-towners and not our population."

Bad crimes... Sure, like most people in the world,

locals here wanted to fall in love, buy houses, raise children and seek the best lives possible.

But it was true, too, that South Florida was one massive melting pot—perhaps like New York City in the last decade. People came from all the Caribbean islands, Central and South America, the countries that had once comprised the Soviet Union, and from all over the world.

Most came in pursuit of a new life and freedom. Some came because a melting pot was simply a good place for criminal activity.

While he people-watched, Jacob replayed everything he had seen the day before in his mind. He remembered what he had heard.

Witnesses hadn't been lying or overly rattled when they had reported that it seemed the shots had come from all over. From the bar, he'd had a good place to observe the whole room. And then, as Ivan had muttered that they could go closer and see, they had done so.

The shooter hadn't been close to Josef Smirnoff—Jacob had been near him and if someone had shot him from up close, he'd have known.

He was pretty sure that the shooters had been stationed in the alcoves on the balcony that surrounded the ground floor, just outside the offices and private rooms on the second floor. The space allowed for customers to enjoy a band from upstairs, without being in the crowd below.

When he'd looked up at the balconies earlier, he hadn't seen anyone on them. The stairs might have been blocked.

Would Jasmine have known that detail? Or would they have shared that information with a new girl?

Jasmine had, beyond a doubt, drawn attention last night. She had been captivatingly beautiful, and she had played the runway perfectly, austere and yet with a sense of fun. She was perfect for the role she was playing.

The band, the models, the excitement… It had all been perfect for the setup. It was really a miracle that no one else had been hit.

He had thought that Jasmine was going after Josef Smirnoff when he had seen her lunge at him—getting close to see that the deed was done, that he was finished off if the bullets hadn't done their work. He'd never forget her surprise when he had tackled her…

Nor his own shock when she had thrown him off.

He was surprised to find himself smiling—he wasn't often taken unaware. Then again, while he'd known that MDPD had police officers working undercover, he hadn't been informed that one of them was working the runway.

A dangerous place.

But she worked it well. She had an in he could never have.

He pictured it all in his mind again. There had been multiple shooters but only one target—Josef Smirnoff. Create panic, and it might well have appeared that Smirnoff had been killed in a rain of bullets that could have been meant for anyone.

Jacob paid his bill and headed out, walking toward Dolphin Galleries. He felt the burner phone in his left pocket vibrate and he quickly pulled it out. Dean Jenkins, his Miami office counterpart, was calling.

"You alone?"

The street was busy, but as Jacob walked, he was

well aware that by "alone," Dean was asking if he was far from those involved with the Deco Gang.

"I am," he said.

"They're doing the autopsy now. Someone apparently had a bead on the bastard's heart. It's amazing that no one else was hurt. Oh, beyond cuts and bruises, I mean. People trampled people. But the bullets that didn't hit Smirnoff hit the walls."

"They only wanted Smirnoff dead. Kill a mobster, and the police might not look so hard. Kill a pretty ingenue, a pop star or a music icon, and the heat never ends."

"Yep. I wanted to let you know that I'm on the ground with the detective from the City of Miami Beach and another guy from Miami-Dade PD. Figured if I was around asking questions I'd be in close contact, and you could act annoyed and harassed."

"Good."

"You met the undercover Miami-Dade cops, right?" Dean asked.

"I did. We've talked."

"Good. The powers that be are stressing communication. They don't want any of you ending up in the swamp."

"Good to hear. I don't think I'd fit into an oil drum. Don't worry, we've got each other's backs."

"Have you been asked to move any money for the organization yet?"

"On my way in to the gallery now," Jacob said. "I expect I'll see someone soon enough."

"It may take some time, with that murder at the club last night, you know."

"A murder that I think they planned. I'd bet they'll contact me today."

"You're on. Keep up with MDPD, all right? Word from the top. Both the cops and our agency are accustomed to undercover operations, but this one is more than dicey."

"At least I get to bathe for this one," Jacob told him.

"There's a bright spot to everything, huh?"

"You bet."

He ended the call, slid the phone back in his pocket and headed toward the gallery.

The sun was shining overhead. People were out on the beach, playing, soaking up the heat. The shadow of last night's murder couldn't ruin a vacation for the visitors who had planned for an entire year.

Besides, it was a shady rich man, a mobster, who had been killed.

He who lives by the sword...

Jacob turned the corner. Ivan Petrov was standing in front of the gallery, studying a piece of modern art. Moe, Curly and Larry—or, rather Alejandro Suarez, Antonio Garibaldi and Sasha Antonovich—were upstairs when Jasmine arrived with Jorge at precisely 10:00 a.m. the next day.

Alejandro was at the top of the stairs. Sasha was at the door to what had once been Josef Smirnoff's office and was now the throne room for Victor Kozak.

Jasmine had made a point of greeting both Alejandro and Sasha. She presumed that Antonio was in the room with Victor, which he was. She saw him when the door to that inner sanctum opened and Natasha Volkov walked out.

The door immediately shut behind her, but not before Jasmine could see that Victor Kozak was seated at what had been Josef Smirnoff's desk.

The king is dead; long live the king, she thought.

This had shades of all kinds of Shakespearean trag-
edy on it. Apparently, Josef Smirnoff had known that
someone had been planning to kill him—he just hadn't
known who. Maybe he had suspected Kozak but not
known. And he probably hadn't imagined that he'd be
gunned down at the celebrity opening for the club.

She knew that Smirnoff hadn't exactly been a good
man. She had heard, though, that he wasn't on the truly
evil side of bad. He'd preferred strong-arm tactics to
murder. He'd rather have his debts paid, and how did a
dead man pay a debt?

Jasmine couldn't defend Smirnoff. However, she believed that Kozak was purely evil. It made her skin
crawl to be near him. She had a feeling he'd kill his own
mother if he saw it as a good career move.

"Ah, you are here! Such a good girl," Natasha said,
slipping an arm around Jasmine's shoulder and moving
her down the hallway. She turned back to Jorge. "You
come, too, pretty boy. You are a good boy, too."

Jorge smiled.

Natasha opened the door into a giant closet–dressing
room combo. There were racks of clothing and rows of
tables with mirrors surrounded by bright lights for the
girls to use. Before the show the day before, the room
had been filled with dressers, stylists and makeup artists.

"So sad. Poor Josef," Natasha said, admitting them
through the door and then closing it. She made a display
of bringing her fingers to her eyes, as if she'd been crying. Her face was not, however, tearstained.

"We are all in shock, in mourning today," Natasha

added. "So, let me pay you for last night and we will talk for a minute, yes? Maybe you can help."

"Definitely," Jasmine said. "Talking would be good. Mr. Smirnoff was so kind to all of us. It's so horrible what happened."

"Terrible," Jorge agreed.

"So." Natasha grabbed a large manila envelope off one of the dressers and took out a sizable wad of cash. She counted off the amount for each of their fees. When Natasha casually handed it over, Jasmine saw it was all in large bills. It seemed like a lot of cash to have lying around.

Natasha indicated a grouping of leather love seats and chairs where models and performers waited once their makeup was complete.

Jorge and Jasmine took chairs.

"You—you were very brave," she said, looking at Jasmine. "I was behind the curtain, but I saw the way you protected Kari and tried to help poor Josef."

"Oh, no, not so brave," Jasmine said. "When I was a child… I was with my parents in the Middle East, and my father taught me to get down, and get everyone around me down, anytime I heard gunshots. It was just instinct."

"I tried to get to Jasmine," Jorge said, "because she's my friend."

"Of course, of course," Natasha said. "But you two and Kari were the ones who were out on the runway when it all happened. What did you see? Of course, I know that the police talked to everyone last night, but… we're so upset about Josef! Perhaps you've remembered something…something that you might have seen?"

Jasmine shook her head. "Oh, Natasha. This is terrible, but I was only thinking about saving myself at first. I didn't see anything at all." Jasmine wished that she wasn't lying. She could easily be passionate because her words were true. She wished to hell that she had seen something—anything.

She had just heard the bullets flying. And seen Josef Smirnoff go down.

"I'm so, so sorry," she said. "Of course, I suppose this means that… Well, if you need anything from me in the future, I'd be so happy to work with you again."

Natasha smiled. "Jasmine, you must not worry. We will always have a need for you. We are a loyal family here! And, Jorge, of course, you, too."

"Thank you," Jorge said earnestly.

"But nothing—nothing at all?" Natasha persisted. "Tell me about your night, from the time you stepped out on the runway."

"It was so wonderful!" Jasmine said. "At first, I could hear the crowd. We were having a great time on the runway, and I heard people laughing and having fun… and then, that sound! I didn't realize at first that I was hearing bullets. And then…then it was as if I knew instantly. My past, maybe," she whispered. "And I went for Kari, and when I saw Josef down on the floor, I wanted to help… He'd been good to me, you know? Then that man—a friend of Josef's, I think—thought that I was trying to hurt Josef, and he…he tackled me."

"And you were angry, of course," Natasha murmured.

"Well, at first, of course, but it was okay after. He apologized to me. He told me he thought that I wanted to hurt Josef. He was very sincere. So apologetic."

"He saw to it that we got back to Jasmine's place safely. I liked him," Jorge said.

"And you, Jasmine? Did you like him?" Natasha asked.

"After we talked, of course. He was very apologetic. He told me that he's new to Miami Beach—new to Miami. He was working up north, but he got tired of snow and ice and had some connections to help him start up in business down here, and so...he was sad that his first time really heading to a fine event ended so tragically."

"So. He made moves on you," Natasha said softly. She wasn't pleased, and Jasmine recognized why.

Jasmine was now a commodity—one controlled by Natasha—even if she wasn't supposed to really understand that yet. This newcomer needed to go through Natasha—her and Victor Kozak now—if he wanted to have Jasmine as his own special escort.

"Oh, no, he didn't make moves," Jasmine said.

"He was a gentleman. Almost as if he was one of your security people. He just saw that we got home safely," Jorge said. He looked at Jasmine. "I thought maybe he liked me better."

"Oh?" Natasha said. "Interesting."

"No, no, Jorge—he didn't like you better!" Jasmine said. She knew that Jorge was smirking inwardly, and yet he was playing it well. They were both saying the right things in order to be able to stay close with Jacob as they ventured further into the world of Deco Gang.

They needed everyone in on this—Federal and local. Jorge had been right.

"You found him to be a nice man?" Natasha asked.

"Very," Jorge said before Jasmine could answer.

"Jorge, I am sorry, I don't think that he's interested in you," Natasha said. "He did express interest in Jasmine. But we shall see. Be nice to him, if he should see you or try to contact you. But if he does so, you must let me know right away."

"Of course," Jasmine said, eyes wide. "I know that you'll watch out for me."

"Yes, of course. We will watch out for you," Natasha said. She smiled. "We are family here. So, now, come with me. There will be another event soon enough. We will mourn Josef, of course. But so many are dependent on us for a living, we cannot stop. We will have a memorial or something this weekend on the beach. You will be part of it. We are family, yes? We don't let our people…down. For now, you will give Victor Kozak your…condolences."

Give him their condolences. If this had been happening just years earlier, they might well have been expected to kneel and kiss Kozak's ring.

She and Jorge both smiled naively. "Definitely," Jasmine said.

They rose; Jasmine led them down the hall.

Antonio and Alejandro were by the door to the office. Jasmine knew that Sasha Antonovich had to still be guarding the door.

Natasha tapped on the door to the office. Kozak called out, "Come in," and they entered.

He was alone, poring over papers that lay on the table before him.

"We're so sorry for your loss," Jasmine ventured timidly when Kozak didn't look up.

"The police are still in the club downstairs," he said, shaking his head. "They want to know about the balconies. I want to help them. I want to find the person who did this to our beloved Josef. But the balconies were closed off. Just with velvet cords, of course, but… Ah, Jasmine! We were all so enchanted with your performance," he said, looking up. "And you, too, of course. You were the perfect foil for the girls," he told Jorge.

"Thank you," Jorge murmured.

"I don't know who was on the balcony," Victor went on. "We'd said there would be no one on the balcony."

"Maybe the police have ways to find out," Jorge suggested in a hopeful voice.

Victor Kozak waved a hand in the air. "Maybe, maybe not. We'll keep up our own line of questioning. Anyway…"

He seemed to stop in midthought and gave his attention to them. "Please, I know that you were hired by Josef, but…it is my sincere hope that you will remain with us. We pay our regular models a retainer, which you will receive while we wait for this…for this painful situation to be behind us. That is, if you still wish to be with us."

"For sure!" Jasmine said.

"Retainer? Me, too?" Jorge asked hopefully.

Kozak glanced over at Natasha. She must have given him her approval with the slightest nod.

"Yes, you were quite the centerpiece for our lovely young girls. We have a reputation for always having beautiful people in our clubs. All you need to do is be around, available to us, and maybe meet some people we'd like to introduce you to. Please, we will be in touch. You may come in tomorrow for your paychecks."

They both thanked him profusely. Natasha led them down to the street.

As they were going out, Kari Anderson was just arriving. She threw her arms around Jasmine, shaking.

"I don't think I had a chance to thank you. You saved my life!" Kari told her.

"Kari, I just made you get down," Jasmine said, flushing and very aware that both Natasha and Sasha were watching the exchange. "Instinct!" she added quickly. "And we're all just so lucky…except for poor Josef."

"I know, it's so terrible," said the young blonde, her empathy real. Jasmine liked Kari. She was an honest kind person who seemed oblivious to her natural beauty. "Josef was always nice. It's so sad. Terrible that people do these things today! Terrible that poor Josef was caught in it all."

Naive—just like Mary, Jasmine thought. Not lacking confidence but unaware of just how much they had to offer.

"Come on up. We will straighten all out with you, Kari," Natasha said. "We will be all right. Victor will see to it," she added. "Now, you two run along and try to enjoy some downtime. Kari, come with me. We will have work for all of you—you needn't stress."

"See you, Kari," Jorge said, waving.

He and Jasmine started down the street while Natasha led Kari past Sasha and up the stairs.

"I worry about her," Jasmine said.

"I worry about all of us," Jorge said. "I was worried about the two of us unarmed during the show. We were taking a major chance."

"We knew there would be cops all over."

"Right. And Josef Smirnoff is dead and bullets were flying everywhere."

She couldn't argue that.

"So, tomorrow, we go back for our checks. Our retainer checks," she murmured.

"And you know we're going to be asked to do something for those checks."

"At least I don't think they're remotely suspicious of us," Jasmine told him.

"Not yet. We're still new."

"Kari came in just ahead of me," Jasmine said. "She...she was a replacement for Mary, I think."

"Here's the thing—what do we do when they want something from us that we don't want to do?" Jorge asked. "We haven't gotten anyone to admit to any criminal activity. If they ask you to be an escort, that's actually legal. So, you go off with someone they set you up with—and that guy wants sex. What do you do? Arrest the guy? That won't get us anywhere. And you sure as hell aren't going to compromise yourself."

"You may be asked first."

"I'm pretty—but not as pretty as you are."

Jasmine laughed. "Beauty is in the eye of the beholder, you know."

"Trust me on this. You'll be first. They'll tread a little more lightly with me."

Jasmine shook her head. "We have to get in more tightly, hear things and find something on them. You're right. They'll deny they have anything to do with illegally selling sex—I'm sure they've got that all worked out." She sighed. "I guess that our FBI connection will do a better job—he'll find out what they're doing with the money."

"How do we prove murder?" Jorge asked softly.

Jasmine lowered her head.

Jorge took her shoulders and spun her around to look at him. "We don't know that Mary is dead."

"I know," she whispered.

She was startled when her phone started to ring; it was a pay-as-you-go phone, one purchased in her cover name, Jasmine Alamein.

She looked at Jorge. "It's Natasha."

"Answer it!"

"Ah, Jasmine, my darling," Natasha said. "I'm so glad to reach you so quickly."

"Yeah, no problem," Jasmine said.

"We have a favor to ask of you. It includes a bonus, naturally."

"What is it?" Jasmine asked. Jorge was staring at her, wary.

"That friend of Josef's—Mr. Marensky. He is new in town. He has asked if you would be so good as to show him around. We'd be happy if you could do so— he came to us, instead of trying to twist our arm for a phone number. You will take him around town, yes? I said that wrong. He wishes to take you to dinner and perhaps you could show him some of the beach. And report to me, of course."

"Yes, for sure. Where do you want me to be when?" Jasmine asked.

"He will call for you at your apartment. Please, make sure your friend is not there when he arrives."

"What time?"

"Eight o'clock tonight."

"Thank you, Natasha. I will be ready."

"Wear something very pretty." Natasha didn't mean pretty. She meant *sexy*.

"I will. Thank you. Thank you!"

"My pleasure. Tomorrow morning you will come back in here."

"Yes, Natasha." Jasmine hung up. Jorge was staring at her. "My first date."

"I was afraid of this."

"She doesn't want you hanging around when my date comes for me."

"Like hell!"

"It's Jacob—*Marensky*."

"Oh." Jorge breathed a sigh of relief.

"I'm just a little worried," Jasmine said.

"About Jacob?"

Jasmine laughed. "Not on that account—I'm not sure he's particularly fond of me."

"You were acting badly."

"I was not—"

"You were."

"Never mind. I'm just wondering what good it's going to do if we just wind up watching one another."

"Trust me. That man has a plan in mind."

"I hope you're right. I'm so worried."

"Jasmine, we just went undercover. You know as well as I do that often cops and agents have to lead a double life for months to get what they're after. Years."

"This can't take that long," she said softly. She didn't add the rest of what she was thinking.

If it did...they might well end up dead themselves.

Chapter Four

Jacob arrived at Jasmine's apartment at precisely 8:00 p.m. She was ready, dressed in a halter dress and wickedly high heels. The assessment he gave her was coolly objective. And his words were even more so.

"You know how to play the part."

"Hey, I'm just a naive young model willing to let a rich guy take me out for an expensive dinner," she told him.

"Jorge?"

"They told me not to have him here."

"What is he doing tonight?"

"Catching up on his favorite cable show," Jasmine said. "Playing it all low."

"At his studio?"

Jasmine nodded and turned away.

Her captain had gone along with this at her say-so. But the FBI seemed to know way more than the police. She was certain that Jacob Wolff knew all about her fake dossier and Jorge's fake dossier, and she felt woefully late to the party.

"Hey." To her surprise, he caught her by the shoulders and spun her around. "This isn't a jurisdictional pissing match, you know. The FBI started planning the minute we heard from Smirnoff. You didn't know because we didn't inform the cops until it was absolutely necessary they knew we were in town. We had no idea you were in the middle of an undercover operation— we've had an eye on these guys for a while. Smirnoff coming in was the opening we needed."

He was right; they'd both had separate operations going on. And she'd wanted this case. She'd talked her captain into it being important. The bodies in the oil drums had proved she was right. Provided they could link them back to the Deco Gang.

"I'm sorry," she murmured.

"I worked something like this in New York not that long ago," he told her. "The Bureau crew I wound up working with hadn't known about me. It's always like that. A need-to-know basis. Fewer people to say things that might get you killed."

"Yes, but now—"

"Now, we're in it together. And now we need to head out. Where would you like to have dinner?"

"Wherever."

He grinned. "I'm supposed to be a very rich guy, you know. Oh, and with the power to push ahead at any given restaurant."

"How rude!"

"Yes, absolutely. But we're playing parts. And we need to play those parts well."

"How have your people gotten to so many restaurants?" Jasmine asked.

"They haven't," he said. "No one will say it, but everyone is afraid of the Deco Gang."

"Ah," Jasmine said. "Well, then, we're in the middle of stone crab season. I say we go for the most popular."

"Sure."

As they left her apartment, he slipped his arm through hers. Jasmine stiffened.

"Play along," he murmured.

"You think they're watching?"

"I think they could be at any given time."

She didn't argue that.

"I didn't bring a car. Taxi or an Uber?" he asked.

"I'm fine walking."

"In those shoes?"

She shrugged. "Not my favorite, but we're going about seven blocks. Over a mile in these? I'd say taxi or Uber!"

They walked past T-shirt shops and other restaurants with tables that spilled out on the sidewalk. It was a beautiful night. Balmy. It had to be in the midseventies. Jasmine could smell the salt on the air, and, over the music that escaped from many an establishment, she could hear the water—or at least she could imagine she heard the waves crashing softly up on the shore. Here where they walked, the sand and water were across busy Collins Avenue; the traffic was almost always bumper-to-bumper. She knew young people often came just to cruise the streets, showing off their souped-up cars.

She didn't get it; never had cared for fancy cars.

People in all styles of dress thronged the sidewalks. Some were decked out to the hilt, planning to visit one of the clubs or see a show. Others were casual, out just to shop or dine in a more casual fashion. While the South Beach neighborhood of Miami Beach was trendy and filled with great deco places, boutiques and more, heading farther north, one crossed Lincoln Road, a pedestrian mall and beyond that, a lot of the more staid grande dame hotels from the heyday era when Al Capone and his mobsters had ruled, and later the fabled Rat Pack had entertained, along with other greats.

The beach was like a chameleon, ready to change for every new decade.

At an old and ever-popular restaurant, known for its stone crabs while in season, they did find they were welcomed by a hostess and discreetly—but far too quickly—shown to a table. Jacob had managed, even with the lines outside wrapping around the building, to get them a private table in a little alcove.

Jacob made a pretense of studying the wine menu. He had known, she was certain, exactly what he wanted from the beginning. He wound up ordering champagne—and club soda, as well. She knew as the evening progressed, the champagne would disappear into leftover club soda.

The waitress was gone—they had both ordered the stone crab claws—and he leaned toward her, taking her hand from across the table, rubbing his thumb lightly over her flesh.

"You talked to your people?" he asked softly.

She nodded. "This afternoon. The three men in the oil drums…one has been there, they estimate, about three years. One several months…and one maybe two weeks or so."

Jacob smiled lightly, his expression expertly at odds with their conversation. "Do you know who they might be? They'll be testing, checking dental records. But so far, they don't match anyone reported missing down here." He hesitated. "We're a land of promise, but… people take advantage of that. I recently worked a case in New York… Here's the thing, and the cause of half the world's problems. When you have nothing at all, you have nothing to lose. People from war-torn countries might be desperate and can be drawn in and then forced to do just about anything." He was quiet for a minute. "Some wind up in oil drums."

"And some," she said, "just want more and more—like Victor Kozak."

"So it appears."

"What do you mean, so it appears?"

"Kozak became kingpin. But when Josef Smirnoff came in to the Bureau, he didn't know who intended to kill him. He just…he was afraid. He ruled so much, controlled so much, and yet must have felt like an ancient king. Someone wanted his throne."

"Just like an ancient king—who could plan to overthrow him unless they had a right to follow in his line?"

"That's true. But… I can't get over how lovely you look in that dress," he said suddenly.

She saw that the waiter had arrived, bearing a large silver champagne bucket filled with ice and a bottle.

"You clean up all right yourself," she said softly. And he did. He was wearing a casual soft taupe jacket over a tailored white shirt. He was a handsome man, she thought—with a bit of the look of a Renaissance poet, except she was certain that while his appearance was that of a tall lean man, he was composed of wire-tight muscle beneath.

The waiter smiled and poured their drinks, and they acted like a couple happily out on a date.

Jacob leaned closer to her again, smiling as he lifted his glass to her. "Josef Smirnoff admitted to dealing drugs, arms dealing, prostitution and money laundering. He swore up and down that he didn't order murder."

Jasmine lifted her glass with a dazzling smile, as well. "And yet, one of those bodies discovered had been there a very long time."

"So, someone might have been getting rid of people without Josef Smirnoff knowing."

"And how could that happen?"

"I don't know. We weren't able to get to Smirnoff for more conversation before he was killed. This had all just sprung into being, you know. It's been a complicated case for us. Smirnoff managed to get hold of an agent in the Miami office, but they didn't have anyone down here that they were certain couldn't be compromised—wouldn't be known by anyone. They appealed to the head offices in Virginia. From there, they called on me. I spent a week immersed in everything related to the Deco Gang, and we were lucky that we could arrange paperwork so it appears that I—as Jacob Marensky—own the Dolphin Galleries."

"So, you didn't know Josef Smirnoff?"

"I can't say that I knew him. But I know what he told people. And he was set up with the US Marshals' office—he would have disappeared into witness protection as soon as we had finished our investigation."

Their dinner was arriving.

"Do you really like stone crabs?" she asked him, hoping that her smile was flirtatious. "They're more of a local delicacy. And here's the thing—the crab lives! They take the claw and toss the crab back in. The claw regrows. That's why they're seasonal."

He lowered his head. His smile was legitimate. "Yes, I've had them, and I actually like them very much."

"Can I get you anything else?" their waiter asked.

They had their crackers, mustard sauces and drawn butter.

"I think we're just fine," Jacob said.

"Lovely," Jasmine agreed.

The waiter left them.

"So, you think someone other than Victor Kozak arranged the murder? You know that the press—and half the people in the country—think he was caught in another act of random violence."

He nodded. "And we have nothing to say."

Jasmine cracked a claw. A piece of shell went flying across the table, hitting Jacob on the left cheek.

"Oh! Sorry!" she said, somewhat mortified.

He laughed. "Not a problem."

"These really aren't date food," Jasmine said. "But then again, we aren't really on a date." She frowned, then made a show of dabbing at his face and laughing. "So, if not Victor Kozak, who would have the power to pull off such a thing as the murder of Josef Smirnoff?"

"It might have been Kozak. If not, there's Ivan Petrov, bartender and manager."

"You think he's high enough on the food chain?"

"Depends on who is in on the coup."

"The only people as close to management as Ivan are the bodyguards—I like to think of them as the Three Stooges."

"On steroids," Jacob said.

"Yes, deadly Stooges," she agreed.

"So, Victor Kozak, Ivan Petrov, Natasha Volkov—and the Stooges," he said.

"I just wonder about the bodyguards. The others are all Russian or Ukrainian, but Alejandro is Colombian, and Antonio is Italian."

"Half Italian," Jacob told her. "His mother is English."

"You do know more than I do."

"They are equal-opportunity crooks," Jacob said drily. "Any group down here can find power elsewhere—even elsewhere around the country."

"Their bookkeeper is from Atlanta," Jasmine murmured.

"Good old Southern boy."

"Girl."

"Pardon?"

"Good old Southern girl," Jasmine said. "And yet…"

"Yet?"

"I don't think she really knows about the criminal enterprises. She gets money after it's been laundered. As far as paperwork goes, they're enterprising citizens, paying their taxes."

"Well, Ivan is deep into it all," Jacob told her. "He was waiting at the gallery when I went in this morning. We made arrangements for the sale of one of the paintings in the gallery."

"As a way to move money?"

"Yeah. He paid way more than the painting is worth. The funds will go into an offshore account. It's all setup."

"So they believe in you?"

"For now…"

He had been studiously cracking a shell. This time, his piece of shell flew across the table—catching Jasmine right in the cleavage.

"Sorry!"

She caught the shell quickly before he could. But the gentleman in him came through; he started to move but stopped. The two of them laughed together. Honest laughter, and it was nice.

"Not really date food," he said. "Unless I were more accomplished at this, of course."

"I don't think you could be much more accomplished," she muttered, afraid that a bit of envy and maybe even bitterness might have made it through in her voice. She caught his curious look. "You speak half a dozen languages," she explained.

He shrugged. "I was just lucky. My family—much like yours—is a mini United Nations. Everyone from everywhere. And I love language. It gets easier to pick up another, if you know the Romance languages, the Latin base always helps for reading, even if it takes a bit. But all languages have rules—well, except for English! It's the hardest. Luckily, it was my first."

"Still…it's impressive."

"You speak Spanish."

"Picked up from growing up in South Florida. Half of my friends are Cuban, Colombian or from somewhere in the islands or South America."

"Or Brazil."

"I do also know a bit of Portuguese," she agreed.

They both smiled again. "So…we're equal-opportunity law enforcement, dealing with equal-opportunity criminals," Jasmine mused.

"So we are," he said. "Let's wander on down Washington Street. We'll stop and have dessert and coffee somewhere else."

"You think we're being followed?"

"I think we're definitely being watched in one way or another."

He paid the check and they left.

"You're from here, right?" he asked her.

"You know all about me, right?" she returned, looking at him.

"Well, I do now. I swear, when I tackled you... I didn't."

"You knew there were cops on the scene."

"They didn't tell me that one of the cops was a woman—modeling as if she were accustomed to the runway. But then you are, correct?"

"You received a full dossier on me after the fact?" Jasmine asked. "I wish that the powers that be might have returned the favor."

"I'm an open book," he told her.

"I'll bet."

"I knew from the time I was a kid I wanted to be in the FBI," Jacob told her. "I had a great uncle who was gunned down—for having the same name as a criminal. He was killed by mistake. Anyway, I got into a military academy, served time in the army and immediately joined the FBI. I've done a lot of undercover work. I seem to blend in well with an accepted and ambiguous foreign criminal look."

"Or latent hippie," she told him.

He grinned.

"If you want to see some of South Florida, I can show you around," she told him.

He smiled, lowering his head. "Great. I grew up here. But you know South Florida better than I do."

She grinned. "I was born here."

"Oh?"

"We traveled a lot—but always lived here. Well, not *here*, but in Miami, in Coconut Grove."

"There are so many areas… An amazing city, really. I think, just four decades or so ago, the population of the area was about three hundred thousand. Now, we're looking at millions." He cast a grimace her way. "Populations always lead to crime," he added.

He could be incredibly mercurial. He slipped an arm around her shoulder and pointed to a café before them. "They're known for their crème brûlée. Shall we?"

"Crème brûlée," she agreed, frowning slightly.

He lowered his head close to hers. "We are being followed," he said, pretending to nuzzle her forehead. "Ten o'clock, just down the street. Our dear friend Alejandro Suarez."

She was careful not to look right away, but let out a tone of delighted laughter and planted a kiss on his cheek.

"Let's have dessert," she said louder.

He took her arm and led her into the café.

"Well," she said as they sat close together. "I'm not sure if we've gotten anywhere, but the stone crab claws were delicious, and this is wonderful crème brûlée."

"Definitely better than some of the undercover work I've done before," he told her. He made a face. "Homeless detail. Sleeping in boxes—and for dinner, French fries out of the garbage."

"Yuck."

"You do what's called for."

"I would have…for this," she murmured.

"So, tell me about Mary. Tell me why you're on this case."

She stared up at him, startled. Somehow, he seemed to know everything. She hesitated and then shrugged.

"Our watchdog has stayed outside," he said softly.

She nodded. He was good at observation; she trusted him.

"Mary," she began. "The Deco Gang has been on our radar for a long time—they've operated out of restaurants, bars and even dry cleaners, moving on all the time. My usual cases keep me on the mainland. MDPD comes in on cases in many of the cities—Miami-Dade County is made up of thirty-four cities now, with more incorporating all the time. Not all the smaller cities have their own major crime divisions, and so we handle a great deal of it. South Beach does have a major crime unit, but the powers that be approved of us taking over this case. Miami Beach cops had a greater risk of being recognized, even undercover. It's not that they tried to hand off work—it was just a better plan. And honestly, until the bodies were found... I might have been the detective taking it the most seriously. Jurisdiction on this is complicated. The oil drums you saw were discovered up in Broward County, by a Seminole law enforcement official."

"There's the Florida Department of Law Enforcement. They could have taken over."

"And those guys are great. But going in on this, it fell to something Miami-Dade would do. We were investigating a disappearance. We were suspicious of the Deco Gang. And when it came to finding a way to slip in and be close enough, the models the clubs use all the time seemed a good cover. I approached my captain about it."

"You were in."

She shrugged. "In all honesty, I was afraid if I mentioned that a friend of mine had been working with the gang's models and then disappeared, it would be a strike against me in terms of being able to take the case. But it actually worked in my favor—I really knew her, I could talk about her and maybe get some information from the other young women working with them. And Mary, well, she's one of the nicest people you'd ever hope to meet. She looks for the good in everyone. Since I'm a cop, she thinks I'm jaded—though I actually think I'm pretty nice, too. Cops don't have to be asses."

"No, they don't," Jacob agreed, clearly somewhat amused.

"But Mary's problem is that she does look for the good. She has to be slapped in the face by bad to see that it exists."

"She probably is a very good person."

"Kari Anderson—the girl on the runway with me when Josef was shot—reminds me of Mary. They're both natural blondes with huge blue eyes and a trusting manner to go with them. Mary was working dinner theater, but not making much money. She saw the ad for models. She did a few shows with the group— Smirnoff's group is behind a number of entertainment offerings. They've been doing legitimate business, too. They own a bunch of other nightclubs. Anyway, Mary got swept up with Natasha and Josef and what she was doing…and saw no evil in it. And she was excited to get paid so well. Florida is a right-to-work state, so dinner theater may be a group requiring Actors' Equity, but then again, it may not be. She was thrilled. She paid her rent two months ahead with her paycheck from one show. And then there was the regular retainer just for being at the clubs, filling them with beautiful young people… It was easy money at first."

"Did she say anything to you about being nervous?"

Jasmine shook her head. "Never." She hesitated. "The last time I talked to Mary, she was excited. She was going to be a star attraction, working their next show. Which was the opening of the club the other night."

"The one you starred in instead."

"Yes. Look, Mary never said anything to me. She wasn't nervous, as far as I know. She just disappeared. A few weeks ago, she was supposed to meet me for lunch. She didn't show up. Mary's parents passed away when she was eighteen. She's on her own, an only child. She and I have been friends forever—we went all the way through grade school and high school together. We have other friends, but no one else has any other information about her. I don't even know how long she's actually been missing. After she missed our date, I called and called. We had an officer from Missing Persons go in to talk to Josef and Natasha, and they both appeared mystified—according to the officer."

"Have you gotten anything?"

"Not yet. The girls are still getting to know me. No one expected what happened to Josef. But apparently, we're all on retainer. Including Jorge."

"Retainer," Jacob murmured.

"I'm not sure what's next. Jorge and I can go in for checks tomorrow."

"Good. I'll stop by at some point." Jacob leaned back. "Well, I believe I'm supposed to walk you back now."

She nodded, oddly sorry that the evening was ending. It was work. Dangerous work.

Work to find Mary.

"You think we're still being watched?" she asked.

"I do."

He paid, stood and drew out her chair. He very politely took her arm and opened the door for her as they exited the café. He slipped an arm around her shoulders.

"Alejandro still around?" Jasmine asked.

"I think he was sitting at one of the outside tables… that's the back of his head behind us. Nope, he's rising now. I'd say he's going to make sure that I take you home and then leave—not overstepping my bounds."

They walked at a lazy pace, his arm around her but with all propriety.

"Interesting," she murmured.

"What's that?"

"How I'm going to discover that they keep control. I mean, as far as they know, I'm just a girl trying to get ahead in modeling. What if I just liked you and wanted to be with you?"

"I don't know. But if I went outside the rules…"

"I'm wondering if we'd both wind up in oil drums. I can see how they'd blame you. You're officially on the inside. But—"

"You're just an innocent. Well, in their eyes."

They'd reached her apartment. She was in a charming place, ground floor, almost in front of the pool. He walked her to the door and then paused. She wound up with her back against the wall by her door. He had a hand on the wall and was leaning against her.

He lowered his face toward hers and gave her a slow careful kiss. She allowed a hand to fall on his chest, and she wished that she didn't feel that there was absolutely nothing wrong with him. His scent was clean and masculine, mixed with the salty cool ocean air. His chest was vital and alive and yet like a rock. His lips were…

He drew away from her.

"I think that was just right. You might want to smile and laugh and then go in."

"Alejandro is watching?"

"He's right out on the street."

"Lovely, what a lovely night," she said, letting her voice carry.

"I'm sure we'll see each other again," Jacob said. "If you're willing…"

"I just have to check my work schedule."

"Of course." He stepped back, and she turned and let herself into her apartment.

She swung the door shut and slid the locks. And then, she stood there for a long, long time. She brought her fingers to her lips. They felt as if they were on fire.

Chapter Five

"You will pay Mr. Chavez twenty-five thousand for the painting," Victor Kozak told Jacob.

They were seated in the office at the rear of the gallery Jacob was pretending to own. Jacob nodded sagely to Kozak. They had already been through the niceties. They both sat with little demitasse cups of espresso. Kozak had admired the shop. Jacob had expressed his appreciation for Kozak's patronage.

"I don't know this artist," Jacob said.

"Trust me. He is excellent."

"And my commission?"

"Fifteen percent."

Jacob let that sit. He smiled at Kozak. "No disrespect. Twenty percent." He was pretty sure that in all such haggling—legal and illegal—Kozak had a higher limit than the figure he'd started with.

"Eighteen," Kozak said.

"I'm looking forward to working with you. Seeing that wonderful art arrives in our country. But if we're to go forward in the future, I believe we need a set rate now. I will be an excellent gallery to procure all the right artists—but I need to survive. The overhead here is quite high," Jacob told him.

Kozak was thoughtful. "All right, then. Twenty percent."

He rose; their dealings were complete. Jacob stood as well and the two men shook hands.

"Have the police come up with anything as yet regarding the shooter? Or shooters?" Jacob asked.

"No, nothing they have shared. You said *shooters*. You think that more than one man was involved?"

"We both know guns," Jacob told Kozak. "Yes, the shots were coming from at least two angles, maybe three."

"Accomplices," Kozak said, shaking his head. "So much violence in this world." He sighed as he lowered his head in sorrow. "Josef was a good man." He shrugged, a half smile on his face. "A good man—for all that we are. He was simply a businessman, and he had integrity in what he did."

Drugs and prostitution, if not murder. But sometimes, even criminals had their ethics.

"All the security," Jacob said, "and still—"

"Don't worry. What the police don't discover, we will," Kozak assured him.

"Naturally," Jacob said.

"I'm so sorry that this happened. Josef…was your friend?"

"We had a few business deals years ago. Art, you know, is always in the eye of the beholder. He'd commissioned a few pieces through me in my galleries before. When I wanted to come south—no more chipping ice off windows, you know—I looked down here and saw that Josef was opening a club. It's always prudent to establish relationships before opening a business anywhere," Jacob said.

"Josef told me about you." Kozak smiled. "And we do nothing without checking out references. I know that Josef trusted you. But now…his body will be released on Friday, they tell me."

"And there will be a funeral?"

"Yes, it will be at a little Russian Orthodox church in the city, not on the beach. A private affair. But you will be invited."

"I appreciate the honor and privilege of saying good-bye to an old friend," Jacob told him. "And with your permission, I will be by this afternoon with a small token for our new friendship."

"That will be fine. The club will reopen Friday night, but invitation only. A very small group to begin. We must show the world that we're now a safe place to be."

"This violence… It can happen anywhere. Lightning doesn't usually strike the same place twice. I believe the club will be fine."

Kozak gave him a rueful grin. "Sometimes, such events make a place a curiosity. Think back to the '80s. Paul Castellano and Thomas Bilotti were gunned down in a hit ordered by Gotti in front of Sparks Steak House in New York. The restaurant is still going strong. Down here, Al Capone was often in a suite at the Biltmore Hotel in Coral Gables. The suite is very expensive, and people still love to take it—even though Thomas 'Fatty' Walsh was gunned down at the hotel, supposedly over a gambling dispute." His smile deepened. "The hotel did go down after hurricanes and the Depression. It became a veteran's hospital. It was empty—and very haunted—but it's back to being very chic today."

"Let's hope we don't all have to go down first."

"Not to worry about us. Josef created a strong group

of business associates. We will be fine." With that, Kozak took his leave.

Jacob walked him to the door. They both smiled at Jacob's "assistant," who was busy behind the old art nouveau desk that served as their register and counter. Katrina smiled back and waved.

She was a perfect choice for this role. Katrina Partridge had been with the Bureau for nearly twenty years. She was in her midforties, attractive and able to carry off both charm and a completely businesslike demeanor. She also knew the art world backward and forward.

When Jacob was gone, she shook her head, indicating they shouldn't talk in the gallery. She pointed to his office, and he followed her there.

"He was walking around a long time. I think he touched a few of the frames, and... I could be wrong. But he could have planted some kind of a bug."

"Good observation, thank you. So, we're being given our first commission," he told her.

"But that's not enough," Katrina said.

"We could bring him down," Jacob told her. "But there will be a work of art, and who is to say what a work of art is worth?"

"Someone who knows art," she said drily.

"But art is subjective."

"So true. Yes, you're right."

"We're after killers," he said softly. "That's what we want to nail them on."

"I know," Katrina said. "And hey, what's not to like about this assignment? I don't have much going on yet—I'm enjoying my downtime. Sand, beach, lovely weather..."

"Still, be careful, Katrina. We can never know when

something may slip. They gunned down a man in a room full of cops and security."

"I'm always careful," she said. She smiled, indicating her back.

She was dressed in a fashionable skirt and blouse ensemble with a handsome tailored jacket. Despite the tailoring, he could see—when she indicated her back— that she was not without her Glock.

He smiled his acknowledgment but found himself worrying about Jasmine Adair.

Modeling. There was no hiding a weapon when dressers were around, making sure that a gown was being worn properly. And she was into it on a personal level—something that was dangerous from the get-go.

He had no right to interfere; her operation had begun before his and they were now required to work together. He had no problem working with police.

It was just that he was attracted to her. He didn't think it possible not to be. She was unique; elegant and a bit reserved, and yet when she smiled, when she laughed, she was warm, vibrant and sensual.

He turned his mind from thoughts of her.

"I'll bring the caviar over in about an hour," he told Katrina.

"All ready, in the container in back. I've dressed it up beautifully, if I do say so myself."

"I'm sure you did," he told her.

They moved back into the gallery. Jacob made a point of informing her that they were commissioning a piece, one that had a buyer already, who was in love with the artist's work.

She made mention of a local up-and-coming artist the buyer might like, as well.

A real customer sauntered into the room. Jacob returned to his office but found himself sitting and doing nothing but thinking.

He had to find a way in that was tighter; he had to be close to Jasmine.

He was still wary, of course. She hadn't turned him into a fool.

Maybe she had. Jacob hadn't felt such an instant attraction…almost a longing…in years.

Not since Sabrina.

"Ah, you are so beautiful, even in mourning," Natasha told Jasmine, admiring the way the draped black dress fell in sweeps to the floor. "Remember, at this, you will be quiet. You will help our guests with their drinks and food but keep a distance. Victor has ordered that this be a solemn occasion. You understand?"

"Yes, Natasha," Jasmine assured her.

Natasha looked over at Jorge, handsome in a conservative black suit. "You two will do well, I believe." She called to the little seamstress who hurried over. "I don't think that the hem needs to come up, but at the waist…a half an inch?"

"Yes, ma'am, of course," the seamstress said. She poked and prodded at Jasmine for a minute, pinning the waist and then nodding.

Jasmine thanked her. The tiny woman helped her slip out of the dress, and carried it away.

As Jasmine reached for her jeans and T-shirt, she was aware that Natasha was assessing her again—as she might assess meat in a market.

"So, last night, you were charming?"

"Yes, he took me for a nice dinner, and I told him about the beach."

"Very good. He likes you."

"I believe so."

Natasha turned away. "You could be asked to do much worse," she said, almost to herself, rather than to Jasmine. "So, now...jeans and a T-shirt. You must dress more...ah, how do I say this? Much prettier, to come in here."

"Business clothes."

"No, the halter dress you wore last night. Very pretty. And heels. No sneakers."

"Definitely, whatever you say."

"Victor would like to see you. I wish there was more time...time for you to go home. Ah, what am I thinking? I still have clothing from the show!" Natasha beamed, and caught Jasmine's hand. "No, no. Don't put your jeans back on."

"Oh...okay."

Natasha left her standing on the little podium where dresses were fitted and headed back to the racks of clothing that remained hanging in the massive closet space. She searched through the racks until she evidently found something that pleased her.

When she returned, she had hangers that bore a sleeveless silk blouse and a red skirt. "These will do," she said.

The skirt was short. Very short.

Jasmine donned the clothing. She smiled, hoping to show that she was feeling friendly with Natasha. "I don't think that the sneakers go with this so well."

"Ah, but of course not! You're an eight and a half, American size, in shoes?"

"Nine," Jasmine told her.

A very large shoe size, apparently, in Natasha's opinion. "Ah, well, you are tall."

She was five-ten. Natasha would be appalled by Jasmine's mom—just five-eight and she wore an eleven.

Natasha brought shoes—four-inch stilettos. "These will be beautiful," she said.

Jasmine slipped on the shoes. She was well over six-feet, now.

"So, come. Victor is happy with you." She turned to Jorge. "You—you will come on Friday evening. The service is at two. Josef will be interred after, and then we will be arriving here."

"Yes, ma'am," Jorge said.

Natasha studied him for a minute and then smiled. "We may have more work for you soon. Showing people Miami Beach—and all its pleasures."

Jasmine knew Jorge well. He didn't miss a beat. "Thank you," he said.

"And, now, you…" Natasha took Jasmine's hand. "Come and see Victor."

"For sure, a pleasure," Jasmine said.

"I'll wait here," Jorge said cheerfully.

"No, Jorge, you are done for today. Antonio will see you out."

Antonio was standing at the door to the large dressing room.

"Call you later!" Jasmine told him cheerfully.

She wasn't feeling so cheerful; she was caught here with nothing, no backup—and she was off to see Victor. She wasn't worried for her life. If she was going to be taken out, they'd have gone after Jorge, too.

Had she done too well with Jacob "Marensky"? Was

she now going to be asked to entertain another of their associates?

There was really no choice but to play it out. She had to wonder if this was where Mary had stood—right before she had disappeared.

With a smile, Jasmine watched Jorge go—and she accompanied Natasha to Victor Kozak's office.

Victor Kozak was not alone.

There was a man in his office. A tall man, he wore a designer suit in charcoal gray. He was perhaps in his midfifties, with iron-gray hair and mustache and watery blue eyes.

They'd both been sitting; Victor behind the desk, the new man in one of the upholstered chairs set before it. They stood politely.

"Ah, Jasmine. I'd like you to meet Mr. Connor," Victor said. "He's visiting from England and knows nothing about Miami Beach. He's hoping you will show him the beach, and to the finest hotel."

JACOB WAS ALREADY on his way to the club when his phone rang. He glanced at the number; he hadn't saved any in his contacts, but rather memorized the last four digits of those he needed to know.

Jorge Fuentes was calling.

"Where are you?" Jorge asked.

"Heading to the club. Why?"

"Head faster. I think they've taken Jasmine in to entertain a client. I mean, she can handle herself, but this is happening way too fast."

"Picking up the pace," Jacob moved forward quickly. "I'll be back in touch as soon as possible."

He didn't run; he might have been observed. But he

could walk fast as hell and he did so. He came to the corner of Washington Street and rounded it, heading to the employee side entrance to the club.

This time, Antonio was leaning against the wall by the door, smoking a cigarette, watching the day.

"Those things will kill you," Jacob said.

"Mr. Marensky. I don't believe we were expecting you."

"I have something for Mr. Kozak. He was just in the shop, you know. I need to get right up there."

Jacob didn't wait for Antonio to respond but hurried past him in a way that meant the goon's only action could be to physically accost him, and the man would still be trying to figure out if Jacob was important enough or not to get through.

Suarez was in the hall.

Jacob made a point of striding past him with a huge grin on his face. "Present for Victor!" he declared, lifting the ice chest filled with caviar that Katrina had so beautifully decorated with multicolored ribbons.

He burst into the office before he could be stopped.

Kozak immediately stood, reaching toward his jacket—and the weapon he surely carried there, Jacob thought. But he didn't draw the weapon.

Good. Jacob was trusted.

Jasmine was there, outfitted like the very expensive and exclusive call girl she was apparently expected to be.

A man had just been leaning over her—either inspecting her or seeking a better look at her cleavage. He was tall and solid, though his face was lined—perhaps from years of worriedly looking over his shoulder. His eyes were a strange, cool blue. Like ice.

"Victor! A present. Forgive me for interrupting. My source delivered this just this morning, and after we spoke—" He paused. "Excuse me, sir. No disrespect intended. I was in a rush— Jasmine!" he said, breaking up his own run of words. "Hello, and thank you again for last evening. You were a wonderful tour guide."

"I was conducting business with Mr. Connor—" Kozak began.

Jacob brought a frown to his face, and then allowed himself to appear deeply disturbed. "No, sir," he said, addressing Connor.

Connor straightened and stared at Kozak. "Kozak, I want—"

"I'm afraid I already have an interest," Jacob said softly.

"She's just a woman," Kozak muttered beneath his breath.

Jacob was glad that Jasmine appeared not to have heard the words. "Forgive me, but, Mr. Kozak, you're a very busy man. This arrangement was made. Yesterday. And at the show, before he was killed, I received promises from Josef Smirnoff."

"Smirnoff is dead," Connor said.

"But not forgotten," Jacob said.

Kozak was, of course, in a tight position. If he hadn't murdered Josef Smirnoff and was taking over as a natural progression, he had to respect promises made by his predecessor.

"Not forgotten, no. And honored," Kozak murmured. Jacob had given him an out—and he was glad to see that the man wanted his "business" and was willing to take the out.

Jacob turned to Connor.

"I'm new, but... I understand this. Miss Alamein and I had dinner last night and arranged for a sightseeing tour this evening. I had forgotten to tell Mr. Kozak about my tickets, but I'm afraid that I did specify this... young woman."

"I can make even better arrangements for you, Mr. Connor," Kozak said. "You must understand, we are in mourning right now. And in honor of Josef, I must follow through on all his promises."

"Fine. Call me when you have found a suitable companion," Connor told Kozak. He was looking at Jacob. Sizing him up. Apparently, he determined that the companionship of a certain woman was not worth a battle. He turned and left without another word.

"So, before you came to me... Josef had promised you this woman," Kozak said.

Jacob didn't look at Jasmine. Knowing her as he was coming to know her, he was amazed that she was managing to just sit still.

"When I saw her on the runway," he said, his voice husky, "I knew I wanted her at that moment. I believe she might have been his last promise."

"Then I will make no other arrangements. But you must remember, Miss Alamein is in my employ. And she will appear when she is needed."

"That is understood."

Kozak walked over to Jasmine. "You will honor this arrangement?" he asked her.

Jasmine stood. In the heels she was wearing, she was eye level with Kozak. She smiled sweetly. "As you wish, Mr. Kozak."

"Fine," Kozak said. "Just remember, you work for me," he added softly.

"Always," she told him earnestly. Jasmine's smile deepened. "And thank you, sir. Thank you. Mr. Marensky and I were able to have the most delicious dinner last night. Far more easily than I might have ever imagined!"

Even Kozak seemed caught by her charm. "My pleasure. So, I believe that Natasha wanted to talk with you one more time. And…" he gave his attention back to Jacob "…Miss Alamein will be ready for you tonight, for these tickets you have."

"I'll wait and escort her home now," Jacob said. "Sir, if you have a minute, the present I brought… I believe you will enjoy it immensely. It is Almas, from the beluga sturgeon—supposed to be some of the finest caviar. I must admit, I am not an expert, but I have been assured by those who are that this is delicious."

"Then you must sit and enjoy it with me," Kozak said. He waved a hand at Jasmine. "See Natasha, see what she needs from you."

Jasmine was dismissed. She left the room.

Jacob looked at Kozak. "I thank you for respecting me—and Josef's memory," he said. "And I would like to do more."

"Oh?"

"I am not without certain skills. I would like your permission to look into Josef's death myself."

BREATHING WAS DIFFICULT.

Jasmine's heart was pounding. She'd been so sure of herself, even in Kozak's office with the very strange *Mr.* Connor all but pawing her, that she'd been figuring out ways to handle the situation herself. Alone with the man, she'd have figured out something…

And blown her cover. And all hope of finding out what had happened to Mary.

She hurried down the hall—smiling at Sasha, on duty there now—to the dressing room. Natasha was at one of the tables, studying her face in the mirror.

She looked at Jasmine, and as she did so, Jasmine had to wonder if the woman's eyes could stretch out of her head, or if she had ears that could extend down a hallway.

Natasha already knew what had happened.

"It's not good," she said. "It's not good at all. One man should not become so possessive."

Jasmine shrugged. "Does it matter?" she asked. "Does it matter if the money is the same?"

"Ah, child, you're new to this," Natasha said.

"Yes, I am. And I am ignorant but willing to learn."

Natasha seemed pleased with her reply. "He will start to think that he owns you and that he would be better off just spiriting you away somewhere. You must be careful and declare your loyalty to us at all times, do you understand?"

"Yes, Natasha. And I am loyal, I promise you."

"And," Natasha added, "you like this Jacob Marensky?"

"He's clean and he smells good. And he is younger."

Natasha waved a hand in the air. "Yes, he is clean and young and smells good. And young can be good. Old men, with their hopes and their prayers and their pills... They have no idea how often those they think they control sit there and do nothing but laugh at their faulty efforts." She shook her head; Jasmine had the feeling she had experienced the worst and earned her way out of it.

"So then, you may have your jeans and your T-shirt. Apparently, Mr. Marensky is a more casual man and you are going on a sightseeing tour." She shuddered as if a sightseeing tour might be akin to torture.

"Thank you," Jasmine said. "I must admit, the shoes...the heels are a lot."

"They make you very tall. Then again, Mr. Marensky is very tall." She waved a hand in the air. "Josef admired the man. Victor believes that he is an admirable man as well, who understands our business but demands that we respect his. You will, of course, report to me."

"Yes, I will."

Jasmine heard voices. A few of the other girls had arrived.

Kari Anderson came into the room, carrying a bundle of clothes. Behind her were Jen Talbot, Renee Dumas and Helen Lee. They were like a palette of beauty—Kari so pale, Jen olive-skinned, Renee almost ebony and Helen extraordinary with her mix of Eurasian features and lustrous long black hair. They were beautiful on a runway.

They had also been hired to please all tastes.

Thus far, though, she hadn't seen any of the women forced into anything. Just pretty girls with an understanding that they could be paid well for their company. She had sat silently herself as Victor had introduced her to Mr. Connor and informed her that he needed a guide and an escort for the evening. What if she had protested?

Had Mary protested?

"I'll just grab my things and change and get out of here," Jasmine said. "And hang these up."

She fled over to the hangers, finding that her clothing had not been hung—just folded as if with distaste and left on the shelving above the racks. She eased out of the shoes and slid out of the skirt.

Kari walked in. "I'm going to need that skirt, I hear," she said.

"Oh?" Jasmine handed her the skirt on its hanger and shimmied the blouse over her head.

"I'm going to go see Mr. Connor," Kari said. She sounded slightly nervous.

"Are you afraid of him?" Jasmine asked in a whisper. "If so—"

"No, no. He's supposed to be very nice."

"I thought he was new."

"No. Mary went out with him. Just dinner. She said he was very nice. Oh, sorry, you didn't know Mary. She was great, but… I guess this wasn't for her. Me, I want the runway. And if it means dating a few losers…" Her voice trailed. "Dating," she repeated drily. "Okay, having sex with a few repulsive specimens… Well, I managed to choose a lot of losers on my own! Might as well have it be worth something in the end, I guess."

"Kari?" Natasha called.

"Excuse me," Kari said to Jasmine. "I have to run!"

Jasmine caught her hand. "Kari—please. Will you call me tomorrow and let me know that you're all right?"

Kari seemed surprised. "Of course, I'll be all right. But thank you. And I will call you—we can maybe have lunch or something?"

"I'd love to have lunch," Jasmine assured her. She hesitated. "It's allowed?"

"Oh, yes. They like us to be friends. Sometimes…"

"Sometimes?"

"Kari!" Natasha called again.

"Later!" Kari told her, and with a swirl of blond hair, she was gone.

KOZAK HAD OPENED a bottle of his special "very Russian" vodka to go with the caviar. Jacob was careful to pretend to sip as much as the crime tsar but imbibe as little as possible.

His time with the man was proving to be very interesting.

Kozak talked about growing up in Russia—about the KGB coming for his father in the middle of the night.

"That must have been very hard on a child," Jacob said.

Kozak shrugged. "My father, he was a killer. When it all broke apart, though…everyone was running. The kind of crime was brutal, from all manner of directions. My mother, bless her, got us out. I never understood. Business is business, but…"

He paused and looked hard at Jacob, very sober despite the vodka he had all but inhaled. "You think you can find Josef's killer?"

Jacob weighed his words carefully. "There have been certain…events in my past that required me to take a closer look at them. I have a talent for uncovering things." He paused. "You really have no idea who killed him?"

Kozak frowned.

"No disrespect," Jacob said quickly. "I liked Josef. We did very good business together. But perhaps, something was going on with the group that was dangerous to all."

"You're talking about the bodies discovered in the Everglades," Kozak said. "There is talk of little but that and the shooting on the news these days. We have even ceased to care about politics, eh? When people are scared…"

He paused and shrugged again. "We had nothing to do with those bodies. Not Josef, not me. And I do not know who killed him. Me, I have kept my boys close—Sasha, Antonio and Alejandro. I have played the game, I have become the king. But you are a newcomer. Down here, that is. Josef trusted you. You know how to stand your ground. You tell me—who killed Josef?"

"I don't know, but as I said, with your permission, I will find out."

"You have my permission—and my blessing. What else do you need?"

"Permission to speak with your boys. And Ivan and Natasha. Whether wittingly or not, Victor, one of them helped the killers."

There was a tap at the door.

"It's me, Mr. Kozak," Jasmine said in a small voice.

"I will see her home," Jacob said, rising and heading to the door. "And I will begin tomorrow. I will find the killer, I promise you."

"Then most definitely, the woman is yours—along with my gratitude," Kozak told him.

Jacob nodded and opened the door. And capturing Jasmine's hand, he hurried down the stairs, Jasmine in his wake.

Chapter Six

"I should have gone with him," Jasmine murmured.

The look Jacob gave her could have turned her to stone. She supposed, in his mind, he had managed not only to save her from a fate worse than death—or actual death, for that matter—but to keep up their under- cover guises, as well.

"No, no," she amended quickly. "You were wonder- ful, magnificent. I mean, you pulled that off, and nor- mal circumstances—"

"Just wait. Wait until we reach your apartment," he said. "At this point, I'm pretty sure it's okay if I come in."

"Are we being followed?"

"Maybe. You never know."

She was surprised when he pulled out his phone. He had such a grip on her with his left hand that she could hear the voice of the man he was calling from his phone in his right hand.

"You got her out?" the voice asked.

Jorge.

"Yes." Jacob glanced her way. "I need tickets, fast. Some kind of sightseeing trip. First available."

"Call you right back."

"Tickets?" Jasmine murmured.

"Tickets."

They were almost to her apartment when the phone rang again. This time, Jorge was speaking more softly.

"Lincoln Road Mall," Jacob relayed.

"We can walk it," Jasmine suggested.

"Then keep walking."

He was angry; she hadn't had a chance to explain yet what she'd meant about wishing she'd gone with Mr. Connor. And on the street the way they were, unaware of how things might go, despite the stand Jacob had just made, he clearly didn't want her talking.

His pace was urgent; she had long legs, and she could trek it, but he was moving fast. They were some distance from the club on Washington Street when he finally seemed to slow—perhaps having burned off some of his energy.

She managed to retrieve her hand from his hold and slide an arm through his, drawing herself close and speaking softly, as if she whispered a lover's words.

"I may have found out how Mary disappeared—and with whom," she told him.

He turned and frowned at her.

"I finally got a second with Kari. She's probably going to wind up going off with this man, Connor. Jacob, Mary met with Connor. She met him—and then she disappeared."

"And you were willing to take that kind of a chance?"

Jasmine swallowed, leaning on his shoulder. "That's what I'm here for. But I didn't find out until after you came and got me out of the room. I saw Kari when I went back to get my own clothing. That's when she told me...and they're going to send her in to be his escort. Jacob, we have to find a way to follow that man. Maybe Jorge—"

"No, Jorge still has an in. And they'd wonder what he was doing. Let me call my office. They'll get someone on it."

He pulled out his phone again. They'd reached Lincoln Road Mall—a pedestrian walkway that offered dozens of shops and restaurants, fun places to dine and enjoy a coffee, a drink, entertainment or an evening.

"It's a private tour company," Jacob said, pointing to a spot by the theaters on Alton Road. "They'll pick us up there."

He veered in that direction, speaking quickly to someone on the phone and giving them the information they had on Connor. Jacob described him to a T. But Jasmine knew he had little else to go on.

She heard rapid questions in return, and then assurances.

"I believe that's ours," Jacob said, pointing to a limo with a sunroof.

The vehicle made a U-turn and pulled to the corner. The driver, a young man in a suit, hopped out and offered them a broad professional smile. "Marensky?" he asked.

"Yes, thank you, Jasmine and Jacob," Jacob said, sliding his phone back into his pocket.

"I'm David Hernandez, your guide for the day!" he said cheerfully. "I'm at your disposal. Now, I understand you're new to the beach, so I'll give you a few suggestions. My first pick is the Ancient Spanish Monastery, but that's north on the beach, so…"

"That's fine," Jacob said quickly. "Is that okay,

honey?" he asked Jasmine, and then he told their guide, "Jasmine knows the place. Me, I'm new."

"I love the Spanish Monastery!" she said. "But I'm not sure I'd be the best guide."

David looked at his watch. "Well, if we move, you can have a couple of hours there. Your assistant ordered a driver and guide until midnight, so—"

"We'll start with the Spanish Monastery," Jacob said.

They slid into the car. With the beach traffic, it was going to take them a few minutes to reach what Jasmine considered to be one of their most intriguing destinations.

"I grew up here, but not on the beach," Jasmine told David.

"Cool. I grew up in the city, by the old Flagler Dog Track—Magic City Casino now," David told them. "People say Miami is young, no history. But we've got tons of it. I could go on forever. But—"

"Please, do, go on forever," Jacob said.

He leaned back in the plush seat of the limo, closing his eyes for a minute. It was the only indication Jasmine had seen that his world could cause him pressure.

He had come in, guns blazing, for her.

She leaned back, as well. She really needed to talk to Captain Lorenzo and give her report. Lorenzo could get cops out after Kari and Connor.

"Of course, South Beach itself is a tourist attraction," David said. "Did you know that it was the original area that was populated? Believe it or not, the beach started out as farmland. The City of Miami itself incorporated on July 28, 1896. Julia Tuttle, our founding mom, had sent an orange blossom to Henry Flagler, convincing him to bring his railroad down—we were almost always frost free!

"The City of Miami Beach was incorporated on March 26, 1915. Now, Miami Beach is comprised of natural and man-made barrier islands. In 1870, Henry and Charles Lum—father and son, by the way, bought a lot of the bracken, sandy, nothing land that's worth billions today. There was a station to help shipwreck victims up north of where you're staying, closer to where we'll be today. They started off with a coconut plantation, but that didn't go so well. Enter some rich Yankees, and the beach started developing.

"Collins Avenue is so named because of an entrepreneur called Collins. He mixed up the crops and got things going. Then with Miami up and running, the railroad coming down and Government Cut created, people were on their way to thinking it would make a great resort area. Enter the Lummus family, who were bankers, and Carl C. Fisher from Indianapolis, who worked with the Collins and Pancoast group, and by the beginning of the twentieth century, Miami Beach was on its way."

David had a great voice—informative, interesting and soothing. Jasmine hadn't realized she had closed her eyes, too—until she opened them and discovered Jacob was looking at her.

"We're on it," he said softly. "The Miami office will speak to your captain and see that the police are aware of this new player."

"I just…" Jasmine paused, looking to the front.

David was going on, talking about the development of the area for tourists. The entrepreneurs had started off developing their crops—avocado, for one—and taking tourists on day trips from the City of Miami. Then came food stands and finally, the Browns Hotel, which was still standing.

"What if this man, Connor, is...a killer?" Jasmine asked quietly. "One of those men who can only get off if he strangles or stabs a woman. What if...?"

"He'll be followed and watched, Jasmine. And, they'll do the same with him as they did with me—just a date, first. Just a date. We'll find out about him, and Kari will be all right."

Kari would be all right. And that meant so much. But what about Mary? She'd been gone nearly a month now.

Jacob started fumbling in his pocket. She realized his phone was buzzing. He answered it in a quiet voice.

David kept speaking. "Collins needed money. He got it from the Lummus guys. He started construction of a wooden bridge. The beach areas went through a number of different names, but you can still find those founding fathers in street names here—and of course, we have Fisher Island, a haven for the very rich. If you really want to find a lot of these founders, we can do that another day.

"You should see the old Miami City Cemetery across on the mainland. It was north of the city limits in 1887 when it was founded. Julia Tuttle is buried there, and oh! If you like Civil War history, we've got some Confederates buried just feet from some Union guys—friends by then, I would think, since they died long after the war. Friends in death, if nothing else."

Jasmine looked at Jacob. He smiled tightly at her. "We have two guys on it. They're trying to dig up something on Connor, but we don't even have a first name for the man."

"He's English. He definitely had an accent."

"I told them that. Jasmine, they're watching Kari. She's at her apartment right now."

"She's an innocent… She's a Mary. She isn't worried about…about anything he might ask her to do. She said she's been with dozens of losers and might as well improve her career chances by going with men chosen for her by Kozak or Natasha. I'll never forgive myself if she gets hurt. I could have gone with Connor."

"She's going to be all right."

Jasmine nodded, taking a deep breath.

David talked on, telling them that when the South Beach area had fallen into a slump, Jackie Gleason had helped to change things doing his famous show from the beach, along with more entrepreneurs who saw the fabulous artistic value of the art deco hotels and buildings.

They were finally nearing their destination.

"The Ancient Spanish Monastery, known officially as the Monastery of St. Bernard de Clairvaux, is really—well, ancient. Construction began in northern Spain in 1133, in a little place near Segovia called Sacramenia. It housed monks for somewhere around seven hundred years, and then there was a revolution and it was sold and became a granary and storage and…not a monastery.

"It came to be here because, in 1925, it was purchased by an American—you guessed it—entrepreneur, Mr. William Randolph Hearst. For a long time, it was known as the world's biggest jigsaw puzzle, because it was shipped to the US as thousands upon thousands of stones.

"Well, then Hearst had some financial problems. He'd wanted to rebuild it at San Simeon, but some of what he'd purchased of the monastery was sold off. The crates—about eleven thousand of them—were in storage in New York. Not to mention there had been an outbreak of hoof-and-mouth disease in Segovia, which meant the packing hay had to be burned and the crates had to be quarantined.

"And then poor Hearst died! More entrepreneurs invested, and all the crates were taken out of storage. Took about a year and a half, they say, to put all the pieces back together. Two businessmen bought them, had them put together and then couldn't afford the fact that the monastery didn't make it right away as a tourist attraction. Financial difficulties again.

"In 1964, it was purchased by Bishop Henry Louttit, who gave it to the diocese of South Florida, which split into three groups. Then it was owned by a very rich and good man, a billionaire and a philanthropist, Colonel Robert Pentland, Jr. He went on that year to give the cloisters to the Bishop of Florida, and voilà! Finally, a church and a tourist attraction. And now, while the monastery is still a great tourist attraction, it's still also an active church. I love going there. It's like stepping back in time."

They arrived. David quickly arranged for their tickets, and Jasmine and Jacob were in, admiring the old stone cloisters and hearing about the historic instruments that were often used in services, seeing some of the artifacts that had come with the monastery—and the carved coats of arms and other relics that had come from other monasteries and venues around Spain.

Then they were out in the gardens, arm in arm, and Jacob was back on the phone again.

"I did get the autopsy information on Smirnoff from my Miami counterpart," Jacob told her as they strolled.

"I realize autopsies are important, but I'm pretty sure I know how Josef Smirnoff died—bullets," Jasmine said.

Jacob nodded. "Yes. But I guess he didn't know he had cancer—colon cancer. According to the ME, Smirnoff must have had it for some time without knowing. He wasn't looking at a long life, even if he'd gone for treatment."

"So, someone murdered him for nothing," Jasmine said. "Kozak was next in line anyway."

Jacob was quiet.

"You don't think it was Kozak?"

"He would just be so obvious. And he denied having anything to do with the bodies in the oil drums."

"Have they finished those autopsies?" Jasmine asked.

Jacob nodded. "They are still waiting on testing. They've gotten fingerprints on the most recent body, but the two other corpses were too decomposed. They think one of the bodies has been there several years."

"I'm assuming they're also trying to trace the oil drums and whatever remnants of clothing they can find?"

Jacob nodded. "They don't have much hope on the oil drums. They were apparently dumped by a major oil company years ago. They were headed to the closest landfill, I imagine. Nice, huh? Anyone could have picked them up."

"But you said they got fingerprints off the most recent corpse?"

He smiled. "As soon as I know, you'll know. Easy now that I've staked my claim on you."

"It does make communication between us a lot easier," Jasmine murmured.

"And hopefully keeps the wolves from baying at your door—and forcing you to show your hand." He grinned at her. "I can appear to be extremely possessive."

She was afraid that her smile was a little fluttery. Because something inside her had fluttered, as well.

His phone rang. He answered and listened intently. "Okay," he said, hanging up. He looked at Jasmine. "Apparently, Mr. Connor doesn't believe in being fashionably late Miami Beach–style. He's at Kari's apartment now."

"So, they're heading to dinner now. We should get back down there—"

"Jasmine, agents are on it."

"I know, but—"

Her phone rang then. She glanced at the number; it was the number that Captain Mac Lorenzo was using for the operation.

"Checking in—and watching out for a valuable asset," he told her.

"I'm fine," Jasmine assured him. "I'm touring the Ancient Spanish Monastery."

"I've spoken with Jorge. We're not pulling either of you out yet. But I also have strict instructions from way high above not to endanger an FBI operation."

"We're not endangering it."

"And you're not to endanger yourself," he reminded her.

"Never, sir," she told him.

"Just make sure you remember the FBI has taken the lead on this, and they're calling the shots."

"I understand." She was careful to keep any remnant of emotion from her voice.

"You're doing all right with interagency communication?"

Jasmine glanced at Jacob. "We're doing just fine, sir."

Jacob must have heard. He arched his brows in a question and reached for the phone.

"Captain Lorenzo, how do you do? Jacob Wolff. We're working on this together well. I don't think we could have planned this out any better."

Jasmine didn't hear what Captain Lorenzo said after that. Jacob handed the phone back to Jasmine and she quickly hung up.

"Thank you for that," she told Jacob.

He shrugged. "I think we are working well together."

"Yes, I guess we are."

"Hey, I'm pretty sure I would have liked you one way or the other. And I do admire your swing. That was a hell of a punch you gave me the other day."

"I didn't know—"

"Maybe that was better. That's the thing with undercover, really. Check in only when you need to or when you need help. Work everything on a need-to-know basis."

He was right, and she knew it. And she could have said she liked him, too. But suddenly, doing so seemed to be a very dangerous part of the operation.

She liked him too much.

Liked the deep set of his eyes, the tone of his voice… the way he touched her. She'd liked the feel of his lips on hers far too much… That brief touch was still a memory that lingered and haunted.

"I still think we should head back," she said.

He looked around. "It's beautiful here. Not just the monastery, I mean South Florida."

"Yeah. But how often do you get down here?"

"I go where they send me," he told her.

She nodded and turned away. Even with the undercover operation underway, they were ships passing at sea. It was disturbing that she was coming to care about him, and almost humiliating the way that she felt...

With him, she would have gladly taken a feigned relationship anywhere.

It was one thing to discover she found him attractive. More, even. Compelling, sensual...a man with the kind of masculinity that moved beyond sense and logic and simply reached into the very core of her being.

It just didn't work to be craving his touch while on the job.

"Well, we've checked in, Jorge knows I'm all right," she said, "and Connor will have Kari on the beach somewhere soon. I'd like to get back to South Beach."

"We can do that," he said.

He took her arm and they headed back. David Hernandez was waiting for them by the limo. Jacob told David he was great, and they would use him in the future, but for the moment, they'd decided just to head back to the hotel. They were going to wander the sand by night.

Hernandez thought that was fine, and he was grateful they'd call on him again. Of course, the man would be pleased. He had the night off now with full pay.

Jasmine and Jacob were both quiet during the drive back. When they reached the cute little boutique hotel where Jacob was staying, Jasmine admired the old lobby.

"You've never been in here before?" he asked her.

She grinned. "When I was in high school, we used to come out here and prowl a few of the clubs and maybe have soda or coffee at a few of the hotels. But I think I've only stayed out here a few times. I'm a native, but that doesn't mean I know every hotel."

"It's nice. Not a chain. And the owners seem to love the deco spirit of the place. I can have coffee on the balcony every morning if I want. I can hear the sound of the surf and watch the palm trees sway—before the rest of the world wakes up and the beach becomes crowded with bodies."

She smiled. "You will see some of the most beautiful bodies in the world out here, you know."

He was quiet for a minute.

"You disagree?"

He smiled awkwardly and shrugged, and then looked at her at last. His light blue eyes seemed to caress the length of her.

Her heart, her soul, her *longing* seemed to jump to her throat.

But he quickly changed moods. "Then again, it's not just perfect bodies. You know that, of course."

"You mean old and wrinkly? We'll all be there someday. I hope when I'm older and drooping everywhere, I still love the beach."

He laughed. "I'm with you on that. I hope when I'm creased and drooping everywhere I can still sit on the sand and watch the sway of the palms and not worry that someone is judging me. I believe everyone has to do what is comfortable for them—and that's part of what I love.

"Yes, there's beauty. Yes, there's the ridiculous. And

there are quiet times, when the sun is rising, when you can look out and feel you're in a private paradise. And then you turn around and the neon of the hotels and the rush of the world comes on in. This place is ever changing, plastic in so many ways and yet real when it comes to the feel of the salt air and those moments when you're in the water, and it's just you and the waves and the sea and the sky."

"Yes," she said softly.

"So, let's take a walk," he said.

They headed out to the beach. Jasmine doffed her sneakers and Jacob rid himself of his shoes and socks, too. They left them by a palm.

Jacob's phone rang.

He listened, and then he told Jasmine, "Connor has Kari out to dinner. He took her to Joe's Stone Crab. They're fine."

"I'm afraid for when they leave. What do we do now?"

"Wait," he said.

"So hard!"

He laughed. "I've been undercover for months at a time. Watching, waiting. And for this case, well, the watching and waiting is a hell of a lot better than usual." He was quiet for a minute. "I recently worked a case where immigrants were brought in and used horribly. It was long on my part, but when it broke, we moved quickly. This may be the same. Thing is, right now, we could get them, or Ivan at least, on money. Then again, they can employ the best legal team known to man. So, we have to take them down big-time—with evidence that prosecutors can take to court."

Jasmine muttered, "So…we wait."

"And play the part," he agreed.

Nightfall was coming in earnest. The sky was fighting darkness and the sun was shooting out rays that seemed to be pure gold and magenta.

Jasmine wasn't sure what got into her. She suddenly broke away from him and ran down the beach, turned and kicked up a spray of the waves that had been washing over their feet.

She caught him with a full body splash, and he yelped and laughed with surprise. Then he came after her.

She squealed and turned to run, but he tackled her and bore her down to the soft damp sand. He leaned over her, looked down into her eyes and then murmured, "Good move. I just saw Sasha up on the boardwalk. We are being watched."

He eased closer. "Can I kiss you?"

Role-playing...

She tangled her fingers into the richness of his hair, pulling him in, and he kissed her.

And then he broke away, laughing, and pulled her to her feet. "I think we gave Sasha a good show, eh?" he asked softly.

"Oh, yeah," she whispered. Once again, her lips were burning.

As they retrieved their shoes and decided on a restaurant for dinner, she couldn't help but wish that the FBI had sent down a much less attractive agent.

Chapter Seven

"His full name is Donald McPherson Connor," Jacob told Jasmine. "He's living at that grand old place down from the club just off of Washington Street—a quiet and dark intersection. The whole sixth floor is his apartment."

They were at her place. He'd done a thorough search for bugs and hadn't found any, and with the way this gang seemed to work, he was pretty sure he wouldn't find anything. In Kozak's words, Jasmine was "just a woman."

Jacob had a feeling that Kozak might be pretty surprised.

Just a woman. In any kind of a fair fight, Jasmine would take Kozak.

But for them, at this moment, it bode well that Kozak and the members of his gang still seemed to live in an archaic world of chauvinism.

"And what else?" Jasmine asked.

"Born in Yorkshire, and he has dual citizenship."

"How does he make his money?"

"He inherited a nice sum and knows how to invest in the stock market."

"So, an older Englishman-turned-American, rich, with nothing to do. Wife? Kids?"

Jasmine had changed from her salt-spray-and-sand-covered clothing to a dark silky maxi dress. She'd come to perch on the sofa by him, hugging her knees to her chest as she looked at him.

"Wife died about ten years ago. They had a daughter but I can't find much on her."

"Criminal past?"

"Nope."

"Any hint of anyone disappearing when he's around?"

"He's been living in Savannah. He's just been down here about two months. They're still looking into him."

"And the agent saw him take Kari back to her apartment and then leave?"

"Yes," Jacob said.

He didn't have to read from his phone; one of his assets was his memory. He could retain what was told to him, which was probably why languages came to him easily. Then again, he loved languages, and all the little rules and differences and nuances within them.

He wished at that moment, though, that he was reading. Because he was left to meet her eyes.

He'd been right that first day, when he'd seen her from afar. Her eyes were green. A brilliant beautiful green, like twin emeralds in a sea of gold. Her face was so perfectly molded he was tempted to reach out and touch it, as he might be tempted to reach out and touch a classic sculpture. Her hair was free, freshly washed and tumbling around her shoulders, still damp. And in the maxi dress, she seemed exceptionally alluring—though he was sure she had donned the article of clothing because it covered her entire body. It felt like a reaction to the skimpy outfit she'd been forced to put on for the "date" with Connor.

"But according to Kari, Mary did escort him," Jasmine pointed out, "and then she disappeared."

"You're going to need to get closer to Kari."

"Well, we're both supposed to report to Natasha tomorrow—Kari and I."

"And I have an excuse to go in. I've gotten Kozak's permission to investigate Smirnoff's murder."

"Have the cops gotten anything? I guess not. I'm pretty sure that, even though the FBI has lead, I'd know about it if anyone had been apprehended for the murder."

"From what I've heard, they're still pretty much in the dark," Jacob said. "Trajectory shows the bullets were fired from the balcony. But everyone working there swears the balconies were closed off. Someone is lying, of course. But no one knows who."

"No guns were found, no casings…no nothing?"

"Nope. And the gunmen—two to three of them, best estimate—entirely disappeared."

Jasmine leaned her chin thoughtfully on her knees. "We could see all the major players when it happened. You were out there with Kozak, Ivan Petrov and the goons, Sasha, Antonio and Alejandro. And Natasha was backstage."

"The killers were hired, obviously. And they were guaranteed a clean getaway. We dusted for prints on the rails and so forth, but there are hundreds of prints. Workmen were there, of course, before the grand opening. Anyone who so much as delivered pizza might have left a print. Smirnoff, from what I understand, loved showing off the place and brought everyone out to those balconies to let them see how they looked down at the floor and the main stage."

She shook her head. "So, we're nowhere."

"No. We're moving forward. You're just impatient."

"I guess so. I mean, I have worked undercover before. But often just for a day or so, getting into the right place, talking to the right people. I admit—it was never anything like this."

"We just keep moving forward."

She nodded. "I guess... I guess I need some sleep."

"Go on."

"You're staying here?"

"I believe I'm entitled now—and I don't want to disappoint anyone by not taking my full measure."

"Ah." She stood, almost leaping away from him. "Pillow and blankets. If I'd known I was having nightly guests, I would have asked for a two-bedroom." She smiled awkwardly and hurried into her bedroom. A moment later, she was back. She plopped down two pillows, sheets and a blanket. "Not sure if you need the blanket, I don't air-condition the place too much. But... Anyway, all right. I'll see you in the morning. Start coffee if you're up first!"

She spoke quickly, almost nervously. It wasn't like her.

"Good night," he said softly.

She left him, and he wished he wasn't playing a role. More than that, he wished he wasn't working. She'd closed the door between them, but he could still see her in his mind's eye.

See her laughter as she kicked up the salt spray.

Feel her beneath him when he tackled her in the sand.

He could see the emerald of her eyes as she'd looked at him before she pulled him in for that blistering kiss.

And he couldn't help but wonder, in his misery, if she just might...just might...be wishing a little bit herself that they had met under different circumstances.

He spent the next hour reminding himself he was a special agent, he loved his job and he had made a difference... They were professional. They played their parts. They brought down the bad guys.

He thought he'd never sleep. He wondered why the hell he had stayed. She could take care of herself. She was trained.

But despite the logic, despite what he knew, he was afraid for her.

He could have returned to his apartment. He knew being here had nothing to do with being professional. If it came to it, he'd give anything to save her life if it was threatened in any way.

Why? He'd worked cases with so many beautiful women and never done more than acknowledge that fact.

Jasmine was different. She had touched something else in him. Something that was more than attraction, even desire.

She was...everything. Everything in a way he hadn't known in over a decade. Not since his wife had died.

JACOB WAS UP when Jasmine emerged in the morning.

She'd spent the night...waiting. She'd thought the door to her bedroom might open at any time. She couldn't decide if she wanted it to or not.

But it did not, and when she finally rose, she found

him already awake. He'd brewed coffee and was sipping a cup, leaning thoughtfully against the refrigerator.

He looked at her as she emerged, his eyes fathomless.

"Three more bodies last night," he said softly.

"What? Where?" she asked. Three bodies. Was one Mary?

He must have seen the fear on her face. "Three men again," he said quickly. "And they weren't found in oil drums. This time, they were found south of the Tamiami Trail. Miami-Dade County, on Miccosukee tribal land."

"Three. Maybe the hired gunmen? If they weren't in oil drums, if they're new… It's possible it isn't related. Will we get identities soon?" Jasmine said.

He hesitated. "No. The bodies are missing heads and hands."

"Oh."

"Cause of death?"

"Unknown, at this point. In my mind, logic suggests they were shot in the head."

"Logic?"

"Execution-style—then the heads were removed. Dumped them in the Everglades." He hesitated. "From what I've been told, they were well ravaged by the animal life. Among other creatures, the vultures had a feast."

"There are few better places to dispose of a body than the Everglades," Jasmine agreed. "But they were definitely…male bodies?"

"Yes, definitely male bodies."

She wandered to the coffeepot and poured herself a cup. She was shaken, but she didn't want to be. She was a detective in a major crime division. But this was personal.

Maybe she shouldn't have been working this investigation. But there had truly been no one better suited to the task of getting in with the Deco Gang.

Jacob came up behind her and placed a hand on her shoulders. "Jasmine, I believe the men found might well have been the shooters. If whoever planned this wanted to make sure no one talked, they had to get rid of the people who actually carried out the deed."

"Yes, that's my gut feeling on it, too," she said. Her hands were still trembling slightly as she held her coffee cup. And she was ridiculously aware of him, right there behind her, the heat of his body, the scent of him.

She had to spin around, composed and determined. "So, today, you start questioning everyone?"

"Today I start questioning everyone."

He had barely spoken when there was a knock on the door.

"Excuse me," she murmured.

As she headed to the door, she was aware Jacob had already showered and dressed completely for the day. He had his hand behind his back, ready to draw his weapon if the guest at the door intended to offer any danger.

No danger was forthcoming; she looked through the peephole. It was Jorge.

She let him in quickly. "Hey."

Jorge glanced at Jacob. He seemed to accept the man's presence as normal.

"I was bringing you the latest news. Captain said he didn't think you should be calling in, even on the burners. Too easy for one of them to catch the phone and check out numbers and get suspicious when nothing on you had an easily trackable number. But I imagine you've gotten the latest?"

"The bodies in the Glades?" she asked.

He nodded and looked at Jacob. "Who do you think did it? Is it Kozak? Natasha? Ivan?"

"I don't know. But I intend to find out." Jacob smiled. "Breakfast first. Somewhere obvious. Somewhere anyone who wishes can see the three of us—me and my escort, provided for me with their blessing, and you, my new love's best friend. Plenty of places in the area. Let's go for a walk and find good food."

"Okay," Jorge said slowly, frowning.

"Then Jasmine needs to check in with Natasha and assure her of my happiness and her own satisfaction with the arrangement—and I get to question the goons."

"And…" Jorge pressed. "Me?"

"I think it's fine if you come in today, just a cheerful dude happy to be with a friend."

"It's a plan," Jorge said.

It wasn't difficult for Jacob to pretend to be out with friends. He liked Jorge very much and thought he was probably a damned good cop. He knew how to fit in to what he was doing, and he didn't need to take the lead. He'd set up the tour for them yesterday in minutes flat and had managed to introduce him and Jasmine on the floor opening night at the club—at the end of a spray of bullets—without giving things away. Jacob also just liked the man.

And as for Jasmine…

He had to be careful.

When they were seated, Jasmine and Jorge were talk-

ing about Miami, and Jasmine was telling Jorge about
their tour guide.

"He was a great guy—a super guide, knew his stuff,"
Jasmine said. "Friendly and informative without being
annoying."

"Hard to imagine this place as a coconut plantation," Jacob said.

"Hard to imagine the whole south of the state as a
'river of grass,'" Jasmine said.

Jacob noted that there was a man seated at a far back
table, eating and reading a newspaper. Watching them.

Jacob picked up his coffee cup and said softly, "Antonio Garibaldi is at the back of the restaurant."

"We were followed here," Jorge said casually.

"And here's the thing," Jasmine said, running her
fingers up Jacob's arm and smiling sensually, "we don't
even know who else might be in the employ of the new
boss, be he Kozak or even someone else."

Jacob leaned closer to her. "We need to find out who
is calling the shots." He planted a quick kiss on her lips
and looked at her lingeringly. Then he stood. "Think
I'll visit the restroom."

He headed to the back of the restaurant and the re-
strooms. But he made a pretense of stopping, as if surprised and pleased to see Garibaldi.

"Hey! I guess I did choose a good place, if you're
here," he said. He pulled out the chair on the other side
of the table and sat.

"Yeah, they do a great breakfast," Garibaldi said.
He was a big man with dark hair and a solid physique,
built as a good bouncer should be. His eyes were quick
and dark. His smile was pained.

"I'm really loving South Florida," Jacob told him.

"And getting to work with Kozak. Of course, I'm as sympathetic as anyone over Smirnoff. He was a good man. What the hell do you think happened? I mean, forgive me, I know you guys are good at your jobs. But how the hell did shooters get up on the balconies?"

Garibaldi looked uncomfortable—he was on the spot. Then he leaned forward. "Hell if I know. Seriously. From the beginning, it was planned that the balconies be roped off. Crowd control. And that day... Smirnoff was giving us our orders. I was watching the front, Suarez had the stage and Antonovich was moving through the crowd. There were cops all over, hired for the occasion. I'll be damned if I can figure it out, and I've tried. Thing is, I was given my orders. The other guys were given their orders. We never saw anyone get up there."

"There has to be an entrance from the offices," Jacob said.

"Sure. There's a door across from Smirnoff's office. That way, when he chose to, he could be in his office, and when he wanted to be part of the crowd, he could come out on the balcony. The cops were all over it. But here's the thing. The door is kept locked. There's a key. And when the cops were all over the place right after the shooting, the door was still locked. Smirnoff kept the key."

"Duplicate keys can be made. I'm sure the cops checked on that," Jacob said.

Garibaldi shrugged. "Whoever may have had a duplicate key, I don't know."

"It was obviously well planned."

Garibaldi appeared to be honestly confused. "You know, sure, it could have been planned. But it seemed like one of those bad things, you know. Some disturbed person just out to hurt anyone—and getting Smirnoff."

"You don't believe that, do you?" Jacob asked.

Garibaldi's voice was soft and low. "I want to believe it," he said.

"But you don't."

"Kozak told us last night that he'd given you permission to question us, see if you couldn't figure something out. I'd like to help you. What do I know? I was in my position. And the shooting started. I was—well, hell. Hate to admit this. I was scared. I think I managed to get people out, get them down. But I got the hell out as fast as I could myself."

"You were armed?"

"I was. But the best gun in the world doesn't do you a bit of good if you don't know what you're supposed to be shooting at."

He seemed to be telling the truth. Jacob never took anyone at face value, but he also noted the man's expressions and body language. He'd have bet that he was being honest.

Garibaldi looked at him and seemed to judge him, as well. "I'm not in this for violence," he said softly. "The money is good..." He shrugged. "I mind my own business and don't care where it comes from. Drugs... People are going to buy them somewhere. The girls... They do what they choose. Natasha talked to Jasmine, and you all had an agreement. Cool. She seems to really like you. So, is that a crime? As for me, I do what I'm told and I keep my nose clean and stay out. I'm just security."

"So you're just supposed to report on us today?" Jacob asked him.

"Yeah. And it's cool. It's obvious you two have more than a business relationship going. That's the way Josef Smirnoff always rolled. Kozak said that it will be business as usual. Of course, he's scared now. Whoever killed Smirnoff could be gunning for him. That's probably why he said you could talk to people. Though, I already told the cops what I told you. The truth."

"Sure. Hey, next time you're watching us, just join us." Jacob shrugged. "She's a cool girl and I like Jorge, too."

"That wouldn't be the way the game is played," Garibaldi said.

"No, I guess not." Jacob stood. "You're a good-looking man with the right stuff. There are tons of other places on the beach that need bouncers, security. If this whole scene is too much for you."

Garibaldi shrugged. "I screwed up once. Didn't check an ID the way I should have. The girl's parents caused a stink. Josef gave me a job. Said I didn't need to ID anyone." He laughed suddenly. "Garibaldi. Nice Italian name. I was born here, my parents were born here and my grandfather came over from Naples to run a tailor shop. No mob ties whatsoever. He was in Worcester, Massachusetts. And didn't even have to pay anyone for a safe working environment.

"Alejandro Suarez, his family came over in the late 1880s. They were cigar makers up in Ybor City, Tampa area. And even Antonovich, he's a third-generation American. We're not…we're not mob. We're not mob-related. I'm here because I have a job. And I do it. Long hours, maybe, but so far, I haven't been asked to do anything other than protect people, watch people and break up fights."

"And what if you had to do something that was illegal?"

"It would depend on what that thing was." Garibaldi hesitated a minute. Then he said quietly, "Hey, man, you're buying art—that you haven't even seen. And we all know about your past."

Jacob nodded. "Yeah. But I play it the way Smirnoff played it. I don't go in for murder. Gets messy—and gets the cops on you."

"Yeah," Garibaldi agreed.

"Sounds like you're a good man. One I'd like to have on my side," Jacob said.

"Thanks," Garibaldi told him.

Jacob left him and returned to his own table. Jasmine and Jorge were having a conversation about the best spas in the area. When he sat down, Jasmine played it perfectly, stroking his arm.

He wished her touch didn't seem to awaken every ounce of longing in his body.

NATASHA WAS WITH Kozak when they arrived.

Jacob was allowed admittance to Kozak's office. Jasmine and Jorge were directed to the dressing room, where they were alone.

Jorge found a stereo system and turned on music. Phil Collins, "In the Air Tonight." Fitting. Shades of the old *Miami Vice* that had really put the area—and many myths about it—on the map.

"Natasha is sleeping with Kozak," Jorge said softly. "She might have been sleeping with Josef Smirnoff, too. At any rate, she was with him for years and years. Trusted. She could have gotten the key and had a copy made."

Natasha came sweeping into the room. She saw Jorge and frowned slightly, then shrugged. "I suppose you say anything in front of Jorge," she said. "Oh, by the way, Jorge, a man has been courting our business, one who may need some entertainment."

"Ready when you are," Jorge said.

"Now, Jasmine, about Mr. Marensky…"

Jasmine smiled and then decided to go another step. She walked over and hugged Natasha.

The woman was not used to hugs. She didn't push Jasmine away, but she didn't hug her back. She awkwardly patted her shoulders. "So, all went well," Natasha said.

"He's lovely," Jasmine said. "Best way to make some money I've ever known!"

"Yes, I believe you. You're very lucky such a man is so captivated by you. It's not always the case, but for you… Yes, I am glad that such a striking man—one whom Josef approved and Victor seems to admire, especially—has taken such a shine to you. But you must realize, my dear, he may tire of you. And move on."

"I know that," Jasmine said. "But for now…he's fun. He wishes to please me."

"And he is far from repulsive in bed, I imagine," Natasha said.

Jasmine didn't let her smile slip. "Oh, so, so, far from repulsive."

"Ah, she's a lucky one," Jorge said.

"Then you will continue as you have been doing. Don't forget… Friday night. Friday is the funeral. And at the funeral, you will be a hostess here, and you mustn't cling to Mr. Marensky at the gathering after the ceremony. After tomorrow night, the club may reopen.

The workers will have cleaned up. No bullet holes will show in the walls by the ceremony. Now, you do understand about Marensky, Jasmine? First, we need you to be working. Second, it's important he remembers that he is graced with your company through us."

"Definitely," Jasmine said. "Understood."

"Then you are free for today. You may go. You, too, Jorge." She handed them each an envelope. Their paychecks. They had no choice but to thank her and leave.

As they walked, they noted they were being followed. It was Alejandro Suarez on their tail this time.

"So, straight to my place, I guess," Jasmine murmured.

"I don't think they're following me."

"What about phones?"

"I have a new one."

"I need to know about Connor. About Connor…and Kari."

Jorge sighed. "Jasmine, we have to trust our fellows. They saw last night that Connor left Kari at her apartment. No sex, nothing. She was fine."

Aware of their follower, Jasmine laughed as if Jorge had said something great and grabbed his arm in fun— as a friend might do. In contrast to her actions, her whisper was intense. "But what are they doing about him?"

"Watching. And waiting," Jorge said. "Jasmine, you knew this wasn't going to be an instant fix, that we'd be out of the loop much of the time. And—"

They had only come a half a block from the club when Jasmine saw Kari headed their way. She released Jorge's arm and cried out with delight, running to see the other girl.

"Kari!" She hugged her. She pulled away and asked softly, "All is well?"

"Fine, it's lovely. Mr. Connor is an absolute gentleman. I'll be seeing him tonight." Kari grinned and said, "Oh, he isn't young and hot like Marensky. But he's fine, very nice. Polite and courteous in a way I haven't seen in years. Happy to have some arm candy while he's out on the town, you know?"

"Good. Well, I guess you knew that, from what Mary said."

"I miss Mary. She was the sweetest!"

"Did she ever say anything to you," Jasmine asked, "anything about going away or even…even about being afraid?"

"No. She was just with us, and then one day she didn't show and didn't come back. Natasha was very upset. She was very fond of Mary, too. Speaking of Natasha, I've got to get in. She wants to see me." But suddenly, Kari gripped Jasmine's hands. "I'm telling you, Mr. Connor is so kind and caring, wanting to know my every wish."

Jasmine realized then that it was the man's very kindness that actually frightened Kari.

Someone so nice. What happened when he wasn't? What might he really want?

Further determined, Jasmine smiled. "Great, Kari," she said loudly. "I guess Jorge and I are going to go home and binge on repeats of *Desperate Housewives*."

"Have fun!"

"You're welcome to join us!"

Kari waved and headed off.

Jasmine headed back and grabbed Jorge's arm. "Something has to be done," she said firmly. "Before tonight!"

Chapter Eight

"I have had that door rekeyed," Kozak told Jacob. "The police asked about it, but it was locked. There was no sign that anyone had forced it. But...how? How did someone get through the balcony without being seen? There were dressers here, makeup artists... But when the show began, everyone was downstairs. Natasha was with the girls backstage. The band members were all downstairs. I didn't have the key! No one had the key—except for Josef Smirnoff."

"Someone obviously copied it," Jacob said flatly.

Kozak shook his head. "I have the only key now. No one knows where I keep it. And I don't intend to tell anyone. Including you. No offense or disrespect intended."

"None taken," Jacob said.

"You are free to look around, but I have to go. Josef's body is at the funeral home. I will make sure he is given the send-off such a man deserves."

"Where will the funeral be?"

"A small Russian Orthodox church, up the way on the beach. And then we will come here." Kozak hesitated. "Will you make the arrangements for it with me today?"

"I thought that I should stay here. We want to know what happened to Josef," Jacob reminded him.

"We do." Kozak sighed deeply. "Yes, you must speak with Antonio, Alejandro and Sasha. The thing is…"

"What is it?"

"They have their place. We work carefully. Of course, they are aware… But we never give them facts. They know people, they know who is important, but we have never given them much on the clients."

"They might have seen something," Jacob said. "Something they don't even know they saw. I've spoken with Antonio. You didn't tell me about the door and the key."

"I didn't. I had to make sure. Josef brought you in, and he assured me you were solid, that you were a powerful man with a long history. I had to come to know you myself." Kozak shrugged. "The police checked the door. They remain with nothing."

"But you know someone within your own ranks had to be involved."

Kozak looked unhappy. "Yes. But whoever did this, they were clever. They hired out. A man doesn't guard what he doesn't see to be in danger."

"No," Jacob agreed, trying to read Kozak.

"You must do what you will. I have hidden nothing on Josef's murder from the police. I will not hide it from you. But I must prepare to bury an old and dear friend."

It was evident that Kozak wanted company while he made arrangements at the funeral home. Perhaps it was even important to go with him.

"I will go with you," Jacob agreed.

As it turned out, Kozak didn't want a driver with

them. He had a big black Cadillac sedan, and he asked
Jacob if he would do the driving.

"You don't want one of the guys to come along?"

"A bodyguard?" Kozak asked. "I think you will do."

They took Collins Avenue north and reached the
funeral home. They were greeted by a solemn man in
a suit, Mr. Derby, the current owner of Sacred Night
Final Rest Parlor.

Derby expressed his condolences, offered them water
or coffee and then tactfully suggested they needed to
choose a coffin. The coffins ranged from a few thousand dollars to just about enough to buy a house—at
the least, a nice automobile.

Jacob was surprised to see tears in Victor Kozak's
eyes. He had either really cared for his friend, or he was
able to pull off a feat many a Hollywood actor could not.

Then again, business was business. He could have
loved the man—and still arranged for his death.

"What do you think, my friend?" Kozak asked Jacob.

"Personally?" Jacob asked. "I believe in a greater
power, but I don't believe the body is anything but a
shell. It makes no difference if a man is laid to rest in
the finest mahogany or the cheapest pine, or if he's cremated and his ashes thrown to the wind. But if you're
worried about the funeral, about our show of respect…
then I'd say this."

Mr. Derby, the funeral director, was eyeing Jacob
with anything but kindness. Still, he seemed to perk
up when Jacob pointed out a fairly expensive coffin,
one that was both handsome, staid and possessed just
the right amount of ornamentation.

"Perfect," Kozak said quietly. "This one is it, sir."

"All right, nice choice," Mr. Derby said. "Now, as to the wake—"

"No wake," Kozak said. "You will bring the body to the church. Closed coffin."

"Sir, my people have done an extraordinary job. You may have a wake. Mr. Smirnoff's face was not impacted, and his suit will cover—"

"No wake. No open coffin," Kozak said. "Josef will be honored and buried."

"As you wish, sir. As you wish. This is a painful time for you as a friend. I do suggest that you consider a viewing, for other friends—"

"No," Kozak said. "Our business is quite complete. We have our own cars for the services. You will bring Josef as arranged to the church. And arrange for the transport from there to the cemetery."

"Yes, Mr. Kozak. Arrangements have been made. He will be brought from the church to the cemetery. Now, the cemetery is over in Miami. You will need police officers for the journey as friends follow for the last services, something which, of course, we take care of for you."

Kozak waved a hand in the air. "Do what is needed."

He was anxious to leave; Jacob held back and assured Derby, "Someone will be by with the final check."

He then followed Victor Kozak back out to the car. The man waited by the passenger's side as Jacob clicked the door open.

Kozak was trembling when he sat. Jacob hurried around to the driver's seat. He didn't have to push; Kozak appeared ready to speak.

"It's not real—I was there. I was there for a hail of bullets. I watched my friend fall, I saw the blood. And yet, it's not real. Not until you see he is laid into the ground. Yes, it is indeed a hard time. You know this. You have laid a wife to rest."

Jacob was still a moment.

A deceased wife was in his fake dossier. It was always best, when creating such a lie, to incorporate many details of life that were real. That helped an agent live the lie that was being created.

"It was a long time ago, right?" Victor Kozak asked.

Yes, a lifetime ago. He'd fallen in love with Sabrina Marshall the minute he had seen her. It had been tenth grade. They'd quickly become an item; he, a high school jock, Sabrina the smart one. They'd married and gone off to college together, and even after graduation when they'd planned their perfect life, talked about starting a family...

The cancer had found her. It had cared nothing about youthful dreams.

"It was a long time ago, yes," Jacob said softly.

A long, long time ago. Many women in between; savvy, bright women, some in business, some in politics, but none in law enforcement.

None like Jasmine, someone he had seen from afar who had nevertheless seemed to enter into his soul. He barely knew her. Maybe, though, he knew her enough.

Maybe, when this was over... When this was all over, Jasmine would no longer be playing a role. She would go back to her passion, being cop in a major crime unit. And he would go where the Bureau sent him, because he was good at what he did, and he did believe, no matter what unbelievable things were going on in the world, that what he did was right. One good man, or maybe many good men, could make the world a better place.

Sabrina had believed that, too.

"I'm sorry," Kozak said.

"So am I," Jacob said softly. "So am I."

"But now, this woman, this Jasmine—she means something to you?"

"Yes," Jacob said simply.

"When Natasha brought her in, I knew, too, there was something about her. Women...most often, they are just part of business, and that's how it must be. So few have that inner fire. But, now and then...one enchants the mind, eh?"

"Yes," Jacob agreed. "This one in particular...there is something that appeals to me on many levels."

"She's all yours," Kozak said.

Jacob lowered his head. He was pretty sure he knew how Jasmine would feel about being granted to a man as payment for his friendship.

Heading back to Washington Street, Jacob cut down Meridian Avenue. As they neared the Holocaust Memorial of the Greater Miami Jewish Federation, Kozak made a little sound.

The memorial was a heart-wrenching, well-conceived artwork, created by survivors, respected and honored by a community. Statues and plaques told a story that tore at the human soul.

Jacob had been there several times through the years. His own past was a checkered piece of all manner of peoples, from the free world and from areas of great subjugation; his Russian mother had a background that included royalty, his Israeli father had parents who had barely made it out of Germany. Jacob was eternally grateful they had chosen the United States as a place to raise their own family—he knew he'd had a relatively easy and privileged start to life.

He was surprised when Kozak asked him to stop.

"You want to get out and walk around?" Jacob asked.

Kozak shook his head. "I just want to look."

Jacob sat next to him in silence.

"World War II. A brutal business. Hitler wanting to exterminate a race of people. Stalin…twenty million Russians were also killed, you know, between the enemy and Stalin."

"Yes, I am aware."

"Young people these days…they don't always know."

"Education is everything," Jacob murmured.

One of the sculptures at the outdoor memorial was especially poignant. It depicted a body, as many bodies had been found. Prisoners had not just gone to the death camps to be gassed and cremated; they'd gone to be a work force, and they'd been all but starved as they worked.

The body was skeletal and depicted in bronze. They were a distance from the sculpture and couldn't see it completely. But Jacob had seen it before. And he knew that Kozak had, too.

Kozak turned to Jacob. "My grandmother survived by hiding in plain sight in Berlin. My grandfather was a Russian soldier, hiding the fact that he was also Jewish. When the Soviet Army closed in on Berlin, my grandfather found my grandmother, who was terrified. She had been in living with a Christian German couple who were appalled by the death and terror around them. She'd been told, however, there was less torture if you quickly admitted what you were. When he found her, she said, *'Juden.'* But you see, my grandfather said,

'*Juden*, yes, I am *Juden*, too.' They were married, and they stayed married for the next forty years. They died in the same year. I believe he died of a broken heart when he lost her, because she passed away first."

"They had years together. It is still a beautiful story," Jacob said.

Kozak turned to him. "I have told you this story because maybe it will help you believe me. I don't kill people. I don't torture, and I don't kill."

Jacob couldn't help himself. Looking at Kozak, he said, "I beg to differ—slightly. Drugs kill."

Kozak waved a hand in the air. "Drugs kill, but people have a choice. But we do nothing where others have not made a choice. The addict must choose life. The drugs exist with or without my participation. We may as well get rich. Am I a good man? No. Am I a cold-blooded killer? No. Take what you will from that. But I did not kill my friend Josef."

Jacob nodded slowly.

Neither spoke for a moment.

He put the car back into gear and drove back south, to Washington Street and the club. They hadn't been away long.

"So, now," Kozak said, "you will find out what happened to Josef, yes?"

"I will do my damnedest," Jacob said.

JORGE REALLY DID put on a Netflix marathon of *Desperate Housewives*.

Jasmine nervously paced the room. "We should be doing something," she said.

"Jasmine, here's the thing. We are doing something,"

Jorge told her. "Okay, so, you're not a fan. What should we watch?"

"I can't. I can't sit still."

"You stink at this."

"Sorry!"

"All right," Jorge said. "I'll check in with Captain Lorenzo. Will that help?"

"Maybe."

He took out his phone and called. Jasmine watched him as he spoke, assuring Lorenzo they were both fine and they were proceeding with the work and their relationship with the FBI was moving along smoothly. Then he asked if anything else had been discovered, listened a while and then thanked Lorenzo and promised he'd be the one in touch.

"Well?" Jasmine demanded, burning with impatience.

"There's a Miccosukee village where they sell handmade clothing, arts and crafts—and have alligator shows," he said.

"I know. It's out on Tamiami Trail, just west of Shark Valley."

"There's a fellow who lives not far from the village. He raises alligators, sells them to various venues for alligator wrestling. Handles them from the time they hatch." Jorge stopped speaking.

"And?"

"One of his young alligators died, and he didn't know why, so there was a necropsy done on the gator."

"And?"

"They found a hand. He reported it. And it's been brought in to the medical examiner, and they believe it belonged to one of the dead men found out there.

They're hoping to get an ID. I don't know a lot about alligator stomach acids, but…well, they're still hoping to get something."

"I know what they're going to find," Jasmine said. "There won't be a match. I'm willing to bet that whoever is doing this is clever enough to have hired undocumented newcomers to do the deed."

"Maybe. Someone desperate and grateful for any work that doesn't go on the books."

Jasmine nodded. "Jorge, what do you think of Natasha?"

"She's all business."

"Yes. And she was in charge of the models. Of the show. And we all suspect she is sleeping with Victor Kozak, but—"

"Maybe she slept with Josef, too. And maybe she was sleeping with Victor because Josef tired of her, and maybe—"

"Maybe!" Jasmine said. "If only we had a definite."

She started to pace again, thinking, trying to remember every move Natasha had made on the day of the show.

Jorge groaned and turned back to *Desperate Housewives*.

"Hey," Jacob said to Alejandro Suarez. He was on guard downstairs, at the door to the club offices and staging area.

"Hey," Suarez said. He studied Jacob. He was puffing on a cigarette, leaned against the wall. He grinned suddenly. "Are you some new kind of enforcer?"

"I'm just an art dealer."

Suarez studied him. "Sure. But hey, I just work here. Kozak said you were going to talk to us."

"Do you remember anyone—anyone you didn't know—at the grand opening?"

Suarez laughed. "Anyone I didn't know? What? Do I look like I rub elbows with the rich and famous regularly?" There must have been something ominous in Jacob's look, because he quickly sobered up.

"Did you see anyone upstairs?" Jacob clarified. "We know that the killers were on the balcony."

"Yeah, that's what the cops said." Suarez sighed, reaching in his jacket pocket for another cigarette. He lit it with his current smoke. The man was a few years younger than Garibaldi and maybe a few inches taller in height. "I came in through the upstairs. We all reported to Josef, who said the balcony would be closed off. That would leave all of us down on the floor with the hired cops—you don't do anything that big without hiring cops."

"Right."

"When I checked in, the girls were all getting dressed. The band members were in the green room, making cracks about the girls. I guess they planned on having them in to party later. That idea went all to hell, huh?"

"You saw the band, Josef Smirnoff, Natasha and the girls. Anyone else?"

"Ivan was already down at the bar. The caterers were never allowed upstairs. Oh, Victor Kozak was downstairs already when I came in, seeing to a last-minute check on the place. When I joined him, he pointed out that the balcony stairways—there's one set near the entrance on both sides—were roped off with velvet cords.

They didn't want people up on the balcony. There's only one door up on the second floor, but it almost leads right into the office, and they didn't want anyone going up because of the office. And he didn't want anybody trying to grab selfies with the girls or the band or anything. If anyone headed toward the stairs, we were to politely stop them. And if they tried again, we were to politely escort them out."

"But no one tried to get up the stairs?"

"There were big signs attached to the velvet cords that said No Admittance. I think most people honor signs like that. Hey, it wasn't supposed to be... It was supposed to be a cool grand opening. No one expected any violence. If anything, we'd have had to throw out a drunk."

"But you saw no one. Nothing?"

Suarez shook his head. "No! I mean, I could have told you before the cops did their investigating that the shooters had to have been on the balcony. But there was a stampede. You know that. I admit, I froze for a second. Then I went to work getting people out."

"Was anyone on the back door—where we are now?"

"I'm assuming it was locked up tight. We were all on the main floor. But..."

"But?"

"I don't know what weapons were used. I was thinking that whoever was up there... Well, if they pocketed their weapons, in all the confusion, they might have come down the stairs and run out with everyone else. Or..." Suarez paused, shaking his head.

"What?"

"They could have come out the back, out of this door. But you see, I don't understand how that would be possible. Cops were already in here. They were crawling all over the area within minutes. I can't believe they wouldn't have seen three men with guns run out this door." Suarez seemed as mystified as Garibaldi had been.

Two down; one to go.

They were great liars—or they had planned their stories well.

Jacob thanked him, then turned and hurried back up the stairs. He found Sasha Antonovich outside the door to Kozak's office. Like Alejandro Suarez, he seemed at ease—bored, probably—as he stood by the door.

"My turn, eh?" Antonovich asked him. He shrugged. "We just look stupid. Kozak said you were going to try to do what the police seem be failing at. So. What can I tell you?"

"What *can* you tell me?"

Antonovich was older than both Suarez and Garibaldi. Remembering all the info he had been given, Jacob knew Antonovich had been with Josef Smirnoff the longest—well over a decade. His hair was beginning to gray, just at the temples. Fine lines were appearing around his light brown eyes, and he wore a weary look.

The man shook his head, his expression grim. "What do I know? That it wasn't just a random shooting? That someone was after Josef? I'm sure you believe that, too. How the hell did they get in? They had to have been on a guest list. I don't know who they were, what they looked like... There were hundreds of people here. They could have been with the caterers, they could have gotten in with the off-duty cops. The cops came from all over the city. Some of them, the Miami Beach guys, were naturally on duty, but in here... Josef wanted lots of security, so we hired people from all over the city. I've been thinking about it, too."

"A dirty cop? Is that what you're thinking?"

"Maybe. Or just someone dressed up like a cop. The other guys might not have known—they came from precincts all over the city. I keep thinking, though, that the guys investigating the shooting had to have thought of all this."

"I imagine they have. I would think they're working all angles."

"Three bodies found down off the Tamiami Trail— no hands, no heads. Sure as hell sounds like a hit to me."

"I agree. I'll bet just about all of law enforcement would."

"Definitely not just a domestic disturbance," Antonovich said, not amused at his own attempt at humor. "The door up here… I was the first one to check it, along with one of Miami Beach's finest. It was locked. If they came through that way, they had a key."

"It's been rekeyed."

"Yeah."

"Well, thanks," Jacob said. He started to walk away.

Antonovich called him back. "Hey," he said softly. "You get that son of a bitch. You get whoever killed Josef. He was all right. Yes, he sold drugs, he sold arms, he sold…women. But he was an okay guy, you know?"

"Sure," Jacob said quietly. He didn't agree that Smirnoff was "an okay guy," but he did believe that a murderer should be brought to justice. Antonovich seemed passionate about catching Smirnoff's killer.

"You're going to the funeral?" Antonovich asked.

"Yes, of course."

"I want to go over to the cemetery. It's old—and

pretty big. Angels and archangels…and small mausoleums and large mausoleums."

"Places for a shooter to hide?" Jacob asked.

Antonovich nodded grimly. "I'll be checking it out,"
he said.

"Good. And good to know."

Jacob turned away. He knew the cemetery, on Eighth
Street, or Calle Ocho, in the city. It was a beautiful
cemetery. Gothic archways, handsome landscaping…
and dozens of places for a shooter to hide—if Kozak
was next in line, and there was still someone making
a power play.

Antonovich appeared to be bitter about Smirnoff's
death, as eager as any to pinpoint a killer. But Jacob just
couldn't be sure what he felt he'd learned.

Either the goons were just hired muscle…or they had
put together a trio of stone-cold killers, just waiting for
the right moment to sweep in.

Which would mean that Victor Kozak was sched-
uled to die, as well.

Chapter Nine

Jorge left Jasmine's apartment at about 4:00 p.m. "I don't think I'm supposed to be hanging around here forever," he told her. "Despite the amount of fun and entertainment you're providing me, I've just got to go."

"What are you going to do?" Jasmine asked.

He smiled. "Hole up in my room with computer files. I'd rather hang around the beach. Check out the scene, hear what I can hear. But I guess that will be nothing. Rats. Guess I'll be hanging out with my computer."

"You don't think that's dangerous?"

"No, Bernie in tech helped me out. I hit a key, and only a genius could find my erased history or files or anything. I'll be okay. You'll be with a hot guy—I won't." He grinned at her.

She didn't grin back.

He walked over to her and hugged her. "Partner, I can feel it. Mary is going to be okay. And you're going to be okay, and I'm going to be okay. Okay? Oh, and pretty man is going to be okay, too."

That one, at last, made her grin. "I'm sure. Fine, go work. And I'll—"

"Keep pacing."

"Yep, I'll keep pacing."

Jorge was gone; she was alone.

She found herself pondering Jacob Wolff. He seemed to know everything about her. Of course, he was with the federal government. She was MDPD—not any lesser, but still, a total difference in privileges and responsibilities. She was, however, sure that if the operation had been planned differently, she'd know much more about him. She didn't even know anything about the fake man, much less the real Jacob Wolff. She was probably lucky she knew his real name.

He probably even knew that her parents were working with a charity rebuilding houses down in Haiti.

She was working up a fair amount of aggravation by the time Jacob Wolff arrived at her apartment; she didn't notice at first that he seemed worn and weary when he walked in.

"Anything? Do you have anything at all?" she asked. "I believe that Connor will be with Kari again tonight— and I'm very afraid for what will happen to her after that."

"We've got field agents watching Connor. They can find nothing to suggest that he's a murderer."

"Oh, really? So, in your usual line of work, people advertise the fact that they're murderers?"

The way he looked at her, she wished she could swallow the words back.

"I don't know anything yet. I have a firm belief that the men just found in the Glades were the killers. I believe they worked for someone who copied the key to the balcony, and they didn't bother to escape that way— they just blended with a panicked crowd that was trampling one another. I actually don't believe Kozak called the shots, but I can't be sure. What have you got?"

"Why do you believe Kozak is innocent—of murder, that is?"

Jacob was looking straight ahead, at the television. "I think he would do a great deal to make money, but I think he's seen enough of death."

"What makes you believe that?"

He turned to look at her. "He has a past very much like my own. My father was born in Israel to parents who barely escaped the Nazis. My maternal grandfather made it out of one of Stalin's purges. I was lucky. I was born here. Almost right here—Mount Sanai. But my parents had to work hard. We were always just scraping by. We were here several years, and then in New York. I went to high school in Manhattan, and on to Columbia University with tuition assistance through the military—and then after my service, the FBI. I've been under the direction of great men with the Bureau for years, always FBI, but recently, FBI in conjunction with Homeland Security—and I've seen what's really, really ugly. So, I allow myself to be wrong. But I talk to people. I try to hear what's beneath what they say. I'm not perfect. I have been fooled now and then, but not often."

"So, you're the only one with a tough past, huh?"

He didn't reply. He looked away. "We'll need a place to go to dinner. We're definitely being watched, and while I'm not worried about our three stooges—who aren't all that stupid, I don't think—we're being watched by someone else, as well. I'm itching to get to the cemetery, but I know I have to trust others. I've called ahead. Miami field agents will be in the cemetery, in the mausoleums, around every angel high enough to cover a man. So, for us, for now…"

She sat next to him. He looked over at her.

She hesitated and then said, "I'm sorry. My past was a piece of cake. My parents are as sweet and kind as a pair of over overgrown lovebirds. I wanted to be a cop because my dad was a cop, and he was influential in catching a serial rapist at work on Eighth Street near Westchester. He somehow managed to teach us about the evils of the world and see the beauty in it, as well. He never whined about me becoming a cop because I was a woman, and neither did my mother. I never wanted for anything. I was helped through college. I... I'm sorry."

He reached across the sofa and took her hand. And they weren't playacting for anyone, because no one was in the room.

"I know," he told her. He grinned. "I've seen your file."

"And I haven't seen yours. I don't even know... Are you married?"

"I was."

"Divorced?"

"No."

"Oh. I'm...sorry."

"It's been a long time," he said.

"Still."

He shrugged and smiled. "You would have liked her."

"I'm sure I would have," she said softly.

He was studying her, to a point where she flushed. "What?"

"I'm a classic case—that's what an analyst would say, I'm pretty sure. Married young, the sweet love of youth, lost that love, plowed into work, kind of a loner. Way too much time undercover for serious relationships..."

She was definitely blushing by then.

"So I've read your file, but there's nothing in there that explains the you that Jorge knows—and told me all about."

"I'm going to kill him."

"Don't. He's your partner. And he loves you."

"Okay, so I don't have a haunted history. And I didn't lose anyone. I mean, I didn't lose a husband or a lover. I just…"

"Well, if you don't go out, you don't meet anyone."

"Seriously, I'm going to kill Jorge."

He grinned. "I really like Jorge. So?"

"Okay, I don't often work undercover. But I do work major crimes. And even though you have shifts with other officers and you work with other agencies, there are times you have to be dedicated to the case instead of getting to know the people you're working with. When you're the one a loved one of a victim is depending on, or you're the one who's gained the trust of a young witness, or…"

Her voice trailed. His elbow was angled on the couch and he was smiling as he watched her.

"Many men find female police detectives to be intimidating," she went on. "And many of those who don't are a little scary themselves. It's not that I don't go out, or I don't believe in going out—"

"Just haven't found the right guy?"

She shrugged, rising nervously. She hadn't expected the evening to turn into a tell-all, especially when she sure as hell couldn't tell the truth about her feelings regarding him.

She walked over to the door. "I guess we'd better go to dinner. Let's see…where haven't we been?"

He stood and met her at the entry. "I don't know. Where do you suggest?" They were facing each other, ridiculously close.

And then, they both heard a shuffling sound, just outside.

"Someone following you?" she mouthed to Jacob.

He carefully looked out. "Maybe," he mouthed back. He drew his gun. He checked the door, and she saw that he had double-bolted it.

To her surprise, he threw the door open.

Night was falling. But the way the apartment building had been laid out, the pool and patio area faced the west, and while the night encroached, the lowering sun created a sky of bold beauty. Soon, the radiant colors would be gone, and it would be the darkness that reigned.

"Ah, what a lovely night. Maybe later..." Jacob said, his voice carrying. And then, still speaking with a full rich voice, he turned to her. "On second thought, why don't we order in tonight?" he asked.

Was there someone out there? A figure, to the side in the shadows, hunkered down in a lawn chair?

The door was fully open. They were on display, and he was looking down at her with his brilliant blue eyes, so handsome and so startling against his dark hair and bronzed face.

Jacob pulled her into his arms and kissed her. And this time, he pulled her close. His mouth came down on hers while his arms encompassed her, his hands sliding down low against her back, drawing her ever closer, his tongue parting her lips and slipping deep within her mouth.

The door slowly closed behind them while they

backed inside the apartment, locked in the passionate embrace.

He was still kissing her as he eased one hand away, once again double-bolting the lock. She heard the sound as the bolts slid into place. And only then did his hold ease, his lips part from hers.

They were still so close. He looked down at her, and she could still feel the dampness of her lips, burning as they seemed to do when he touched her.

"I think…" she murmured, and he leaned closer, as if to hear her. His lips were almost upon hers again, his body was all but touching hers. To her amazement, she almost smiled, and she said softly, "Oh, screw this!"

She moved back into his arms. She was tall, but she moved up on tiptoe, the length of her body against his. She moved her mouth that one inch closer, found his lips and kissed him, parting his mouth, delving deep within it with her tongue, initiating all. She was stunned by her own movements, but more so by the depth of the longing and desire that was sweeping through her.

The kiss deepened and deepened. She pressed closer to him, flush against him, and felt his hands travel down the length of her body. The kiss broke, and he eased back slightly.

She felt she was panting like an idiot, and he had moved away. A flush of heat broke over her, and her limbs began to tremble. She had to force herself to bring her eyes to his, but when she did, she saw he was still watching her, intensely alert. He smiled slightly and said, "Ummmm." He was still holding her, and then he arched a brow and whispered, "Oh, screw this."

He swept her up, higher, into his arms. His mouth found hers again, but he moved as he kissed her, across the floor, toward the apartment bedroom. In seconds, they were lying down together on the bed. He braced himself over her, and said softly, "Only if it's what you really want."

She smiled. His pausing to question her, to be very sure, added to her sense of attraction and desperation.

She reached out, drawing his face down to hers again. She replied with her hands on his face, caressing his face as she drew him to her. "Yes. So much." They kissed again…just kissed, and then he straddled above her, doffing his jacket. The Glock he carried was evident then, and he reached back for the gun and holster, leaning over to set them on the dresser.

He looked down at her a moment.

"Mine's inside the bedside drawer, to the left," she told him. Now they both knew where to reach if they were threatened in any way at any time.

That solved, he struggled from his shirt; she rose up to help him. He was still in trousers, socks and shoes. He halfway rolled from her, divesting his clothing, and she slipped out of the cool knit dress she'd been wearing, as well as her bra and panties.

To her surprise, he suddenly made an urgent sound, almost like a growl, rising to meet her again.

Naked flesh against naked flesh, he whispered, "So wrong of me. I knew the moment I saw you on the runway that you were extraordinary, you were grace and laughter and beauty, and I wanted you, but I didn't know what it would mean when I knew you…"

When his mouth found hers again, she felt the burn that had teased her lips become something of a raging wildfire that snaked down the length of her body. She allowed herself to roam free with her hands, loving the curve of his shoulders, the clench of muscle in his shoulders and down his back. She felt his body harden against her own, and she couldn't wrap herself tightly enough to him, to be both almost in his skin and touch him just the same.

They fell back on the bed together and she lay on top of him, landing kisses on his neck and his shoulders, the hard planes of his stomach, and moving lower against his body.

His hands grabbed her back, and they flipped in the bed. His mouth fell upon her throat and her breasts and lingered and teased and caressed. Those kisses continued downward, and she arched and writhed against him, finding his flesh and returning each touch of passion and hunger and longing.

She thought she would burn to a cinder, she was so alive, burning with a need unlike anything she'd ever known, wanting the play to go on forever, yet desperate that something be touched, that he be within her, as well.

And then he was, and they were moving, and moving, and moving...

They rolled, their lips melded together again and the rock of his hips was incredible. The sense of him within her was almost more than she could bear, the absolute sweetness, the rise of that fire, that longing to be ever more a part of him. Rising...and bursting out upon her like a flow of liquid gold.

The night seemed to sweep in all around her for long moments as she felt little bits of ecstasy shoot through her, ebbing bit by incredible bit, until she felt the damp sheen of their flesh, still so taut together, the rise and fall of her breath, the rock-hard pounding of her heart.

And him, still holding her, still clinging in the darkness to the awesome beauty of what had been. So real, flesh and blood and pulse and their gasps for air...

They didn't speak at first; they just breathed.

And then he whispered softly, "I don't think I'll be putting that in the report."

She smiled and turned to him. "I understand you're often by the book. Forgive me."

"Forgive you?" He straddled her again, catching her hands and leaning low, his eyes alight with humor and tenderness. "Ah, my dear Detective Adair. It is I who must ask forgiveness. On second thought, no. Can't ask forgiveness. This was—"

"Incredible," she whispered.

"More than incredible. I don't know the words... Maybe there are none."

She pulled him back to her, and the kiss they shared was sweet and tender, and still, she knew, could arouse again at any second.

He pulled away and got out of bed suddenly. Light from the living room swept into the bedroom and she could see the full leanly muscled perfection of his tightly honed body in the doorway. He wasn't self-conscious as he padded out to the living room. Curious, she rose up on an arm.

Then he was back, every movement sleek and fluid, and he fell down beside her again. "Checking the door," he murmured.

"There's still someone out there?" she asked.

"Sitting by the pool. We'll order in," he told her.

He moved toward her and she jumped back suddenly, stricken. She'd been so enraptured with the man she'd been lucky enough to come to know that she had all but forgotten this wasn't an ordinary job.

She was looking for Mary. And even though Mary still seemed beyond her reach...

"Kari!" she exclaimed. "I'm worried, Jacob. What about Kari—and Mr. Connor?"

"I'll call in," he assured her. He found his jacket where he'd flung it earlier and dug his phone out of the pocket. After a minute, he had the info.

"Kari is back at her apartment."

"She's all right? And they're back inside?"

"Just Kari is back at her place. Connor took her out for a steak dinner and then a moonlit stroll on the beach. Then he brought her home. He left shortly, a smile on his face."

"Oh," Jasmine said. "Jacob, you don't think she'll be in any trouble with the gang for...for not sleeping with him?"

"No, I don't think she'll be in trouble."

Jasmine was still unsure. "He's being watched, Jasmine. Kari will be okay. Someone will get to Connor soon enough."

"Kari was worried though. I think she felt something was off. And I can't forget about Mary..."

"We'll find Mary. I swear it," he told her.

She believed him. And miraculously, she could move forward with her own night, grateful that the young blonde woman was all right. For now.

And there was nothing they could do. Not for the night.

She moved forward, catching his face, looking up into the dazzling blue of his eyes. "Thank you."

He kissed her again, that tender kiss... But the kiss

deepened, and then it began to travel, and he was kissing her breasts again, affording each the most tender caresses, and her belly and thighs, bringing that erotic fire with every touch.

She let the night seize her again, and she returned his caresses, unable to stop seeking more and more of him, know the taste of his skin, the taste of him.

They embraced tightly, and he was within her, and they rolled, and she was atop him, and this time they laughed and teased and whispered.

And then they lay together again, just breathing, still afrire, savoring the beauty of the darkness of the night, the coolness of the sheets beneath their bodies.

She was the one to sit up and straddle him this time.

He smiled, catching her hands with his. "Leave it to a cop to always want to be on top." He rolled her over, covering her with his body.

"And leave it to a Fed to think he must be in control."

"This Fed," he said softly, "is just happy to be with you."

She smiled back at him, wishing that the night would never end; that this was all they needed in reality and that the world would go away.

It could not.

He rolled from her, standing. "Food—we need to order food."

"I am hungry," she agreed.

She leaped out of bed, reaching to the foot of it for the caftan robe she kept there. He found his boxers but bothered with nothing else. He was already out in the living room, his phone drawn from his pocket. He looked at her. "I have a delivery service so, Chinese, Indian, Italian… Steaks? Seafood? What's your pleasure?"

You are my pleasure! she thought.

She managed not to say it out loud. "I'm easy. Food-wise," she added quickly. "Anything."

"Wow. I found one with pizza and champagne. Now there's an interesting combo. But I don't think that champagne... Not tonight."

"Not tonight," she agreed.

It was one thing to be drunk on desire when you were supposed to be drunk on desire. But quite another to have anything that might alter the mind with a goon outside on the porch.

"I don't believe we're in any danger, but I've seen things change quickly," he told her. "Ah, Thai food!"

"Perfect."

She stood near him and looked over his shoulder as he went through the offerings. They decided on one noodle dish and one rice dish.

Jasmine suddenly felt extremely awkward.

"Coffee!" she said. "I should make some coffee."

She started to walk into the kitchen. He caught her arm and pulled her back to him, holding her there, looking into her eyes. "Please, don't go away from me," he said softly.

She knew he didn't mean she shouldn't go into the kitchen and make coffee.

"I...it sounds like a line," she told him, "but I've never...in my life...just done this so quickly... I guess I don't know how to act."

"And I hope you believe me. I've always drawn a line. Until tonight."

She stood on her toes and kissed his lips lightly. "I won't go away," she promised.

She made coffee; Thai food arrived. Jacob made a

point of answering the door still clad just in his boxers. He was careful to double-bolt the door again, and then to bring his Glock back out to sit on the table while they ate.

"You know, I'm a damned good markswoman," she told him.

He smiled at her. "I'd expect no less." He picked at a strand of the noodles. "Oh, by the way, Kozak gave you to me today." His smiled deepened as he saw her stiffen. "Sorry. All in a role."

She hesitated. "But in truth, I give myself where I choose."

"And so do I," he told her.

She laughed softly. Much of the Thai food went uneaten; they wound up laughing over a noodle they had both chosen.

And then they wound up in one another's arms again.

THERE WAS A knock on the door.

Jacob rolled out of bed, instantly awake. He grabbed his trousers and then his gun. Jasmine followed him out of bed in a flash, slipping on a robe, going for her own weapon.

He took a quick glance at the clock on the nightstand: 9:00 a.m. He headed out of the bedroom quickly, with Jasmine on his heels.

But one look out the peephole had Jacob unlocking the door. "It's all right. A friend," he told her.

Jorge stepped in, looked at both of them and then smiled.

"Method acting!" he said. "I like it. Just wondering what the hell took you two so long."

Chapter Ten

The funeral service was long. Speaking in Russian, the priest delivered the service with all respect and care—while the man might have known about Smirnoff and his deeds, he didn't judge when it came time for a man to meet his Maker. It was actually beautiful, though Jacob was sure many in the congregation had no idea what was being said.

Victor Kozak gave an emotional speech about his friend, and he did so in English for the benefit of the mourners who had gathered.

Many had come out to pay their respects—not so many would be invited to the celebration of life that would come later, at the club. Equally, not so many would travel with the funeral train that would follow the hearse to the cemetery.

Jacob had spoken with his Miami counterpart, Dean Jenkins. He knew agents were already waiting at the cemetery.

It would be a fine day for an attempt on Victor Kozak's life.

Jenkins also filled him in on what was happening with events at the morgue, and with the local crime scene technicians.

"They identified one of the dead men, from the hand they got out of the alligator's gullet. Ain't technology great? Although, to be honest, it wasn't fingerprints or anything like that. One of my guys working in Little Havana recognized the ring.

"The victim was Leonardo Gonzalez—an undocumented Venezuelan immigrant. He and a few of his fellows had traveled through Mexico and, according to our agent, onto a cruise ship and into Miami. He'd been a contract killer at home and was looking for work in Little Havana. He was happy to work for anyone but was looking for connections in the Little Havana area because he didn't speak any English.

"Anyway...according to our sources, he was the kind of really bad guy taking serious advantage of the criminal activity going on down there right now, but he might have crossed another crime lord, meaning it was time for him to get out. But he had his own little gang. I'm working under the assumption our other two headless bodies are associates of his."

"Thanks— Anything new on Donald McPherson Connor?"

"We followed him. He was a perfect gentleman with the young lady. And he left her at her door. An agent is still outside. He could have followed Connor, or he could have kept his eye on her. He chose to protect the one we know to be an innocent. Anyway, we have a new crew out on the streets today. Oh, they're checking in at your art gallery, too, making sure that Special Agent Partridge is doing okay."

"Thanks. Hey, should I be getting a new phone?"

"Not to worry, I'm listed as a local artist. You any closer?" Jenkins asked him.

"I don't know. I'm going to see what happens at the funeral."

They ended their call, and Jacob joined the mourners, making himself one with Ivan Petrov and the three goons.

Jasmine was not invited to this part of the day; she would be at the club, preparing to work with the food and drinks that would be served. He tried not to worry. He knew she was an accomplished policewoman, and he believed she was an excellent markswoman. She was also vulnerable, though he had warned her that she should be wary at all times—and armed if any way possible.

She knew that, of course.

Kozak hadn't asked Jacob to drive to the cemetery; he wanted him next to him in his car, behind the driver, who would be Antonovich.

Jacob couldn't help but wonder if Kozak was afraid that Antonovich could shoot them both if Jacob was driving—he'd be easy prey for a man sitting behind him.

They arrived safely at the cemetery. It was just west of the downtown area known as Calle Ocho. The cemetery had recently joined with two different companies that had been offering funeral arrangements and grave sites since the 1850s back in Cuba. It was at the edge of a neighborhood close to downtown known as Little Havana.

But like most of Miami, anyone and everyone might be here.

They entered through Gothic arches. The grounds were sweeping, well tended and beautiful. Trees cast shady spots everywhere, and the park stretched for long blocks. They drove around a winding trail until they reached the canopy that stood over the area where the body of Josef Smirnoff would be laid to rest.

The cars parked; Jacob got out and waited for Kozak

to emerge from the car, as well. He looked around. A lovely marble angel stood guard over a nearby family lot; a small family mausoleum stood about fifty yards away. Another, about a hundred yards farther out.

They were under a gracious old oak, near to a grouping of military headstones. Down a bit farther was a large concrete memorial to a man who had been a Mason and with the Mahi Shrine. His memorial gave witness to the fact that he had spent forty years as a Shriner, dedicating his time to raising funds for the children's hospital.

Probably a great guy. Right now, Jacob had to be certain that his memorial wasn't hiding a sniper.

He continued his scan of the area. The large mausoleum with its beautiful stained-glass windows, known to house many, many bodies, was perhaps a hundred yards behind them. A great place for a sniper to hide.

He reminded himself that the Miami agents knew this cemetery, where to be and where to watch.

And still he was on high alert.

"There, Mr. Kozak," Antonovich said, coming around to Kozak's side. "The chairs in front, sir. Those are for you and those who were close to Josef."

Sticking to Kozak's side like a piece of lint, Jacob led the man to the chairs.

Josef Smirnoff might not have been a cold-blooded killer, but he sure as hell had been a criminal. Victor Kozak had taken over from him, and while he might not be a cold-blooded killer either, he was also a major criminal.

But the showing of respectable people at the cemetery was large enough; the local news media brought trucks to the winding road that led through the very large cemetery—another place for a shooter to hide.

Politicians and other respectable citizens arrived to say goodbye to Smirnoff.

Jacob sat back as the priest gave the graveside prayers. He had to have faith in his fellow agents. But just as he had settled—still alert and ready—a late-comer arrived at the grave site.

It was the man who so disturbed Jasmine.

Donald McPherson Connor.

THE CLUB WAS a bustle of activity when Jasmine arrived, even though it was early. The catering company per-sonnel included two chefs, two wine stewards and six members of a cleanup crew.

Jasmine and Jorge reported right away to the dress-ing room. The servers were suited out appropriately—men in tuxes, women in similar versions with short skirts instead of pants—and shown the various food stations and the additional bars.

"Remember, today, you serve quickly, politely and quietly. We honor Josef," Natasha instructed. "You all understand? Behavior is beyond circumspect."

Stopping by one of the makeup tables where Jasmine had just harnessed her own hair in a braid at the back of her neck, Jorge told her, "Five City of Miami Beach cops, all aware to watch for trouble—hired on by Kozak." He lowered his head to her, pretending to smooth back a piece of her hair. "The chef at the first table is a plant—FBI. We have representation from MDPD as well—Detective Birch. You've worked with her. She'll be on the arm of one of our young politicians."

"Sounds good," Jasmine murmured. "Then again, how many cops were prowling the show when Josef was killed?"

"There's a cop at the balcony door. If anyone is going to start shooting, it won't be from the balcony." He leaned closer still, pretending to flick a piece of nonexistent lint from her brow. "FBI is crawling over the cemetery, too. Thing is, the killer must know. Unless he—or she—is really an egotistical bastard, nothing will happen today."

Nothing would happen. This would go on...

Jorge grinned suddenly. "You look different."

"I don't dress this way often."

"No, it's the way your eyes are shining."

"Jorge."

"It's nice to see you happy."

She looked at him and then lowered her head, ruefully smiling. "I'd like to see you happy."

"Hey, you may. I'm not watched, not the way you are," he told her. "I had some dinner out last night. Sat on the beach."

"Jorge, you have to be—"

"I was careful. Trust me."

He grinned, and she knew it was the truth.

"Jorge, I need you!" Natasha called. "Now, you will take the large silver tray—you have nice long arms. Move through the crowd but offer up the food. Do not interfere with people who are talking. You let them stop. Think of yourselves as courteous machines."

Jorge moved on. Jasmine saw Kari at the next dressing table and she stood, heading over to her.

"Need help with anything?" she asked.

"Nope," Kari said, looking up. "I never can do false eyelashes right, but Natasha says we shouldn't wear them today."

"They're miserable things anyway."

"I agree."

"So, how are you?" Jasmine asked her softly.

"Good. Great, really."

"Great?" Jasmine asked.

Kari smiled. "I know that he's old, but honestly, if I were, say, forty-five instead of twenty-two, well... He has such a great accent. He talked to me about books and plays and he told me so much history about this place that I didn't know... He's kind, Jasmine. So very kind."

"Great to hear. I thought he made you a bit nervous. Are you okay with him now? When do you see him again?"

"Tonight. Later, of course. I told him—and I'm sure Natasha told him—that the club models were working the funeral, and we wouldn't be available until the entire celebration of life came to an end. He told me that, no matter what the hour, he'd like to see me." Kari hesitated a moment and then whispered, "I don't know why I was worried. Jasmine, we had the best dinner. Such a lovely night. He's truly so well educated. And then I thought he would want more. I thought he would want me to sleep with him. Oh! And he talked about Mary. He said she was such a lovely person—he was sure she went on to resume her education. They had talked about school and always having a backup to modeling or acting. He believes she might have headed out to California."

California? Or the pit of an alligator's stomach, somewhere out in the Everglades.

"I guess he's worked with or been a client of these people for a while," Jasmine said.

"Not so long. He told me that the group here—well,

Josef Smirnoff first, and now Victor Kozak—knew how
to find the most cultured women. He likes to go to the
theater and the opera and art shows, and…he needs the
right escorts."

"How nice."

"He loves music and musicals, voices!"

The opera…or screams as a woman died beneath
a knife?

"Jasmine, he's really such a gentleman. I thought he
might be the type to immediately demand that we sleep
together, that…"

"What?"

"That he might want me to do weird things." Her
voice dropped to a whisper. "You know, weird sexual
things. Scary things." She swallowed. "You know…au-
toerotic asphyxiation, or maybe not even scary things,
just disgusting things. But he didn't even press sleeping
with me." She paused, seeming a little uncomfortable,
then went on quietly. "We're not specifically *ordered*
to sleep with the clients, but there's an understanding
that they get what they want if they're paying the price.
And that trickles down to us in money and…in pres-
tige on the runway. It's no secret that Natasha's highest
earners get the best gigs. But…this guy, no pressure.
I'm babbling. I guess I am still maybe a little nervous."

"Kari, you have my number, right? If not, I'll make
sure that you do now."

Kari pulled out her phone and Jasmine quickly gave
her the number to her burner phone.

"We're having lunch, right?" Kari asked.

"Lunch, yes, but keep your phone near. If you're
afraid at any point, you call me immediately!"

Kari frowned, but then smiled. "You can call me, too,

you know, except that..: Well! You seem just fine, and I imagine…" She broke off and laughed suddenly, leaning forward. "I might have been willing to pay some big bucks myself for that blue-eyed wonder who chose you."

Jasmine smiled weakly.

"You're okay, right?" Kari asked. "I mean, with him."

"Yes, I'm just fine," Jasmine managed.

"What is he like, that Jacob? Those eyes of his… If he ever looked at me the way he looks at you, wow. I'd be putty."

"Putty," Jasmine repeated. "That's me."

"Girls!" Natasha called. "Time to take your stations. Sasha has called—the services at the grave site are ending. We will be ready, the most gracious of hosts and hostesses."

And so, they were on. They all trailed out of the dressing room.

Natasha was by the balcony door; it was open for them to head down the stairs.

Jasmine smiled as she passed Natasha. Only Kozak was supposed to have a key. But Victor wasn't here. And Ivan was downstairs, setting up the main bar, giving orders to the catering company.

Jasmine hurried downstairs along with the others. She knew that somehow, she would get that information to Jacob.

Lightning didn't strike twice…

Unless sometimes, it did.

No BULLETS RANG out at the cemetery.

The priest, resplendent in his robes, carried through the service. Women had been given roses; they walked past the coffin to drop them down upon it.

"I need a moment," Kozak told his companions.

He was at the coffin alone, except for the four cemetery workers who waited discreetly to see that the coffin was lowered six feet under. The hearse was preparing to leave. Antonovich, Suarez and Garibaldi waited while other mourners filed out to their cars.

Donald McPherson Connor was starting to walk away.

Jacob was a distance from Victor Kozak as it was; he wouldn't be any farther from the man if he walked toward Connor. He excused himself to the trio of bodyguards.

"Mr. Connor!" Jacob called out.

The man stopped walking and looked back at him, eyeing him distastefully. Jacob noticed that he was lean but fit.

Probably plenty strong. Certainly strong enough against a slim blonde girl.

Connor was evidently irritated at having been stopped—by Jacob, at any rate. "Yes, Mr. Marensky, what is it?"

"Well, I just wish to apologize, and I hope that we don't keep bad blood between us. I was, in fact, hoping that you found Miss Anderson to be up to your expectations."

"Miss Anderson is a truly lovely woman. I am enjoying her company."

Jacob forced a smile. "Excellent. She is quite beautiful."

"Not as intriguing as Miss Alamein though," Connor said. He was an oddly dignified man—soft-spoken. "So, Mr. Marenksy, what exactly do you do in relation to the Gold Sun Club?"

Then again, Jacob had seen some of the most innocent and soft-spoken men and women possible turn out to be vicious and as cold as ice.

"We have shared business interests. I run an art gallery," Jacob said.

"So I hear," Connor said, his British accent a little clipped.

"I'd welcome you for a visit. See if there's anything that catches your eye. Just what is your enterprise, sir?"

The man's smile tightened. "No enterprise—other than the stock market. Now there, sir, is bloody criminal action from the get-go, and yet quite legal."

"Ah, I believed that you had worked with Josef—and now Victor."

"I simply require a certain kind of companion."

"I see," Jacob said, still smiling. Just what was it that he required? "Well, sir, I shall see you at the club. I just wished to clear the air between us. Please understand, my arrangements had been made first."

"Oh, yes, I understand perfectly, Mr. Marensky." Connor was still looking at him with watery blue hatred.

"Jacob?" Kozak was calling to him.

"Excuse me," Jacob said, spinning around to return to Victor Kozak's side.

"We must be leaving now," Kozak said.

"Yes, of course."

"You and Connor are good then?" Kozak asked him softly.

"Oh, as good as we can be, Victor. As good as we can be."

"Please, then…" Kozak indicated the road through the cemetery; theirs was the only car that remained. "Sasha, you will drive."

"Yes, sir," Antonovich said, sliding into the driver's seat.

Garibaldi took the front seat by him. Kozak slid into the back, between Suarez and Jacob. The car rolled out of the cemetery, onto Southwest Eighth Street and then headed for I-95 and the extension out to South Beach.

The funeral itself had gone off without a hitch. Now, all they had to do was make it through the reception—the celebration of life where the mourners would come together and Smirnoff would receive his last honors.

Smirnoff, Kozak and their peers really were criminals. Jacob had seen one too many a decent person cajoled into and then hooked on drugs. And abusing the trust of hopeful girls was reprehensible. But Jacob wanted Kozak prosecuted and locked away—not on a slab with a bullet in his head.

As the car rolled up to Kozak's special parking place at the back of the property, Jacob felt Kozak's hand wind into a vice on his arm.

The man looked at him, and there was fear in his eyes, quickly masked as Garibaldi came around and opened the door.

Jacob got out.

"My friend, I know you will change things!" Kozak said. He caught Jacob's arm again, turning to show him where they were. "Cops—down there, at the end of the block. That guy with the long hair and the beggar's cup at this end? A cop." He pulled Jacob along to show him the men to whom he was referring.

And then he whispered to Jacob, "Here. This is where they will try to kill me. Somewhere here, at the club."

Chapter Eleven

It always amazed Jasmine to see the people who came out for such an event—the last rites for a man they had to have known conducted criminal activities. She was also certain many people on the guest list had not sat through the long religious ceremony at the church, nor attended the final graveside services.

The club was busy within minutes of the door opening.

Ivan stood at the main doors dressed in his best designer suit. Natasha was at his side tonight, ready to greet everyone as they came in; she had finished her busywork, prepared her various crews and was ready to be the grand hostess.

Jasmine had been given a tray of canapés to carry around, and she did so smoothly and easily. Though maintaining her demeanor as a courteous robot was not as easy as it might have been—Kozak and the goons and Jacob had yet to come into the club.

When they finally did, she breathed an inward sigh of relief.

She tried to maneuver herself around to Jacob's position casually, making it part of her regular sweep of the room. When she made it to an area near the street entrance, he was still standing with Kozak and the bodyguards.

"Gentlemen," she said quietly, offering up her tray.

The bodyguards quickly reached for the little quiches. Jacob inclined his head slightly and took a canapé, as well.

Kozak turned to her. "What I need is a drink, Jasmine. Will you get me a vodka? I'm sure that Natasha has seen to it that our hired bartender knows what is my special reserve."

"Yes, of course," Jasmine said.

But Natasha swept by at that moment, giving her a serious frown. "Jasmine, you are to move among our guests."

"Yes, Natasha," she said.

"Natasha," Kozak said softly. "We have many people working the floor. I would like Jasmine to go and get me my drink."

"Victor, I can do that for you," Natasha said.

"You are the hostess. Let Jasmine go," Kozak said. "It's time that I...that I welcome our guests and give my little speech here, eh? But one vodka first!"

Jasmine headed off to the bar. The man there gave her an appreciative look and she smiled in return. "I need a drink for Mr. Kozak—his special reserve. He believes you'll know what it is."

"Yep," the bartender said. "I've been given the bottle and serious instructions. It's a unique vintage from Russia, not sold in the United States." He grinned at her, reaching beneath the bar for the bottle. He got a glass and said, "Just two ice cubes. Rich men and their drinks."

"Thanks," she told him.

"I live to serve. Come see me again!"

She nodded and started to hurry away but turned

back. "Did you meet with Mr. Kozak before this event? Did he give you the bottle?" she asked.

He shook his head. "I met with the praying mantis. Oh, sorry—the entire catering company met with Natasha. She gave us strict instructions."

"And the bottle of vodka?"

"No, it was here where she said it would be when I came in. Hey, sorry, I hope she's not a friend of yours— I'm an actor and this catering company keeps me in cash while I'm pounding the pavement. I'm sorry. Please, I didn't mean to be offensive."

"You need to be a lot more careful."

"Please, don't get me fired."

"I won't, but... Never mind. Thank you."

Once again, she turned away, but then something about the situation seemed disturbing. "Would you mind? Give me four more drinks, just like this one but with regular vodka. Something good, just not Kozak's special reserve."

"Anything for you."

She smiled. And prayed that she and Jacob had come to know one another in their undercover roles as well as they had come to know one another personally.

Kozak and Jacob, with Garibaldi, Suarez, and Antonovich behind them, were heading toward the stage. Jasmine took a step back, her heart pounding, wondering if she was wrong and if she might just cause the entire operation to implode—and put them all, including the guests, in serious danger.

But her hunch was strong. She had seen Natasha with the key.

Natasha was definitely sleeping with Kozak—but had she been sleeping with Josef Smirnoff before? Was she part of what came with taking over the business because she wouldn't be ousted herself?

Jasmine walked toward the men.

"Special for Mr. Kozak, and gentlemen, I believe it was a long day for you, as well. I hope I have not displeased you, Mr. Kozak."

She looked at Jacob, just lowering her eyes at the glass he was to take, and gave the barest shake of her head. He shouldn't drink it. He would know—surely, he would know!

Jacob's striking blue eyes fell on hers. Before Kozak could answer, he said, "That was very thoughtful of you."

"Nice, sweet, as always," Antonovich said happily, and he looked at Kozak.

"Definitely. One vodka, boss, eh?" Suarez asked.

"One vodka," Kozak agreed.

Jasmine dared look around as the men took their drinks. An up-and-coming beach politician was entering with a lovely young news reporter on his arm. Natasha was doing her duty and greeting them.

"I must get to the stage," Kozak said.

"I'll get you there swiftly," Jacob assured him.

Jasmine flashed a smile to all of them. "I'd best get to my canapés," she said. She started to walk away.

"A second?" Jacob asked, looking at Kozak for permission, as well.

"Yes, then you will walk with me, stand by me, at my back," Kozak said.

Jacob smiled and stepped away with Jasmine. She had her chance. "Natasha had the key tonight," she said. "Might be important. Kozak wasn't here. I don't think they plan a shooting."

"Poison in the vodka?"

"I could be wrong."

"Thanks. You gave it to me."

"You knew!"

"I knew," he assured her, and then he squeezed her hand and stepped back.

"To the stage," Kozak said. He seemed very nervous. *As he should be!* Jasmine thought.

As he walked away, Kozak took a sip of his vodka. He frowned instantly. The man did know the taste of his special reserve.

And that wasn't his special reserve.

But Jacob guided him toward the stage. Jasmine saw Jacob casually and discreetly set his own glass down on a waiter's tray.

The waiter was Jorge. He looked across the room at her and nodded.

JACOB STOOD JUST behind Victor Kozak as the man took the microphone, thanking everyone for coming, and for honoring Josef Smirnoff. He told a few tales about his friend and talked about the way Smirnoff had loved Miami Beach and how the club had been a dream for him.

"Sparkling like the Miami sun!" Victor said. "He was my business partner. He was my friend. In his honor, we will rename the club—it will be *Josef's* when it opens to the public tomorrow night. While we faced senseless violence and his death here, we are a powerful people. We are South Floridians, whether we were born here or we were lucky enough to enter this country and find this paradise as our home. We are strong. And, in his name, we will prevail!"

As Kozak spoke, Jacob kept his eyes on the room.

He also mused that Kozak didn't think that peddling escorts or drug dealing were really bad things to do. Illegal, but not bad.

He saw the police—in uniform, and undercover—and the agents in the room. And he knew each of them was watching for the first sign, so much as a hint, of the barrel of a gun or someone reaching into a pocket.

But he was pretty sure Jasmine was right; guns would not be blazing. A killer must right now be waiting for whatever poison might have been in the special reserve to work.

"Make it quick," Jacob managed to whisper.

Kozak took heed. He quickly asked the crowd to honor Smirnoff's memory and enjoy his dream. Then Jacob took his arm and led him from the stage.

"Tell your men you feel sick," he said. "That I'm going to get you upstairs."

Kozak heeded him once again. "I am unwell! Sasha, you will watch the east stairs. Antonio, you will watch the west. Alejandro, you will take between them. I am… I must sit down. Alone. The day… It has been too long. Mr. Marensky will see me upstairs to my office. Tell Ivan and Natasha they must remain the finest hosts."

"Yes, sir," Garibaldi said quickly.

"Hurry, and stumble as we walk up," Jacob said quietly to Kozak.

Antonovich nodded to the policeman at the base of the stairs; the man noticed Kozak, nodded in return and unlatched the velvet barrier. Jacob set his arm on Kozak's back and they headed up the stairs. Halfway up, Kozak pretended to stumble.

"Good, good, we keep going," Jacob murmured.

They passed the expected security. They made it to

the door, and Jacob passed through it quickly. A cop met them in the hall.

"Getting Mr. Kozak to his office," Jacob told him.

The cop nodded.

They opened the door to the office—despite the massive security, Jacob entered first.

The office was empty. He had expected it would be. The killer would be waiting for Kozak to fall downstairs.

And everyone would think the day had been just too difficult for Victor Kozak. The man drank, he liked his cigars, and maybe he liked some of his smuggled product, too. His heart could just give out, after a day like today.

And the poison wouldn't be found during an autopsy, since such substances would not fall into the realm of regular tests.

Kozak sat behind his desk and sighed deeply. "I really could use a drink!"

"I'm sure you keep something in here. Then again, I'm sure there are others who know you keep something in here," Jacob warned him.

"So. I will not drink. What do I do?" Kozak asked.

"We wait here. We see if someone comes. Maybe we call an ambulance. We let the crowd know you're in the emergency room, barely hanging on."

Kozak drummed his fingers on his desk, smiling. He stared at Jacob.

"You are not an art dealer, are you, Mr. Marensky? As a matter of fact, your name isn't even Marensky, is it?"

The night seemed very, very long.

Jasmine moved about the floor as she had been directed, watching the stairs now and then. She saw Jorge with one of the catering crew, an FBI plant, and knew the vodka was probably already on its way to be tested.

But the bartender, she was sure, had just been hired on for the night.

She saw the other girls milling about the room, doing exactly what they had been told to do. They were pretty and silent and moving like robots. She watched the stairs. And to her relief, people began to leave.

While the club had been open and music—soft, somber music, much of it Russian—had played through the night, there was no dancing. After the speech, after the food and free-flowing alcohol, there was little else to do.

People murmured about coming when the club was up and running again. Big names in music had been booked before Smirnoff's death—they were probably still on the agenda.

She was doing her last round with coffees and coffee liqueurs when she saw the man, Donald McPherson Connor, stop Kari Anderson and talk to her. Then he slipped out the door.

A moment later, Kari followed.

Jasmine walked back to the bar quickly, ready to dispose of her tray and head out.

But there was a man at the bar. A little man with big glasses, a nerdy smile and wild bushy hair. "Don't," he said softly, then called to the bartender. "Another, my friend!"

"Pardon?" Jasmine asked, setting her tray down. She didn't care what he was saying; Jacob had Kozak upstairs. Things were coming to a head. And Kari was leaving with a man who just might be a very sick murderer.

"No, we're on it," the little man said. He spoke more loudly. "I mean, man, you're not just a beauty, lady, you are really cool looking. Those eyes of yours—emeralds!" He lowered his voice while pretending to study her eyes. "Special Agent Dean Jenkins, working in association with Wolff. We have a man following Connor and Miss Anderson. Keep your cover."

"That's very nice of you, sir," she said. "I work for the club. We don't date customers."

Garibaldi came up behind her. "Is there a problem?" he asked, glaring at the man who had just identified himself to her as FBI.

Dean Jenkins lifted his hands. "No, sir. No problem. I'm totally a hands-off guy, just complimenting beauty."

"He was very sweet. No problem at all," Jasmine said quickly.

To her relief, Garibaldi ambled away.

Jasmine turned with her tray of coffee cups and coffee drinks.

Natasha was standing there. "All is well?"

"Yes, of course."

"Have you seen Mr. Marensky?" Natasha asked her.

"I believe he went up with Mr. Kozak. He wasn't feeling well."

"They are upstairs? Still?"

Jasmine didn't have to answer. She heard the sound of an ambulance screaming through the night. People began to chatter nervously.

"Oh, my God! Victor!" Natasha cried. She turned and raced for the stairs. She was stopped by Garibaldi, with whom she argued. But this time, Garibaldi had apparently been given strict instructions by Kozak himself.

The wailing sirens stopped.

Natasha kept arguing with Garibaldi. Ivan was coming to join her, a strange look on his face. Was he frowning...or was that a look of satisfaction?

No one was near Jasmine at that moment. She heard a soft whisper at her ear.

Dean Jenkins was standing just behind her. "Jacob is with Kozak. They're heading to the hospital. Word will be out that he collapsed and that they're afraid of a heart attack."

Jasmine let him know she had heard him, nodding slightly, watching along with the others. She moved away from him. As she did so, she felt her phone vibrate in her pocket. She quickly made her way close to the bar, behind a structural beam, and answered it, halfway expecting Jacob.

But it wasn't Jacob.

"Jasmine!"

It was Kari Anderson.

"Jasmine, I need to tell you—"

"Kari, what? Kari?"

Jasmine looked at her phone; the call had ended. The line was dead.

"So, I WILL DIE. Or I will go to prison for the rest of my life," Kozak said, sighing softly. He shrugged. He was lying in the back of an ambulance. Comfortable.

It was a real ambulance. But they weren't real paramedics manning the vehicle, though they would really take Kozak to the hospital, where he would really be admitted.

Jacob had feared that Natasha or Ivan might have made their way upstairs before he'd managed to get Kozak out, but the ambulance had arrived just in time—and Kozak had been shoved right in and the vehicle had taken off into the night. Within moments of closing the ambulance doors, Jacob had revealed to him that he was FBI.

"Victor, the whole operation has to go down," Jacob told him. "I'm sure if you give the district attorney any help you can, he'll make the best arrangements possible."

"I can give you cartels. Names of the men who come and go with drugs and drug money."

"I'm not the DA," Jacob said.

"And I discovered that I do want to live, however long that may be," Kozak told him. He sighed. "My friend, will you do one thing for me?"

"This will be out of my hands now, Victor."

But Victor smiled. "This is a small thing. Before I am locked away, will you see to it that I get just one more…"

"One more what?"

"Shot of my good vodka!"

"I will do my best, Victor. I'm sure you have an attorney, and… I don't know. But for now, your best service is to give us the men who did put those bodies in the oil drums and who left the headless men in the Everglades."

"They want me dead."

"All the more reason we need anything you have to find out just who is calling the shots."

Jacob felt his phone vibrating in his pocket.

Jasmine? She had saved the night, somehow suspecting there might be poison in the vodka. But her cover might be jeopardized…

He answered the phone quickly.

It was Dean Jenkins. "She's gone after Connor, Jacob. Your detective associate."

"What? How? When?"

"The commotion started with the siren. She disappeared. And she saw Kari take off after Connor. We have a man on him, of course, and I'm on my way out, but—"

Jacob leaped up and hurried to the front of the ambulance. "Stop, let me out—quickly!" he said.

"Yes, sir. But—"

"Proceed, get him to a room, guards all around," Jacob said.

"Will do," the driver promised.

The ambulance jerked to a halt. Jacob jumped out and began to run. He had blocks to run, blocks filled with tourists, diners, children...

But at least Connor's apartment was north of the club. At least...

Jasmine was a cop; a good cop. She'd be all right. She'd think it out.

She was also emotional. She was afraid Mary had disappeared because Connor had done something horrible to her. Afraid that same horrible thing might happen to Kari...

"Hey!" a man protested.

Jacob just nudged past him and quickened his pace.

THANKS TO DEAN JENKINS, Jorge and all the other police and agents working the case, Jasmine knew where to go. Connor's room. She knew the street, the hotel complex and the number.

Naturally, it was on a side street—one that was poorly lit, for the beach. One that was a bit austere, where the rich came to stay, unburdened by the noise and ruckus of the average working-man tourist.

She ran up to the building. She could see the lobby through the plate-glass windows that surrounded the handsome interior. It was an old deco place redone— velvet upholstered chairs and a check-in reception that wasn't a counter but a desk. She could see a man with a newspaper in the lobby, watching the door.

FBI. The man watching Donald McPherson Connor? If so, he was nowhere near close enough.

Jasmine hesitated, taking a deep breath. One more time—one more try.

She pulled out her cell and dialed Kari's number. It rang once and went straight to voice mail.

She pocketed her phone and tried for a regal and nonchalant manner. She waited for the clerk to walk back into the office behind the desk.

Then she sashayed through as if she belonged there, despite her elaborate if dignified waitress uniform. She didn't know the man with the newspaper; he didn't know her. She offered him a brilliant smile and sauntered on through to the elevator.

She realized, in the elevator, that Connor had taken the penthouse; a floor all to himself. She was surprised when the elevator let her choose the top floor without any additional security.

The doors opened into a charming vestibule, rather than a hallway. It was as if she had arrived at someone's grand house. Handsome double doors led into the apartment itself.

She tried knocking, her heart beating a thousand drums a second. It would be illegal for her just to enter. She certainly couldn't force it open.

She waited…and no one came. The door might well be unlocked in such a building—in a good neighborhood, with security in the lobby.

And if she said she entered because she thought she heard a cry…

Just as Jasmine reached for the handle, the door opened.

Connor stood there, a gun in his hand.

"Ah, Jasmine," he said. "We've been waiting for you."

AS HE RAN, Jacob envisioned every manner of horror. His breath was coming hard; his calves were burning.

He knew he had made the right choice, running. It was the weekend on the beach, cars were bumper-to-bumper. For some reason there was an element of local society who thought it was cool to drive down Collins Avenue and show off their cars, some elegant, some souped-up, some convertibles, and some...just cars. Some with music blaring, and some discreetly quiet.

He was moving far faster than the cars.

And still...

He pictured Jasmine, bursting in on Connor. And Connor, ready for her, shots blazing before she could enter the room; Jasmine shooting back, maybe even taking the man down, as well. Injuring him, maybe killing him, but then lying there in a pool of blood, dark hair streaming through it, almost blue-black in contrast to the color of blood, eyes brilliant emerald as she stared into the night, and yet...sightless.

He had to stop thinking that way. He wasn't prone to panic; he'd have never survived his past.

His phone rang; he answered it anxiously, still running. It was Dean Jenkins.

"Natasha, Ivan, and the trio have headed to the hospital. I was just escorted out of the club. It went into lockdown. I found a place behind a dumpster by the cars. They all left together in the limo."

"Thanks. But no one goes in to see Kozak. They can be herded into a waiting room. They can't be near him. They can't know he's not really poisoned."

"We've got a 'doctor' ready to talk to them. As far as they'll know, Kozak is being airlifted to a trauma center where they're fighting to save his life."

"Thanks, Jenkins."

"Anything on your end yet?"

Apparently, Jenkins couldn't hear the way that he was panting. Just one more corner...

"Almost there."

He turned the corner and saw Connor's building, grand touches of Mediterranean-style along with the fine art deco architecture.

He ran through protocol in his mind—there was no right way to burst in on the man. This was a small part of what was going on; they didn't know who had killed Josef, who had tried to kill Kozak. The operation was in a crisis situation at the moment—and he needed to keep his cover.

He ran to the front, stopped briefly for a long breath and to gather his composure. He saw the agent with his newspaper—and the tiny dolphin tie tack that identified him. A clerk in a handsome suit sat at the desk.

There was no time; Jacob entered the lobby, headed over to the man he'd never met, and greeted him. "Henry, how are you doing?"

"Great—fine fishing today. The kids come in tomorrow. We're going to take them over to Key Biscayne to see the lighthouse and then back to the Seaquarium— let them swim with some dolphins."

"Sounds like a plan. I've done the dolphin thing myself…" Jacob watched as the clerk headed to a back room. "How long?"

"Connor—just twenty minutes or so. Kari Anderson— fifteen. And then, another woman, just a matter of minutes."

Minutes…

Jacob headed for the elevator. It only took seconds for a bullet to find its mark. But as he reached the elevator, he realized the other agent had leaped to his feet to join him.

"I'm here now," Jacob said. "If I need backup, you'll know. If I'm not down—"

"Wait, there's just something you need to hear first," the agent said.

CONNOR NEVER HAD a chance to use his weapon.

Jasmine judged her distance—and the awkward way the man was holding the gun. She ducked low and took a flying leap at him, catching his legs, toppling him.

She'd been right; he was no gunslinger himself; he was completely inept. His gun went flying and he let out a yelp that made him sound like a wounded kitten.

She straddled him, pinning him down. "Where's Kari? What have you done with her?"

"What have I done with her?" He seemed stunned.

"You bastard, what have you done with her?"

It would be unethical, but…she was still playing a role. She'd taken him, and she meant to get the truth from him, beat it out of him if she had to. She could get away with this—one high-class escort worried about another, attacking a man…

But just as she was about to deliver a good right to his jaw, she heard her name called.

She looked up.

Kari was standing in the archway to the next room.

At the same time, she felt strong arms wrap around her waist, drawing her off of Connor. She twisted and fought and turned—

Jacob!

Jacob, stopping her, when she had the man down… "Let me go!" she demanded furiously.

"Jasmine, Jasmine, it's all right, you don't understand!" Kari cried. She rushed over to Connor, going down on her knees and trying to help the man up.

Astonished, Jasmine turned to Jacob. "What in God's name is happening?" she demanded, wrenching free from him. "Has everyone gone mad?"

Jacob turned and closed and locked the door and then looked at her.

For one moment, she felt extreme panic. Were they all in on it? Was Jacob a turncoat, had he somehow tricked the federal government, was this all…?

No! She believed in him, she knew him, knew this couldn't be.

"I admit, I don't fully know myself," Jacob said. "But we need to give Mr. Connor a chance to explain."

Connor was up on his feet, standing next to Kari— who was protectively holding his arm. "What is going on?" Connor asked.

"You first," Jacob told him.

"I'm just a citizen," Connor said. "Trying to…do the right thing."

Kari spoke up then, passionately. "Donald's daughter came to Miami Beach and wound up modeling with the group." She let out a long breath. "She was found dead on the beach. Drug overdose."

"I hire them to get them out," Connor whispered.

"But…but…" Jasmine began.

"Nan, my daughter, talked to me. She was frightened. She said that she couldn't forget what she had seen, and she was afraid that someone knew she knew about the cocaine, and…then she was found dead. She wasn't an addict. She didn't do drugs. I called the police—there was an investigation, and it went nowhere. The officers tried, but Nan wasn't found anywhere near the club, she'd been out with friends, she'd said she was leaving, and…they killed her. I know they killed her. And I couldn't get justice, so—"

"Donald made arrangements for me to get away—far away. Hide out, and then start over," Kari said softly. "I wanted to get ahead so badly, be rich and famous… be loved. I did things I'm not proud of. And I couldn't see any way out. But… Donald is a savior!"

"I need some kind of proof," Jacob said. "And if this is all true, Mr. Connor, I am so sorry and, of course, so grateful, and you're a fool, as well. You're risking your own life."

"My life does not matter so much anymore," Connor said flatly. "I have proof—our airline tickets. I was taking Kari to London tonight and then on to Yorkshire, to settle her with my family there."

Jasmine stared at them all, incredulous. And then it hit her. Connor's daughter…dead.

"Mary," she murmured.

"Mary?" Connor said. "Mary Ahearn?"

Jasmine stared at him.

Connor smiled. "Lovely young woman. She tried to help me find out which one of those horrible people was responsible for Nan's death. She tried to find out what was going on."

"So, you gave her a death sentence, too," Jasmine whispered.

He shook his head, looking a bit confused but still smiling. "Mary is alive and well. She's at my estate in Yorkshire, happily working on a play she's been longing to write. Of course, she'd love to be acting, and she's very fond of British theater, so she just might want to stay on. I asked her not to contact anyone from her former life until we were sure she was safe."

Jasmine would have fallen over. She felt Jacob's strength as his arms came around her.

He was staring across the room at Connor. "We will have to verify your information. And I hope you're telling the truth. If so, I swear to you, we will get justice for your daughter. I'm setting you up with an agent to get safely out of the country. I don't think you'll be bothered tonight—there's too much else going on right now."

"Why did you call me? Why did you hang up?" Jasmine demanded of Kari.

"My—my phone died! I figured I'd call you and let you know I was leaving as soon as possible," Kari said. "And then we were getting my things, and Donald promised he'd come back and get you out, but he thought you were safe, that Jacob might be a criminal, but he'd be watching over you and then somehow, he'd get to you and—I'm so sorry!"

"One thing, please," Connor said.

"What?" Jacob demanded.

"Who the hell are you people?" Connor asked.

Chapter Twelve

It felt odd that it had just been that afternoon that Josef Smirnoff had been lain to rest. The ceremony at the club had taken place, and Jacob had ushered Kozak out in an ambulance, pretending the man was at death's door.

While Jacob and Jasmine were at Connor's suite, Kozak had gone into the hospital—and then out another door. He had immediately been ushered out to a FBI facility out west in Miami, in a little area with scores of ranch houses built in the 1970s, heading west off the canal that bordered the Tamiami Trail all the way across the south end of the peninsula to Naples, Florida.

Agents watching the hospitals—the beach hospital where Kozak had first been taken and the county hospital with the trauma center where he'd supposedly been brought later—had kept up with Jacob; Jasmine had been in touch with the MDPD who had in turn been in touch with the Miami Beach department, and everyone was on alert in case another attempt was made on the life of their new informant.

The entire inner core of Kozak's circle had arrived at the beach hospital, only to be assured that everything was being done, but that no one could see Victor Kozak. They had left together, but now Ivan and Natasha were back at the club with only Antonovich to watch over the doors. Natasha had been a mess, so Jasmine and Jacob were told—and had to be sedated when she was told that Kozak was on the verge of death.

Jacob had received many calls from both Ivan and Natasha, but he had told them both that he also had been kicked out of the hospital for having grown too insistent on seeing a man when an intensive care crew was busy trying to save him.

It was well after midnight by the time Donald McPherson Connor and Kari Anderson had been escorted to the airport—and safely onto their plane. Jasmine had gone from being ready to rip the man's throat out to being his best friend—they'd wound up talking and talking.

Kari had told her she'd wanted to say more, but she couldn't. She'd been afraid of what Jasmine might say or do, not at all certain that Jacob wasn't on the rise through the gang—or that Jasmine wasn't already completely beneath his control.

Connor had spoken about his own grief and then about dealing with it in the most constructive way he could.

"You really took chances," Jacob had told him.

"Not so much. I wasn't in on anything. I was just a client. Not someone making money—I was someone giving them money." He paused and shrugged. "And money is something I have. But it means nothing when you don't have the ones you love to share it with."

Jacob had to admit, he was a bit in awe of the man himself. Grief and loss often destroyed the loving survivors; Connor had channeled his resources and himself into saving others.

Naturally, Jacob hadn't immediately trusted what he heard, but with the information Connor gave him, the FBI offices were able to verify his story. The man did own a huge estate in Yorkshire. In truth, he had a title. He also held dual citizenship and spent as much time in the States—recently in the pursuit of saving the lives of young women—as in Great Britain.

And so it was two in the morning when Jacob and Jasmine returned to her apartment. She didn't seem the least bit tired. She was keyed up and alive, filled with energy.

"She's all right, Jacob! Mary is fine. She's in England…and I've been so, so afraid!"

He was sitting on the sofa, wiped out. She'd been all but flying around the room. In her happiness, that flight took her to fall down on his lap, sweeping her arms around him, her smile bright and her eyes as dazzling an emerald as could ever be imagined.

Her touch removed a great deal of his own exhaustion.

"She's alive, and you have to meet her. Oh, Jacob, to think I wanted to skin that man alive, that I thought he was part of…" Her voice trailed off and she frowned.

"What?" he asked, reaching out to stroke back a long lock of her hair.

"We're no closer to the truth. Nan Connor was afraid because she was a witness to a huge cocaine deal. But we don't know who saw her, and there's no way we can find out. We're pretending that Kozak is dying, but none of the gang has risen up to try to take over."

"Jasmine, as far as I know, they wouldn't dare do so. They don't believe that Kozak is dead as of yet, and they won't dare play their cards until they do."

"Where do we go from here?"

"Everything is in motion. I don't even call the shots from here on out. I'll go out tomorrow to interrogate Kozak, but it's going to be up to men with much higher positions than mine to determine what our next steps are. Kozak was grateful just to be alive." He paused, looking at her. "That was an amazing save tonight—the poison in the vodka. How did you know?"

"When he talked about his special reserve, it occurred to me that he'd be the only one drinking it. I'd hoped I'd find out who had brought the bottle and handed it to the bartender, but the guy was from the catering company and he said the bar had been set up when he got there, with the instructions that the special reserve stuff was for Kozak and Kozak only."

"Impressive." He smiled, watching her eyes. "You are a veritable beast. I thought you were going to rip Connor's head off. We're lucky you didn't shoot. He had a gun, right? You need to slow down—you could have gotten yourself killed."

"I could see he didn't know what he was doing with the gun," Jasmine said. Then she frowned. "How did you know that he wasn't going to kill anyone?"

"The agent watching him, Special Agent Daubs, Miami Criminal Division. He'd overheard Connor and Kari talking. And he watched them. Said he was a pretty good judge of men, and I guess he was."

"I'm glad," Jasmine said softly.

"So now, once again, we wait. Tomorrow, I'll spend some time out with Kozak. And you and Jorge and others will be on the beach, waiting, ready to move if anything does break—play your part. But don't go anywhere near the club."

"I still have my uniform."

"If they call you, let me know right away. And for now—"

"Tonight?" she asked seriously.

"Sleep would be on the agenda."

"Ah, yes, sleep."

"Perhaps some rigorous exercise to speed the process," he suggested.

"We are still playing roles," she murmured.

"Jorge did say we were method actors."

"We can always work on method," she whispered.

Jacob wondered vaguely what it was about a special woman, that her slightest whisper, the nuance in her words, her lightest touch, could awaken everything in a man. There was no one in the world anything like her, he thought.

She stood, reaching for his hand. He rose, smiling. In the bedroom, they both saw to their weapons first. They barely touched, shedding their clothing in a hurry.

He went down on the bed, patting the mattress, and for a moment, she stood, sleek and stunning as a silhouette in the pale light from the hallway. She moved with grace, coming to him, and then she was next to him, in his arms, and if anything, they were more frantic that night to touch and to tease and to taste one another. To make love.

Later, when they should have been drifting off to sleep, she rose up on an elbow, looking at him, empathy in the ever-brilliant sheen of her eyes. "Forgive me, but…"

He knew what she wanted to know. So, he told her about growing up in Miami at first and moving to New

York. Falling in love with Sabrina in high school, college, the service…

"Going off to the Middle East," he said. "She was always so worried about me. And she was vibrant. Full of life. We were happy. I'd done my service and I knew I wanted to head into the FBI Academy. I was certain I'd make it. We never thought… Well, she was diagnosed, and three months later, was gone."

"I am so, so sorry."

"It was over ten years ago now," he told her, rolling to better see her face, stroke her cheek. "But you… hmm. Can't figure how you manage to be unattached. Of course, Jorge told me that you do have a tendency to shut a guy down before he can ask you out."

"Jorge talks way too much."

He laughed softly and pulled her into his arms. "That's all right," he told her. "I'm not an easy man to shut down."

She grinned, indicating their positions. "I didn't try very hard to shut you down."

He laughed and she was in his arms again.

SHE WAS NO good at waiting. She would never make it full time in undercover work.

Jasmine actually tried to sleep after Jacob left. His phone had rung far too early, letting him know that a car was coming to take him to the safe house where Kozak was being guarded. But sleep was impossible. She made coffee, washed and dried her hair and was tempted to try to do her own nails, since she had a rare moment of downtime. She reminded herself how incredibly happy she was—how grateful.

Mary was fine, alive and well. Kari was fine, too.

They'd met a man who was trying to prevent future wrongs.

Still, someone within the gang was truly cold-blooded. At least eight people were dead because of the person within who considered murder to be a stepping-stone to criminal power.

If only Jacob were there to bounce her theories off of. They worked well together. Even when they were just playing roles. But the roles had become so much more. She'd found someone who seemed to really care about her, who could be with her, for all that she was, for what she did.

These roles would come to an end. That didn't mean they had to stop seeing each other, but her life, her work, was here. And his life and work were in New York.

It was foolish to think about the future. In the middle of this, she couldn't even be certain that either of them had a future. She had faith in herself and faith in him and all their colleagues—but no one entered into law enforcement without recognizing the dangers.

Worrying about the future was not helping her keep from crawling up the walls.

She couldn't call a friend and go out. She was still undercover. And Jacob had told her not to go near the club.

She was on her third cup of coffee when she realized that she could call Jorge. She was so antsy she'd probably annoy him, but Jorge never seemed to mind. As the thought occurred to her, she felt her phone ring.

"Jorge!"

"Hey, gorgeous, whatcha doing?"

"I was about to call you. I'm waiting. Doing what I was told to do. Climbing the walls. Being such a desperate cop I'm ready to watch a marathon of *Desperate Housewives* with you."

"Well, I have a reprieve for you. I'm on my way. All sanctioned. Come out to the corner. I'll be by for you."

"Perfect. Jeans okay?"

"Jeans and sneakers. Great. See you in five minutes."

"This is cleared with Captain Lorenzo—and the FBI?"

"Yeah, we're supposed to be heading to a music venue controlled by the gang. Top groups. Acting like normal people. Waiting like the rest of the folks around us, finding out if Kozak is going to make it. Gauging their reactions."

"Okay!" Jasmine rang off and shoved her phone into her cross-body handbag. She hurried out, carefully locking her apartment, all but running by the bathers out by the pool, aware of the bright sun and the waving palms.

A car pulled over to the curb; it wasn't a car she knew, but an impressive SUV. FBI issue for work down here?

Jorge rolled down the passenger-side window. "Hop in!" he said cheerfully.

"Where did you get the car?" she asked.

"City of Miami Beach," he said. He was smiling broadly, but she frowned. Something about him didn't seem quite right.

But while she and Jorge might never have discussed their personal lives, they were solid working partners. They always had one another's back. He would die for her...

It wasn't until she was inext to the car that she realized Jorge wasn't alone in the car.

There was a man in the back, but Jasmine's focus

went to the fact that he had the business edge of a serious knife against the throat of a woman he'd shoved down in the seat. The young woman was trying desperately hard not to snuffle or cry out, with that blade so close to her artery.

It was Helen Lee, the sweet and lovely young woman with whom she and Kari had shared the runway.

Helen was absolutely terrified.

The man with the knife smiled. She was not entirely surprised to see who it was.

"Welcome, Jasmine. Now, Jorge, drive. And no tricks, no running us off the road. You wouldn't want my hand to slip. You wouldn't want to see this blade slice right through Helen's throat, would you? Jorge—drive. Now. Jasmine, smile. Please. It will keep my hand so much steadier."

Jasmine's gun was in her purse, but she couldn't reach for it then. So was her phone. She believed that the man would slit Helen's throat.

As she slid into the car, she kept her bag clutched tightly in her hands.

FROM THE OUTSIDE, it looked like any other house. It sat off 122nd Avenue and Southwest Eighth Street—the Tamiami Trail there and farther west—or Calle Ocho when you headed way back east toward downtown Miami.

Built in the 1970s, it was a ranch-style home like many of the others surrounding them. It had a large lot, but so did several other houses in the area. This house, however, had a little gazebo out front, covered with vines—a fine place for an agent to keep guard—and a large garage and a few storage sheds out back.

The living room was like any other living room. It had a sofa and some plush chairs and a stereo system and a large-screen TV. The windows were all barred— but then, so were many of the other houses in the area, a deterrent to would-be burglars.

Just like so many other houses, there were signs on the fence that warned Beware of Dogs, and the dogs were the kind for which people should be wary. Signs also warned about the house being protected by a local security company, one used by many of the other residents of the area.

There was a kitchen, usually well stocked. There was a well-appointed gym, but then again, other people had home gyms. A dining room sat between the living room and the kitchen. The house boasted four bedrooms.

One of those bedrooms had no bed.

It had a table and chairs, and it was where guests were often required to engage in conversation with those who had brought them here.

Kozak sat in one chair. Jacob sat in another. Also at the table was Dean Jenkins—the man Josef Smirnoff had first approached in fear for his life.

One other man had joined them, Carl Merrill, a prosecutor from the United States Office of the Attorney General.

"As I told Jacob—before I realized how determined my would-be murderer was—I have never killed anyone," Kozak said.

"Your actions have resulted in the deaths of many," Merrill said.

"I can give you so much," Kozak told him. "But I must have a deal. I must."

"What is that you think you can give me? We've got

you, head of an organized crime gang, and enough evidence of your activities to prosecute," Merrill asked.

"Names. I can give you the names of men who look squeaky-clean, who are working with the cartels out of South America. There are bigger fish than me in Miami."

"Victor," Jacob said, "you can't even give us the name of the man who wants you dead, who wants to take over the Deco Gang. Let's see—he's been working for you. And we know he forced a lethal dose of cocaine into a young woman who was a model for you. And he's likely responsible for at least three corpses in oil drums in Broward County and three headless corpses in the Everglades."

Kozak spun on him. "I don't kill. And I don't order executions!" he said angrily. "If I knew, could a murderer have come so close, would I have been about to drink poison?"

"Deals have yet to be made, Victor. We need help now. Who locked the door to the balcony on the day that Josef Smirnoff was killed?" Jacob asked.

"Josef." Kozak sighed. "I can't go to a federal prison…not in the general population. We had reputations. There are too many men who might think me guilty of crimes I did not commit. A man in my position does not deny violent acts to others of his kind. A reputation is everything. I let mine grow as it would."

Jenkins leaned forward. "Victor, let's start here. Did you know that Smirnoff contacted me?"

"No, I did not."

"Had he been acting nervous in any way?"

Kozak appeared to think about that and slowly shook

his head. His voice was husky when he spoke. "If he was afraid, he would not have shown it anyway."

"Do you believe he suspected you?" Jacob asked.

"If so, he shouldn't have."

"Was he sleeping with Natasha—were they a real couple?"

Kozak hesitated on that one. "Yes, she was…strong. And good."

"So, you inherited Natasha along with the leadership," Jacob said. "She had the key to the balcony yesterday."

"There is only one key. She had it because I would not be present."

"Do you think it is Natasha who might be trying to kill you? Would she be hard enough to have one of her girls killed—and to order the execution of those men?"

Kozak smiled. "Natasha, she is a woman. But in business…this business? Natasha serves," he said softly.

Jacob had to wonder at that.

But Kozak was convinced of the truth of his words. He shook his head. "I don't know, I really don't know. As they say, keep your friends close, but your enemies closer. I have kept my people close. I don't know how they can be hiring these killers, desperate people."

There was a knock at the door. The agent who was the house's "owner" stepped in. "Special Agent Wolff, a word."

"Now?"

"Yes, sir. Now."

Jacob politely excused himself. Outside the room, he realized the agent was anxious.

"It's a call from Captain Lorenzo, sir, MDPD. Our

men on the beach were following a car out of the club, but they lost them on the causeway. I—"

He stopped talking and handed Jacob the phone.

The man on the line quickly, tersely, identified himself as Captain Mac Lorenzo.

"I don't know how she did it, but Jasmine managed to contact this number and leave her phone on. She's in a car—they're headed west somewhere. Jorge is driving, Jasmine is in the front. There's a man in back, and from what I can hear, he's taking them somewhere. It sounds as if they're headed for an execution. We've got men on it, but they keep losing them. I've already asked the Feds to hop on it as quickly as possible, but you were close to that group. I'm hoping you might know where they're being taken."

Jacob froze for a split second; he felt as if the life had been stripped out of him.

"I need the exact location those headless bodies were found," Jacob said. "Speak fast, I'm already moving. And keep the others back. If the killer feels cornered, he'll kill whoever he has close out of spite. Get me backup, but keep the backup back."

Lorenzo kept talking. Before he finished another sentence, Jacob was in a car and heading west down the Tamiami Trail.

"Not so slow that the police notice us. There's no need to risk another of the city's finest."

Hearing the voice of the man in the back, Jorge cast a quick glance toward Jasmine. His eyes were filled with agony. She knew how he felt.

A quick look in back assured her there was already

a fine line of blood creating a jagged necklace along Helen Lee's throat.

Jasmine and Jorge would both fight, play for time, for the life of another, as long as they were both still breathing.

There was no way to let him know she'd gotten her hand into her purse, and that she was pretty sure she'd hit the number one; a priority call that would hit the phone Lorenzo had just for communication with her.

But would Lorenzo know where they were going? How could he know when she didn't know?

West. They were headed west. Jorge was driving as slowly as he could reasonably manage without drawing the man's ire or suspicion. He was in no rush to bring them to their destination. They were off the beach now, across the causeway on a long, long drive that seemed to be taking them out to the Everglades.

It was a land a few of the hardiest knew well, where airboat rides could be found, where the Miccosukee kept a restaurant and reservation lands, where visitors could find out about their lives and their pasts.

A place where, no matter how many hearty souls worked and even lived, there were acres upon acres that was nothing but wetland, part of the great "river of grass," filled with water moccasins and alligators, even pythons and boas.

"To the Everglades," she said aloud, as they whipped past the Miccosukee casino.

She turned around and stared at Ivan Petrov.

"You want to kill Jorge and me. Why?"

He eyed her coldly and then smiled. "I don't believe that Kozak is dead. He's the one who brought Marensky in. You did something with his drink. Marensky called the ambulance, and now…now they do not report that Kozak is dead."

"Whatever your argument with me, why Helen?" she asked.

His smiled deepened. "She happened to be there," he said.

Ivan Petrov. They should have figured; they had looked at Kozak, at Natasha, at the goons… They would have gotten to Ivan. He was never off the list.

"I need some guarantee you're going to keep Helen alive," Jasmine said. "Then Jorge and I will do as you ask."

"You are with the government," Petrov said.

"I swear to you, I am not an FBI agent. Neither is Jorge."

"Then you are trying to take the lead, playing up to Kozak. Well, they have cold feet. The enterprise will never be what it should be under Kozak. He is a weakling—he doesn't know how to remove what festers among us. Drive, Jorge. And turn around, Miss Jasmine."

The casino was behind them. Minutes were counting down. They were coming up to Shark Valley when Petrov told Jorge to slow the car down.

He couldn't be going to Shark Valley! There were trails and bike paths, tourists and rangers all about. Unless he meant to kill anyone in his way.

They didn't turn into Shark Valley. They passed the entrance, and the Miccosukee restaurant to the right on the road.

Then suddenly, Kozak said, "Here."

Here? She knew of no road here…

"Now!" Petrov commanded.

Helen let out a scream as the knife pierced her flesh. Jorge turned.

Jacob was met by Mickey Cypress of the Miccosukee Police. The man was in his early forties, lean, bronze and no-nonsense. He'd been waiting for Jacob right outside the entrance to Shark Valley.

"You don't want to go exactly where the bodies were found," he told Jacob. "The Everglades is literally a river, and the bodies were carried until they were snagged by the mangrove roots." He had a map out on his phone and he pointed to a spot that seemed to be just beyond a canal where they stood.

Jacob glanced at the map. Suddenly, two giant male alligators went into some kind of a battle in the canal.

"Leave them alone, completely alone," Cypress told him. "There's a marshy trail we can take through here, and a small hammock. That's where I think we'll find their killing grounds. There was no road there before, but some fairly solid ground. I think they created their own way."

Cars drove up next to them. Men in suits got out— the backup.

Cypress looked at him. They were probably good agents; they just didn't look ready for a trek into the water and marshy land.

"Special Agent Wolff!" one of them called.

Jacob looked at Cypress.

"I'm with you," Cypress said. "Um, if you're trying for stealth…"

Jacob nodded and headed back to the agent calling to him. He asked him to hold their position and keep a line of contact open. He walked back to Cypress.

The local cop told him, "Trust me, I know how to get there. I was the first on call when the bodies were found. I've been on this."

"I trust you," Jacob assured him. "We need to hurry. I got after them right away, but they still had a head start."

"Then we move."

Cypress started over a small land bridge, just feet from the male alligators defending their turf. Water came cascading over them from a massive flip of a tail.

They kept walking.

IVAN PETROV HAD his knife—and a gun on his belt. He kept the knife at Helen's throat.

Jasmine clung to her purse.

"Drop it!" Petrov commanded. His knife moved ever so slightly.

Helen gulped out a cry. Tears were streaming down her face—silent tears. She tried not to sob and stared at Jasmine—any movement would cause a great chafe of the knife against her throat. Her eyes were both imploring and hopeless.

"Go!" Petrov commanded. Jorge walked ahead; Jasmine behind him. He sheathed the knife and drew his gun.

"I don't understand, Ivan. Who were the people in the oil drums?" Jasmine asked.

"Well, I will tell you," Petrov said. "The first, his name was Terry Meyers. He thought he should manage the club—and the women. That was long ago, when Smirnoff had barely begun to settle into South Florida. Smirnoff was, in fact, surprised when Meyers failed to arrive for a meeting. The second, well, he failed to show with a payment. He made me look bad. You can't deal with people who don't deliver on goods or who don't make their payments. It's bad for business if you don't follow through. Same deal for the third loser."

"The three who weren't in the drums," she said. "They were the ones who killed Josef."

"Yes, actually, they were very good. I was sorry to see them go. But you see, they couldn't live. If they had been apprehended, well… I did hire them personally."

"You admired them so much, you beheaded them," Jasmine murmured.

Jorge glanced back at her; she was doing the right thing, keeping him talking. There were two of them. They could survive this. They had to get Helen in a safe position, and then they could rush Petrov—he couldn't shoot them both at the same time.

But they had to get Helen away from him first.

Jorge suddenly stopped, letting out a shout.

"Move!" Petrov commanded.

"There's a gator ahead in the path," Jorge said, falling back by Jasmine.

"That's fine," Petrov said, dragging Helen around and waving his gun at the small gator on the trail. "We're almost there." He fired the gun toward the gator. The creature moved off into the surrounding bracken.

There was some kind of a structure there, a broken-down shack, a remnant, Jasmine thought, from the time when various Florida hunters had come out and kept little camps.

It was now or never—Petrov had just fired the gun, he was looking away, he was holding Helen, but the gun wasn't directly at her throat.

Jasmine didn't let out a sound; she made a silent leap for the man.

She bore him down to the ground. Helen slipped

free, screaming hysterically. She began to run back in the direction from which they had come, screaming all the while.

Petrov's gun hand was flailing; in a second, the barrel would be aiming at Jasmine's face.

But Jorge was there, stomping on the man's wrist, kicking at the gun. It went flying into a gator hole, filled high with water.

But Petrov wasn't going down easily. He caught Jasmine and flipped her down to the muddy earth.

Jorge kicked his head.

Petrov had the knife on his belt now; Jasmine went for it. Seizing it from Petrov, she sliced his hand. He cried out as blood gushed.

And then, a gunshot fired. They all went still.

The knife still tightly in her grip, Jasmine turned to the sound.

Standing casually now before the rotting wood of the old shack was Natasha. She shook her head.

"Men. They are worthless, eh? They continually think they are in charge, and they have no idea. Ivan! A silly girl and these two. You have a gun, you have a knife, and they best you. What would you have done without me, Ivan?"

She shook her head again at Ivan, but then smiled at Jasmine. "Yes, you are one who knows how to manipulate a man, eh? It's the only way, until you have seized the position of real power. And then they will bow down before you, and they will become your toys, and you will command them. It's a pity you must die. It will be hard for me... Oh, maybe not so hard, because now Ivan and I will have to crawl through this wretched swamp looking for that silly Helen. If she doesn't kill herself first. Maybe it will not be so hard. I will kill your friend first, so you can watch him die, and he will not have to watch you die? How is that?"

"I should have known you were the one with ice-cold blood running in your veins—right from the beginning," Jasmine said.

Natasha shrugged. "Me? I am not so much the killer. I like others to do the killing."

"And then you kill the killers."

Natasha smiled. "Ivan killed the killers. I simply cut off their hands and their heads…and fed them to the swamp. Enough talk." She took aim.

But Natasha couldn't have known what hit her.

He came from behind. His arm came down on hers and Natasha screamed with shock and pain as she lost her grip on the gun, as she was tackled to the ground.

Jasmine stared.

Jacob was there. Impossibly, Jacob was there. He'd slipped around silently from behind the hut, and he was now reading Natasha her rights and handcuffing her, heedless of the fact that he was on her back and pressing her face into the mud.

He looked at Jasmine, his recitation breaking. He nodded toward Petrov, who was trying to turn and escape.

Jasmine turned to Petrov, but another man—never before sensed nor seen—went sliding past her.

"Not to worry. I've got that one."

Jacob yanked Natasha to her feet. He spoke into his phone. Jasmine and Jorge were still just standing there, incredulous to be alive, when men—a little ridiculously dressed in fine blue suits and leather loafers—came running through the brush.

"Got her, sir," one of them said to Jacob, taking Natasha. He was young, younger than Jasmine. A brand-new agent, she thought, but ready to do whatever was asked of him, including running through a swampy, mucky river in his office attire.

He was gone; Natasha was dragged away. And then they heard shouts; Ivan had been apprehended, as well.

"Helen—Helen Lee is running through the swamp," Jasmine called out, her voice echoing through the mangroves and pines.

One of the agents came back. "No, ma'am, we've got her. She's fine. A little scratched up and still hysterical, but…we've got her. She's going to be okay."

"Hey, I'm coming with you," Jorge said. "She knows me. I'll get her calmed down."

And then, for a moment, Jasmine and Jacob were standing there alone. A large white crane swooped in and settled down near them, seeing a fish in the shallow gator holes that surrounded them on the small hammock.

Slowly, Jasmine smiled. "Your timing is impeccable."

He let out a long soft sigh, and then he grinned. "So I've been told."

She raced across the mud and the muck that separated them and threw herself into his arms. And they indulged in one long kiss, both shaking.

"You are kick-ass," he told her.

"But not even a kick-ass can work alone," she whispered. "You saved our lives."

"Only because you were doing a good enough job saving your own life," he assured her. "Lord, help me, this may be ridiculous, but I think I love you."

"This may be more ridiculous," she said.

"What?"

"I know I love you!" she told him.

"Special Agent Wolff? Detective?" They were being summoned.

Hand in hand, they started back along the path. "Paperwork," Jacob murmured.

"And then?" she asked.

He wiped a spot of mud off her face. "Showers," he said. "Definitely showers."

She smiled and he paused just one more minute, turning her to him.

"And then," he said, blue eyes dazzling down on her, "then figuring out our lives. If that's all right with you, of course."

She rose on her toes and lightly kissed his lips.

She could have done much, much more, but others were waiting—and there were some very large predators near them. The human ones might be down, but while she wasn't afraid of the creatures here, she wasn't stupid enough to get in their way either.

She broke the kiss and looked into his clear eyes. "It's all right with me."

Epilogue

The woman hurrying toward him along the long stone path over the castle's moat was truly one of the most stunning creatures Jacob Wolff had ever seen. His initial opinion of Jasmine had never changed.

Her skin was pure bronze, as sleek and as dazzling as the deepest sunray. When she smiled at him, he could see that her eyes were light. Green, he knew, an emerald green, and a sharp contrast to her skin. She had amazing hair, long and so shimmering that it was as close to pure black as it was possible to be; so dark it almost had a glint of violet. She was long-legged, lean and yet exquisitely shaped, even in jeans, sweater, boots and a parka.

She didn't pause when she met him. She threw her arms around him and leaped up so he had to catch her, and laughed as he spun with her in the rising sunlight that did little to dispel the chill of the damp day. No one saw them.

Donald McPherson Connor's "estate" had proved to be a castle. Small, admittedly, but *a bit of an historic home*, as Donald called it, and far out in the countryside of northern England.

"Best vacation ever!" she told him, sliding down to stand.

He looked behind her. They were no longer alone.

He'd headed out for a walk on the grounds right after morning coffee; Jasmine had stayed behind to wait for Mary and Jorge—the two had been in a lengthy discussion of just how cold it might get during the day, and throwing her hands up, Jasmine had indicated he should go ahead.

His hike had been serene. The countryside seemed to stretch endlessly, beautiful rolling land with horses and sheep and cattle.

He'd had vacation time built up—you couldn't just hop off to an amusement park or the mountains or the French Riviera in the middle of work when you were deep in an undercover operation. He felt this time off was well deserved, for himself and for Jasmine. It had been impossible for them to turn down Donald Connor's suggestion that they come to visit Mary.

They had a suite in the tiny castle. No windows facing a beach, but instead an arrow slit that looked out over a stretch of land that was misty and green. They had long nights together and days with amazing friends.

Jorge and Mary caught up with them. "Off to the theater, if you're sure you don't mind the walk," she said.

Mary was as gentle and sweet a woman as Jasmine had said, wide-eyed and kind, with blond hair as long as Jasmine's raven tresses. Mary had cried when she'd come to the airport to meet them; she'd been so sorry to have frightened Jasmine, to have put her in danger. But Donald had explained that he was just an ordinary citizen—he'd needed Mary to not say a word to anyone until she was safely out of the clutches of the Deco Gang. She'd been lucky to have an up-to-date passport.

Mary told them that Natasha had instructed her they had more escort work, and the intended client was a man she had seen come and go with different suitcases. She had suspected the man was part of their drug operation. And by then she knew that the girls weren't really models, that the so-called models were being prostituted, and that she just might not be able to do all of the things expected of her. And that if they suspected that she knew too much—or anything at all—she just might wind up dead.

Jasmine explained to her over and over again that it was all right—they'd put a stop to it all, and possibly saved many more lives.

Natasha had gone through people quickly. In her mind, so it seemed, people were as disposable as silverware or linens that were no longer needed.

There was, of course, a note of sadness to it all. They could do nothing for Donald's daughter; she was gone. But while he couldn't be happy, the man was grateful and satisfied. Her killers would find justice.

"A walk is great," Jacob assured her.

"Okay, so maybe these ugly shoes are good," Jorge said, slipping an arm around Mary's shoulders. The two of them moved slightly ahead. Mary began telling Jorge about the history of the area and how old the theater they were about to attend was.

Jasmine looked up at Jacob and smiled. "It's a children's play we're seeing, you know."

"Mary wrote it—I can't wait to see it. Donald will join us there?"

"Exactly," Jasmine said.

Mary suddenly stopped. She looked back, grinning. "Hey, I was talking to Donald this morning, earlier. He thinks you guys should have your wedding here."

Jasmine stopped dead. "Mary, we're visitors here. And we haven't—" she looked at Jacob, a flush rising to her cheeks "—we haven't even…"

Talked about marriage.

They had talked about everything else. A long-distance relationship seemed like half measures. But then, what to do? Jasmine loved the people with whom she worked, and she loved Miami. Jacob understood. They were looking into a transfer for him to the Miami office.

It had only been a few weeks since they'd survived the murder attempt in the Everglades; they'd been mulling over all possibilities in the meantime. And of course, finishing the endless paperwork, the United States Attorney General, the police, evidence, witnesses and everything else that went with the end of such a complicated case.

Kozak was going into witness protection; both Ivan and Natasha would be prosecuted for the murders they had committed. Victor Kozak had given the authorities all they needed to apprehend a number of the drug smugglers in Miami Beach, and information regarding them that might lead to solving many of the cold cases on file across Greater Miami.

Antonovich, Garibaldi and Suarez had worked for Kozak, and though they had faced stiff interrogations, they hadn't actually been proved guilty of any crimes. Jacob hoped that the three would find better employment.

Petrov still had a problem believing he was going

down—he'd tried to throw everything on Natasha, but in turn, Natasha had tried to throw everything on him.

The man had been a fool, Jacob had told Jasmine, when they had been alone and curled together one night. He'd underestimated the power of a woman. And, smiling, he'd assured her, "That's something I never would do."

Now, Jacob grabbed her hand, forcing her to look at him. "I don't know—the wedding here. What do you think?"

"I..." Jasmine looked at him.

Jorge let out a sound of frustration. "Oh, come on! You know there's going to be a wedding. Seriously, who else could either of you live with forever and ever, huh?"

He was right. You were very, very lucky in life when you found that one person who complemented you in every way.

Jacob looked into her eyes, so strong, so gentle, so giving... Dazzling.

He figured he could answer for both of them. "I don't really care where we get married. As long as we do. And I do need to get you all to New York. I have a friend—I've worked with him and the love of his life, and her family owns an Irish pub on Broadway. Her brother is also an actor and can score all kinds of theater tickets, Mary."

"New York—oh, I would love it! But first—a wedding in a castle. We'll let you do the honeymoon alone, and then an after-honeymoon in New York. Perfect!" Mary caught Jorge's hand and the two walked on ahead.

Jacob caught Jasmine's hand. He went down on a knee. "Detective Adair, will you marry me? In a castle, at the courthouse, Miami, New York...wherever? I cannot begin to imagine my life without you. It can be here, there or anywhere."

Jasmine came down on a knee, as well. "My dearest Special Agent Wolff, yes. Here, there, anywhere," she assured him. "I can't imagine my life ever again without you!"

He leaned forward, and they kissed. And kissed...

Until Jorge called back to them. "Hey! Time for that later. We're going to miss the play."

Laughing, Jasmine rose and pulled him to his feet. "The rest of our lives," she said.

"The rest of our lives," he agreed.

* * * * *

Also by B.J. Daniels

HQN

Buckhorn, Montana

Out of the Storm
From the Shadows
At the Crossroads

Montana Justice

Restless Hearts
Heartbreaker
Heart of Gold

Sterling's Montana

Stroke of Luck
Luck of the Draw
Just His Luck

Harlequin Intrigue

A Colt Brothers Investigation

Murder Gone Cold
Sticking to Her Guns
Christmas Ransom

McCalls' Montana

The Cowgirl in Question
Cowboy Accomplice
Ambushed!
High-Caliber Cowboy
Shotgun Surrender

Visit her Author Profile page at Harlequin.com,
or bjdaniels.com, for more titles!

COWBOY ACCOMPLICE

B.J. Daniels

This book is for my cousin Sandra Johnson Olinger.
Last summer she came to Montana, bringing with
her all the memories of a summer we spent
camped on Hebgen Lake so many years ago.
Thank you, Sandy.
And thanks for listening to the stories I wrote
in the tent beside the lake when we were kids
and encouraging me to follow my dream.
There is nothing like family.
Thanks for reminding me of that.

Prologue

Outside Mexico City

He sat on the edge of the bed in the dim mirrorless room, his face swathed in bandages, his mind several thousand miles away. He'd been waiting more years, through more surgeries and more pain than his mind could stand. When he closed his eyes he could still hear the crackle of the flames, feel the intense heat, smell his searing flesh.

"Señor Smith?"

He turned to see Dr. Ramon, a small, nervous white-cloaked figure, framed in the doorway.

"Are you ready?" the doctor asked in Spanish as he stepped in, the door closing behind him.

Ready? He'd been ready for years. He said nothing as the plastic surgeon pulled back the curtain. Sunlight streamed into the room, momentarily blinding him. He closed his eyes as Dr. Ramon put down a black medical bag on the edge of the bed beside him.

Slowly, carefully, the doctor began to peel away the bandages, his fingers trembling. They both knew what was at stake here.

Señor Smith as he was called here closed his eyes,

having given up hope a long time ago that his face might ever be normal again.

A cool breeze caressed his cheek as the last bandage fell away. With a pain far greater than any physical one he'd ever known, he opened his eyes.

The doctor had stepped back and was now studying his handiwork, his face expressionless. "You are a new man," he said finally, his gaze skittering away at the intensity of his patient's look.

Señor Smith had heard such words before. He didn't want or need false hope. False hope had gotten other even more prestigious surgeons killed.

He reached his hand out for the mirror he knew the doctor had brought in his bag. His hand was steady as he took it. Hope made a person tremble. He had nothing but fear at what monstrous visage he would now see in the glass.

Slowly he held up the hand mirror and stared into the face of the new stranger he found there. To his surprise, this stranger wasn't hideous. Nor was he handsome. He was…average. The face of a man no one would look at twice on a street corner or across a crowded room.

He could feel the doctor waiting for his reaction, perhaps by now having heard what had happened to the other surgeons.

"It is perfect," he said, looking from the mirror to Dr. Ramon.

The doctor breathed a ragged sigh of relief. "Bueno, bueno. You are free to leave, Señor." He picked up his bag from the bed. "Vaya con dias." Go with God.

Señor Smith nodded and looked in the mirror again at his new face. He would go all right, only he wouldn't be going with God. He'd been to hell and right now he'd sell his soul just to go home again.

Except he'd sold his soul years ago, he thought with a rueful smile. He was going home. And with a face no one would ever recognize, a body that had become hard and lean.

Like the Phoenix rising from the ashes, he had survived it all with only one dream in mind. Vengeance.

He couldn't wait to see the look of surprise on J. T. McCall's face. J.T. wouldn't see him coming. Until it was too late.

Chapter One

Regina Holland glared down the empty two-lane high-way, wishing a car would appear. Wishing anything would appear. Even a horse-drawn wagon. She was beyond being picky at this point.

But of course there wasn't any traffic now. She kicked the flat tire on her rented red convertible with the toe of her high heel and instantly regretted it when she saw the dark smudge of black on her expensive red shoe. She cursed her luck as she bent down to thumb at the smudge.

She'd been in the state for three days and her luck had gone from bad to worse. It had seemed such a simple task in the beginning. How hard could it be to find a cowboy in Montana? She had two weeks to find him. If she failed, she could kiss her dream goodbye. Everything was riding on this. Her entire future.

Regina knew exactly what she wanted and as was her character, she wasn't about to quit until she got it. Somewhere in Montana was her cowboy. All she had to do was find him.

Straightening, she tugged down the skirt of her expensive designer suit and scowled at the tire. Oh, she'd found her share of cowboys all right. Men of every size, shape and disposition but definitely not "The One."

But right now she swore she'd take the first cowboy who drove up with a jack and the wherewithal to change her tire. Unfortunately, it didn't look like any were going to come riding up. No John Wayne on the horizon. Not even a rodeo clown. The highway was empty and she could see both ways for miles.

A pickup had come by but hadn't stopped even when she'd tried to wave down the man behind the wheel. He'd acted as if he hadn't seen her. So much for western hospitality.

A few miles away, she thought she could make out a couple of buildings, possibly a town. Not much of one from what she could see, but at least it looked like something.

She could walk in this heat and these heels or—she glanced at the bag of tools she'd found in the trunk—or she could try to change the tire herself.

She looked down the highway again. Heat rose off the blacktop and an intense sun beat down from an all-too-expansive clear blue sky. She knew the moment she started to walk in these heels, vultures would begin to circle.

She picked up the bag of tools with two well-manicured fingers, spilling an assortment of metal objects onto the ground. How hard could it be to change a tire? She had degrees in business and advertising from Berkeley, for crying out loud.

Twenty minutes, and two chipped nails later, Regina knew how hard it could be. Impossible. She was squatting by the tire, trying to figure out how to get the stupid bolts off, when she heard the sound of a truck coming up the road. It appeared like a mirage, a large dirty brown shape floating on the highway's heat waves.

Regina didn't know how long she'd been squatting by the flat tire, but she found that her muscles had permanently locked in that pitiful crouched position. She could only lift an arm and wave frantically as the vehicle bore down on her.

The truck roared past and she thought for one horrible moment, that the driver wouldn't stop. To her relief, she heard the screech of brakes, heard the truck pull over a dozen yards in front of her car. She was bent over assessing a run in her silk stockings when she heard the driver approach.

A pair of boots and the bottom of a pair of jeans stepped into her line of vision. Both the boots and the jeans were worn and muddy. At least she hoped that was mud. The boots stopped before they reached her, then turned away. For one awful moment she thought he was leaving. Instead he called to someone she assumed was back at his truck.

"I told you to stay there, Jennie," he ordered gruffly. "Do as I tell you for once or next time I'm leaving you at home."

Her gaze and her eyebrow came up at the same time. She'd heard some Montana men still bossed their wives but he should be ashamed, talking to a woman like that.

She thought about telling him so in no uncertain terms. Then she remembered her flat tire and bit her glossed lower lip as the man swiveled back around to her.

"Need some help?" he asked in a soft western drawl. Great voice. Regina took in the cowboy with a trained eye starting at his boots, noting with professional detachment the way he filled out his jeans. Muscled thighs. Long legs. She let her gaze travel up those legs past the slim hips, the narrow waist, to the man's wide chest. Nice. Real nice. His broad shoulders beneath the western shirt literally blocked out the sun.

His face was in shadow under his battered black cowboy hat. Didn't the good guys always wear white hats?

"Oh, I could definitely use some help," Regina said, a little breathless, trying not to flutter her lashes. How far would she go to get this tire changed? She hated to think.

He shoved back his hat. Handsome too, if you liked that rough around the edges type. Such a waste since it wasn't his strong masculine jaw, his spacious shoulders or his seductively low voice that she was looking for.

"If you've got air in your spare, it shouldn't take but a few minutes," he said and stepped past her to bend over to inspect her tire.

Regina sucked in a breath as she eyed the man's posterior. It was positively perfect. "I can't tell you how much this means to me." She practically shouted in glee, amazed at her change of luck. She'd found him. The One.

J. T. McCALL went to work changing the tire and trying to hide his amusement. He'd been having a bad day, actually a bad couple of months, but he had to admit this little distraction was definitely elevating his mood.

He hadn't believed it when he'd first seen her dressed all in red, wearing the loftiest pair of high heels he'd ever seen, standing beside a matching red convertible in the middle of nowhere.

What was a woman dressed like that doing just outside Antelope Flats, Montana? Boy was she lost.

He flicked a look at her over his shoulder, mentally shaking his head. Wait until he told Buck, his elderly ranch foreman, about this. Buck wasn't going to believe it.

He felt her gaze on him as he made short work of changing the tire. "Where ya headed?" he asked, unable to curb his curiosity.

"Antelope Flats."

"Really?" He couldn't imagine what business this woman could possibly have in the tiny ranching town up the road. It was so small it didn't even have cable TV. For J.T., after weeks on the ranch, it was the big city but for this woman— "All done."

He loaded the flat tire and the tools into the trunk and slammed the lid, then took another good look at her as he wiped his dirty hands on his jeans. She was definitely easy on the eyes.

"I can't tell you how much I appreciate this," she gushed.

"My pleasure." He figured she'd try to slip him money but he'd be darned if he'd take even the price of a cold beer at the Mello Dee. No, just seeing her the way she looked right now was plenty thanks. Standing there, teetering on her heels in the middle of the highway, a lock of her dark hair fleeing from her tight little no-nonsense French roll or whatever women called those things, and a smudge of dirt on that perfectly made-up face.

"I'd like to do something for you," she said.

He shook his head. "Consider it your welcome to Antelope Flats."

"You're from here?" she asked, eyeing him speculatively.

"Ranch just back up the road. Name's J. T. McCall," he said, not sure he liked the way she was looking at him. He started to step around her.

"Really, I must insist. You've been so kind," she said quickly, blocking his exit. "In fact, I have something in mind."

He raised a brow and grinned, telling himself this wasn't happening and if it was, *no one* would believe it.

"Of course, I'd have to see you in the saddle," she added.

"I beg your pardon?"

Her eyes widened. "You do ride a horse, don't you?"

Torn between feeling insulted and curious about where she was headed with this, he said, "I guess you could say I ride."

"Good." She looked pleased. "Because I'm in Montana looking for a cowboy." She flashed him a flawless smile, all teeth, all perfect. "And I think *you're* that cowboy."

If she thought he'd be thrilled to hear this, she was sadly mistaken. He'd already encountered one city girl who'd come to Montana looking for a real-life cowboy. Once was plenty enough.

"I appreciate the thought," he said more politely than he felt. "But, I'm not your cowboy." He started past her.

She caught his arm with one of those well-manicured hands, the nails the same red as her outfit. The hand was white as new snow, the skin soft-looking. This woman hadn't done one day of hard manual labor in her life.

"Wait," she cried. "You don't know what I'm offering you."

"I'm afraid I do," he said, carefully removing her hand from his arm. "No offense, but I'm just not interested."

"No!" she cried. "*That's* not it." Frowning, she brushed back a lock of hair and put another dark smudge on her cheek. The imperfection made her more appealing somehow.

"I'm looking for a cowboy to do a television commercial for my jeans company, not—" She waved a hand through the air, her cheeks flushed.

She wanted him for a blue jeans commercial?

"You understand that you'd have to audition," she explained. "I can't promise that you'd make the cut but—"

"Audition?"

"To see how you look on a horse." She narrowed her gaze at him as if she was worried he wasn't getting it.

Oh, he was getting it all right.

"You see, it would be a close-up shot," she said, hurrying on. "Your face wouldn't show, just your—" She glanced below his elk horn belt buckle.

He followed her gaze, shocked. "My *what?*"

"Your...backside. It would be a close-up of it in the jeans on the horse. Your posterior, which I might add, is perfect. For the commercial," she quickly amended.

Well, now he really was insulted. He'd never had a woman proposition him before. Well, at least not like this. And he realized he didn't like it. She was sizing him up like a piece of beef on the hoof. Or maybe he just didn't like the fact that she was only interested in his "south end."

"Thanks just the same," he said as he tipped his hat. He and his perfect posterior were leaving.

She seemed surprised. "But the commercial will be shown on *national* television," she said trotting unsteadily along beside him toward his truck. "You'd be paid, of course, and you'd get to keep the jeans."

"Get paid *and* get to keep the jeans?" he asked sarcastically.

"Yes," she said smiling. "And if it worked out, this could lead to all kinds of opportunities. This could open the door for a whole new career for you, Mr. McCall."

He almost stopped walking to tell her what he thought, but he was trying to be a gentleman. That's why he'd pulled his truck over to help her in the first place.

"Wait," she cried. "At least let me give you my card."

"Lady, I hate to be rude, but I really don't have time for this," he said turning back to her, but she'd already trotted back to get her card for him.

He waited at the rear of his muddy flatbed truck, shaking his head in wonder. "I'm not going to change my mind," he called to her, not sure if the woman heard him, but doubting she would listen anyway.

He watched her lean into the car, providing him with a nice view of her tight-skirted bottom. Now *that* backside would make a wonderful commercial, he thought, momentarily distracted.

Before he could stop her, she'd rushed back to thrust her card into his hand. "I really think you should reconsider. This commercial pays more than you probably make in a year chasing cows," she said taking in his attire—and his truck.

That did it. He glanced down at the card, just long

enough to see her name. Regina Holland. Regina? What kind of name was that? And her address. Los Angeles. He should have known.

"Listen up, Reggie, I happen to *like* chasing cows. And right now I have six hundred head to chase down from summer pasture, my camp cook is out with a broken leg and I don't want my butt anywhere but in a saddle heading into the high country before dark. Is that clear enough for you?"

He shoved the card—now slightly crumpled from being balled in his fist—back into her hand and went to his truck, jerking open the door.

"Reggie?" he heard her mutter behind him. Then she called after him: "Perhaps you should discuss it with your wife, Jennie."

His wife? He shook his head. "Good girl, Jennie," he said, patting the mutt before pushing her over to her side of the pickup seat. "What would make the woman think I was married to a mongrel dog?" He had a feeling he should be even more insulted.

Glancing back as he pulled out onto the highway, he saw that Regina Holland was standing in the middle of the road, looking as lost as when he'd found her. His irritation dissolved and he chuckled to himself as he shifted into second and put some distance between him and the red sports car.

No, he thought shaking his head, no one was going to believe this. Not that anyone would ever hear about it. He sure had no intention of ever telling a living soul now that he realized what the woman wanted. Perfect behind, his butt. He'd never live down the razzing he'd get. Never in a million years.

He topped a rise in the road and Regina Holland disappeared from his rearview mirror. Gone, if not forgotten.

All morning he'd been trying not to stew and he had a hell of a lot to stew over. Something was going on at the ranch and had been even before his mother returned. For almost all of his thirty-six years, he'd been led to believe that his mother was dead. Hell, he and his brother Cash, the only two of the McCall kids who actually remembered their mother, had been putting flowers on her grave every Sunday.

Then out of the blue, Shelby McCall shows up at the ranch and announces she's not only alive, but that she and Asa cooked up her demise because they couldn't live with each other and yet didn't want the kids to have the stigma of divorce hanging over them.

J.T. had never heard such bull in his life. On top of that, he and his three brothers had always thought that their little sister Dusty was the result of an affair their father had had years ago.

Turned out, Dusty was the result of Asa and Shelby getting together to "discuss" things.

Well, now Shelby was back at the ranch, tongues were waggling in three counties, his brother Cash, the sheriff, was trying to keep them both from going to prison for fraud, Dusty wasn't speaking to either of their parents and something was up between Shelby and Asa.

J.T. hadn't been able to put his finger on it. But he'd seen the looks that passed between them. He had a bad feeling they had another secret that would make the first pale in comparison.

If all of that wasn't bad enough, his brother Rourke had gotten out of prison a few months ago, come home, stirred things up good when he not only fell in love, but also cleared his name by finding the real killer who'd helped send him to prison eleven years ago.

The McCalls had always been the talk at the Longhorn Café in town. J.T. knew it was one of the reasons his brother Cash had become sheriff. He was tired of being one of the "wild" McCalls.

Of the bunch, J.T. looked like a saint. Probably because he'd had to take over the running of the ranch after Asa's heart attack. Rourke had been in prison, Cash was sheriff and his little brother Brandon was too busy sowing his oats.

Some days, J.T. resented the hell out of the family's reputation because everyone still painted all the McCalls with the same brush. The McCalls were the cowboys that fathers warned their daughters about. Western born and bred, they were a rough-and-tumble bunch, no doubt about that. Always fighting amongst themselves like a den of wildcats, but joining together in times of trouble.

And J.T. had a bad feeling this was a time of trouble as he drove toward Antelope Flats.

This morning a neighboring rancher had told him he'd seen something "odd" on their adjoining summer range in the Bighorn Mountains a week ago.

"It was one of your cows," Bob Humphries said after the two of them were seated in the Sundown Ranch office, the door closed. "Something had killed it."

Losing cattle to mountain lions, grizzlies or wolves wasn't that uncommon. He wondered why Bob had driven all the way out to the ranch to tell him this.

Bob met his gaze. "An animal didn't kill that cow," he said as if he could tell what J.T. was thinking. "It had been burned."

J.T. sucked in a breath, pulse pounding, the weight on his chest like a Mac truck.

"It reminded me of what happened about ten years ago," Bob said, worry furrowing his brow. "But those fellows are dead, right?"

J.T. could only nod.

"I suppose it could have been lightning," Bob said, still looking worried. "But I thought I should tell you since you're headed up there today."

Now as he neared town, J.T. glanced toward the Bighorns. The long range of mountains glistened against the cloudless blue sky.

He'd always loved this time of the year and looked forward to leaving the heat of the valley for the cool of the cow camp miles from a road. He liked the hard work of gathering the cattle and driving them back down to the ranch, but it was the camp's isolation that always appealed to him the most. No phone. No electricity. Nothing but the peace and quiet of the mountains, long hours in the saddle, sacking out at night in the line shack while the men slept in wall tents. The sound of the campfire, men talking cattle, the quiet that a man could find in the darkness of night up there.

But as he looked at the mountains where he would be spending the next few days, an icy chill skittered up his spine.

He shook it off and thought instead of the woman in red who'd wanted his butt. Much better than thinking about the dead men who had haunted his dreams for the past nine years.

REGINA STOOD IN the middle of the blacktop, her face as red as her outfit. Jennie was a *dog!* The first time she'd glanced toward the truck, all she'd caught was a glimpse of red hair in the front seat. The back window was so muddy—

She felt sick. She knew she shouldn't have tried to do business in the middle of the highway. But the cowboy was perfect and she'd just wanted to get him before he got away.

If he looked as good in a saddle as he did bent over her flat tire, he would launch the jeans line and she could write her own ticket. She'd known she wanted a real cowboy. Not one of those Hollywood models. No, she needed the real thing, shot in his environment with panoramic views of the real west, cattle and all, behind his perfect behind.

And she'd found just the man for the job.

And she'd just let him walk away.

Not a chance, she thought as she looked after the truck. She'd never backed down from a challenge in her life. And her life had been rife with challenges, she thought. Getting this man to do the commercial was child's play given the other obstacles in her life that she'd overcome.

She'd been too confident that he'd accept her offer, she thought as she walked back to the rental car. She fought the urge to chase him down and set him straight on a few things. His rejection stung, especially when he'd thought she was offering herself. But she'd been rejected before. Not quite so offhandedly though.

She climbed in, dropped the visor and looked in the mirror, shocked at her appearance. Wiping furiously she tried to get the greasy smudges off her cheek with a tissue. Her clothing was wrinkled, her makeup a mess, her hair in disarray.

He must have thought she was a nutcase. That's why he'd turned down her offer. The way she looked, she didn't blame him for not believing her. And she'd probably come on a little strong. But she'd been so grateful to him for changing her tire—and his posterior *had* been so perfect....

She tucked a wayward strand of hair back behind her ear. Maybe she shouldn't have told him he had to audition. But she'd only said that so he wouldn't know how much she wanted him. She was pretty sure she could get this guy for a song. Coming in way under budget wouldn't hurt. Everything was riding on this.

Reaching into her purse, she pulled out her cell phone and dialed Way Out West Jeans. No service. What kind of place was this?

She started the car and looked down the highway, barely able to make out the rear end of the man's truck disappearing into the distance. What were her chances of finding another one like him?

She knew the answer to that. Whereas finding him again wouldn't be a problem. She'd seen the logo on the side of the muddy truck. Sundown Ranch. And he'd told her where he was headed. A cattle roundup in the mountains. Could she have asked for anything more ideal?

After he knew that her offer was legit, he'd be grateful that she'd tracked him down. Only a fool would turn down a chance like the one she was giving him.

She smiled as she headed toward Antelope Flats. Even if he still thought he didn't want to be the new "look" of Way Out West Jeans, she'd change his mind. The man had no idea what lengths she would go to— especially when she was desperate—to get what she wanted.

But he was about to find out, she thought, as she drove into the small western town and spotted a phone booth. She couldn't remember the last time she'd seen one of those.

Getting out of the car, she stepped into the glass-sided booth and dialed the company's 800-number.

"I found the perfect butt," she said when Anthony answered.

"Gina, darling, you know what that kind of talk does to me," he joked. Anthony was gay, her best friend and the best head of advertising she'd ever known. "So when do I get to meet him?"

"He's a bit rough around the edges," she hedged.

"You are making my mouth water."

She laughed. "He's straight. As an arrow."

"You're sure?"

She couldn't say how she knew, but yes, "I'm sure. There is one tiny little problem."

"I don't like the sound of this. You know what a tight deadline we're under here, darling."

"He needs a little convincing."

"Oh, well, then I'm not worried," he said, sounding relieved. "No man can turn you down."

She hoped he was right about that. "I'll call again as soon as I have the contract in hand," she told him. "It might take a couple of days. Also there is no cell phone service here."

"Ta-ta, darling. Call when you have the contract in hand."

She smiled as she hung up and looked down the street. Parked not a block away was a newer pickup with the same Sundown Ranch logo on the side. Getting back into her rental car she drove down the block and parked next to the truck. It sat in front of what appeared to be the only restaurant in town, the Longhorn Café.

Regina put the top up on the convertible and after locking it, headed toward the café entrance. Just as she started to open the door, a man came out, startling her.

Their gazes met. Something about him seemed familiar. He pushed past her, skipping out onto the sidewalk without even an "excuse me."

She stared after him, trying to remember where she'd seen him before, and then it hit her. He was the man who'd driven right past her on the highway, the one she'd tried to flag down to help her with her flat tire. He hadn't paid any more attention to her then than he did now as he disappeared into the general mercantile next door. How rude.

Fortunately not all Montana men were like him, she thought, as she stepped into the café and glanced around for the man she imagined would be driving the Sundown Ranch pickup outside.

The café was nearly empty except for one large round table at the back. Its half-dozen occupants had looked up as she'd entered and were still watching her with interest as she started toward the older man in western wear and a white cowboy hat sitting at the table with the younger cowboys.

"Am I correct in my presumption that you are the gentleman driving that vehicle?" Regina inquired.

He was a large man, strong-looking, his face weathered, heavy gray brow over kind brown eyes and his western clothing freshly laundered and ironed, distinguishing him from the other men at the table. He had a thick gray mustache that drooped at each end. He looked like someone's grandfather.

He pushed back his cowboy hat and blinked at her before glancing out the window at the Sundown Ranch pickup. When he looked at her again, he blushed. "Ah… um that's my truck if that's what you're asking, miss."

The younger cowboys at the table were nudging each other and grinning as if they hadn't seen a woman for a while.

She ignored them as she held out her hand to the distinguished elderly cowboy. "I'm Regina Holland and you're…?"

"Buck Brannigan," he stammered. "Foreman of the Sundown Ranch."

She flashed him a smile. "Just the man I was looking for."

Chapter Two

Later that evening as J.T. rode his horse up to the cow camp high in the Bighorn Mountains, he decided to check out the dead cow Bob Humphries had told him about. Mostly, he hoped to put his mind to rest.

He'd left his new puppy Jennie at home. The other two older ranch dogs had gone with his sister Dusty and his dad to round up the smaller herd of longhorn cattle they kept on another range. He missed having at least one dog with him on the roundup but the new puppy wasn't trained to round up cattle and he'd have had to be watching Jennie all the time to make sure she didn't get into trouble.

He had enough to worry about. He'd had to leave the hiring of the roundup cow hands and cook up to ranch foreman Buck Brannigan.

Buck had assured him he had it covered. J.T. should have been relieved to hear this but something in Buck's tone had caused him concern. Finding good hands this late in the fall was tough and finding a good cook was next to impossible, especially around Antelope Flats.

J.T. hated to think what men Buck had come up with given that most of the hands he normally used for roundup from summer range had already moved on by now.

He should have had the cattle down weeks ago. But his brother Rourke hadn't just fallen in love with Longhorn Café owner Cassidy Miller. The two had gotten married. If it hadn't been for the wedding, J.T. would have gotten the cattle down from the high country earlier. But Rourke had asked him to be his best man and the wedding had been only last week.

As he rode higher into the mountains, he saw his breath and swore he could almost smell snow in the air. In this country, the weather could change in a heartbeat and often did. Once the snow started in the fall, it often stayed in the high mountains until spring. With luck he could get the six hundred head of cattle rounded up and down before winter set in.

But as he neared the spot where Bob had seen the dead cow, J.T. wasn't feeling particularly lucky.

The late-afternoon sun felt warm on his back as it bled through the pines. He caught the scent of burned grass on the breeze before he saw the edge of the charred area.

He drew his horse up and dismounted. Over the years, there'd been days he had pushed what had happened that fall at the cow camp out of his mind. Murder was hard to forget. But this had been more horrifying than murder. Much more.

And it had started with one dead cow.

He ground tied his horse and walked through the deep golden grass. On the ride up, he'd convinced himself that lightning had killed the cow. Although rare, it happened sometimes, especially in an open area like this high on a mountainside. Much better to believe it was just a freak occurrence of nature than the work of some deranged man.

But as he neared the burned grass, he saw that the cow was gone. There were tracks where it had been dragged off. He shuddered, remembering the burned man who had also been dragged off into the woods and the grizzly tracks they'd found nearby.

J.T. glanced toward the dense pines. It was too late to go looking for the cow, even if he'd been so inclined. He turned and walked back to his horse, anxious to get to the line camp before dark.

As he rode deeper into the Bighorns, he couldn't shake the feeling that something—or someone—was watching him. Maybe even tracking him. An animal? Or a man?

He didn't relax until he glimpsed the light of the campfire through the pines. The men had built a fire in the pit in an open area between the wall tents and the line shack. Shadows pooled black under the cool dark pines and the familiar scent of the crackling fire drifted on the breeze, beckoning him with warmth and light.

Everything looked just as it had for years. The two wall tents were pitched a good distance to the right of the fire pit. The cook's cabin, a log structure almost hidden by the pines, sat back some off to the right. The ranch hands slept on cots in the tents. The boss and foreman took the bunks in the cabin with the cook.

Past the campfire and down the hillside sat the hulking outline of the old stock truck. He was glad to see that the truck had made it up the rough trail. It would probably be its last year. He'd put off buying another truck because this one had been doing roundups almost as long as he had and there was something about that that he liked.

As he turned his horse toward the corrals, he felt his earlier unease settle over him like a chill. Something was very wrong. The camp was too quiet. Usually the hands would be standing around the campfire, talking about cattle or horses, telling tales and arguing about something. And typically, his foreman would be right in the middle of it, Buck's big deep bellow carrying out over the pines like a welcoming greeting.

Instead, the men were whispering among themselves and Buck was nowhere to be seen.

Riding over to the corral, he dismounted. Something had happened and whatever it was, it must not be good. The cowhands' horses milled in the corral. Eight horses, six the hands had ridden up individually during the day from the trailhead. The two extra horses Buck had brought up in the stock truck.

As J.T. began to unsaddle his horse, Buck came out of the line shack and headed toward him as if he'd been waiting anxiously for his arrival. Not a good sign. J.T. tried to read the look on the elderly foreman's weathered face. Worry? Guilt? Or a little of both? Whatever it was, J.T. feared it spelled trouble.

He waited for his foreman to bring him the bad news as he busied himself unsaddling his horse. His first thought was that Buck had lied about finding a camp cook. Their regular one had broken his leg riding some fool mechanical bull. Without a camp cook, they'd be forced to eat Buck's cooking, which was no option at all. Ranch hands worked better on a full stomach and there was a lot less grumbling.

Buck's cooking was so bad that the men would want

to lynch J.T. from the nearest tree within a day, so Buck damned sure better have gotten them a cook.

"Okay, what's wrong?" he asked as Buck sidled up to the corral fence.

A mountain of a man, large, gruff and more capable than any hand J.T. had ever known, Buck had been with the Sundown Ranch since before J.T. was born. Buck was family and family meant everything to a McCall.

But J.T. swore that if Buck hadn't found a cook he'd shoot him.

"What makes you think somethin's wrong?" Buck asked, taking the defensive, another bad sign.

J.T. wished he didn't know Buck so well as he studied the older man in the dim light that spilled through the trees from the campfire. He would have sworn that the men over by the fire were straining to hear what was being said. Oh yeah, J.T. didn't like this at all.

He stepped closer to Buck, not wanting to be overheard, and realized he'd been mistaken. The look on the foreman's face wasn't worry. Nor guilt. Buck looked sheepish.

J.T. swore. He couldn't help but remember Buck's cockiness a few days earlier: "I'll find you a camp cook or eat my hat."

"Tell me you found a cook," J.T. demanded, trying to keep his voice down.

"Well, I need to talk to you about that," Buck said.

If it came down to a choice, *he'd* rather eat Buck's hat than Buck's cooking. "What's to talk about? You either hired a cook or you didn't."

"Have I *ever* not done something I said I would?" Buck demanded.

J.T. shot him a let's-not-go-there look and counted

heads around the campfire. Six men sitting on upended logs around the fire, all as silent as falling snow. An owl hooted in a treetop close by. Behind him, one of the horses in the corral whinnied in answer.

"Do I know any of the men you hired?" he asked Buck, that earlier uneasiness turning to dread as he let his horse loose in the corral with the others.

"A couple. I was lucky to find *any*. Hell, I had one lined up but he got hurt in a bar fight and another one—"

"I wish I hadn't asked." He could tell by the foreman's excuses that he'd had to scrape the bottom of the barrel to get six hands together for this roundup. He hated to think how bad the six might be.

"Let's get this over with," he said, hefting his saddle and saddlebag with his gear in it, as he headed for the campfire.

The men all got to their feet as J.T. approached with Buck trailing along behind him.

"Evenin'," he said to the assortment of men standing around the campfire resting his saddle and saddlebag on a log by the fire. "I'm J. T. McCall." At a glance, he'd seen the men ranged from late twenties to late thirties. They seemed to study him with interest.

"Luke Adams." A thirty-something, slim cowboy held out his hand.

J.T. took it, feeling that he knew the man. At thirty-six, J.T. had been doing roundups for thirty years so the faces of past cowhands sometimes blurred in his memory as did most of the cattle drives. But something about this man.... "You worked for us before?"

Luke seemed surprised he would remember. "Almost ten years ago."

The memory fell into place, dropping like his heart in his chest. Luke Adams had been one of the cowhands who'd left camp after the first trouble nine years ago. Luke had been one of the smart ones.

While J.T. had never been superstitious, it still gave him an odd feeling that one of the cowhands from that tragic cattle roundup had signed on for this year's.

"I haven't seen you around Antelope Flats," J.T. said, wondering where Luke had been all these years.

Luke shook his head. "Went down to New Mexico for a while."

He nodded, feeling uneasy as he studied him in the firelight before moving to the next man.

"Roy Shields," the man next to Luke said quietly, then awkwardly pulled off his hat before sticking out his hand. Roy was slim and wiry-looking with thin red hair, early to late thirties, one of those people it was hard to tell his age.

His grip was strong but not callused. He looked like a cowhand, one of the quiet ones that seldom gave him any trouble. But how did the saying go, still waters run deep? Roy could have been familiar. The man hurriedly shook his hand, keeping his eyes downcast. J.T. made a note to watch him.

"Cotton Heywood," the next man said eagerly reaching to shake J.T.'s hand. He was one of the local ranch hands who worked in the area. He had a full head of white-blond hair, which explained his nickname.

"Good to see you again, Cotton," J.T. said, trying to remember the latest scuttlebutt he'd heard about the man. Cotton had gotten into some kind of trouble at another rancher's cow camp, but for the life of him, J.T.

couldn't remember what. He seldom paid any attention to rancher gossip, but now he wished he had.

J.T. looked to the next man.

"Nevada Black," said a strong-looking man with dark hair and eyes. His hand wasn't callused either. He gave J.T. a knowing smirk. "That's my real name. I was born at a blackjack table."

"You have any experience on cattle roundups?" J.T. asked.

"I took a few years off, but I've been rounding up cattle since I was a boy," Nevada said. He rattled off a series of ranches in Nevada and northern California where he'd worked.

J.T. nodded and looked to the next man.

"Slim Walker," said the gangly cowboy. He held out his hand and when J.T. took it, he couldn't stop himself from pulling back. Slim nodded, then stretched out both hands in the firelight for everyone to see. "Burned them. Got knocked into a campfire at a kegger." He shrugged. "Gave up drinking after that."

J.T. barely heard the man over his thundering pulse. He tried to hide his embarrassment and quickly looked to the last man.

The sixth cowhand stood back a little from the fire as if he'd been watching J.T. make his way around to him and waiting.

"Will Jarvis," he said slowly stepping forward, removing his hat. He had thin brown hair and was the oldest of the bunch, late thirties like J.T. himself.

J.T. studied the man's face as he shook his hand. Something about him was familiar but he couldn't put his finger on it. The man's hand was smooth and cool. He was no ranch hand. Buck really *had* been desperate.

"Glad you're all here," J.T. said, not sure of that at all as he tried to shake the bad feeling that had been with him from the moment Bob Humphries told him about the dead, burned cow. "We have a lot of cattle to round up over the next few days. I suggest you turn in right after supper. We start at first light."

As he glanced toward the cabin, he realized he didn't smell food cooking, just smoke, and shot a look at Buck before picking up his saddle and gear and heading in that direction.

Behind him, he had the strangest feeling that the men around the fire were not only watching him, but also waiting for something to happen.

"Maybe we should talk for a minute before you go into the cabin," Buck said as he caught up to him.

"Why is that, Buck?" he asked without slowing his stride. J.T. had always liked to get whatever was waiting for him over with as quickly as possible. "If you got a cook, then what—" The rest of his words died on his lips as he saw the camp cook through the cabin window. "What the—"

"Now, boss—"

J.T. shoved his saddle and gear at Buck without a word and, with long purposeful strides, stormed across the porch and into the line shack. "What are *you* doing here?"

It was a stupid question since Reggie whatever-her-name-was stood at the cookstove with a pan in her hand. She was dressed in fancy western wear, all spanking new and all in that same shade of red that had blinded him on the road earlier today.

"You know each other?" Buck asked in surprise from the doorway.

J.T. swung around long enough to slam the door—
with Buck on the other side of it. Slowly, trying to control his temper, he turned back to the woman standing
in his line shack. "What *are* you doing here?"

"Isn't it obvious?" she asked. "I wanted to give you
another chance to reconsider my offer so I hired on as
your camp cook." She held out her hand. "Regina Holland. I wasn't sure you remembered from my card."

He ignored her hand. He could not believe the woman's nerve. Had she no sense at all? Coming up to his
cow camp after him? And worse, signing on as the
cook. Women didn't belong in a cow camp. He was
going to kill Buck.

"Listen, lady, it is one thing to be cute on the highway but not in my line camp," he snapped. She really
had no idea what she'd done. Or who she was dealing
with.

"I'm not being cute," she said, frowning as she lowered her hand. "I'm *very* serious."

She couldn't have looked less serious in that urban
cowboy getup if she'd tried. "I already turned down
your offer flat," he ground out from between gritted
teeth as he tried to keep his voice down. "*All* of your
offers. How much more plain can I be?"

He knew the men outside were straining to hear what
was going on. A *woman* in cow camp? Worse, a woman
who looked like this? A woman with designs that had
nothing to do with cooking. A recipe for disaster if
there ever was one.

She lifted her chin, standing her ground as she
looked up at him. Without her high heels, he towered
over her. He also outweighed her by almost a hundred
pounds. But she didn't seem to notice—or care.

"You didn't give me a chance back on the highway today," she said, seemingly unconcerned by the ferocious angry scowl he was giving her. "If you'd just listen to what I'm willing to give you—"

"You listen to me, *Reggie,*" he said, biting off each word as he stepped closer. "I told you I'm—"

"This is an opportunity—"

"...not interested and I'm not going to—"

"...that doesn't come—"

"...change my mind and I don't want to hear—"

"...along every day—"

"Reggie!" he shouted, forgetting how important it was to keep their conversation private.

She flinched but still had the audacity to mutter, "... of the year. And it's Regina," she snapped. "*Not* Reggie, *McCall.*"

McCall? He swore under his breath.

She took a breath. "Couldn't we just start over?" She gave him a breathtaking smile and spoke in a soft seductive tone. "I feel like we got off on the wrong foot."

He recalled how odd the men had been acting around the campfire. A knife of alarm buried itself in his chest. Had she already announced what she was doing here? He told himself he wouldn't be responsible for what he did to her.

"Did you say anything to the men about..." He couldn't bring himself to say the words given that Buck probably had his ear to the door not to even mention the cowhands eavesdropping around the fire. He needed these men to look up to him over the next few days, to respect him and follow his orders without fail. He didn't need them checking out his butt and laughing behind his back.

"About my offer?" she asked with wide-eyed innocence.

He'd wring her pretty little neck. "So help me, if you said one word—"

"I haven't told *anyone*."

"Not even Buck?"

She shook her head.

He hated to think what story she'd concocted to get Buck to give her the cook job. His instant relief that she hadn't told everyone was short-lived. She hadn't told anyone *yet*. "Get your things. You're going back to town. *Now*."

"At least give me a chance to apologize," she said touching his sleeve. He pulled free, stepping back to ward her off. "I'm sorry. When I heard you talking to Jennie, I just assumed she was your wife."

He groaned, remembering telling his new puppy Jennie to stay in the pickup or be left at home. That's why Reggie thought Jennie was his wife? And just when he thought she couldn't insult him further.

"I also want to apologize for assuming by your attire and truck that you were a poor cowhand—"

"Stop while you're *behind*," J.T. snapped, instantly regretting his unfortunate choice of word.

She flushed. She was trying so hard he almost felt sorry for her. Almost. "I don't see why you're so upset," she said, actually sounding puzzled. "I'm offering you *fame*."

Just what he always wanted. A famous butt. "And I'm offering you a chance to clear out of here before—"

"If I could just make you realize what an asset you have in your—"

"All right, Ms. Holland!" There was no getting

through to this woman. "The answer is no. I accept all of your…apologies. But the answer is still *no*. So since there is nothing else for you here—"

He was so close to her that he could smell her perfume. Something expensive and unforgettable. Her eyes were the color of the Montana sky. He dragged his gaze away to the floor and noticed that even her boots were red! She had "dude" written all over her and looked as out of place as a fancy skyscraper on this mountaintop. But what really graveled him was that she looked as sexy in this getup as she had in the expensive suit earlier.

"What's with you and red?" he had to ask.

She looked down at her outfit. She really did fit the western shirt nicely. "It's my signature color."

He should have known.

"Well, unless you want your signature color to be dirt-brown I suggest you step away from that cookstove." She didn't move.

"You don't like red?"

How had he gotten sidetracked from the real issue here to red? He didn't care if the woman wore nothing at all. He groaned as his imagination flashed on *that* image.

"I want you to just get back in your—" He looked out the window to the pines below the line shack suddenly realizing he had no idea how she'd gotten here. No way could she drive here in her sports car. It took one hell of a four-wheel drive truck to make it up the rough trail to the camp—and only in good weather. Once it rained or snowed—

"How did you get up here?" he asked, his heart in his throat.

"I rode up in the supply truck with Buck."

She could have told him Martians had dropped her off at the camp and he would have been less skeptical. "Buck brought you up?" Had Buck lost his mind? The only way to get rid of her would be to send her down on horseback or drive all the way back down the mountain in the supply truck. J.T. swore under his breath.

Well, at least no harm had really been done, he told himself. He would lose Buck for half a day but this situation could be resolved.

"Buck?" he called. The door to the cabin instantly opened and Buck stuck his head in the door. "Go start the truck. You're taking Ms. Holland back to town."

Buck shot a sympathetic glance to Reggie, but had the good sense not to argue before he ducked back out the door.

"I don't think you realize how important this is. Can't we please discuss it like rational adults?"

"No. Get your stuff. You're out of here."

"What will you do for a camp cook?" she asked.

"We'll manage."

She studied him for a moment, fire in her eyes, then turned and went to the set of bunk beds in the corner. A huge expensive suitcase was open on one of the lower bunks. He caught sight of a bunch of frilly lingerie. He groaned inwardly. A woman like this in a cow camp? He was going to kill Buck.

"I wish you would reconsider," she said, looking close to tears. "This could open all kinds of doors for you. It could very well make you famous. Everyone wants fifteen minutes of fame."

"Not this man. Or his butt." He moved beside her,

closed the suitcase and picked it up. "Shall we?" he said, motioning toward the door.

Before she could move, Buck opened the cabin door. "Boss?" His face was pale and drawn as he motioned J.T. over. Worse, Buck only called him boss when there was trouble.

Now what?

"The truck won't start," Buck said. "When I looked under the hood—"

J.T. didn't wait for the rest. He shoved past the foreman and headed down the hillside to the old stock truck. That truck had never let him down even when it was forty below zero and blizzarding outside. He could hear Buck behind him, muttering to himself.

Buck had left the hood up, a flashlight lay across the top of the radiator. J.T. picked it up and shone it at the engine and swore.

"That's what I was trying to tell you," Buck said. "Someone took the distributor cap."

Was it possible someone had taken the part as a joke? This sort of thing was definitely not funny. Any fool knew there could be an emergency that would prevent one of them from riding out of here on horseback and they would need the truck to get out.

J.T. turned slowly to look at Buck. "You don't know anything about this?"

Buck looked shocked by the question. "Why would I do something this stupid?"

To help that woman in my line shack. But he knew Buck was right. He wouldn't do anything this danger-ous. Not even for a beautiful woman.

"I was thinking about the last time something like this happened," Buck said quietly, glancing toward the campfire. "The truck had been disabled that time too, right?" Buck hadn't been on that roundup nine years ago. But like everyone else in four states, he'd heard about it.

"The tires were slashed," J.T. said. The method used was different, but the end result was the same. "And the hands involved are all dead." One crazy, two greedy fools. All dying horrible deaths. And for what? He glanced toward the line shack. "This has to be that woman's doing. She's the only one who benefits from this—and the only one who doesn't realize how dangerous it is." She'd already proved how low she would stoop to get what she wanted. She'd done this to prevent him from sending her packing.

"You're right," Buck said, sounding relieved.

This had to be her doing. But he couldn't stop thinking about the cow Bob Humphries had found. Also Reggie didn't look like the kind of woman who would know a distributor cap from a hubcap, he thought, remembering how she hadn't even been able to change her own tire. But in hindsight, that had probably just been a ruse to get him to stop and help her.

Had to be Reggie's doing, J.T. told himself as he slammed the hood. He refused to think something else was going on here and that she wasn't the only one who didn't want any of them leaving here.

But as he headed for the cabin, he felt his skin crawl as he glanced past the camp into the darkness of the pines and imagined someone hiding out there watching them, waiting to pick them off one by one. Just like last time.

Chapter Three

Buck caught up to him just before he reached the line shack and stopped him. "You won't be too hard on her, will you?"

J.T. stared at the older man in astonishment. Either Buck Brannigan was getting soft in the head or that woman had gotten to him. Either was unbelievable having known Buck all his life.

"Did you just temporarily lose your mind or were you drunk when you hired her?" J.T. demanded, more upset than he would have been under normal circumstances. He couldn't shake the uneasy feeling that had settled in his gut after seeing where the cow had been burned and dragged off into the woods. A missing distributor cap and a disabled truck. A crew he didn't know—or necessarily trust. Hell, he had more than enough to worry about without having a woman in camp. Especially *that* woman.

"You said, find a cook," Buck said stubbornly. "I found a cook. And let me tell you, I had one heck of a time but I knew better than to show up without one so when Regina walked into the Longhorn and begged me for the job..."

J.T. swore. There was only one way she had known about the job opening. J.T. had opened his big mouth and told her. But Buck still shouldn't have hired her.

"Any man with even one good eye can see that that woman doesn't belong off concrete sidewalks, let alone in a cow camp," J.T. snapped.

Buck rubbed his grizzled jaw with a large paw of a hand, then grinned. "Heck, J.T., she was such a determined little thing and cuter than a white-faced heifer. She talked me into hiring her before I knew what had happened. She said she was desperate for the job and we *do* need a cook. I thought, what could it hurt?"

They both looked back toward the truck.

"Sorry, boss," Buck said again.

J.T. just shook his head. "I want you to ride out at first light. Come back with the other four-wheel drive truck. When you get back, you take Ms. Holland to town and find us another cook if you can. Either way I want you back here by early afternoon."

Buck nodded looking contrite. "You didn't mention how you knew her."

"No, I didn't," J.T. said and glanced toward the fire. The men were all pretending not to be watching—or listening—to what was going on. None of them had complained that they hadn't had dinner yet. Under normal circumstances there would be some powerful bellyaching going on. Nothing about this roundup was normal.

He thought about the warm bunk beds waiting in the cabin as he glanced over at the wall tents where he would be sleeping instead. Damn this woman.

Reggie begged to be a camp cook? Well, J.T. would oblige. She could cook supper over the woodstove, then they'd see how she felt about being a camp cook.

He leveled his gaze at Buck. "You'd better hope she's the best darned cook this side of Miles City, starting with supper tonight."

"She was just so desperate," Buck said again.

"Yeah," J.T. said, "but desperate to do what?" He was wondering if her story about the TV commercial was even true. Maybe there was something else she was after. Something even worse than his perfect posterior.

Buck chewed at the end of his thick mustache. "I might be a fool but I can't imagine that woman in there taking the truck part."

"*Might* be a fool?" J.T. let out a snort. Buck was no pushover, quite the contrary, except somehow Reggie had the old cowboy wrapped around her finger. But he had to agree with Buck, even if she'd faked her incompetence when it came to tire changing, he still couldn't see her stealing the truck's distributor cap—not with seven men in camp watching her every move.

"If she's really behind this," Buck said, "then someone must be helping her. I suppose it could be someone who followed us up here and camped nearby. Or someone in camp."

"My thought exactly," J.T. said as he looked from the campfire back to Buck. "No one in this camp better be trying to help her, Buck. I'm warning you and you better warn the men."

"I can't believe the men wouldn't know how dangerous this is," Buck said. Without the truck, the only way off this mountain was on horseback. A twenty-mile ride to the ranch. If anyone got sick or hurt—

Maybe someone had followed them up here and was camped nearby. "I'll ride out and take a look in the morning, if I can't talk her out of the distributor cap tonight." He glanced toward the cabin. "You have no idea what that woman is capable of."

Buck lifted a heavy gray brow. "But you do?"

He ignored the question and Buck's curiosity. "Let me handle this. If she's behind taking that distributor cap—"

"Just don't be too tough on her, okay?"

J.T. shot the foreman a warning look and stomped to the cabin.

Reggie had rolled her suitcase as far as the door.

"The truck doesn't run," he said.

She looked alarmed. "How do we get out of here?"

"I could have Buck saddle up a horse for you."

Her eyes widened in even more alarm. "You would send me off this mountain in the dark on a *horse?*"

"In a heartbeat. All you have to do is follow the trail fifteen miles down to the county road. From there just go east. You shouldn't have any trouble finding the ranch. One of my brothers will give you a ride into town to your car from there."

She looked at him as if she couldn't believe he was serious.

He wasn't. He was angry and upset but there was no way this woman could find her way back to the ranch even in broad daylight with street signs to follow. She'd sooner fall off a cliff or stumble into the river and drown herself and one of his horses. For the horse's sake, he couldn't do it.

But it was tempting. Especially if she was responsible for the disabled truck. And if she wasn't? Well, then he wanted to get her out of here and as quickly as possible because he didn't have a clue what was going on.

"You can't send me off this mountain on a horse," she said again.

He thought he saw tears in her eyes. Had she finally realized that she'd gotten herself into something she couldn't handle?

Her voice dropped to a whisper. "I don't know how to ride a horse."

J.T. looked at her. Of course she didn't ride. Any fool could have guessed that. "You do know how to walk though, don't you? It's probably only twenty miles to the ranch as the crow flies."

She practically gasped.

Fighting the urge to throttle the woman *and* Buck, he said, "You can stay here tonight." As if he had a choice. He was tempted to throw her to the wolves. Not literally, but at least make her sleep in one of the wall tents tonight on a cot instead of the warm cabin where *he* should have been sleeping, he thought with a curse.

"Buck is riding down in the morning," he said. "He'll bring back a truck and take you to town. In the meantime, you're the camp cook. Buck?" he called.

Buck was waiting outside the door listening, of course. "Yes, Boss?"

The words were almost impossible to get out, knowing that Buck and Reggie cooking together could be lethal. But he wasn't going to stay in here with her. No way.

"Help Ms. Holland with dinner," he ordered.

Buck grinned. "You got it, boss."

"She can stay in the cabin. You and I will take one of the wall tents."

"I'm sorry to put you out of your cabin," Reggie said sweetly enough to give a man a toothache. "I can sleep in the tent."

Like she had ever slept in a tent on a cot in her life, J.T. thought.

"I don't mind staying in the tent," Buck said quickly.

All J.T. could do was shake his head in wonder. There was nothing worse than a sentimental old fool.

Except for a young one, he thought with disgust as he left the cabin. Buck must be getting old. There'd been a time when even a woman like Reggie Holland couldn't have conned a man like Buck Brannigan. What was the world coming to?

J.T. marched over to the fire, apologized that supper was running late and explained the new sleeping arrangements. He'd expected the men to complain and loudly.

"No problem, boss," Cotton said grinning as he glanced toward the cabin. "Let me know if there is anything I can do to help Ms. Holland."

This was why women didn't belong in a cow camp.

Slim and Luke quickly offered their assistance as well.

J.T. groaned under his breath and reminded himself that she would be gone by tomorrow. But he couldn't help but worry that she hadn't given up. What would she try next? He hated to think. Especially if she had an accomplice in one of his men.

Well, before the night was over, J.T. figured he could talk Reggie into handing over the distributor cap and the name of her accomplice. Both would be out of here at first light.

As buck explained cooking over a woodstove, Reggie tried to tell herself that she'd won round one.

So she had to cook supper. A slight drawback. Maybe she would wow J.T. McCall. True, she had never cooked anything in her life other than taking something out of a container and popping it into the microwave. She'd never had time to learn. But she *was* fearless. And determined not to leave this camp until she had McCall signed to the commercial. Her future depended on it.

Not just her future, she reminded herself. A lot of

people were depending on her to pull this off. This entire advertising campaign was her idea, a desperate last-ditch effort to save the company—and her job.

If the campaign succeeded, Way Out West Jeans would go public and no longer just be a tiny obscure family-owned company. Regina's future would be secure.

If it failed, the employees would be without jobs and Way Out West Jeans would have to close its doors, the hundred-year-old company bankrupt.

She was determined that wasn't going to happen. No matter what she had to do.

She needed authenticity and J. T. McCall and his Sundown Ranch were it. She'd been flabbergasted when Buck had shown her the ranch before they'd come up the mountain. Thank goodness for Buck.

She'd overheard just enough of the conversation outside the cabin between McCall and Buck to know that without Buck she'd be on her way down the mountain in the dark either on the back of one of those horses in the corral or on foot.

How lucky that the truck hadn't started. And how lucky that Buck Brannigan had been sympathetic to her story about needing this job. He'd probably heard the real desperation in her voice. She *did* need this. Just not the job she'd been hired on to do.

She felt a little guilty for putting Buck in what was obviously an awkward situation with his boss. But she got the feeling that Buck was one of the few people who wasn't afraid of J. T. McCall.

She found Buck's bashfulness cute, along with his "Aw shucks ma'am," hat-in-hand protective politeness. For a moment, she wondered what her life would have been like if she'd had a father like Buck.

Shoving that thought away, she concentrated on the task at hand, cooking over the woodstove and assuring Buck she could handle this while he moved his stuff out of the cabin and into the tent.

"You *can* cook, right?" Buck had asked her earlier at the Longhorn Café.

She'd known all she had to do was answer the man's question correctly. "I'm a woman, aren't I?"

That seemed to appease him, just as she knew it would. A lot of men thought all women were born being able to cook and clean. Not in her family, that was for sure.

No, her talents lay somewhere else. That's why, given time, she had no doubt that she could persuade even a man as mulish as J. T. McCall that he'd be a fool to just sit on his assets.

But she didn't have much time. Only until tomorrow when Buck returned. Shoot, she'd closed impossible deals in a lot less time than that, she told herself. Whether she liked it or not, she was her mother's daughter.

In the meantime, she would cook supper following the instructions Buck had given her. She just hoped cooking proved easier than changing a flat tire.

WHEN J.T. WALKED into the line shack cabin for supper, the air reeked of smoke even though all the windows were open and a stiff breeze was blowing through the place.

He didn't have to ask how the new cook had done. As he settled into the chair at the head of the table, he spotted a large platter of incinerated steaks, black and shrunken and no longer resembling anything edible.

The cowhands who'd earlier seemed overjoyed to

have a pretty female cook in camp were now eyeing the burnt steaks warily.

"You want to pass the steaks around?" Buck asked, sounding as if he had a sore throat.

J.T. noticed how Buck avoided his gaze as J.T. picked up the platter of cremated meat. Silence filled the cabin. He sensed the men around the table watching him as if waiting to see what his response would be. He knew if the cook had been a male, everyone in this room would be complaining, J.T. at the top of the list. Yet another reason a woman didn't belong in a cow camp.

J.T. looked from the platter to Reggie. She stood in the corner not far from the woodstove, hanging back in the shadows as if trying to make herself smaller. Loose hair hung in limp tendrils around her face, a large dark smudge of charcoal graced her cheek and her new duds looked as if she'd been in a mud wrestling match—and lost. So much for her signature color. All in all, she appeared exhausted. And close to tears.

But it was the expression on her face that was his undoing. She looked downright contrite. He watched her inspect a red, inflamed fingertip, then bring it to her mouth to suck on the burn, and he felt a rush of sympathy for her.

Earlier he'd threatened to throw her to the wolves, but he realized now that that's exactly what he'd done by allowing her to pretend to be the camp cook. He doubted she'd ever cooked in her life, let alone over a woodstove.

Cursing himself, he looked down at the ruined meat on the platter. "Steaks huh, great," he said between gritted teeth as he slid one of the charred chunks of once grade A beef onto his plate before passing the platter to the man next to him, Cotton Heywood.

Cotton quickly helped himself to a steak. "Looks good! Boy am I hungry."

The spell broken, each man complimented Reggie as the meat made its way around the table, each man except for Will Jarvis. He stared at the steak remains, then let his gaze lift to J.T.'s for a long moment before finally stabbing one and dropping it to his plate.

J.T. watched him, still fighting the feeling that there was something familiar about the man.

When J.T. glanced up, he found Reggie's gaze on him. While she still looked duly chastened, he glimpsed gratitude in her blue eyes. He wanted to tell her that he was only keeping peace in his camp, not saving her, but he doubted she'd believe it any more than he did.

He mentally shook his head. This woman had the ability to make a man want to wring her neck one minute and take her in his arms and comfort her the next. Women like her were damned dangerous.

"You *are* going to join us, aren't you, Ms. Holland?" he asked, reminding himself that this was her doing. She'd gotten herself into this. And if she thought she was going to get out of eating what she'd cooked, she was sadly mistaken. He wouldn't force his men to eat anything the cook wouldn't also be required to eat.

"I'm not very hungry," she said in a quiet, almost timid voice.

He'd just bet she wasn't considering what she'd done to this food. He studied her. Was she ready to give up? He could only hope. "I insist you have something to eat."

Luke Adams got up to pull out a chair for her. Even though the men had to know this woman was going to ruin their food as long as she was here, they all smiled over at her as she sat down. But how could they not feel sympathy for her? She looked as pathetic as a rain-drenched stray kitten. He wondered which of the men had taken the distributor cap for her. The woman was persuasive enough, she could have talked any one of them into it, J.T. realized—even Will Jarvis, the most cantankerous of the bunch it seemed.

Buck passed a bowl full of something small, shriveled and crispy brown. J.T. frowned down at them, trying to figure out what food they'd originally been. The brown nuggets resembled large hard nuts.

"Do you want some butter on your baked potato?" Buck asked with more pleasantness than J.T. had ever heard in the big man's tone.

So that's what they'd once been? He would never have thought it possible to make a potato look like this. He wondered what she'd done to them. And decided he didn't want to know.

He was almost afraid to take the large bowl Buck offered him next, but was relieved to see that he recognized the food in it. Baked beans. He scooped a healthy serving onto his plate, glad at least something would be edible. How much damage could Reggie do to a can of pork and beans?

He started to take a bite, but stopped, disturbed to realize what else Reggie's presence had done. Cow camps revolved around male custom. The conversation at the table should have been about critters, who'd be riding the draws looking for strays tomorrow, who'd be wrangling the horses. Instead the men ate in silence.

Nor were they wolfing down their food, though who could blame them. Still some of them were actually using napkins and employing the utensils in the way they were designed.

J.T. shook his head. Reggie was destroying century-old rituals, making grown men behave against their nature, and he didn't like it.

He sawed off a piece of steak and took a bite. It tasted like charred cheap shoe leather. He chewed and chewed and finally forced the bite down with beans. Big mistake. Fire shot through his mouth and down his throat. Choking, he grabbed his water glass, his wild-eyed murderous gaze leaping to Buck.

Buck kept his head down as if intent on his food. Everyone else at the table also seemed unduly interested in their plates.

He downed his water, then glared across the table at Reggie, fire in his eyes as well as his mouth. The woman was going to kill them all. Any woman who could do this much damage to food wouldn't even blink when it came to disabling a truck.

Was all of this just a plot to get him to change his mind and do the commercial? My God, the woman would stoop to anything.

She appeared busy pushing her food around her plate. Smart not to eat it. She glanced up as if she felt his gaze on her. She stared at him in concern. Was she worried that he might leap across the table and throttle her or that he might die right before her eyes? He knew his face must be bright red, his eyes were running water and he could not stop choking.

"Buck said you liked a lot of green pepper in your beans," she said into the strained silence. No doubt the men were quietly choking to death as well. "So I found a bag of chopped peppers and put them all in. I think they might have been the wrong peppers."

No kidding.

Buck let out an uncharacteristic little laugh. "There were two different bags of peppers in the cooler. I should have shown her which ones to use. I think she used the jalapenos."

"Yeah," J.T. said, narrowing his gaze at her. Was it an honest mistake? Or had she purposely done this? No one would be *that* cruel, would she?

Well, she'd underestimated him. There was nothing she could do to get him to change his mind. Not poison him. Not kill his taste buds. Not starve him. Nothing. He would get her out of here tomorrow and Buck would bring back a real cook. Now that J.T. knew what she was capable of, he wasn't letting her near the stove again. He would cook breakfast himself.

"I like my beans hot," Cotton piped up. "They're spicy but real good." He smiled at Reggie.

Luke and Slim jumped to Reggie's defense as well. J.T. watched them eat the beans, their eyes tearing with each bite, lies on their lips, their politeness costing them dearly.

He would have felt sorry for them except for one thing. Reggie was losing that chastened look. Their compassion and polite compliments seemed to be giving her renewed strength. When J.T. looked down the table at her, he saw that spark of determination, still fairly dim, but burning again in her eyes.

It was the last thing he wanted to see burning there.

"Here, Luke, have some more beans," J.T. said, passing him the bowl. "There's enough for all of you to have seconds." He watched each man take his share as the bowl was passed around the table. How could they not without hurting Reggie's tender feelings?

Everyone except Will Jarvis and Nevada Black helped themselves to more beans.

"I've never been a big fan of beans," Nevada said. Nor burnt steak and potatoes, it seemed. His plate looked untouched.

Same with Will, only he didn't bother to say anything as he passed on the beans.

J.T. didn't blame the men. He was feeling a little guilty about making the others eat more of the horribly hot beans. It wasn't their fault that they'd gotten caught in the middle of this war between him and Reggie and they didn't even know what was really at stake. J.T. wasn't even sure he did. He just couldn't let them get too taken with this woman before he could get her out of here.

He felt her reproachful gaze on him as the beans reached her and she scraped the last of them onto her plate. Defiantly, she ate them, her gaze fixed on him. He watched her, knowing how much each forkful cost her, and yet, other than unshed tears swimming in her big blue eyes, she didn't let it show. She ate every bite.

The men did the same.

If Reggie had wanted to make him feel like a heel, she'd succeeded. Worse yet, her defiant act had only managed to do just what he'd feared. It had allied the men to her. Even Will and Nevada were watching her with a look of something like respect. Damn this woman was impossible! She already had Buck on her side, now she had them all eating out of her hand, so to speak.

Earlier he'd thought her beaten, close to crying, ready to cave in. He saw now that Reggie Holland didn't fall to defeat easily. He'd not only underestimated her tenacity, he found himself admiring it and at the same time fearing it. How far would the woman go to get what she wanted? And how many of his men would she use to do it?

The disabled truck nagged at him. He looked around the table, trying to imagine what any of the cowhands had to gain by taking the distributor cap. Cotton, Slim and Luke weren't paying attention to anyone but Reggie.

Will Jarvis seemed to be watching everyone at the table while picking at his food with distaste. Roy, head down, was eating quietly, but then Roy did everything quietly, it seemed. Nevada Black was eating what he could salvage of the meal, but he didn't look happy about it.

Of the men, Nevada Black looked like the one who had probably done some time. He seemed the most likely to have disabled the truck. But for what possible motive? J.T. wouldn't be surprised if Nevada Black was gone in the morning. He didn't look like a man who put up with much.

Neither did Will Jarvis. Both men were older and no doubt less tolerant. Unless they needed this job desperately, they would hit the road if the conditions didn't improve.

Luke, Slim and Cotton were a whole other story. Any of the three could have come to Reggie's rescue and disabled the truck.

J.T. let his gaze come back to Reggie. She had to have known he would send her packing as soon as he found her at the line shack. She'd gotten to stay here tonight only because of the missing distributor cap. And she was the one person who supposedly didn't ride a horse.

She looked up at him, resolve burning again in those eyes like a hot blue flame. He shouldn't be surprised by anything this woman did, but he found himself surprised over and over again. He'd never met anyone like her and hoped he never did again.

He cursed under his breath as he watched each of the men take his plate and utensils over to the large galvanized tub full of hot dishwater on the stove, something they would never have done for a male cook. Several tipped their hats to Reggie and actually thanked her for cooking, then hung around as if not wanting to leave.

She bestowed one of her drop-a-man-to-his-knees smiles on each of them. Even Will Jarvis who had hardly touched his meal returned her smile, though grudgingly.

J.T. couldn't blame them. Reggie looked like a waif. You wanted to take her in your arms and tell her everything was going to be all right. She seemed so tired that he had to wonder what was keeping her on her feet as she got ready to do the dishes. She meant to finish the job she'd started, even if it killed her. And for a moment, he thought about seeing if it would.

"Cotton, why don't you and Slim clean up the dishes tonight," J.T. suggested. "Luke, you can see to the horses." Everyone but Reggie knew it was an order. "I need to talk to Ms. Holland and I think she's done quite enough for one day."

If the men were surprised by his irregular order or resented it, they didn't show it. Doing dishes in a cow camp was strictly the cook's domain, but Reggie had already destroyed most of the established codes of the west, why not break a few more?

J.T. saw Cotton and Slim exchange knowing smirks as they set about their work. They thought something was going on between him and Reggie! He wanted to deny it. Well, at least tell them that what they thought was going on wasn't.

But he knew better than to open his mouth. Protesting would only dig the hole he was in deeper.

He was just thankful that Buck would be leaving early in the morning and Reggie would be history by afternoon. Even if her cooking didn't kill them all, he couldn't have her here. Pretty soon, she'd have the men fighting over her. Or worse.

Sending Buck into town would put the roundup behind a little, but it would be worth it. Things could get back to normal. Even if Buck didn't find a cook, J.T. would rather hear the men complain about Buck's cooking than put up with this.

Buck looked worried as J.T. ushered Reggie out the door of the line shack. What did the old coot think he was going to do to her? Take her out and shoot her? Let Buck think the worst since he was the one who'd gotten them into this mess.

No, J.T. thought, he couldn't blame it all on Buck. He should have made it clearer to her on the highway this afternoon that he was never going to change his mind. And he should never have mentioned to her that he needed a camp cook. Nor should he have let Reggie cook tonight.

Discouraging this woman wasn't easy but he had to try. He couldn't let her continue with this charade. She was wasting her time and his. He would make her see that. Somehow.

He'd convince her to return the distributor cap and send her back to town with Buck tonight in the truck. The sooner she was out of the camp the better. Especially since he had a bad feeling about this roundup.

The last time he'd had that feeling, five men had died.

Chapter Four

Regina shivered as she stepped out into the night. The cute little western jacket she'd bought at the Antelope Flats general store did little to chase away the cold. She had never known such darkness as she moved through the trees away from the light of the cabin. She stumbled and would have fallen headlong if J.T. hadn't caught her arm and righted her.

"It's just so dark," she said and realized he was standing only inches from her.

"Your eyes will adjust," he said softly, his voice sending a different kind of chill through her.

She could feel his gaze on her face. She hugged herself and gulped the cold night air, feeling like an alien who'd landed in a strange, hostile environment. Nothing looked familiar: not the terrain, not the men, not the clothing and certainly not the food, especially after she'd finished cooking it.

She hadn't eaten red meat in years—until tonight. But she would have choked on it before she'd have let J.T. think she wasn't going to eat it because it was burned to a crisp.

Not even the atmosphere of this place agreed with her. Air she couldn't see made her suspicious. The high altitude left her dizzy. And the boots hurt her feet. She didn't even want to think about the accommodations.

J.T. had announced she could sleep in the cabin as if he was doing her a favor. Now that she'd had a good look at it, she would beg to differ.

On top of that, she ached all over. Her fingers were burned. And she feared she'd never get rid of the smell of smoke and grease on her skin, especially as she hadn't seen a place to bathe. Or relieve herself other than what appeared to be an outhouse a couple dozen yards off the hillside in the pines. Like she was going out there in the dark.

But she'd asked for this. True, it was the most drastic thing she'd ever done, but it would be worth it. Once she had McCall under contract.

"We need to talk," he said.

She could see his face more clearly as her eyes adjusted to the darkness. A sliver of moon hung in the dark velvet sky above the lofty pines. A splattering of bright glittering stars twinkled across the vast skyscape. She'd never seen anything like it before and she found everything about this place too intense. Especially J. T. McCall.

Regina couldn't remember a time she'd felt so inept. Or so lost. But she wouldn't quit. Nor would she admit defeat, although she could see he was hoping for just that.

"I'm sorry about dinner," she said quickly. "I'll do better in the morning."

He stared at her, clearly surprised. "You'd actually put yourself through that again?" So he *had* thought she'd given up.

Not that there hadn't been a few moments when it

had crossed her mind. Like when Buck had pointed to the woodstove and told her she was to cook on that fire-breathing, smoke-belching dragon in the corner.

Cook what? He'd outlined the meal and how the woodstove worked. It had sounded simple enough. Although, so had the microwave the first time she'd used it. Thanks to modern technology, she'd managed to turn grated cheddar cheese into orange plastic at the touch of a button.

The woodstove was far from modern technology, but about the time the steaks caught fire, she realized she could do a lot more damage with a woodstove.

"I hired on as camp cook," she said firmly. "I'll finish the job."

"Over my dead body—and I suspect if I ate any more of your cooking that would be the case."

"What are you trying to say?"

"You can't cook."

She couldn't argue that. "I can learn."

"Not fast enough."

She lifted her chin and met his gaze. "You'd be amazed what I am capable of when I set my mind to it."

"That's what I'm worried about." He sighed. "Look, until Buck returns with a truck, I don't want you going near the cookstove."

She started to open her mouth.

"No arguments. I'm sorry you wasted your time coming up here in the first place. Once back in Antelope Flats you can continue your search for your…cowboy."

"I've found the only cowboy I want."

He shook his head.

"I'm risking everything for this advertising campaign," she said, surprised by her candor and the slight break in her voice. "If this doesn't work out, I'm finished and a lot of other people will lose their jobs."

He eyed her as if this was just another ploy. "I'm sorry to hear that. You just found the wrong cowboy. Cut your losses. The sooner you get out of here, the sooner you can find someone else for the commercial." He held up his hand to ward off her next argument. "This is a battle you can't win. You're leaving. Either by truck, on horseback or on foot. Your choice. You won't change my mind and as far as the camp cook job, you're fired."

She'd known this might happen, especially after he'd experienced her cooking. She'd just hoped it wouldn't come to this. She glanced back toward the cabin. "Maybe you're right." Was that a sigh of relief she heard? "But perhaps one of your men might know of a cowboy who would be interested in the job after hearing that you turned down the offer."

"You aren't trying to blackmail me, are you?"

She could tell from his tone that blackmailing J. T. McCall wouldn't be a good idea. He might be surprised if he knew just how desperate she was. Or maybe he wouldn't.

He stood immobile, pale as the moon, jaw clenched, a deadly look in his eyes.

A sliver of guilt pricked her conscience. She did her best to ignore it. After he made the commercial, he'd be glad she'd been so determined. They would both be. Okay, at least she would be for sure.

"I would not take kindly to being blackmailed," he said in a tone that was soft like a silk glove with a fist in it.

His warning tone sent a chill through her, but she couldn't back down. "Think of it as incentive."

"I should turn you over my knee and—" He stepped toward her menacingly.

She drew back. Surely he wouldn't actually do such a thing? But what did she know about Montana cowboys?

"You try to blackmail me and I swear I will personally take you down this mountain tonight if I have to drag you every step of the way."

She nodded, trusting he meant it. "Fine, then I guess I'll be leaving tomorrow after Buck gets back."

"If you're smart, you'll go tonight."

"I thought the truck wasn't running."

"Reggie, if you know where the distributor cap is, now would be a good time to cough it up."

She stared at him. "You think *I* took it?"

"You or one of the cowhands you conned into it. You're the only person ignorant enough to pull a stunt like that and the only one who has gained by it."

She felt as if he'd slapped her. "What kind of person do you think I am?"

"Scheming, manipulative, devious, conniving and underhanded," he said.

She felt her cheeks flame, surprised that his opinion of her was so low—worse that it bothered her. "You forgot uncompromising."

He sighed again. "What can I do to make you stop this?"

"Give my offer some serious thought." She held up her hand. "Just tell me you will think about it. If you still don't want to do the commercial by the time Buck returns tomorrow, then I will leave and you will never see me again. I give you my word."

"Your word?" He let out a laugh. "I have a better idea. You give me the truck part, I pay you a week's wages and I won't make you walk out of here. I'll drive you myself tonight."

She cocked her head at him. "You're afraid you'll change your mind about my offer if I stay the night?"

A muscle in his jaw jumped. His eyes, a paler blue than her own, turned as hard and cold as ice. "Ms. Holland, this is a cow camp. I have six hundred cattle to get out of these mountains before the snow falls, which could be tomorrow. I have men who need to keep their minds on their jobs. In order to do that, they need a dry place to sleep, food they can actually eat and no distractions. You are a distraction."

She smiled. Maybe she *was* getting to him. "Thank you."

"That wasn't a compliment. Please, just give me the truck part. Even if you were to stay up here the rest of the week you would never convince me to do your commercial."

He actually sounded as if he meant it.

"I wish I had this distributor cap thingy," she said honestly. She could feel his gaze on her. He didn't believe her.

"Fine," he said, sounding even angrier. "You want to keep up this charade, you got it. As long as you stay, you're the camp cook. Breakfast is at daybreak."

She shuddered involuntarily. Daybreak? What time was that? "You're rehiring me?"

"We generally have ham, bacon, pancakes, eggs and hashbrowns."

Holy cow. She should have known a continental

breakfast would be too much to hope for. "Anything else?"

"Make the eggs fried, over easy."

"Why not."

He raised a brow. "You think you're up to frying an egg on a woodstove, Reggie?"

"I'm ready for whatever you throw at me, McCall." She didn't want to even think about *seeing* an egg that early in the morning let alone *cooking* one. "Anyway, Buck says it's possible to cook *anything* on a wood-stove. It's just all a matter of getting the heat adjusted."

"Is that what Buck says?" He muttered something under his breath she couldn't hear and was glad of it. He pulled off his hat and raked a hand through his hair in obvious frustration. "Dammit, woman, don't you know you're in over your head?"

She said nothing. If this evening were any indication, she had a pretty good idea of what she'd gotten herself into.

He shoved his hat back on his head. "You're making a very big mistake and so is your accomplice." With that, he turned and stalked toward the camp.

As she watched McCall's perfect posterior walk away from her, she felt a stab of real doubt. Was he right? Was she wasting her time? Would he *ever* agree to the commercial?

She tried hard not to think about daybreak or eggs or this accomplice he suspected. But if she hadn't taken his stupid distributor cap he kept talking about, then someone had. But who? Buck? Was he trying to help her?

Or was there someone else in the camp who didn't want her or anyone else leaving tonight?

She shivered as she hurried back toward the lights of the cabin, afraid she really had gotten in over her head this time.

IN THE WEE hours of the morning, J.T. woke to the sound of someone walking around outside his tent. He slipped quietly from his sleeping bag, pulled on his jeans and boots and stepped out of the wall tent. Clouds hung low over the pines, making the night even darker, as if someone had dropped a blanket over the mountaintop. The last embers of the campfire cast an orange glow between the tents and the cabin. Beyond was blackness.

The horses whinnied softly in the corral. He looked in the direction of the line shack, suddenly worried about Reggie. Was it possible that she and one of the cowhands were in this together? But she hadn't known any of the ranch hands before yesterday. Or had she?

He'd just assumed that she'd conned one of them into helping her once she got to the cow camp. But what if the plan had nothing to do with a TV jeans commercial? Then what? Rustling? That had been the plan nine years ago.

J.T. heard the creak of a porch floorboard and worked his way through the pines to the opposite side of the structure.

The darkness was complete, the air heavy and cold. He could see his breath as he worked his way along the side of the cabin.

He'd just reached the porch railing along the side when he spotted a ghostlike figure at the edge of the trees. He froze, pretty sure he couldn't be seen from where he stood in the darkness.

The figure took a few tentative steps deeper into the

woods. There was no mistaking the size, shape or the way she moved. Reggie. She leaned forward into the pines as if looking for something. Someone?

As she stepped deeper into the darkness and trees, he lost sight of her, but he could hear her whispering to someone.

He cursed himself. Who was she talking to? The person who had disabled the truck? He let out a silent oath as he realized this might have been a setup from the get-go. Had she known he'd be going into town yesterday and been waiting for him with that flat tire? No man could have driven past her, not the way she looked. But why go to so much trouble? So she could end up at his line shack. Her and her accomplice.

He told himself he was being paranoid, but then was reminded of the dead cow, the missing distributor cap, the feeling he couldn't shake that the incidents were just the tip of the iceberg.

She came back out of the pines, barefoot, tiptoeing, holding up the hem of her long white nightgown. The fabric hugging her curves, leaving little to the imagination.

He cursed the effect it had on him as he watched her run back inside the line shack and quietly close the door and lock it, and hated to think what effect she had on whoever she'd been meeting in the woods.

He stayed hidden for a long while, waiting to see who came out of the trees. No one did. But the person she'd been talking to could have sneaked back around to his wall tent easily enough without being seen.

"Everything all right?" Buck whispered drowsily as J.T. reentered into the wall tent.

J.T. hoped so. "Just checking things," he said, slipping into his sleeping bag on the cot. He lay there staring up into the darkness, listening to the soft whinny of the horses, the whisper of the night breeze in the pines, the occasional pop of the dying campfire, wondering who the hell Reggie was and what she really wanted with him. Also who she'd roped into helping her.

He had no way to check out her story—or her. Nor could he find out more about the men Buck had hired. Not until he returned to the ranch and that would be days from now. Too late. Even if he owned a cell phone, it didn't work up here. There was no service even in Antelope Flats.

As he lay there, he couldn't help but think about the cattle roundup nine years ago. That one had been cursed, Buck used to say. "Weren't nobody's fault what happened up at that line shack. Sometimes things just happen and no one on this earth can stop it."

J.T. didn't believe that any more than he believed in curses. But he did believe there was evil in the world, evil in some men, and he knew only too well what could happen when you put a handful of strangers in an isolated place miles from civilization and that evil showed up with a grudge and a knife.

He closed his eyes and tried to get some sleep. In the dream, a woman in a bright red dress danced while behind her the line shack burned, flames shooting into the black night sky and a man stood in the darkness watching her, waiting.

J.T. woke to the smell of smoke. Through the canvas of the wall tent, he heard the crackle of flames and saw the glow. Fire!

He rolled over. Buck's cot was empty. He must have already gotten up and left for town.

Heart racing, J.T. pulled on his jeans and boots and lunged out the tent door headlong into the steel-gray morning, convinced one of the wall tents or the line shack was on fire.

Will Jarvis looked up in surprise beside the campfire.

J.T. stumbled to a stop, his pulse thundering in his ears as he tried to calm himself. The line shack wasn't on fire nor the other wall tent. History wasn't repeating itself.

"Everything all right?" Will asked, his tone almost mocking.

J.T. knew he must have looked like a fool the way he'd come barreling out of his tent. He glanced toward the line shack. Dark.

He pulled on his jacket as he walked over to the fire, needing the warmth and taking the opportunity to find out what he could about Will Jarvis.

"Smells like snow," Will said, sniffing the breeze before turning to warm his hands over the fire.

"Let's hope not," J.T. said, his mood not improving. He was tired and cranky. What little sleep he'd gotten had been haunted with nightmares. He hadn't been able to get Reggie off his mind, especially after seeing her sneaking out to talk to someone in the middle of the night.

Obviously there was more going on than he knew. The sooner he got her off this mountain, the better.

With luck, Buck would be back before noon. J.T. had told Reggie last night that she had to cook breakfast. Fortunately, it was only a threat. He'd make breakfast and by the time he got back in the evening for supper, the new cook Buck found would have dinner ready and Regina Holland would be history.

So why did he feel so disagreeable this morning? Because he couldn't forget that someone had helped Reggie. Possibly someone in this very camp. He couldn't forget that Reggie had been talking to someone in the woods last night. An accomplice. But an accomplice to what?

He took a deep breath of the morning air. Will was right. The weather was changing. It wouldn't be long and snow would blanket these mountains and stay for the long winter months to come.

"You been on a lot of cattle roundups?" J.T. asked Will, trying not to sound suspicious. But he was suspicious of all the cowhands now and there was something about Will....

"I've been on my share."

"What ranches?"

Will looked over at him and shook his head. "Some in Colorado and Wyoming. None you would know."

J.T. wanted to be the judge of that. He waited.

"The Pine Butte, the Triple Bar Three, Big Spring Station."

All ranches J.T. had heard of. All ranches pretty much anyone would have heard of. Which meant Will could be lying through his teeth, knowing there was no way to check....

J.T. heard a rustle from the second wall tent and Slim Walker and Cotton Heywood came out, followed by Roy Shields and Nevada Black. After a few minutes of standing around the campfire, J.T. asked about Luke Adams.

"Haven't seen him," Slim said. "He was already up

and gone when I woke." Roy and Cotton nodded in agreement and everyone looked to Will Jarvis.

"His cot was empty when I got up and made the fire," Will said.

J.T. took a look in the wall tent. Luke's gear was gone and when he walked over to the corral, he wasn't surprised to find Luke Adams's horse gone as well. What the hell?

Maybe after last night's dinner Luke decided he didn't need any more of this. Luke just hadn't seemed like the type to leave in the middle of the night.

Now J.T. was a man short. Worse, he didn't like the way Luke had left—without a word. Was it a coincidence that Luke Adams was gone and Reggie had been talking to someone in the woods in the middle of the night? J.T. highly doubted it as he headed for the line shack.

Shafts of pearl-gray shot down through the tops of the pines, turning the early morning dew to diamonds.

As he neared the cabin, he found himself getting angrier by the minute. The woman had lied and somehow disabled his truck and even tried to blackmail him! She was definitely after his ass all right. But he doubted it had anything to do with a TV commercial. She was trying to sabotage his cattle roundup. Had already done a pretty good job of it. He'd had to send Buck back to the ranch and now he was short another hand with Luke gone.

What the hell was J.T. going to do with her? He knew what he'd like to do with her—and it wasn't let her cook.

He just couldn't let her get to him. Look what she'd done to poor unsuspecting Buck. All that delicate softness, curvaceous sweetness and apparent defenselessness sucked a man in. He remembered the way she'd been last night after that awful meal, all doe-eyed and apologetic. It still annoyed him that she'd made him feel guilty as if all of this was his fault.

As he stepped up onto the porch, he wondered what devious plots she'd been hatching last night. He paused just outside the door. He didn't need to announce his entrance. After all, it was *his* cabin. But he still scooped up an armload of firewood before noisily stomping his feet on the porch. He didn't want to catch her naked, that was for damned sure.

He started to open the door, but stopped himself. Irritated, he knocked.

When he didn't get an answer, he opened the door a crack. "Ms. Holland?"

To his surprise, the fire in the stove crackled warmly, casting a faint glow over the room. He took a couple of steps into the room, reminded that he was walking into her bedroom. "Ms. Holland?"

Still not a sound. He cleared his throat and called out again wondering if it was possible that she'd taken off with Luke Adams.

No hint of daybreak bled through the windows and he realized that she'd draped towels over them for curtains. As his eyes adjusted to the semidarkness, he could make out a lump burrowed under a pile of covers on the first bottom bunk. He figured she'd be dead to the world after last night—no doubt her first real manual labor.

He stomped over to the woodstove, making enough racket to raise the dead—if not a Los Angeles talent agent. If that really was what she was.

She didn't stir—not until he stumbled over something out in the middle of the floor. A series of objects thudded loudly and something rolled across the floor.

Cursing under his breath, he worked his way around the far edge of the floor to the woodstove, dropped his armload of wood unceremoniously and felt around for a match. From the bunk came a loud groan.

He lit the lantern. Reggie was completely covered by blankets, not even her head visible.

"Buck?" came a faint sleepy voice from deep in the bunk.

"No," J.T. snapped, sounding as irascible as he felt. Buck was on his way to Antelope Flats because of her. Reggie was on her own. And look what had happened last night when Buck had *helped* her cook.

"Oh, McCall," she said from under the blankets, not sounding in the least pleased that it was him.

He held up the lantern to see what he'd tripped over. All of the canned goods and food supplies Buck had brought up were now stacked in a semicircle around Reggie's bunk on the floor.

"What in the—?" J.T. shook his head as he stepped closer. Why in the world would she literally surround herself with groceries?

He swung the lantern around to shine it on the bottom bunk. All he could see of her was one bare arm sticking out of the mountain of blankets. The arm was curled around a ten-pound bag of flour. J.T. frowned in nothing short of true bewilderment.

"Why is all the food on the floor?" he asked patiently.

Reggie's head poked out from under the blankets, she blinked as if blinded by the firelight—or him, then she ducked back under with a louder groan.

He smiled, cheered immensely that he'd woken her from her beauty sleep. The fact that he was the last person she wanted to see this morning made it all the better.

She looked out at him, blinking away sleep, seeming to find it hard to focus on him.

In the lantern light she looked a lot better than he felt. It annoyed him greatly.

"How were your accommodations?" he asked, hoping she'd gotten less sleep than he had, especially since she'd had that late-night secret summit in the woods. He wanted to demand who she'd been talking to out in the woods last night but he decided to keep that piece of information to himself a little longer. First he would watch her with the cowhands. Better to let her think she had gotten away with her late-night rendezvous. "Sleep well?"

"Like a baby." She blinked those big blue eyes at him, clearly lying through her teeth. "What time is it?"

"Time to start breakfast."

Her gaze went to the window. "It's still dark outside."

He didn't tell her that normally the cook got up way before daybreak to start the fire. It took an hour before the fire was ready to cook on.

Fortunately, she'd kept the fire going so breakfast wouldn't be as late as he'd figured.

"As camp cook," he said, "you have to get up earlier than anyone else and usually go to bed later."

She tried to sit up and then seemed to realize she still had her arm around the bag of flour. She sneaked a quick look at him, then haughtily freed her arm and glaring at him, sat up, banging her head on the overhead bunk. "Ouch." She rubbed her forehead and eyed him as if this too were his fault. "Well, aren't you going to say something smart?"

He tried not to laugh. Served her right. If she hadn't been glaring at him—

"If you will just go away and let me get up and dressed...."

"Not so fast." The more he looked at the semicircle of staples, the more curious—and concerned—he'd become. "You haven't told me what the food is doing around your bed. I'm sure there is a simple explanation." He highly doubted it since it was Reggie. He wasn't sure what exasperated him more about her, the fact that she looked so good in the morning or that she really thought she could evade his question.

She glanced at the supplies on the floor and chewed for a moment on her lower lip. "Have it your way—" She threw back the covers, swung her legs over the side of the bed and stood up.

Just the sight of her killed every coherent thought except one: Wow.

The white silken gown fell over her curves like melting butter on flapjacks, making it hard to tell where the gown began and skin ended. To make matters worse, there was her hair. Yesterday it had been wrapped in a tight little bun or whatever at the nape of her neck. Now it floated around her pale shoulders, dark and luxurious.

He turned his back to her, going to the woodstove to stoke the fire, a fire of his own burning hot inside him. He was about to excuse himself and give her a chance to get dressed when she padded barefoot over to where he stood by the woodstove.

She had pulled another garment over the gown, something in the same thought-stealing silk that did

little to hide her own assets. He tried to keep his gaze
on her face. It was soft and cute as a newborn calf and
just as harmless looking. Appearances could be *so* de-
ceiving. Her fragrance floated around him. Perfume
and—he frowned—dish soap? "What are you doing?"

She shot him a look as she picked up one of the skillets from the counter behind her. "I'm getting breakfast."

"Not dressed like *that!*" It was the pure impractical-
ity of the ensemble that infuriated him, not the effect
it had on him. Worse, he feared she knew exactly what
she was doing to him and she was enjoying it a lot more
than he was. "Anyway, I fired you."

She seemed to ignore him as she dropped the skil-
let on the back of the woodstove and went to dig in the
cooler. "Then you rehired me. Is it always this cold up
here?"

Cold? The cabin felt suffocatingly hot. "Maybe if
you were dressed appropriately—"

She shivered and went back to the bunk to get her
socks and boots. He watched her wince as she pulled
them on. They looked ridiculous with the expensive pei-
gnoir. And as ridiculous and out of place as Reggie herself had looked in the red suit yesterday on the roadside.
The same way she didn't fit in here at the line camp.

Getting to her feet again, she looked like the only
thing keeping her upright was pure stubbornness alone.
Why didn't she have the good sense to give up now?
Why didn't he?

He watched her draw one fingertip into her mouth,
the same one he'd noticed she'd burned the night before. He felt himself weaken.

"I have some balm for your burns," he heard himself say. "You can put it on your boot blisters as well."

She looked over at him in surprise. The gratitude in her gaze grabbed hold of him in a death grip. She bit her lip as if she might feel a little guilty for putting him through this. Or maybe it was just him who was feeling guilty. Could he be wrong about her motives?

J.T. stepped to one of the smaller coolers just off the porch and came back with a chunk of cheese. He held it out to her. "Eat this."

Regina took the cheese and did as she was told before she even thought to question him. As she chewed, she looked up at him, realizing that people just did what J. T. McCall told them to do and he expected nothing less. He wasn't used to anyone not following his orders. No wonder he'd been so angry with her.

The cheese helped, she felt more awake, not quite so tired. She figured that was his intention. "Thank you."

He wasn't like anyone she'd ever known. His looks alone made him stand out. A blond, blue-eyed handsome cowboy. The real thing. Just what she needed.

And yet he was nothing like she'd originally thought she wanted. He drove an old dirty pickup, wore worn clothing, often had mud and manure on his boots and jeans and smelled of sweat and horseflesh, leather and dust. And she'd never met a sexier man in her life.

No man had ever stirred the desires in her that McCall did. When this was over, she knew she would look back on it and wonder if she'd lost her mind in Montana. She could just imagine what her mother would say if she knew that her daughter was having such thoughts about a man like J. T. McCall.

Not that she would ever let a sexual desire make her

stray from her purpose. Too much was at stake for a roll in the hay—literally—with such a man. But she couldn't help but wonder what it would be like.

And he was attracted to her. He'd just about died when she'd gotten out of bed in her nightgown. She smiled to herself at the memory.

If everything in her life wasn't riding on this advertising campaign....

She could just hear Anthony. "Gina, baby, what could it hurt? You can't work all the time."

But looking at McCall, she knew it could hurt. He wasn't the kind of man you just bedded and walked away from unscathed. Not that she'd ever just bedded a man. She hardly had time even to date. Her grandmother was always telling her she'd be an old maid if she didn't forget about work for a moment and think about a man.

Well, she was thinking about a man right now. And her thoughts would have shocked her grandmother. Maybe not. But they definitely shocked Regina.

J.T. DIDN'T LIKE that look in her eyes. "I'll go get that balm," he said as he retreated backward until he felt the doorknob digging into his behind. "Get dressed. Don't touch that stove. I'll make breakfast." He felt much too heroic.

That's why her next words floored him.

"I'd really like to see you ride today," she said. "Do you think that would be possible?"

Her words stunned him. She couldn't be serious. The guilt he'd felt just an instant before took off like a wild stallion on open range. It took any sympathy he'd felt for her with it as well.

"You just don't know when to quit, do you?" He stepped to her, forgetting for the moment how she was dressed. Or not dressed, as the case was. "I'm going to tell you this one more time. I don't know what you're really up to, but I want you out of my cow camp."

"What I'm up to? I told you what I want. All you have to do is agree to the commercial and you won't ever have to see me again."

So she was sticking to that story. "I thought you had to see me ride first before you could make me the offer?"

She seemed to realize her mistake. "I do. Why else would I want to see you ride?"

"My question exactly." She looked so innocent standing there in her negligee and cowboy boots—"Whatever it is you're really after, give it up, Reggie. I told you, no one can be more stubborn or determined than me. Not even you."

She smiled, baby blues twinkling. "I guess that's the one thing we have in common, McCall. We're both tenacious to a fault."

"Wrong, Reggie," he said as he towered over her. "With you, it's a fault. With me, it's my best quality." He tipped his hat and headed for the door.

But as usual, Reggie got in the last word.

"Believe me, McCall, your pigheadedness isn't your greatest asset. If it were, I wouldn't be here."

Chapter Five

Blurry-eyed, Regina sat down slowly on the lower bunk and pulled off her boots so she could get her jeans on. She ached all over. A faint blush of light sifted down through the pines beyond a gap in her makeshift towel curtains at the window. She felt like the walking dead, her boot-blistered feet aching, her eyes sandpapery, her fingers burned and red.

But she'd done her best not to let McCall see it. She looked at the bunk, wanting sleep, but not even tempted to get back into that hard bunk. Even if her pride would have let her. She was going to make pancakes. Come hell or high water.

She dressed in her new cowboy clothes, not that they looked new anymore. She wished now that she'd just bought a plain western shirt, a pair of her own jeans and some brown boots so she fit in more. The thought surprised her. What was happening to her? She was a Holland. Their whole goal in life was to stand out.

Dressed, she picked up all the food supplies she'd left on the floor. As she began to mix the ingredients for pancakes she felt like she was having a recurring nightmare. She'd stayed up most of the night practicing making pancakes, one batch after another. She'd been determined to show J. T. McCall that she wasn't as helpless as he thought.

Part of her wanted to shock him. The other part wanted to please him. That was the part that worried her.

Before last night she'd never made pancakes in her life, but fortunately she'd discovered a recipe on the back of the flour sack and other recipes on boxes and cans of food and she *could* read.

After she was sure everyone had gone to bed, she'd gotten up, covered the windows with towels and, working by flashlight, had practiced making pancakes. One batch after another. She hated to think how many mistakes she'd made and had to dispose of before she finally got a pancake that looked like the one on the flour sack.

Now she put more wood on the fire and looked down at her pancake batter and smiled. Her only concern was the amount of supplies she'd used. She hoped they didn't run out of food. But there seemed to be enough for an army and Buck would be bringing back a truck so they could go get more, right?

She tried not to think about Buck's arrival—and her forced departure. She didn't have much time and she was rather at a loss as to how to proceed. J. T. McCall didn't need the money, didn't want the fame and wasn't even flattered by the offer. She would never have believed such a man existed if she hadn't met him.

What McCall was, she realized, was incredibly stubborn. It would take dynamite to dislodge him once he'd made up his mind. And according to him, his mind was as set as cement.

There was the thump of boots on the porch, a step she

recognized, then a soft knock at the door. She reached up to tuck an errant lock of hair behind her ear. "Come in, McCall."

J.T. OPENED THE DOOR, another armload of firewood and the balm for her blisters, expecting he would need to get Reggie out of bed. Again.

To his surprise, she was dressed and standing at the cookstove. Nothing appeared to be on fire. In fact, she seemed to have breakfast almost ready.

He'd taken a little extra time to give her a chance to get up and dressed. After saddling his horse, he rode the perimeter of the camp looking for any sign that he and his crew might not be alone up here.

He found none. No tracks. No sign of a newly used campfire ring. No sign of a spot where a tent might have been erected. He hadn't realized how long he'd been gone.

Since he'd planned to cook something simple when he returned, he hadn't worried. He never expected to see Reggie cooking. Especially over a stove where there was no flaming food.

Cooking was supposed to have been punishment for Reggie. The last thing he wanted was to see her looking competent at that cookstove, to see her looking as if she belonged here.

He checked out the pancakes she had going on the griddle. They actually looked like pancakes. She also had some ham and bacon fried up on the back of the stove. It wasn't even burned.

He glanced at the lower bunk. She'd picked up all the canned goods and supplies around it.

She followed his gaze and seemed to blush. "I was practice-cooking, all right?"

"Practice-cooking?" he echoed.

"I read the recipes off the backs of the bags, cans and boxes of food. Then I practiced preparing a few dishes. That's all."

That's all? In the lantern light, he could see an array of freshly cleaned pots and pans on the counter in the kitchen. That's why she smelled of dish soap this morning. He couldn't help but smile.

"What's so funny?"

He shook his head. He knew he must be looking at her as if she'd just single-handedly forged a mission to Mars. He couldn't help it. Nor would he have been more surprised.

Why would she stay up half the night reading recipes off the backs of containers and practice-cooking when he'd fired her and by lunchtime she was out of here? He sobered. This woman's persistence knew no boundaries.

He felt his dread deepening and told himself that Buck would return by early afternoon at the latest and Reggie would just be a memory. One he wouldn't soon forget.

"Do you mind if we didn't have eggs this morning?" she asked.

All he could do was shake his head. Earlier he'd thought of things he wanted to say to her but they'd all flown right out of his head. He just stood looking at her, overwhelmed by the woman's doggedness, but grudgingly impressed. She was truly a babe in the woods but she was trying so hard, he had to admire her grit.

"Here, I brought you this," he said holding out the balm.

She took it with a look of such gratitude that he had to look away so she didn't see how guilty he felt.

"What do you have against city girls?" she asked as she flipped one of the pancakes. It was a beautiful golden brown and smelled wonderful. Almost as good as Reggie, dish soap and all.

For a moment he was taken aback by her question though. He was going to tell her it was none of her business but then she looked at him, those big blue eyes drawing him in.

"I... I almost married a woman from the city."

Reggie lifted a brow. "You were in love with her."

He thought about lying, but nodded. "She wanted a cowboy and the fantasy, but she soon realized what she didn't want—the reality of my lifestyle." He turned away and saw that she'd set the table already. Or had she set it last night when she was practice-cooking and he just hadn't noticed?

"She broke your heart."

He wished he had told her it was none of her business and left it at that. "She just made me realize that the last thing I needed was a city girl on a Montana cattle ranch."

To his surprise Reggie was silent. For that he was grateful. She flipped the pancakes and looked up at him, the spatula in her hand. He knew he must be staring at her, but he couldn't help himself.

He was hoping to hell she didn't have anything to do with Luke Adams's disappearance. And he was also trying to understand what it was about this woman....

REGINA MET HIS gaze and suddenly felt like giggling. It was his baffled expression, her own lack of sleep, the ridiculousness of her situation and the fact that she'd stayed up all night teaching herself to make *pancakes* to get a cowboy's perfect posterior in a pair of her jeans. If her grandmother could see her now.

She tried to hold back the giggle but it escaped.

"Reggie?"

To her horror, she started giggling and couldn't stop. Tears ran down her face and her body shook with laughter.

McCall was staring at her as if she'd lost her mind and then he did the strangest damned thing, he laughed. J. T. McCall laughing.

It came as such a surprise, the sound of it, the rich lyrical depth of it, she stopped giggling and looked at him and then to her shock, began to cry, huge sobs that racked her body.

He moved to her. "Finally sunk in, huh."

She nodded, crying and laughing until she took a breath and was sane again.

He reached over to thumb a tear from her cheek.

"You must think I'm the biggest idiot you've ever met," she said.

He shook his head. "But you are the most determined *woman* I've ever met." He thumbed away another tear. "And one of the bravest."

She smiled and he stood there just looking at her.

"Want to tell me anything before I call the men in for breakfast?" he asked, his voice sounding hoarse.

Tell him something? Like the fact that she wished he'd kiss her. Is that what he meant? Or was he still thinking she had the truck part?

She saw that was more what he had in mind. And to think that a second ago she'd thought he might want to kiss her as much as she had wanted him to. She really had lost her mind.

He edged backward to the door, never taking his eyes from her as if he feared what she might do next. Then turning, he left.

Men. She would never understand them.

She stopped long enough to hurriedly apply the balm to her blistered feet and fingers. It helped, giving her hope that after breakfast her feet would feel good enough that she could sneak off and watch him ride. She already knew he would look great in the saddle. But she wasn't just doing it for the commercial.

The truth was the more she was around McCall, the more curious she became about the man. Not that she wasn't still determined to have him for her commercial. What would it hurt to learn more about him? She was curious about his life—a life he wouldn't even trade for fame and fortune.

She shook off the exhaustion and poured the last of the not-bad-looking pancake batter onto the griddle as if born to do it, then stood back and watched the cakes bubble. She could make pancakes!

Even after all her practicing, it still amazed her. Might not mean much to some people, but to her it was nothing short of a miracle.

She flipped the pancakes with an expertise born of practice and pain the night before. The pancakes had cooked to a rich golden brown. She smiled to herself again, feeling as if she'd really accomplished something, feeling good in spite of the burned fingers, blistered feet and sore back and legs.

The only thing that could make this day any better would be for J. T. McCall to agree to do the commer-

cial before Buck got back. She realized that was probably the only reason J.T. was being even civil to her. He
knew he would be rid of her soon.

Well, she wasn't down and out yet. Somehow she
would change his mind before Buck's return. Going at it
head-on hadn't worked. Perhaps there was another way.
Although it wasn't her nature but it just might work.

The cowhands came in slowly, as if afraid of what
they'd find. Who could blame them after last night's
meal. It had frightened her more than them. She'd been
the one who'd had to extinguish the flaming food.

She watched the men file in. There was the tall
blond, Cotton, then Slim, the lanky cowboy with the
scarred hands. Burns? She had an acquaintance who'd
burned himself with chemicals while working at a meth
lab. He had scars like that.

Then there was Roy, the quiet one and Nevada, the one
who looked like an ex-con to her. Not his face, but something about the way he carried himself. And then there
was Will. Will Jarvis. If J.T. wanted to know who had
taken his stupid distributor cap he should look to Will.
The man had passed her on the highway yesterday. She
distrusted a man who wouldn't help a damsel in distress.

The men all seemed to brighten when they were able
to recognize the food on the table. The men all took
their places. All except for Luke Adams, the shy one.

As J.T. joined the men at the table, she put the plate
with pancakes next to him, took her chair and waited.
J.T. filled his plate and passed the food.

She wondered where Luke was, but was relieved to
see the men filling their plates without McCall having
to hold a gun to their heads.

But the true test would be McCall. She stole a look at him, anxious for him to take a bite of the pancakes.

Instead, he looked pointedly at her empty plate. She couldn't possibly eat at this ridiculous hour of the morning, could she? With his gaze still on her, she took two small pancakes and a strip of bacon.

Foregoing butter or syrup, she took a tiny bite of the pancake, feeling like a monarch's official food taster. She blinked in surprise. She took another bite, a larger one, and then quickly finished off the pancake. It was *delicious*.

She helped herself to a couple more and decided a little butter wouldn't hurt her. She'd work off the calories before the day was over, she was sure of that. She drizzled some of the huckleberry syrup over the top of her short stack, amazed at just the thought that *she'd* made these.

She took a bite, closed her eyes and let out a moan of delight. When was the last time she'd had pancakes, let alone *butter* and *syrup* on them? Breakfast in L.A. was usually a cup of coffee on the run. She would swear that she'd never had pancakes that tasted this good.

She opened her eyes and realized that J.T. was staring at her, an amused expression on his face. She quickly wiped away her look of ecstasy then the buttery syrup from her lips with her tongue.

She waited, her heart in her throat, annoyed at how much she wanted him to say he liked them.

J.T. took a bite of his pancake, chewed, stopped, looked up at her in surprise. "Not bad." He gave her a slight nod, then a smile.

She looked down, trying to hide how pleased she was.

J.T. LOOKED AROUND the table, worried. Over the years he'd had cowhands leave. Some missed girlfriends, others didn't like the work. Some got into fights with one of the other cowhands and left. Some just couldn't take all the quiet.

None of those reasons seemed to fit Luke Adams, but J.T. knew he could be wrong. He hoped to hell he was wrong about a lot of things he suspected.

"Luke didn't say anything about leaving last night?" J.T. asked as he cut a bite of ham with his knife.

He looked around the table, carefully avoiding looking at Reggie. All he got from the men were head shakes or shrugs in answer to his question.

"He get into a fight or argument with anyone?"

Head shakes, shrugs.

"Luke left?" Reggie asked, sounding surprised.

"So it seems," he said.

She glanced around the table, then asked Slim to pass her the pancakes.

"No one heard him leave the tent?" J.T. asked. Apparently not. He let his gaze light on Reggie. She had her head down, seeming more interested in her pancakes then Luke's departure.

"You know where Luke might have gone, Ms. Holland?"

Her head jerked up. She blinked. "How would *I* know?" She had a dab of syrup on her lower lip.

"I thought you might have heard or seen him leave since you were up late?"

She shook her head, her tongue coming out to lick away the syrup.

She might have been the last person to see him, he wanted to say, but didn't pursue it in front of the others. He'd been watching her with the cowhands and he hadn't seen anything pass between them, not even a suspicious look.

Luke's disappearance seemed to indicate he'd been the person she'd met in the woods last night; the person who'd disabled the truck for her. If so, they were obviously in this together. Whatever *this* was. Was it possible she wanted him to make a jeans commercial *that* badly? It had to be something else.

"Maybe he just got up early and went for a ride," Reggie suggested. "Or maybe he went with Buck."

"Buck would have said something if he'd known Luke was leaving. Doesn't it seem odd to you that Luke would take off without a word to anyone?" he asked her.

Her eyes widened. She shrugged. "Everything here seems odd to me."

His gaze killed the splattering of laughter that erupted around the table from her comment. "Well, I don't want anyone else leaving here without me knowing about it." He looked to the men. "I want you to work closely, keeping the others in sight today. Also keep a look out for Luke in case he just wandered off. I don't want anyone else getting lost."

J.T. saw Will Jarvis glance over at Slim. Slim was busy eating and didn't seem to notice, but J.T. did. "Luke didn't mention anything about leaving to you, did he, Slim?"

Slim looked up in obvious surprise. His Adam's apple worked for a moment. "I might have heard someone get up last night, but whoever it was came back a little while later."

It seemed no one had heard Luke leave. The six men had all been sleeping in the same tent. He wondered how Luke had been able to leave, gear, horse and all, without anyone being the wiser.

His gaze settled on Reggie. He also wondered what she and presumably Luke Adams might have had to discuss in the middle of the night in the woods. Maybe she was just thanking him for helping her. Because if Luke was the man she'd been whispering to in the dark, J.T. would lay odds Luke had also been the man to take the distributor cap.

REGINA COULD FEEL McCall's gaze on her. He thought she had something to do with Luke leaving? She'd never laid eyes on Luke Adams or any of the rest of them before yesterday. But she could see trying to convince McCall otherwise would be futile.

What exactly was he accusing her of, anyway? He already thought she'd done something to the truck to keep it from running so she could stay the night. Now he thought she'd done something to Luke?

She excused herself and got up to start the dishes. She had a pretty good idea that J.T. wasn't going to have the men help her. She was right. As soon as they all finished their breakfasts, he told everyone to get saddled up.

Chairs scraped and boots thumped across the floor to the door. She didn't bother to turn as they all left.

"I would suggest you stay in the cabin until Buck returns with a truck," J.T. said behind her, startling her. She thought he'd left with the others.

She nodded and kept washing the dishes. Stay in the cabin. He must be kidding. She had no intention of missing the chance to see him ride. She had pictured it in her mind given the way he carried himself, all that confidence and competence, all that arrogance.

But in order to see him in the saddle, she'd have to get out of this cabin soon after the men left. She wished now that she'd paid more attention to how far away the cattle were when Buck was explaining how the cowboys rounded them up.

"I don't want you wandering off and getting lost," J.T. was saying.

He was still here? She nodded again and when she still felt him waiting behind her, she gave up and turned to look at him.

He handed her a dirty plate from the table. As she reached for it, her fingers brushed his.

They both released the plate. It clattered to the floor but didn't break. Regina jumped back, startled, her gaze going to his. Other than the color, she'd never really noticed his eyes before. Probably because she'd only been interested in his butt.

Now she saw that part of what made him so handsome was his eyes. They were a pale deep blue, but with flecks of gold. The eyes alone could have held her attention. But something in his gaze—

Suddenly the cabin seemed ridiculously hot. She swallowed, unable to take her eyes from his, although it felt as if all the heat in the room was being generated by his gaze.

Her insides seemed to soften, while at the same time, she felt as if she couldn't catch her breath. Then over the erratic thudding of her heart, she heard the room grow painfully still.

It all happened in an instant. So quickly that Regina wasn't really sure she hadn't imagined it.

J.T. jerked his gaze away, cleared his throat and stooped to pick up the plate as one of his men appeared in the doorway to ask something about riding the ridge-line.

J.T. barked out the answer, his sumptuous, deep voice a little hoarse sounding.

The man—she saw out of the corner of her eye it was the young blonde Cotton—drew back in surprise, then seemed to leave quickly so J.T. didn't see his knowing grin.

J.T. dropped the plate into the hot sudsy dishwater.

Regina began to wash the plate as if nothing had happened. Nothing *had* happened, had it? Then why did her face feel flushed and her hands seem to shake as she washed the plate? All because a man had *looked* at her?

When she finally did turn around she found McCall long gone. She set to washing the pans and skillets, keeping hot water going on with the fire so she could finish her job as quickly as possible and catch J.T. in the saddle.

Through the window she could see that it was growing light out, the sun coming up, the pines shimmering like green silk in the early morning light. The last time she'd seen the sun come up, she'd been out all night.

She stood staring out the window, surprised by how breathtaking the view was, then shook herself. What was she thinking? If she hoped to see J.T. ride— She quickly dried her hands.

But as she started toward the door, she heard a thud like something hitting the side of the cabin. Her gaze flew to the window but she saw nothing through the glass. Could it have been one of the men? Not likely.

She'd heard them ride out a while ago. It had probably just been a tree limb blowing in the breeze.

Cautiously, she opened the door. The porch was empty. She stared out at the trees. But there was no breeze. It hadn't been a limb hitting the side of the cabin. Whatever she'd heard was nowhere to be seen.

She looked out toward the corral. Only two horses remained. No cowboys. She stood at the porch railing listening. She heard no sign of the men or the cows. She realized she didn't even know which direction they'd ridden off in or how far away they had gone. Mostly, she realized, she didn't like the idea of going out there alone.

It wasn't like her to be afraid, but it was as if she sensed something waiting in the woods, something more dangerous than anything she'd ever encountered in L.A.

Not that she would let that stop her. Buck would be back soon. She didn't have much time and she wanted to see McCall ride. She knew once she saw him in the saddle nothing on this earth could keep her from talking him into doing the commercial.

But as she pushed wide the cabin door, she saw a large dark shadow fall across the porch. J.T.? Had he been waiting outside, knowing she wouldn't do as he'd told her?

Or had he come back because of earlier and what had happened between them. *Had* something happened? He must have thought so for him to come back.

Her heart did a little flutter at the thought as she leaned around the edge of the door expecting to see him standing just off the porch, the sun behind him.

At first it didn't register what she saw—or heard.

She let out a shriek of alarm. A huge bear rummaged

in the dirt just off the end of the tiny porch—just feet from her.

She stumbled back into the cabin, slamming the door behind her. She could hear the bear snorting and scraping at the earth next to the porch.

What if it decided to come into the cabin?

She glanced around, looking for a way out. The windows didn't open and there was only the one door—the one with the bear just outside. She was trapped!

Frantically she looked around for a weapon, then let out an oath. What was she thinking? Even if she'd found a rifle she didn't have the faintest idea how to shoot one. Nor was she apt to shoot the bear even if she did.

Belatedly, she remembered something Buck had told her when she'd asked if there were any bears in the mountains.

Chapter Six

J.T. had sent the cowhands off to start rounding up the cattle. He wanted a few minutes alone to cuss and fuss and mentally kick himself—and to take a look around their tent.

What the hell had happened back in the cabin? One minute he was looking at Reggie and the next—

He swore under his breath, shaking his head at his own foolishness. One minute he'd just been looking at her, thinking what a handful the woman was, remembering the way she'd enjoyed her pancakes, and the next minute—hell, he didn't know what he'd been thinking the next minute.

He couldn't have been thinking at all to be thinking anything about a woman like her. A fool city girl. Worse, one with designs on him. At least this one had been honest from the get-go. All she wanted were his... assets.

So she'd stayed up most of the night and taught herself how to make pancakes and hadn't burned breakfast to a crisp. So what? No reason to go all soft on her.

She was a damned fine-looking woman so who could blame him for being attracted to her if that's what it had been for that split second when their fingers had touched?

Whatever it had been, it wasn't going to happen again. He needed to keep his distance from her. Who knew what womanly wiles she would use on him if he weakened even the slightest. He already knew what lengths she would go to. At least he thought he did.

What really ticked him off was that she'd made him forget all about her late-night rendezvous. He had meant to ask her, not that he thought she would tell him the truth.

But as he led his horse over to the second wall tent, he couldn't help worrying that she hadn't been behind taking the distributor cap. So how did he explain her wandering around in the night whispering to someone in the trees?

He started to open the tent and stopped, thinking he heard a noise. He glanced toward the cabin. He was tempted to check on her and make sure she was all right. Uh-uh. He wasn't going near that cabin or Reggie. It didn't matter what she was doing out in the dark last night or who she was talking to. Buck would return and take her to town. By the time he and the men came in for supper, she would be gone.

So what was his problem? He knew it was the idea of leaving her alone even for a few hours. Who knew what kind of trouble she could get into?

He glanced around, feeling as if someone was watching him. He knew he couldn't be seen through the pines from the cabin. Reggie would probably still be doing the dishes anyway. Taking another glance around, seeing no one, he entered the tent. The cowhands should all be out rounding up cattle, trying to keep each other in sight. So no one could sneak back for any reason, right?

He knew what was nagging at him. Luke Adams. He was surprised that the cowhand would leave in the middle of the night without a word. Especially if Luke was the person Reggie had been whispering to out in the woods. Luke's disappearance on top of the disabled truck left him feeling all the more uneasy.

He'd already checked and knew Luke's gear was gone. But still he wanted to have a look around the tent.

He checked each man's gear but didn't find anything out of the ordinary. He straightened, hitting his shoulder on the tent frame. He thought he heard a sound, a soft rustle, like something shifting over his head. He looked up and noticed something odd—an object had been stuck between the layers of canvas in the frame. He wouldn't have noticed it at all if he hadn't hit his shoulder and dislodged it.

He reached up and sliding his hand into the space touched cold metal. His heart leaped to his throat as he pulled out the 9 mm pistol.

J.T. knew that each man had a rifle or pistol on him when he was gathering cattle. Sometimes a man had to put down an injured cow. Or scare off a bear or mountain lion. Even put down a horse with a broken leg.

His camp rule, which he was sure Buck had shared with the men, was no alcohol. And no firearms in the tent or cabin. He'd heard too many stories from his father and grandfather about cowhands getting drunk and having shootouts in the middle of cow camp.

So why had one of the cowhands *hidden* a gun in the tent? As he stared at the gun he wondered not only who it belonged to but also what the owner was planning to do with it.

Sticking the pistol into his coat pocket, he stepped from the tent, glanced around and saw no one, then went to his own tent and hid the pistol beneath his cot for the time being.

As he exited his tent and started toward his horse, he heard a noise come from the cabin. He told himself he was just imagining the banging sound, looking for an excuse to go back to the cabin and Reggie.

As he looked toward the cabin, he realized he half-expected to see it on fire. It was that damned nightmare he'd had last night.

Through the trees he could see a portion of the building and the only smoke rising out of it was through the chimney. But the memory of the nightmare coupled with everything else left him anxious.

The banging sound seemed to be getting louder.

He stared at the cabin, telling himself not to go back there. He had six hundred head of cattle to get out of these mountains before the snow hit and the sooner the better, all things considered.

But it was impossible to ignore this much racket. And there was no doubt that the incessant banging was coming from the cabin.

He shook his head and headed toward the sound. What in the devil was she up to now?

REGINA HAD RUSHED to the kitchen, grabbed the largest pan she could find and a good-sized spoon. Out on the porch, she heard the creak of a floorboard groan under the weight of the bear. It was on the porch!

She began to pound the bottom of the pan with the

spoon like a mad woman. To her horror, the ear-splitting banging didn't seem to faze the bear. She beat the pan harder and realized she would have to open the door. Obviously, the bear couldn't hear it well enough.

Hadn't she read somewhere that bears ate people in Montana? Grizzly bears. Was this a grizzly? Probably, with her luck. From the size of the bear, it looked as if it could get into the cabin without any problem and she had no doubt that it would break in if she didn't scare it away.

She beat the pan as hard as she could, her heart pounding louder than the spoon on the bottom of the pan. Moving quietly to the door, she opened it a crack and looked out. She couldn't see its shadow on the porch anymore. Maybe she'd chased it off.

She stepped farther out on the porch. No sign of the bear but she kept beating the pan just in case as she inched along the porch to the side of the cabin.

The bear reared up in surprise to see her. Not half as surprised as she was to see it. She turned and ran, afraid to slow down to make the ninety-degree turn back into the cabin let alone to get the door closed and locked before the bear burst into the cabin.

Her feet barely touched the porch as she flew across it expecting to feel the bear's breath on her neck any moment.

Climb a tree! She was looking for a tree she could climb, pounding the pan as hard as she could as she ran, afraid to look back—

Something clawed at her shoulder with enough force to spin her around. She shrieked, and instinctively closed her eyes and swung the pan. She heard the pan thump off something solid and swung again.

J.T. LET OUT an oath and grabbed for her, but she nailed him again with the pan, knocking his hat into the dust. "Dammit, Reggie! What in the hell is wrong with you?"

She opened her eyes. They were bigger and bluer than ever in her pale, frightened face. "I thought—" She seemed to be trying to catch her breath, her substantial chest moving up and down with the effort.

He rubbed the knot rising on his forehead with one hand and leaned down to pick up his hat from the dirt with the other. "Are you nuts?"

She grimaced as her gaze went to his bruised forehead. "Sorry."

"Yeah." He gingerly settled his hat back on his head and took the pan and spoon from her. The woman had beat huge craters into the bottom of the aluminum pan. He frowned at her. "Why in the world were you—"

"Buck told me to do it."

He eyed her. "Are you sure you got the directions right? What exactly were you trying to cook?"

She mugged an unamused face at him and stepped around him to point back toward the cabin. "I was trying to scare the bear away."

He turned. "What bear?"

"It must have gone into the cabin."

He shot her a disbelieving look. "You're sure it was a bear?"

"I know a bear when I see one. I think it's a grizzly."

He nodded, skeptical on all counts. "Come on," he said impatiently as he started toward the cabin.

At the porch, Reggie hung back. He shook his head as he crossed the porch. The woman was going to be the death of him. As he peered around the doorjamb, he was relieved to see that there was no bear in the cabin but he heard something around the corner.

Moving to the end of the porch, he looked around the corner and spotted a small black bear rummaging in something along the side of the cabin. He turned to find Reggie had joined him, hiding behind him for protection.

"Buck told you to bang on a pan if you saw a bear?" he asked incredulously. He hated to think what she'd have done if he'd given her a real weapon.

"It's a grizzly, isn't it," she whispered.

"No, it's just a young black bear."

"Just?"

He stomped his boots on the flooring. "Go on, get!" he called out to the bear.

The bear lifted its head. J.T. could feel Reggie's body pressed against his back, her fingers digging into his ribs as she held on.

"I said, get!" he hollered again and tossed the battered pot at the bear's rump. It startled the young bear. He loped off into the pines.

"It's gone," J.T. said to Reggie, but he wondered what the bear had been so interested in beside the cabin.

Reggie loosened her hold on him and he stepped off the porch to investigate. He hadn't gone far when he saw what the bear had been in to. It looked as if a hen house had exploded, there were so many eggshells on the ground. With a groan, he turned to look back at Reggie. She was standing at the edge of the porch, still looking scared.

"You didn't throw food out here, did you?" he asked, knowing full well that she had.

"Food?" she repeated.

He watched her wet her lips, calling more attention to

her mouth than he really needed her to do. She glanced after the bear, then at the eggshells on the ground and the marks where the bear had torn up the earth. For a moment, she only chewed at that soft-looking plump lower lip.

"I wouldn't exactly call what I tossed out *food,*" she said slowly. "Just some practice pancakes and a…few eggshells."

He shook his head at her. "Reggie…" He took a breath, trying to control his temper. "This is bear country. You put out food and you're going to attract bears and I don't think that's what you want to do."

Her eyes came up to meet his. For a moment, he almost lost himself in all that sky-blue.

"Not only that, having bears in camp is real hard on pans," he said, no longer able to hide a grin.

"Very funny." She did not look amused.

He reminded himself that she was a city girl and as out of her element as she could get. If he went to L.A., there would probably be things that would scare him and make him look foolish.

He handed her the spoon and went to pick up the pan and clean up the garbage to keep the bear from coming back. As he did, he found himself fighting back a grin at just the memory of her charging through the woods, banging that pan. The woman was something, he'd give her that.

Men often underestimated women. Not that he thought any man was prepared for a woman like Reggie. Look what she'd done to poor unsuspecting Buck. Look what she'd done to him. He remembered the way she'd looked last night in the cabin, all doe-eyed and apologetic. It still annoyed him how she'd made him feel guilty as if it were his fault she was here.

He heard her behind him and turned to hand her the battered pan.

She glanced again in the direction where the bear had disappeared. "What do I do if the bear comes back?"

He heard the worry in her voice. "He shouldn't unless you cook up something for him again."

She mugged a face at J.T. The color had come back into her cheeks and she no longer looked frightened, but her eyes were still large and bottomless and clear as a high mountain lake. It was hard not to take a dip in them.

He realized that the bear had been a blessing of sorts. "But if I were you, I'd stay in the cabin just in case," he said, knowing that's exactly what a city girl would do after seeing a bear. And at least with her locked in the cabin, he shouldn't have to worry about her. Unless she really did set the cabin on fire or tried to cook or— Best not to think about it.

"Just try to stay out of trouble," he said, then turned and headed for his horse. His head hurt from where she'd hit him and he still had cattle to round up. He hoped to hell Buck hurried back.

REGINA STOOD ON the porch, torn between doing exactly what he'd said—locking herself in the cabin until he returned—and seeing him in the saddle.

She hurried to the edge of the porch, peered around the corner and watched as he strode back to where he'd left his huge horse. She watched him swing up into the saddle. If she'd had any doubts how his buns would look on a horse, she didn't anymore. He was perfect. The consummate cowboy keister.

Now all she had to do was find a way to get him to do the commercial, she thought as she watched him ride away. For the first time, she realized that might not happen. She might fail. She shoved the thought away. Over her dead body!

She stood at the edge of the porch watching him ride up the hillside, mentally willing him to turn, to look back. If he didn't turn, there was no way he was going to do the commercial. If he did—

He was almost to a stand of white-barked trees, the golden leaves flickering in the morning breeze, when he looked back.

She quickly ducked behind the corner of the cabin, smiling. J.T. McCall wasn't as immune to her as he pretended. She was getting to him.

Feeling better, she turned, glad to see that there was no bear at the end of the porch. But as she started to take a step, she heard a sound. The crack of a twig off in the trees, then another. Something was out there. Something big enough to break a stick.

Heart pounding, she glanced over her shoulder, expecting to see the bear behind her. Or something worse, although she couldn't imagine what that would be.

Hearing the crack of another limb breaking, she turned, thinking it might be one of the men who'd come back for something.

She looked toward the tents, the trees blocking her view, then up the hillside toward the corrals. Nothing.

Listening, she waited, thinking that if it was one of the men he would say something to her. She heard no sounds of the men or the cows. She didn't know which direction they'd ridden off in or how far away they'd gone. Mostly, she realized, she was vulnerable out there for whatever might be in the woods.

She hurried back inside the cabin and locked the

door. J.T. hadn't said when they'd be back. She tossed another log on the woodstove and eyed the lower bunk. It was the best she was going to do.

J.T. RODE TOWARD the sound of lowing cattle. As he came up over a rise, he saw the undulating herd below him in the wide pasture and stopped to get his feet back under him. This was what he had been born to do. Be a rancher. He loved the sight and sound of the herd, preferred to be on a horse than in a pickup and would fight any man—or woman—who tried to take it from him. And had.

He knew that was what was worrying him. That history was starting to repeat itself. The dead cow. Truck trouble. One cowhand already gone. It hadn't happened in the same way nine years ago but the similarity was enough to scare him. On top of that, there was Reggie. Maybe that worried him the most because he felt protective toward her. Hell, someone had to protect the woman.

Nevada rode toward him and J.T. knew at once that something was wrong. "I found a dead cow I thought you might want to take a look at."

J.T. nodded and followed Nevada back through the towering pines. It was cool and dark under the dense green boughs where the morning sun hadn't reached yet. He breathed in the pine scent, filling his nostrils with it, knowing that soon he would be smelling burned hide.

The cow lay on its side at the edge of a small ravine. It had been killed, its side slit open, its innards removed and then a fire built in the carcass.

"Have you ever seen anything like this?" Nevada asked, sounding spooked.

Unfortunately J.T. had. "It's someone's idea of a prank."

Nevada looked at him as if he had to be insane. "This isn't a prank. This is a warning."

J.T. nodded and looked Nevada in the eyes. "I think someone's trying to sabotage my roundup. Or at least make me think they are."

"Rustlers?"

That would be anyone's first thought. "Possibly. Could just be someone messing with me. I would prefer you didn't mention this to the others."

Nevada held his gaze for a long moment, then nodded.

"I would also understand if you wanted to draw your pay and get the hell out of here," J.T. said.

Nevada seemed surprised. He laughed. "Not a chance. I wouldn't mind meeting up with the fellow who did this."

"Me, too," J.T. said and listened for sounds of the other men. "That's one reason I want everyone to keep an eye out for the other men."

Nevada pushed back his hat and looked back through the pines toward the herd. "You think it's one of your men."

"I hope to hell not, but I haven't seen any sign of anyone else around," J.T. said, wondering if he was telling Nevada because he trusted him. Or because he didn't.

"I'll watch my back," Nevada said and rode off to join the others.

J.T. sat on his horse for a moment, fighting the urge to go back and check on Reggie and listening for the sound of a truck engine coming up the mountain. Then he spotted a half-dozen strays down in a ravine and past them, what looked like a rope noose hanging from a tree.

Chapter Seven

Regina woke cramped in a ball beneath the blankets. The fire in the stove had died and the cabin felt chilly. What time was it anyway? The sun was now shining low in the window on the opposite side of the cabin.

She sat up, careful not to bang her head again, and listened, wondering if a sound had awakened her. Or just the numbing silence.

Getting up, she put more of the balm on her blisters, then pulled on her boots and went to the door. Shouldn't Buck be here by now? She'd expected McCall to come back by now. Maybe she wasn't getting to him as much as she'd hoped.

She ventured out onto the porch, remembering that awful feeling earlier. There had been something out there, she was sure of that. But now, she heard a comforting sound. Cows mooing.

J.T. would be where the cows were, right? She had to admit, she knew nothing about gathering cattle but she knew she wanted to see what he did and the mooing didn't sound that far away. And there was no sign of the bear.

She promised herself she wouldn't go far, although the cool air felt good and the balm he'd given her and the Band-Aids she'd found in a first-aid kit made walking possible.

The landscape felt less threatening with the sun coming through the branches to splash the bed of dried needles below in pale gold. The pine boughs shimmered, a silken soft green, and a light breeze flapped playfully at the hem of her western shirt. Overhead, large white cumulus clouds bobbed along in a sea of infinite blue.

As she wound her way through the pines, she took deep breaths of the clear mountain air, surprised that it seemed a little less alien. In fact, even the countryside felt less hostile.

She followed the sound of the cows, weaving in and out of the trees and around huge rocks, thinking about how different it was from Los Angeles, how different the men were in Montana.

She'd reached the edge of a ravine when she suddenly realized she had no idea where she was. Behind her all she could see was trees and rocks and they all looked alike. No cabin.

In front of her there was nothing but more trees and rocks. No street signs. No taxi cabs. No other cabins. And nobody around to ask.

Worse yet, she was having trouble pinpointing exactly where the sound of the cattle was coming from. The mooing seemed to echo through the pines and she had the frightening feeling that the mooing might carry for miles.

Fighting panic, she wondered how anyone would ever find her. Would J.T. even look? Should she try to find her way back? Or keep going in hopes of finding the cattle and help?

Suddenly her blisters were killing her. Why hadn't she paid more attention to where she was going?

Close to tears, she walked over to a rock at the edge of a clearing. From here she could see a stand of white-barked trees, the leaves golden. She could hear their soft rattle in the breeze, like thin gold coins.

She tried to calm herself. She couldn't have gone very far. Of course she'd be able to find her way back. Anyone who would drive in L.A. could handle this.

But she did wonder how long it would take before someone came looking for her if she couldn't. She wished she'd thought to leave a trail of bread crumbs, but then, that would probably have just led a bear to her.

She heard a noise. Something large crashing through the trees on the other side of the clearing. A large dark object came running out of the pines, kicking up the fallen gold leaves. She let out a cry as she saw that it was a horse, its mouth foaming, its eyes wild. It ran at her.

Her heart in her throat, she stumbled to her feet and tried to get out of the horse's path. In her hurry, she didn't see the tree root. The next thing she knew she was face down on the ground—and in pain.

"Oh." She'd hit the ground hard but it was her ankle that hurt. She'd twisted it badly as she'd fallen. As she lay in the dirt she wondered if this was where McCall would find her body come spring.

She sat up. She'd be damned if she would just lie in the dirt and wait for someone to find her. Using the tree trunk for support, she worked her way to standing on her good ankle. She tried her other ankle and groaned.

One thing was clear, she wasn't going far.

This had been a fool thing to do. Following McCall out here. She looked around, trying to decide which direction to try to walk in. The last thing she wanted was to run into that horse again. She didn't know there were wild horses out here. What was she saying? She didn't have any idea what was out here in the wild.

She turned, startled again as a half-dozen brown-and-white faced cows trotted past to drop out of sight.

The cows brought tears of relief to her eyes but nothing like the voice she heard behind them. Limping, she followed the cows to the edge of the clearing and saw that they had dropped down into a small rocky ravine.

Bracing herself against a small pine, she stood on the edge in the pines as the cowboy's voice floated up to her.

"Go on, get up there," J.T. called softly to the cows as he rode into sight below her.

At first all she saw was his worn black hat and a glimpse of his yellow-checked western shirt and blue jean jacket through the brush.

She could hear other cattle now and saw through the pine boughs dozens of cows in a wide open meadow farther down the mountain—in the direction J.T. was headed. Her gaze quickly returned to him as he came into full view below her.

She had planned to call out to him but instead she stayed unmoving in the shelter of the pine, watching him herd the cows through the bottom of the ravine. There seemed to be little wasted motion and she wondered how many times he'd done this particular task before.

"Get up there," he called almost affectionately to the cows.

He was directly below her now. She watched, taken aback by how commanding he looked in the saddle. Bigger than life. And yet so natural, as if he and the horse were one.

She felt a pull inside her so strong that at first it felt as alien as everything else in Montana.

AN EERIE FEELING raised the fine hairs on the nape of J.T.'s neck. The feeling was so strong he actually reached back to rub his neck. For a moment there he thought he'd felt Reggie's gaze on his fanny the way he could sense a bad storm or trouble coming. With storms and trouble though, he was seldom wrong. With this, he hoped to heaven he was mistaken.

Reggie was back at the cabin. For once she would do as he asked. Hell, she'd be scared to death to wander out by herself after that bear incident.

But he turned anyway, unable to resist the power of the feeling that he was being watched. No, not watched, scrutinized. And by a pair of big blue eyes.

He brought his horse up short at the sight of her standing under the pine just above him, his first reaction pleasure. His second, worry and anger.

She was smiling a self-satisfied, knowing smile. It took him a moment to fully comprehend the extent of that smile, the flush of her cheeks, the glow in her gaze.

"Damned woman," he muttered under his breath. She'd come out here to see how he sat the saddle. What had made him think she'd behave sensibly? "I thought I told you to stay in the cabin?"

Her smile deepened. "I wanted to see you work."

He hadn't felt even a little self-conscious under a woman's gaze in years. Until now. She had a look he'd seen often enough on coyotes. He didn't particularly like the predatory way she was considering him or the way it made him feel. Especially since he was damned sure her scrutiny was aimed at his south end.

"It was a fool thing to do," he snapped. "It's a wonder you didn't get lost, fall off a cliff, drown in the creek, twist an—"

"I *am* lost and I did twist my ankle," she interrupted. "That's why I'm so glad to see you."

He swore under his breath. She seemed way too happy to see him—even for a lost city girl. This had been his "audition" for the TV jeans commercial he wasn't going to do. Not that that made any difference to Reggie. Not even the arduous job of camp cook could dissuade this woman. And from the radiance of her smile, he'd lay odds that he'd passed her screen test.

So why did he get the feeling she wanted more than him in a commercial? His cattle? He couldn't see her throwing her lot in with rustlers, but what did he know. If not his cattle, then what?

"Stay here," he ordered her. "Don't move until I come back. Do you think you can do that?"

"I wouldn't know where to go and my blisters hurt too much to move and I can barely walk on my ankle."

"Great." He drove the cattle on down to the herd in the pasture. When he rode back, he was surprised to find her sitting where he'd left her, as good as her word, and he'd realized he'd ordered her just as he had his dog Jennie. His face burned in shame that he'd been insulted because she'd originally thought Jennie was his wife and he'd ordered her to stay in the truck.

Her conception of Montana cowboys would be based on him. He groaned inwardly at the thought and wondered what to do with her now. He'd thought things couldn't get worse but Reggie was proof they could.

As he dismounted, he noticed that her face was flushed. She'd never looked so beautiful sitting there in the sunlight. He saw a fire burning in her eyes. Damn. She hadn't given up on him doing her commercial. If anything she looked all the more determined, he thought as he joined her under the wide sweeping arms of the pine.

The day was hot, the sun nearly at its apex. Rays of heat cut through the not yet bare aspens, making the fallen leaves shimmer beneath their feet. The leaves overhead rattled like dry paper.

She started to get up. "McCall, I need to tell you—"

He nodded, reached down and pulled her to her feet. Determined not to let her get in another word about that damned commercial or whatever she was after, he pulled her to her feet and kissed her, successfully shutting her up.

And being a man who liked to finish what he'd started...

It wasn't until he'd thoroughly kissed her that he realized the folly of his actions. By then he'd completely lost himself in the sweet, soft pliant warmth of her lips, in the deep, dark, wet secrets of her mouth.

All he knew was that it felt good and right and, if he was being honest, something he'd wanted to do since he'd seen her on the highway.

When he finally came to his senses, he jerked back. What had he been thinking? Had he lost his mind?

He had to hold her to keep her from slumping to the ground, having forgotten about her twisted ankle. She reached up to touch a finger to her lips and took a ragged breath that made her chest rise, her body tremble. Then ever so slowly, she smiled.

Damn, he thought. He'd just done the worse thing he could have.

REGINA HAD ALWAYS prided herself on her quick recovery rate. But it took a moment to get her feet back under her after *that* kiss even without a sprained ankle.

"What was that about, McCall?" Not that she was complaining, mind you. It was just such a surprise. The kiss. Even more surprising, its effect on her.

Her heart still pounded fiercely and her limbs felt like running water. Good thing he was still holding her. What had he put into that kiss? She felt almost...intoxicated as she met his equally stunned gaze.

"It was just a kiss," he snapped, as if the kiss had had no effect on him.

"You just keep telling yourself that, McCall." She'd like a replay just to see if it had been as amazing as she thought. But then another kiss like that would only lead to trouble. "Unless that kiss was your way of saying yes."

"What?" J.T. said, letting go of her and stepping back.

"Your way of saying yes to the commercial." She laughed so he'd know she was just trying to lighten the mood between them.

He didn't seem to get the joke. "How could you possibly get that out of one silly little meaningless kiss?"

"I was *joking.*" Silly, little, meaningless kiss? He was starting to irritate her, but she knew she was more upset with herself than him. She didn't fraternize with blue jeans models. Even those who hadn't given in yet.

"I would think a woman like you would have kissed enough men to know that was just a kiss, nothing more," he said, shoving back his hat in obvious frustration.

She'd been kissed by a fair amount of men. But none of them had kissed her like *that.* Nor had she kissed them back like *that.* Maybe she'd been dating the wrong men. Wait a minute. *A woman like you?* What was that supposed to mean?

"In my experience, McCall, a kiss, no matter how

small, means *something*," she snarled, now clearly more irritated with him than herself. She brushed past him and headed off through the trees in what she hoped was the direction of the cabin, limping and in pain, but determined to walk all the way back without his help. He could just stuff his forgettable kiss.

She took a couple of steps and stumbled. Unfortunately, her legs hadn't forgotten that damned kiss either.

"You can't walk all the way back to the cabin with a sprained ankle and blisters," he said and cursed as he grabbed her to keep her from falling. "Come on."

She barely had time to cry in protest before he swept her up into his arms. At first she thought he planned to carry her back to the cabin. But then she realized what he had in mind was much worse.

He whistled and his horse trotted over to them. "You can't walk so you have to ride."

The beast looked even larger close up. "Not a *horse*."

"A horse is your *only* option. I'm not going to carry you. Anyway, Killer isn't just any horse."

Killer? "Really, I can walk. I'll just—" Before she could say more, he tossed her up into the saddle like a sack of potatoes. She grabbed the saddle horn, afraid she'd go right on off the other side. "His name is Killer? Why would you name him killer unless—"

"You'll be fine," J.T. said, humor back in his voice.

She looked down at the man as she teetered precariously, miles from the ground, straddling a wild brute named Killer on the slipperiest saddle on earth. J.T. was enjoying her discomfort. The bastard.

If she'd felt weak at his kiss, it was nothing compared to being on his horse. "You forget," she said a little breathlessly. "I don't know how to ride." Did she dare mention her fear of large animals?

"Do you know how to sit?" he inquired. "Because that's all you have to do."

Before she could answer, he swung up behind her on the horse. The horse shuddered under them and took a step. She let out a shriek.

Killer seemed to roll his eyes at her. He obviously wasn't any happier about this than she was.

"How did... Killer get his name?" she asked.

"You don't want to know," J.T. said and nudged the horse with his heels.

The horse began to move. Regina felt as if she was going to slide off. She clamped her legs tight around the beast. Killer jumped forward.

"Easy," J.T. said, wrapping an arm around her as he worked the reins and the horse settled back down. "Unless you'd like to get us both bucked off I'd suggest you not do that again."

She barely heard him over the pounding of her heart.

"Maybe now you'll have the good sense to stay at the cabin until Buck comes back for you," he said.

She would have sworn she heard him chuckle to himself. Well at least someone was enjoying this, she thought, as she clung to the saddle horn and tried not to look down.

She had better luck with that than trying not to think about the man behind her.

Good sense? If she had good sense she wouldn't have come up with this last-ditch ad campaign, she wouldn't have set her sights on J. T. McCall's perfect posterior, she wouldn't have hired on as his camp cook, and she certainly would have never let him kiss her—let alone throw her on his horse.

She tried to relax, leaning back a little into him, feeling tired and resigned to whatever her fate might be on the back of Killer. She'd made so many mistakes with the man, including kissing him back the way she had, even death didn't look so bad.

"Sit still," he ordered, his voice sounding strange to her.

She ran her tongue over her lips, not surprised to find his kiss branded there. She felt suddenly soft and vulnerable and…so female it hurt.

McCall was angry with her. She'd no doubt destroyed any hope of getting him to model the jeans. She didn't even want to think what would happen if she returned to California without the perfect cowboy butt contract in hand.

Worse, she'd probably get bucked or fall off this horse and be killed and never get out of the mountains, let alone Montana, the way things were going.

She was fighting the urge to cry when the horse rocked. She shifted her weight, and with a start felt McCall's arm tighten around her. He pulled her back against him and heard the change in his breathing.

Silly little meaningless kiss indeed.

She was smiling to herself when she looked up and saw the horse that had almost run her down.

"What the hell," she heard McCall say behind her.

"That's what I was trying to tell you back there before you kissed me," she said. "That wild horse almost ran me down. That's how I twisted my ankle."

"That's not a wild horse," he said behind her and she heard fear in his voice. "That's Luke Adams's horse."

Chapter Eight

J.T. slipped quietly off his horse and reached up to lift Reggie down. He motioned for her to be quiet and stay back as he approached Luke's mount.

The horse's coat was lathered. He moved slowly toward it. "Easy, boy. Easy."

The horse rolled his eyes and backed away. J.T. carefully opened the corral gate, then began to work his way around to the other side of the horse.

As he did, he tried to make sense of what he was seeing. Luke's horse. No saddle. The horse had come back here, had been standing next to the corral when they'd ridden up. J.T. could only assume that Luke hadn't gotten far from camp. But if he'd been riding the horse, it would have had a saddle on it.

With the corral gate open, J.T. stood back. One of the horses in the corral whinnied, catching Luke's horse's attention. J.T. worked his way closer to the horse, then slipped off his hat and shooed it toward the open corral.

The horse shied, then trotted into the corral.

He closed the corral gate.

Where was Luke and what had happened? And the big question: where was Luke's saddle? It should have been on the horse if Luke had been thrown or the horse spooked for some reason.

He glanced toward an old tack box at the back of the cabin. The lid wasn't quite closed. He walked to it and lifted the lid. Luke's saddle and gear were inside. He closed the lid and stood, trying to make sense of it.

Luke hadn't really left? He'd just wanted everyone to think he had? Or someone else wanted them to believe it.

"Why would Luke's horse come back here?" Reggie asked when he walked back over to where he'd left her.

He shook his head as he began to unsaddle his horse. Fear vibrated through him like a low frequency hum. Buck should have been back by now.

As he released his horse into the corral with the others, he saw Reggie glance down the hill where the old truck was still parked. No newer four-wheel-drive rig. No Buck. He was relieved to see that she seemed as surprised by that as he was.

What could have happened that Buck was running this late? The foreman knew how important it was that he get right back here. Buck was no fool. He would have hightailed it back to the camp. Unless something had kept him from it. Or someone.

"I would kill for a bath," Reggie said behind him.

Her choice of words jarred him out of his thoughts. He turned to look at her as he picked up his saddle. The afternoon sun had sunk into the pines. Long shadows spilled across the camp. They had plenty of time before the others would be back for dinner.

She looked tired, her clothes filthy. He'd bet they were the only ones she'd brought that were even close to appropriate in that big suitcase of hers. He met her blue eyes and, even though he fought it, felt sorry for her. She'd really had no idea what she was getting herself into and she'd held up pretty well, all things considered.

Hell, she was a city girl. Stronger and with more courage than the other one he'd known, that was for sure.

She looked up at him. Her lips parted slightly and right then he would have given her anything—short of agreeing to do her commercial. Was that really all she wanted from him?

"There's a creek not far from here," he said. "But you can't go alone."

She lifted a brow in question.

He shook his head. "I've already got Luke missing. From now on I don't want anyone leaving this camp alone. Especially you."

She smiled, giving him a look he didn't like. She'd already figured out that he would always be paired with her. He would have trusted her safety with Buck—but Buck hadn't come back. And now J.T. didn't trust Reggie with anyone but himself. He was bound and determined to get this woman off this mountain and back to civilization in one piece.

"How badly do you want a bath?" he asked.

Her brow shot up again.

"I need some straight answers out of you," he said.

"For a bath? I'll get my stuff."

"I'll dump my saddle and meet you on the porch." As he was passing the cowhands' tent, he saw that the door was untied. Through the breach, he could see something on the floor just inside.

His heart began to race. Like a sleepwalker he moved

toward the tent and what looked like a body lying on the tent floor.

Clothes. A bundle of clothing lay on the floor. Past it more clothes had been strewn around the tent, but to his relief there were no bodies. He stared at the mess. It appeared that someone had gone through all of the cowhands' belongings. Who? And maybe more important, why? Was the person looking for the gun? Or something else?

He moved to his own tent and opened the flap that acted as a door. His and Buck's possessions were just as they'd left them. He dropped his saddle inside the tent and took the 9 mm pistol from where he'd hidden it. Checking to make sure it was loaded, he stuck it into his jacket pocket, then closing the flap, turned back to the cowhands' tent.

Whoever had ransacked the tent had been looking for something. If not the gun, then possibly money? Not likely since where would a cowhand spend cash up here?

No, it must have been something else, although he couldn't imagine what, other than the gun, as he closed the tent flap and walked toward the cabin. If his hired hands had done as he'd told them, they'd spent the day keeping the others within sight. That would narrow down the suspects.

But he knew that a cowhand could disappear down a gully chasing cows and the others could lose track of time while doing their own work. Any one of them could have sneaked back here and that's what scared him. Reggie had been here alone. Until she decided to take a walk.

Had her walk been a blessing in disguise?

He glanced at his watch, wanting to hear the whine

of a truck engine coming up the mountain. Worry settled like a heavy dark blanket over him as he tried to imagine what kind of trouble Buck might have run into.

Reggie came out on the porch as he approached. Her step seemed a little lighter. No doubt due to just the thought of a bath. He was glad to see that the bear didn't appear to have come back.

"Here, let me help you," he said, taking the bag with who knew what in it from her and slipping her arm around his waist to take the weight off her sprained ankle.

They moved slowly through the thick green canopy of pines in companionable silence, the sound of the creek growing louder and louder.

WATER. REGINA COULD hear the rush of it, smell it in the air. She practically ran when, through the trees, she spotted the stream pooling in the rocks.

She heard McCall chuckle next to her. Her excitement at even the prospect of a bath must show. She hadn't even tried to talk to him about the commercial on their walk through the woods. True, she was almost too tired to argue about it.

"There's a nice pool the right depth through there," he said when they reached the river. "I'll wait for you over here. Do you know how to sing?"

The question took her by surprise. "What?"

"Sing. If you sing, I promise not to look. That way I'll know you're all right."

He actually looked serious.

She nodded, more intent on the bath than anything else. If she had to sing, she'd sing. She limped toward the spot where he'd indicated and began to sing, "My home's in Montana, I wear a bandana, my spurs are of silver, my pony is gray." Those were the only words she knew. She hummed loudly, turning to see what he was doing.

He had sat down under a large pine, arms folded, his back against the trunk, his hat over his eyes.

She stripped down, the retreating sun warm on her back. She knew the water would be cold.

She kept humming, wavering only a little when she stuck her foot in the water and felt how cold it was. Wading out into the water to where a circle of rocks formed a deep pool in the stream, she lowered herself in slowly.

It wasn't bad once you were all in. She breathed in the damp, pine-scented air and dunked below the surface to wet her hair.

J.T. PUSHED BACK his hat at the sound of the sudden silence. He sat up and looked toward the pool.

She surfaced just then, coming up in a shower of water, her hair a dark wave, her back slim and pale.

"Hum," he called to her and leaned back, pulling the hat down over his eyes.

This had been a terrible idea, he thought, listening to her hum, sounding happy. After that one glimpse he could imagine her sudsing her hair, chest deep in the creek.

The ache he felt surprised him. It was pure sexual. Hell, he was a normal, red-blooded male. But the desire to protect her was even stronger.

"Stopping humming to rinse hair," she called.

He counted to ten and was getting nervous, when he heard a splash. He waited for her to hum. Hum, dammit, woman.

"My home's in Montana," she sang and he realized she was closer than she'd been. She was no longer in the creek, but standing on the rocks directly in front of him.

He didn't dare move, listening as she sang softly, her voice growing nearer and nearer until he could smell her clean scent. Her damp hair brushed across his hand resting on his knee.

Still he didn't move, didn't breathe.

He felt her fingers on the brim of his hat, felt her shove back the brim.

He opened his eyes.

She had knelt down, and was leaning toward him so her hair hung down on each side of her face.

Her gaze was on his, bluer than his own eyes.

He let out the breath he'd been holding slowly, still not moving.

"Thank you," she whispered.

He let himself smile. "You're welcome," he whispered, afraid she would kiss him, afraid she wouldn't.

He sat up, determined not to let her distract him again. He had to have answers. Especially after the noose he'd found in the woods today.

"Reggie, I need you to be honest with me."

She leaned back, looking disappointed that he hadn't kissed her again.

"I have been honest—"

"Listen to me. We're a long way from the ranch, even farther from town, we don't have a way to get out of here except on horseback because the truck won't run." He paused, his gaze holding hers. "This is very dangerous, Regina."

Regina? She could hear the fear in his voice. It echoed in her chest and she had the feeling that something else had happened. "I thought Buck was bringing a truck back?"

His gaze bored into hers. "I'm afraid something has happened to him."

She swallowed, tears stinging her eyes at the thought. She liked Buck. He'd been kind to her. If something really had happened to him, it was her fault. He would never have left the mountain alone except for her. She felt sick.

"Regina, if you know what's going on here, I need you to tell me now," he said quietly.

She realized she liked it better when he called her Reggie. "You think I had something to do with Buck's disappearance, too?" She shook her head. "How is that possible?"

"You tell me. Is this really about a TV commercial?"

"Yes. What else?"

"That's what I was hoping you would tell me." Clearly he didn't believe a word she said. "Who did you meet in the woods last night?"

She blinked. "What?"

"I saw you meet someone in the trees outside the cabin last night," he said, sounding angry. "I heard you talking to him."

She was shaking her head. "Last night?" She remembered the only time she'd ventured past the porch. "I went to the bathroom."

"The outhouse is back the other way."

She felt her cheeks warm. "The outhouse was too far away. I went into the trees."

"Who were you talking to?"

She stared at him. "No one."

"I *heard* you."

328   Cowboy Accomplice

She thought for a moment, remembering walking around out there barefooted, stepping on prickly pine needles and twigs, muttering to herself…. "I was talking to myself."

"You weren't talking to Luke?"

"Luke?" she echoed. "I wasn't talking to Luke or anyone else."

He glanced toward the creek. "Did you happen to go in the men's tent for any reason?"

She couldn't believe this questioning. "No. Why would I?"

"I don't know. Someone ransacked the tent."

She stared at him in shock. First someone fixed the truck so it wouldn't run and now someone went through the cowhands' tent? Worse, J.T. was acting as if he didn't believe that Luke just quit without notice and rode out of camp before anyone else got up.

"You're worried because his horse came back," she said.

He nodded. "I found his saddle, tack and gear in the box at the back of the cabin. I think he just wanted us to believe he left. Or someone else did."

She stared at him. "Why would anyone do that?"

He shook his head.

"If something is going on here, it has nothing to do with me," she said, wishing he would believe that.

"All you want from me is a TV commercial?" he said.

She hesitated only a moment. "That's it."

J.T. had seen her hesitate. She wanted something else but he still didn't think it had anything to do with his cattle or this roundup. The way she was looking at him… "You promised you'd be honest. You want something else from me. What is it?"

"I want to learn to ride a horse."

"What?"

"I want to learn to ride a horse."

"I thought you were afraid of horses?"

She nodded, rocking back a little on her heels as she flashed him a knock-you-to-your-knees smile. "I was but after riding with you, I've changed my mind."

"If this is some new plot—"

"Isn't it possible that I might want to learn to ride a horse and it has nothing to do with the commercial?"

"No." He felt a chill. Dark shadows pooled under the pines, the sun gone. "We need to get back to camp and start supper."

Her disappointment was so acute and so clear in her face that he almost weakened. Rising, he helped her to her feet, wrapped one of her arms around his waist as he helped her back to the cabin.

"I think you underestimate me," she said as they neared the porch.

He hoped not. "You can take riding lessons when you get back to L.A.," he said, realizing that he liked thinking of her as a city girl who didn't fit in here, could never fit in here. It distanced him from her and he wanted that distance between them. She *was* a city girl and she *didn't* fit in here. It was that simple. And even if she did learn to ride, what would that change? Nothing.

"But what would be the point once you're back in L.A.?" he added.

"I watched you ride and I want to be able to feel that confident in the saddle," she said seeming to ignore his jibe.

He could tell she was still afraid of horses. Why the sudden interest in learning to ride? "I've been riding a horse since I was a toddler," he said, waiting for her to bring up the commercial. That was where she was going with this, wasn't it?

But she didn't.

Nothing about this woman should surprise him and yet it did.

"I could start learning to ride here in Montana and then continue with classes in Los Angeles."

"Do they have horses in California, let alone enough open space to ride them?" he asked facetiously as he wove his way through the pines.

"Have you ever been to California?"

"I've never felt the need to leave Montana."

"Well, you might want to someday," she said smoothly.

He didn't have to look to know she was arching one brow. He could feel the heat of her look and hear the invitation in her voice as clearly as if it had been engraved and hand delivered. And he cursed himself silently for kissing her earlier. Who knew what he'd gotten this woman thinking now.

"In the meantime, would you teach me to ride?" she asked.

"What?" He knew he must sound like a moron but keeping up with this woman was giving him whiplash. Would he teach her to ride? He helped her up on the porch and looked into her face. Her eyes were that deep bottomless blue he was so fond of. "Hell, no. What do I look like? An equestrian center?" But even as he said it, he realized it wasn't such a bad idea. She might have to ride out of here. And soon.

What would he do if Buck didn't return? He shoved the thought away. He knew Buck. If there was any way in hell, the old foreman would be back.

"Did you forget that I have six hundred head of cattle to round up and get out of these mountains before the snow falls?" he demanded.

"Sorry, I just thought when you weren't rounding up cows…"

"I need to get dinner going," he said over his shoulder. "The men will be coming in hungry."

She still didn't say anything as she went inside. He heard the rattle of pots and pans as he gathered an armload of firewood.

He could hear the low of the cattle just over the hill and knew the men wouldn't be far behind. He just hoped to hell no more of them went missing. He wondered which one had hidden the gun in the tent fold. More important, why.

REGGIE LOOKED UP as J.T. came through the door. She had a fire going in the woodstove and was peeling potatoes. He looked worried. "What's wrong?" she asked.

He shook his head and took the peeler from her and showed her how to use it correctly.

"Thanks," she said. It worked much better the way it was supposed to be used.

He sat down at the table across from her and leaned toward her before glancing toward the lower bunk bed. "You have some sort of identification with you?"

She told herself she shouldn't be surprised. But it bothered her that he didn't trust her. Okay, maybe she could understand his lack of faith, all things considered. But since when did going after what you wanted automatically make you a liar and a thief and whatever else he thought of her?

She got up and went to the bunk, found her red

leather purse in her suitcase and took out her wallet. She handed it to him without opening it.

He held the wallet in his hand for a moment, his eyes on her. She stood, feeling like a child before the principal as he slowly unzipped the small leather wallet. She watched him flip through it, stop on her California driver's license, then continue flipping through the plastic photo holders.

She felt as if he were going through her underwear drawer. Her whole life was in that wallet.

"You work for Way Out West Jeans," he said. "You never told me the company's name."

"You never gave me the chance."

He was still holding the wallet. "Who is this?"

She stepped closer to glance at the photograph of an attractive woman standing next to an amazingly handsome man. The photo was old, the edges worn and wrinkled. "My mother and father."

"Nice-looking people."

"My dad died when I was two. I was raised by my mother and grandmother." Why had she told him that?

"I'm sorry." He flipped back to her other photographs, glancing from each then to her as if he was looking for a resemblance.

"Friends," she said and reached for the wallet. "I was an only child."

He looked embarrassed for going through her things as he handed back the wallet. "I'm sorry I didn't believe you about the jeans."

She turned and went back to the bed to put her wallet away. He hadn't moved. She could practically hear him struggling to come up with something to say to her. No matter what he thought, she hadn't really lied to get this job, but she could see where he might think she had.

"I talked Buck into giving me the cook job and led him to believe I could cook, but I had nothing to do with the truck not running or anything else," she said as she looked over her shoulder at him.

He had turned and was taking a package of meat from the cooler.

She stared at his broad back realizing what he thought of her. That she was a cold-blooded bitch who used people to get what she wanted no matter the cost. Why should she care what he thought of her? Tears stung her eyes.

Worse, his opinion of her hit a little too close to home. "You have no idea how competitive the jeans market is or what it's like being a woman in that world."

He said nothing as he put the potatoes she'd peeled on to boil.

"This advertising campaign means everything," she said, surprised she was close to crying.

He turned then to look at her. *"Everything?"*

She swallowed. "It's critical to the future of the company and to my future." She stopped as she realized how desperate she sounded. "I thought a man like you could understand working hard for something you believe in."

"A man like me? You don't know me at all if you think I would use any means to get what I wanted," he snapped.

"I've had to work hard for everything I've ever gotten. You, McCall, know nothing about me or my life or what I've been through to get to where I—"

A tree limb brushed against the window. They both turned at the sound. Outside the wind had come up.

Pine boughs now swayed. One thumped softly against the window.

J.T. went back to his cooking. She turned away and wiped hastily at her tears, angry with herself for crying, angry at him for thinking so little of her.

He was wrong. She did know who he was. Not just the eldest son of Asa McCall and the man who ran the Sundown Ranch. She'd seen his kindness, his compassion, his strength and his determination. She'd seen how the men respected him. He inspired loyalty. The man could even cook.

She'd spent the years since college creating the Wild West to sell jeans. But now that she was *in* the Wild West, she saw that it was nothing like she'd thought. She'd fantasized about a cowboy's life for her jeans. But J. T. McCall was nothing like it and now she found herself fantasizing about the man.

She wanted to know this man better and it didn't have anything to do with the kiss earlier. Well, hardly anything.

But she also realized that by going after what she wanted—J. T. McCall's backside—she might have jeopardized his cattle roundup, not to mention ruined any chance of getting him for the commercial and made a lasting bad impression on him. She might also be responsible for whatever had happened to Buck.

She wanted a chance to make things right and gain J.T.'s respect, to show him she wasn't as inept as he thought she was. If she hoped to win his respect she'd have to show him that she could survive in his world and that meant being able to ride a horse. The mere thought terrified her. The only thing she had loved about being on his horse had been having J.T. behind her holding her. She tried not to think about riding alone, without J.T. not only behind her, but not even holding the reins.

J.T. would teach her to ride, she was pretty sure of that, and she was a quick study.

Of course, once she could ride a horse, he would send her down the mountain and she would lose any chance—as if she hadn't already—of changing his mind about the commercial.

But she had to prove to him that he was wrong about her. She would overcome her fears. Even if it killed her.

J.T. STUDIED EACH cowhand as he came into the cabin for supper.

Nevada Black stormed in first. "Someone ransacked our tent." He sounded angry as he took his chair.

J.T. nodded. "It was like that when I got back." He sat down at the table and began to pass the platters of food around. "Any idea what they were looking for?"

Nevada looked surprised by the question. "I guess that would depend on what was in the tent." He glanced at the other men.

Will Jarvis didn't even bother to look up. Roy glanced at J.T., then took the bowl of potatoes and began to dish up his plate. Slim and Cotton exchanged shrugs.

"Was there anything of value left in the tent?" J.T. asked and watched for a reaction. After his trip to the creek with Reggie, he'd hidden the 9 mm pistol in the cabin.

All the men shook their heads as they served their plates and began eating.

He'd hoped that one of them would admit to hiding the gun in the tent. The fact that no one did made him all the more worried that the danger was coming from inside not outside the camp.

"I asked you to keep in sight of each other," he said, but could see before anyone said anything that there had been times when the men had lost sight of each other. He could almost feel the suspicion, which alone could drive a wedge between the men and make matters worse. If that were possible.

"I was thinking it might have been a bear who messed up our tent," Roy Shields offered, his face coloring. It was the first time Roy had said that many words since J.T. had met him. "I saw prints on the way back to camp."

Cotton groaned. "I did have some cookies my girlfriend sent and they're gone."

"It wouldn't be the first time we had a bear in camp," Slim chimed in, the group seeming to relax a little.

"You all know this is bear country and we need to keep a clean camp," J.T. said and looked pointedly at Reggie.

"Sorry, Mr. McCall," Cotton said.

The talk around the table turned to cows and how many had been rounded up. Tomorrow they would begin gathering the rest of the strays. With luck they could be out of here the next morning.

J.T. noticed that the men all seemed tired while Reggie appeared to be getting her second wind. He didn't see that as a good sign.

He felt a little guilty for what he'd said to her earlier. He hadn't meant to come down so hard on her. Maybe she wasn't responsible for the disabled truck, or for whatever had happened to Luke Adams, or Buck not returning yet. But he had a bad feeling that someone in this camp was and he feared it was the owner of the gun he'd found.

Chapter Nine

All the men cleared out right after dinner, including J.T. Regina could hear some of the men standing around the fire, a couple of them talking quietly. She could see the flicker of the campfire through the window and their silhouettes.

J.T. wasn't one of the men standing around the fire. She wondered where he'd gone. She wished he'd stuck around. She'd hoped to talk to him. It dawned on her that if he continued to be suspicious that she was behind the things that had been going on in the camp, he wouldn't be looking for the real culprit.

She'd seen how worried he was about Buck. She hoped he was wrong and that the elderly foreman was just running late for some reason. She couldn't bear it if anything happened to Buck because of her.

She finished the dishes and stepped out on the porch, needing a breath of fresh air. The bath in the creek had been wonderful. She felt like a new woman and smiled, remembering J.T. under that tree. His eyes were the palest blue she'd ever seen in a face that was rugged and so sexy it made her knees weak. J.T. had insisted on wrapping her sprained ankle, which felt much better.

She heard someone approach from the darkness of the pines and knew without looking that it was him.

"Come on," J.T. said and motioned for her to follow him.

She didn't question where they were going, just stepped off the porch, glad for his company tonight. She followed him along the dark edge of the cabin on the side away from the campfire, away from the men. Her ankle ached, but she wasn't about to complain.

He stopped at the edge of the corral. She saw that he'd moved the other horses into the corral next to it.

Stars popped out in the clear midnight-blue sky over the tops of the pines. Tonight the sky seemed even bigger, the stars brighter. Or was it just being here with McCall? She felt awed, humbled under such a sky, everything that had motivated her to this point in her life seeming insignificant.

"The first thing you need to learn is how to saddle a horse," he said quietly as he picked up his saddle, which was straddling the corral fence, and shoved it at her.

Her knees practically buckled. The saddle was heavy, much heavier than she'd expected. She could feel his look of disdain and hurriedly righted herself, hefting the saddle a little higher, getting under it. She'd be damned if she'd drop it.

She followed him over to where he had his horse tied to the corral railing.

"It takes a little effort to get the saddle on," he said.

She imagined so given that she was way down here and the horse's back was way up there. She took a breath and tried to lift the saddle up and onto the horse's back. The saddle went over the top, almost taking her with it.

He retrieved the saddle and handed it to her without a

word. This time she got the saddle in the right place and practically swelled with pride at her accomplishment.

He straightened the saddle and proceeded to show her how to cinch it down and put on the bridle.

The horse, of course, moved away, snorting and giving her a look that said, over his dead body. She grabbed the rope Killer was tied to and pulled the beast closer. She refused to groan. At least out loud.

"Good job. You're stronger than you look," J.T. said, with maybe a little admiration in his tone, when she'd finished. "Okay, let's adjust the stirrups. It's time to get on the horse."

Her heart was thundering in her chest, her hands shaking as she took the reins he handed her.

"Don't drop these. This is how you control the horse, okay?"

She nodded, staring at the horse, remembering that feeling of being out of control when she was astride the monstrous thing. She swallowed and repeated her resolve to learn to ride.

Reaching up to grab the saddle horn, she put her foot into one of the stirrups and pulled herself up, swinging her leg over, grinning in surprise to find herself astride the horse.

McCall smiled.

The horse shuddered and hopped over a few feet to the side. She quickly dropped the reins and hunched over the saddle horn, gripping it with white knuckles.

She heard J.T. groan.

"What did I tell you about the reins?" he asked handing them to her again.

"Don't drop them."

He nodded and looked up at her, shaking his head as if she were hopeless.

He got the horse moving and showed her how to hold the reins in one hand and lay them to one side of the horse's neck. To her amazement the horse turned.

"Good," he said.

She tried turning the horse the other way. Shoot, it was like driving a car. Kinda.

"Okay, walk him around the corral." McCall climbed up on the corral to watch.

She rode around the corral and even let go of the breath she'd been holding when she didn't immediately slide off. Or get bucked off.

After a dozen laps, she brought the horse to a stop next to J.T. She couldn't see his face in the darkness but she could feel his gaze.

"Good job. How's the ankle?"

"Fine," she lied.

"Right. Better call it a night."

A twig cracked off in the woods behind them. The horse shuddered. J.T. brushed her leg as he steadied the horse.

"Okay, let's see you get off by yourself," he said quietly as if he was listening to something beyond them. "Think you can get down and unsaddle him?"

She nodded. The horse felt warm against her calves. She reached down to run her hand over his neck. Nice boy. It surprised her. She didn't want to get down yet. The truth was, she didn't want this time with J.T. to end.

"You never told me how he got the name Killer," she said, remembering just what she was sitting on.

J.T. drew his attention back to her. "His full name is *Lady* Killer."

"Why would you— You were just trying to scare me?"

"I was angry with you for taking off by yourself. I was trying to teach you a lesson."

"I'm sorry." She really meant it. "I didn't realize when I talked Buck into hiring me as your camp cook the trouble I was causing."

"I know."

"I know you're worried about Buck," she said. "Can't you ride down and check on him?"

J.T. shook his head. "I can't leave here."

"But don't the men know what to do while you're gone?" She could feel his gaze on her. She knew what she was suggesting. If he went, he'd come back with a four-wheel-drive truck and insist she leave. Any chance she had of talking him into the commercial would be over. "I'm worried about Buck, too."

J.T. THOUGHT SHE couldn't surprise him. He looked up at her. She didn't look afraid of the horse anymore. She seemed to have forgotten that she was even on it. But he feared there was much worse in the night to be afraid of.

She swung down out of the saddle and reached for the ground with her foot, the one attached to the sprained ankle. The moment it touched earth, she fell backward.

He caught her, his hands curling around her waist, keeping her close. Past her, he could see the campfire through the pines but no one around it. Earlier all five men had been standing around it. The fire had burned down to glowing coals now. Everyone had gone to bed. Maybe.

"If I left and came back with a truck you'd be free

to go search for another jeans model," he said quietly as she turned in his hands to face him.

She shook her head and smiled ruefully. "Anyone else would just be settling."

"I thought this was your big chance, that it meant everything to you."

"There'll be other commercials," she said, her voice wavering a little.

He wanted to believe her. "This cowboy thing was your idea?"

She nodded. "Most of our models are professionals who look like...models."

He knew without asking. "You have a deadline coming up soon?"

"It doesn't matter."

Of course it mattered. He got the feeling that if she blew this assignment, it would have very bad consequences on her career and he knew how much her career meant to her. Everything, she'd said.

"Ride out in the morning," she said now. "I can make breakfast for the men. Hey, I might surprise you."

He could count on that. He laughed softly and pulled her closer. "I can't leave you here," he whispered against her mouth. "It's too dangerous."

REGINA THOUGHT SHE heard a noise in the darkness over the trees. It sounded like the crack of a twig, only this time it was closer. Much closer.

He must have heard it, too. He drew back. "Go to the cabin." He dropped his voice. "Keep the door locked."

If he was trying to scare her, he was doing a darned good job of it. She hurried back to the cabin, taking the path on the campfire side this time, her ankle aching badly now. She heard the murmur of voices in the cowhands' wall tent, but saw no one.

The porch side of the cabin was dark. She hurried along the worn boards to the door. She'd left the lantern on in the cabin and was welcomed by its warm glow as she rushed inside. Because the cabin was small and only one room, she saw at a glance that it was empty. Hurriedly, she locked the door behind her and stood for a moment trying to catch her breath.

J.T. said he couldn't leave because of her. Because it was too *dangerous*. What did he mean by that? Surely he wasn't just trying to scare her into giving him the distributor cap from the truck. She wouldn't put it past him. After all, he'd told her his horse's name was *Killer*.

But they'd both heard something out in the woods. And Luke's horse had come back, his saddle and gear stuffed in a box outside the cabin to make it look as if he'd left. Had that been Luke out there spying on them? Listening?

She touched her tongue to her lips and hugged herself, still excited by the horseback ride and the kiss. She must be losing her mind. But then so must McCall. How else could she explain the kiss? How did she explain any of J.T.'s kisses, she thought with a sigh.

With only towels on the windows, she felt too vulnerable with the lantern on. She went to the bunk, found her small flashlight and extinguished the lantern. For a few minutes, she stood in the dark, watching the gap between the window frame and the towel. Nothing but tree limbs moved beyond the glass.

She turned on her flashlight and put more wood in the stove. She wasn't tired at all—not after that long nap she'd had.

Was she really resigned to finding another model for her jeans commercial? If she was trapped up here much longer it wouldn't make any difference. Unless she had a model by the end of the month, she could just kiss the promotion goodbye. But so much more had been riding on this advertising plan. She tried not to think about it.

She couldn't search for another cowboy posterior until she could get off this mountain. But she knew what she'd told McCall was true. She'd just be settling if she chose another cowboy. She would always know that she'd gone for second best—and that had never been her style.

So why wasn't she in a complete panic? She told herself it was because there was nothing she could do, but she knew there was a lot more to it. McCall had changed everything. The six-foot-four man with blond hair and blue eyes and the best behind she'd ever seen had spoiled her for another cowboy. Or another man.

She listened, hoping she would hear his footfalls on the porch soon. She was worried about him. If Buck didn't return soon, what would J.T. do? She knew he was trying to get as many cattle rounded up as possible but he seemed…scared. Not for himself but for her and his cowhands. And she knew him well enough to know that J. T. McCall wouldn't scare easily.

She thought about everything that had happened at the cow camp. None of the incidents should have had him that frightened. There had to be more going on than he'd told her.

J.T. WALKED THE perimeter of the camp, telling himself the sound he'd heard was a deer or an elk. He circled back to the corral, the camp quiet, and unsaddled his horse and carried the saddle to the big tent.

On the way, he looked in on the cowhands.

All five cots appeared to be occupied. He closed the tent door, sure at least one of men had seen him checking on them. Will Jarvis. Was he awake because he'd just climbed into his sleeping bag?

The campfire had burned down. No light burned in the cabin. Maybe Reggie's walk had been good for her, made her too tired to do any roaming tonight.

But still he had to go check on her. He left his saddle in the tent and walked toward the cabin feeling strangely vulnerable because of her. She was his Achilles' heel. He wanted desperately to go look for Buck, but he couldn't leave her. Nor was he sure he could protect her.

The men would take care of themselves as best they could if they had to. They'd known what they were getting into when they'd signed on. There was always some danger involved whenever you were this far up in the mountains. And they could all ride. Any one of them could get out of here in a matter of hours by horse.

But Reggie… He hated to think how ill-equipped she was to survive here. Especially since she didn't ride a horse and he could tell that her ankle was hurting her more than she wanted him to know.

He reached the cabin and tapped softly on a windowpane, waited and tapped again. He wasn't about to go to the door. The last thing he could trust himself not to do would be to go inside where it was warm, where Reggie would be possibly wearing that heart-stopping negligee—

Her face appeared in the window, startling him. She looked pale.

"Are you all right?" he mouthed.

She nodded and gave him a smile. "You?"

He had to smile. "I'm fine. Did you bolt the door?"

She nodded again and motioned did he want to come in?

He shook his head a little too vigorously because she laughed. "Good night."

"Good night," she mouthed back. She did have a great mouth.

He quickly turned and walked toward the tent, smiling to himself.

Now if Buck and Luke Adams would just show up. But he knew he wouldn't stop worrying until this roundup was over, until Reggie was safe, until he knew who had sabotaged the truck and killed the cows.

He wished a cell phone did work up here. He would call the ranch and see what had happened to Buck.

But a phone call wouldn't solve the mystery of what had happened to Luke. J.T. thought the cowhand had left in the middle of the night because he'd realized he'd made a mistake by coming back here, the memory of what had happened nine years ago too much for him.

But with Luke's horse returning, his saddle and gear stuffed in the box behind the cabin, J.T. was worried that Luke hadn't left running scared. Luke hadn't even left under his own power.

J.T. stopped to listen to the night. Hearing nothing unusual, he stepped into his tent and tied the canvas door closed. He pulled off his boots and jeans and crawled into his sleeping bag, knowing he wouldn't get much sleep tonight.

As he closed his eyes, he listened for the sound of a truck coming up the mountainside. Prayed for it. What he wouldn't give to see Buck's weathered old face right now and know he was safe.

Just before daylight, J.T. heard a sound that bolted him upright in bed. A terrified shriek.

J.T. pulled on his boots and dove from the tent wearing only his long underwear. It took him a moment to realize the sound hadn't come from the cabin where he'd expected it had.

The wall tent door next to his flew open, the air filling with cries and cussing as the men lunged out into the darkness half-dressed.

"What is it?" J.T. demanded as everyone circled, Roy snapping on a flashlight and shining it on Cotton.

"Rattlesnake," Cotton said from between gritted teeth and leaned down to pull up the leg of his long underwear. "The son of a bitch got me."

J.T. stared at the bite mark in the glow of the flashlight. There weren't any rattlesnakes up this high in the mountains. Especially in October. He could feel everyone looking at him, no doubt thinking the same thing.

"What's wrong?" Reggie called from the cabin porch, sounding scared. "McCall?"

"Go back in the cabin! I'll be there in a minute," J.T. hollered back. He swore as he turned to go out into the trees. He picked up a limb and returned. Roy handed him the flashlight without a word. Carefully, he stepped into the tent.

The flashlight beam illuminated only a small circle of golden light. He quickly shined the light around the tent, the beam skittering over the canvas floor. No snake.

Gingerly, he moved along the cots, shaking out each sleeping bag. He hadn't gone far when he heard the distinctive rattle and froze.

Leaning down slowly, he shined the light under the cots. He could hear the men outside, talking among themselves, still sounding scared, high on adrenaline, all but Cotton glad it hadn't been them.

The light picked up a pair of eyes, prehistoric looking. The large greenish-colored snake was coiled in the corner behind a duffel bag.

He stepped closer, shoving the cot and the bag aside. The tent filled with the sound of the deadly rattle as he moved nearer, the limb ready.

The snake struck, lunging its long thick-scaled body at him. He dodged to the side and trapped the snake against the side of the wall tent with the limb.

After several attempts, he was able to pin the snake's head so he could reach down and grasp it behind the head.

It was a big heavy prairie rattler, a good five feet long. Lifting it, he carried the snake out of the tent. The men all stepped back, giving him a wide berth as he took the snake deep into the woods. The beam of the flashlight bobbed ahead through the darkness, the snake growing heavy, his fingers fatigued from the pressure needed to keep the reptile from biting him.

In the quiet darkness away from the camp, he finally released the snake. Someone had to have brought this snake up the mountain, kept it hidden outside of camp and then put it in the tent tonight. To what? Scare the men? Or scare him?

J.T. swore. Well, he was scared and angry. He watched the snake slither away into the trees, following it with the flashlight beam, trying to understand what the hell was happening in his camp.

Then slowly, he turned back, studying the ground in the thin light, looking for a sign that anyone was camped nearby. Any sign that they weren't alone up here.

But the only tracks in the soft earth were his own. When he'd ridden the perimeter of the camp, he hadn't found anything either. All of which led him to believe the one thing he had feared from the beginning, that the trouble was coming from *within* his camp. One of his own men was doing this.

He told himself that so far it had just been pranks. No one had been killed. At least as far as he knew. The men had ridden up separately to the line shack. Any one of them could have brought the snake, kept it hidden out in the woods in a container and then let it loose in the tent tonight. But if that was the case, the fool had taken the chance that he might be the one who was bitten. Only a crazy person would take a chance like that.

J.T. thought of the only man he'd considered truly crazy. That man had died on this very mountain nine years ago. Killed by his own madness. Just the thought of Claude Ryan chilled J.T. to his marrow.

Was that what this was about? Someone wanted him to relive that cattle roundup of nine years ago, recreating it not exactly but just close enough that J.T. wouldn't know what was going to happen next? That he couldn't be sure it was really happening—until it was too late?

Nevada was inspecting Cotton's bite in the glow of the lantern inside the wall tent when J.T. returned. It was obvious the men had thoroughly searched the tent to make sure there were no more snakes, but no one was going back to sleep in the hours until daylight.

"He needs to get to a doctor," Nevada said, looking up as J.T. ducked in through the tent doorway.

Isn't this what J.T. had feared when the truck hadn't run? The men were looking at him, waiting for him to tell him which one of them could drive Cotton to the hospital.

"The truck doesn't run," he said. "Buck went down yesterday morning to get a part for the truck and bring back another vehicle."

Slim looked up in surprise. "What's wrong with it?"

J.T. sighed. "Someone took the distributor cap."

The men all looked at each other.

"When is Buck coming back?" Will asked.

Good question. "He should have been back by now," J.T. said. He had to be straight with them. If he was right, they were in danger. No cattle roundup was worth getting men killed.

"Any of you who want to leave, I understand," he said. "We'll round up what cattle we can this morning and then herd them down this afternoon for anyone who wants to stay."

"What about the strays?" Nevada asked. "There must be a good fifty head out there."

"We'll have to leave them," J.T. said, his mind made up. "We head out by ten. That way we can reach the ranch by early afternoon." Unless someone tried to stop them. He just prayed that nothing else happened between now and then.

Reggie would have to ride down. With her sprained ankle, it would make it difficult—and painful, but there was no other way. He just wished he had a horse up here that was more suitable for a rank beginner. But they would be trailing the cattle out, moving slow. And the woman had grit.

He looked at Cotton. "You think you can ride out now?"

Cotton nodded. Clearly he just wanted away from here—and to get medical attention, even though few people died of snakebites. But J.T. knew they were painful and could make a man really sick. He didn't want to take any chances. He had a first-aid kit in the cabin, but nothing for rattlesnake bites. He hadn't thought snakes would be a problem since there weren't any poisonous snakes at this altitude.

"I'll go with him," Slim said, sounding upset and scared.

"What about the rest of you?" J.T. asked, studying the men's faces in the lantern light. The rattlesnake hadn't been an accident. Like him, they were probably wondering who'd put it in the tent and why. Was Cotton the intended victim or one of them?

Will, Roy and Nevada looked at each other, suspicion in their expressions, but no one else appeared to be leaving.

J.T. tried to hide his relief. Part of him wanted to send them all out with Cotton, but he suspected that whoever was doing this would just be waiting up the road for him. And then there was Reggie. She had no idea what she'd blundered into. These men would have at least heard about what had happened up here nine years ago and maybe suspect it was happening again. Reggie didn't have a clue.

"Make sure Cotton gets to the ranch," he said to

Slim. "One of my brothers will take him to the hospital from there and see that you are both paid."

Slim nodded and glanced around the tent, his fear almost palpable. J.T. understood a healthy fear of snakes, but clearly Slim was more afraid of the men with whom he'd been sharing the tent.

J.T. watched Slim pick up both his gear and Cotton's, then duck out the tent door to go saddle their horses. Slim was practically running to get out of camp.

Is that what had happened to Luke? Had something scared him away as well? Something that reminded him of nine years ago and what had happened? But a man wouldn't leave his gear or his saddle or his horse.

J.T. glanced at his watch. "I'll get breakfast going." It would be light in a couple of hours and none of them would be able to get any sleep anyway. "Thanks for staying on."

He ducked out the tent door and walked to his own to finish getting dressed. He could hear the men rustling about in the other tent. No conversation now. They would all be leery of each other. Probably for the best, he thought. They would be watching each other like hawks, making it hard for one of them to pull another stunt like the snake.

Outside again, J.T. walked up to the corral as Cotton and Slim were getting ready to leave. He pulled Cotton aside, the one cowhand he knew and thought he could trust. "When you get to the ranch, would you ask my father to send Cash up?"

Cotton's eyes widened a little at the mention of the sheriff's name. He nodded and glanced warily over at Slim.

"Good luck," J.T. said, hoping neither of them needed

it. As they rode away into the darkness, he fought the fear that neither of them would ever reach the ranch.

If Buck had made it that far, even if he was injured, one of J.T.'s brothers would have driven up to make sure everyone was all right and give him the news about Buck.

That meant Buck had never reached the ranch.

With growing dread, J.T. headed for the cabin. Lantern light bled from the small paned windows. He moved toward the light and Reggie, anxious to see her. He couldn't help but think about what would have happened if the snake had been put in the cabin instead of the men's wall tent.

Chapter Ten

Regina had the fire going in the stove when she heard J.T.'s footfalls on the porch. "Come in," she said at his soft knock. He looked horrible. Her heart lurched at the sight of him. "What's happened?"

"There was an accident. Cotton was bit by a rattlesnake."

A rattlesnake? She shivered.

"Slim is riding out with him." He moved to the stove, warmed his hands. She could see that his hands were steady but he was obviously shaken. It had been one thing after another. First the truck not running, then Luke disappearing and Buck not returning. Now Cotton and Slim were leaving?

"Someone put the snake in the tent," he said, his voice so low she had to lean toward him to hear it.

"Why would someone do that?" she asked horrified.

"Maybe as a prank," he said. "Maybe to sabotage the cattle roundup." He shrugged. "I've decided to move the cattle down today."

"You'll have them rounded up by then?"

"Enough of them," he said. He sounded weary. And worried. "I'm sorry about your ankle, but you're going to have to ride a horse out of here, Regina."

Regina? He must be serious. She nodded. "I'll do whatever you need me to do."

He smiled at that as if he wished she'd done that in the beginning. So did she. Coming up here had been a mistake. McCall was right about that. She was no closer to signing him to the advertising contract than she'd been on the highway days ago.

She would have to ride all fifteen miles down this mountain on a horse. She would have to return to L.A. defeated. She would never find another cowboy like J. T. McCall even if she had the time to look. She'd failed. But right now she was even more worried about Buck. "Maybe Buck will get back before we leave," she said, praying that would be the case.

J.T.'s look said she shouldn't count on that.

Her heart fell. Unexpected tears blurred her vision. "What do you think happened to him?"

McCall shook his head.

What was going on? "Are the rest of the men staying?" she asked, wondering how J.T. would get the cattle down if they all left.

"For the time being."

She reached for one of the large cast-iron skillets on the stove. "Should we start breakfast?" It wasn't light out and, according to her watch, it wouldn't be for several hours.

He nodded. "We'll get an early start, right at daybreak," he said almost to himself. "I want you to be ready to ride as soon as I return," he said to her.

She looked around the cabin. "What about my suitcase, my clothes?"

He shook his head. "I'll come back for everything once you're safe."

Safe.

He took off his coat, hung it by the door and set about making breakfast. She helped, working beside him, trying hard not to think about Buck. What had happened to him? What was going to happen to all of them before they got out of here? Worse, would whoever was doing this let them leave?

Will, Nevada and Roy came in and took their places at the table with barely a nod in her direction. They all ate, heads down, a jittery silence filling the room even though the food wasn't burned. But she knew just the sight of the four empty chairs made them all solemn. That and the fear that more of them would be missing if they didn't get out of here soon.

"You want me to try to get some of the other strays we saw down in that ravine?" Nevada asked. "I can catch up if you move the herd out before I get back."

J.T. shook his head. "Once we get the main herd down, I can come back for the others."

Will was shaking his head. "In a day's time you aren't going to be able to get back up into this country." He nodded at their surprised looks and motioned to his left leg, his hand going to his thigh. "A snowstorm is coming in. A big one. I have a bad leg. It's never wrong. The weather's about to change."

"Let's just hope we can get the cattle out before it hits," J.T. said.

Roy was quiet as usual, but when he did look up, Regina thought he looked worried.

She broke the awkward silence that followed by getting up to do the dishes. After a moment, the men all pushed back their chairs, brought their dishes over to her, then filed out. All except J.T.

"I want you to stay here. Keep the door locked," he said behind her.

She nodded, scared by the fear she heard in his tone. She kept washing the dishes so he didn't see that her hands were trembling. He'd warned her she was in over her head.

"I'll be back for you soon," he said but seemed to hesitate. "Will you be all right until then?"

"If you're trying to scare me—"

"I didn't mean to." He sighed and raked a hand through his hair. "You just need to be careful." He studied her face, looking worried that she might become hysterical at any moment. Not that she didn't have the potential.

"I'll be fine." But even as she said the words, she worried that she might be wrong about that. She wanted to throw herself into his arms. Just to be held for a moment and then she really would be fine. For the time she was wrapped in his arms anyway.

"Regina?"

Why didn't he call her Reggie? That would have made her mad, made her not want to cry.

He leaned in to look at her, his expression puzzled. He must have seen her trying hard not to cry. He made a face. "Don't…"

He put his arm around her awkwardly as if this man who could run a ranch, round up six hundred head of cattle and boss grown men around didn't have a clue what to do with one five-foot-six-inch woman.

She leaned into him, pressing against his broad solid chest. His arms came around her, pulling her to him with obvious reluctance.

She didn't care. She didn't even like him most of

the time but right now it felt wonderful just being held, being sheltered in all that warmth and strength, feeling safe, no longer feeling alone and scared.

He seemed to soften, his arms molding her to him.

He bent his head and she felt his breath in her hair. "Oh, Reggie," he whispered. "What am I going to do with you?"

He seemed to breathe her in, dropping his head to hers, his cheek against the top of her head. She was completely enclosed by his arms, his body, cocooned in his protective embrace. She couldn't remember ever feeling so safe. She would have stayed there forever.

But boots thumped across the porch outside. McCall opened his arms, took her shoulders in his big hands and held her in front of him at arm's length.

"Ready when you are," Nevada called.

"Give me a few minutes," J.T. called back, then seemed to wait until he heard Nevada's boots retreat back down the porch.

His expression softened as he looked at her. "Sit down. *Please*," he added. "I need to tell you something. I'm not trying to frighten you. But I think you should know this."

She nodded as she sat down, even more afraid of what he was going to tell her.

"Nine years ago three men came up with a plan to rustle my cattle," J.T. began, his jaw tight, his face pale. "The plan was to get rid of as many of my men as possible to make the odds better once we had the cattle down the mountain where they had semitrailers waiting."

She stared at him. This roundup had started with six men and was now down to three. "They killed them?"

He shook his head. "Only the ones they couldn't get

rid of other ways. They camped nearby and hit us at night, taking out the men one at a time, scaring some off, killing several. I didn't know what was happening. At first I thought the cowhands had just left." Like Luke, he didn't say but she heard it anyway. "The things that happened seemed like accidents," he continued. "Until I realized they'd disabled the truck. I set up a trap, caught them in an old cabin down by the truck where we used to keep supplies."

She held her breath.

"During the gunfight that ensued, a kerosene lantern inside the cabin was knocked over. The fire burned quickly, the cabin was old, the timbers dry. The men could have gotten out. But they wouldn't give themselves up."

"They burned to death?" she asked, aghast at the thought of being trapped in a cabin that was on fire.

"We found two bodies inside. The third man got away but we knew he was badly burned. We knew he couldn't have made it off the mountain alone."

"You never found his body?"

J.T. shook his head. "But we found some of his clothing and marks in the dirt where he'd been dragged off."

She grimaced. "By what?"

"A bear. A grizzly. There were prints in the dirt near the scraps of clothing we found."

She thought she might be sick. "I thought you said there weren't any grizzlies up here."

He shook his head. "I said the bear you fed pancakes to wasn't a grizzly." He stepped over to the woodstove to throw on another log. "There was an investigation nine years ago. My brother Cash was and still is sheriff so the state held the inquest. Legally, the case was closed because the three men were dead. There were semitrailers found near the county road on the way out of here where they'd planned to load the cattle."

She stared at his broad back. "Steal the cattle?"

He nodded.

"You think it's happening *again*," she said, shocked to realize that's exactly what he had to be thinking— and with good reason.

"The incidents are similar enough."

"But how, if the men are dead?"

He turned to look at her. "Someone connected to that old incident could be trying to get revenge. It's the only thing that makes any sense."

"But it wasn't your fault."

"It was my roundup. I'm responsible for everyone under my hire."

Like her. Except he hadn't hired her exactly and certainly didn't want her up here. She was beginning to understand why he was so upset, so worried. This was no place for a woman.

"If it really is about revenge, why has it taken them nine years?" she asked, not wanting to think about the spot she'd put J.T. in by being here, complicating things. And no wonder he'd thought she had something to do with what was going on. She shows up and look what happens.

"The time frame bothers me too," he said. "Why wait? Maybe because I wouldn't be expecting it, not after all this time." He shrugged. "I hope I'm wrong about what's going on up here. But in case I'm not, I wanted you to know."

She nodded, not sure how knowing this helped her. She'd been scared before. Now she was terrified. "You think they're hiding out in the woods like last time?"

If he was trying to keep her in the cabin, he didn't have to worry.

To her surprise, he shook his head. "I think the person doing this is here in camp."

She stared at him in shock. "There are only three men left."

He nodded and walked over to a cabinet in the corner. Opening it, he fished around in back.

To her amazement, he took out a gun.

"Have you ever fired a 9 mm pistol?" he asked, sounding hopeful.

She shook her head, hating to see the disappointment on his face.

"I'm not planning on you ever having to use it, okay? But I want you to know how—just in case."

She nodded as he pressed the gun into her hand. She listened as he instructed her on how to fire it. She wasn't sure what frightened her most. That he feared she would need it. Or that she might have to shoot someone.

As J.T. RODE out of camp with the three men, he couldn't shake the feeling that he shouldn't be leaving Reggie alone. Maybe especially with a gun. But he couldn't leave her unarmed and he had to get ready to move the cattle down.

He had thought about taking her with him but they had a long ride ahead of them later this afternoon and with her ankle, the ride would be painful enough without making her ride this morning as well.

The only way he could be sure she was all right would have been to stay with her. Since he couldn't do that, he hoped that by keeping an eye on the last three cowhands she would be safe. As long as he was right about the trouble he was having coming from within the ranks—not from the outside, then all he had to do was keep track of the men.

He had his rifle in the scabbard on his saddle. He noticed that the other men had their weapons as well as they rode out of camp.

He'd considered sending Reggie down the mountain with Cotton and Slim, but he knew he couldn't do that. Cotton was hurt and would be suffering the effects of the snakebite. Slim had been acting too scared. J.T. couldn't even be sure that Slim would stay with Cotton and get him to the ranch and medical help. And the truth was he didn't trust anyone.

At this point, he just hoped that with any luck, he would meet up with his brother Sheriff Cash McCall on the way down the mountain this afternoon. That is, if Cotton made it to the ranch with the message.

He tried not to think about the alternative. Just as he tried not to dwell on getting Reggie off this mountain. He couldn't ride double with her. Not twenty miles. She would have to ride her own horse and no matter what she said about wanting to learn to ride, he had seen how afraid she was of horses. As long as she didn't do anything foolish—

He groaned. What could have been more foolish than following him up here in the first place? At least with everything going on, she'd given up on the commercial. He supposed that was something.

Ahead, Slim and Will cut into the trees to pick up three stray cows. He looked around for Roy. He didn't want to lose any more men. Nor did he want any of the three to double back to the cabin. With relief, he saw Roy through the trees, rounding up several more cows.

On the mountain below him, the main herd milled in the large meadow where he and the men had left them yesterday. Their coats shone in the sun, a dark rich brown and stark white. He'd been around cattle all his life but right now they were as beautiful as anything he'd ever seen. He loved this way of life. Anger boiled up in him at the thought that someone was trying to take it away from him—and using his men to do it. Just like last time.

He told himself that by this afternoon he would have the cattle and the crew back at the ranch. If he could just hold things together until then. He headed into the trees to cut a couple of strays back toward the herd, anxious to get back to Reggie and head down the mountain to the ranch.

He couldn't wait to see the ranch house where he'd been born and raised. Only a few days ago, he'd been glad to leave. With his father Asa McCall acting strangely, his mother Shelby back from the dead, Dusty mad and pouting, Brandon stuck on the ranch working to pay off some gambling debts, Rourke away on his honeymoon, Cash living in town and keeping busy being sheriff, J.T. had wanted as far away from the ranch as he could get.

But even with the craziness at the ranch, J.T. would give anything to be riding up to it right now. He had half a million dollars worth of beef to get off this mountain. The Sundown Ranch was a working ranch that depended on the sale of the cattle each year to keep going.

He had to get the cattle down. And, he reminded himself, maybe whoever was behind the incidents would quit now that they were moving the cattle down. No one had been seriously hurt. This time. So far.

Right. He thought about Buck. He couldn't be sure that was true. Worse, as he watched the cattle milling below him, he couldn't shake the feeling that the incidents hadn't been random, that they were leading up to something bigger. He hoped to hell he was wrong.

The one thing he couldn't ignore was the chance that whoever was doing this had the same plan Billy Joe Duncan, Leroy Johnson and Claude Ryan had had nine years ago.

The only one he'd known was Claude Ryan. Clearly, it had been Claude's plan and he'd found two men to help pull it off. With Claude it had been personal. Claude had been nurturing his grudge against J.T. since they were kids.

He'd died trying to even some score that J.T. had never even understood. It was Claude's face J.T. saw in his nightmares. Claude on fire, his face melting in the flames at the window, his gaze filled with hate as he screamed that he would kill J.T.

That kind of hate scared J.T. more than he wanted to admit. Fueled by that hate and madness, was it any wonder that Claude had been the one who'd escaped the burning cabin and had dragged himself partway down the mountain?

J.T. couldn't imagine the last hours of Claude's life. Had he still been alive when his body had been dragged off into the trees by the bear to be devoured?

Not even Claude deserved that.

REGGIE HAD JUST finished the dishes and packed the necessities for the ride down the mountain. She glanced at her watch, anxious for J.T. to return. It seemed like weeks since she'd seen J.T. kneeling beside her rental car, changing her tire. Changing her life, she thought.

Her head snapped up as she smelled it. She had gotten one of the windows open a crack earlier when she was doing the dishes. Now she wasn't surprised to see smoke blowing in. She could hear the flames licking at the dry wood. Her heart leaped to her throat. The cabin was on fire!

Fire had killed the three rustlers and now the line shack was on fire. Her mind raced. Was it possible she could put the fire out? With what though?

She could hear the crackling of the flames. Smoke billowed past the window and began to bleed through the cracks along the back wall. Her eyes and throat burned as the cabin began to fill with smoke. The whole place could go up in flames at any moment. She had to get out of here!

She limped to the bed, grabbed her jacket and saw the gun where she'd left it on the mattress. As she reached for it, she knew the fire was no accident. Someone was trying to scare her. Or kill her.

Scooping up the gun, she tried to remember everything J.T. had told her about firing it. Her hand shook and she hurried to the door, her ankle throbbing, but nothing like even the thought of being burned alive in this cabin.

She unlocked the door and tried to push it open. The door wouldn't budge. What was wrong? The door had always opened easily. Fear paralyzed her. She threw herself against the door. It still didn't move. Rational thought intervened. Someone had barricaded the door.

Smoke moved like fog around her waist-deep and quickly climbing. She had to get out. The windows were small and paned and her only way out. She hoped she could squeeze out that way. Otherwise, she was trapped in the burning cabin.

Regina rushed to the window farthest from the burning part of the building and began to break out the glass and wooden panes with the butt of the pistol. The glass was old and brittle, the wooden panes weathered.

The cabin was full of smoke now, her eyes blurred, she could barely breathe. Covering her mouth, she dropped the pistol out the window and then climbed after it. The space was tight. She was half out when she heard something inside the cabin fall with a crash as the fire spread.

Her hips stuck in the small window. With all the strength she could muster, she pushed against the side of the cabin, forcing the rest of her body from the window.

She tumbled headfirst into the dirt and lay there for a moment, the breath knocked out of her, coughing and crying. Her hips were scraped and cut from the broken glass. Her hands were scraped and bleeding.

But she was alive. She sucked in the fresh air as she picked up the pistol and scrambled to her feet. The cabin was ablaze, the heat and smoke forcing her back. She stared at the flames for a moment, then turned and looked around the camp, sensing that she wasn't alone.

She couldn't see him but she could feel him watching her. He hadn't expected her to escape. Or had he?

The air felt colder than it had earlier. She moved through the trees, keeping the pistol in front of her, wanting him to see it, wanting him to know she would kill him, praying she would have the courage to pull the trigger.

She stumbled and almost fell. Ignoring the pain that shot up from her ankle, the ache in her chest that made her cough and the tears that blurred her eyes, she ran for her life.

Chapter Eleven

J.T. spotted the fourth dead cow not far from the line shack. As he approached he caught the smell of charred fur. His heart dropped at the sight of the burned cow lying in the open meadow.

"Bastard," he breathed and dismounted. He'd seen this same work before so he wasn't surprised that the cow had been bludgeoned to death, then set on fire. He could still smell the accelerant used to start it. What a waste. And for what? Just to frighten him? Or to warn him? Either way, the person behind this had already succeeded at both.

He remembered a run-in he'd had with Claude Ryan years ago. Claude had been drunk and looking for a fight. He'd always had a chip on his shoulder when it came to J.T. They were the same age, had been in the same class all the way through grade school and high school.

But while J.T. had gone away to college, Claude had stayed and become a bouncer at the Cowboy Bar. In the years before that, Claude and his father had lived in an old house on the edge of town that always smelled of skunks. His mother had run off with a trucker when he was nine and his father had been killed in an accident at the sawmill where he'd worked when Claude was nineteen. Claude had blown what little money he'd gotten from the insurance company.

Claude had never made it a secret that he resented J.T. and felt everything had been handed to him while Claude had had to scrape and scrap for everything he got.

"Life isn't fair," he'd told J.T. that night their paths had crossed. "Why is it that you were born into a ranch and I was born into crap?" Claude asked him.

J.T. hadn't wanted to get into a fight so he'd tried to walk past Claude, but Claude had grabbed his arm.

"You don't deserve it," Claude blubbered. "Someday I'm going to take it all away from you." He'd let go of him then and stumbled back. "My kind of existence breeds killers. Did you know that? I have nothing to lose and you have everything. That scare you, J.T.? It ought to."

It hadn't then because he'd thought it was just the booze talking. Claude had been in his face numerous times over the years for little slights. If J.T. got better grades or made the football team and Claude didn't, Claude blamed his life circumstance—and he blamed J.T. as if he measured himself by J.T. and always found himself wanting.

As he looked down at the dead cow, J.T. wondered if stalkers didn't have this same type of obsession. They fixated on one person, blaming them for everything wrong in their lives.

But Claude was dead, he reminded himself. He'd seen the spot where the body had been dragged through the dirt and dead pine needles. He'd seen the grizzly tracks.

He'd looked for Claude's remains, planning to at least bury the man at the cemetery outside of town. But he'd never found them. Not unusual in a country this vast. The bear could have carried the carcass miles away.

He turned his horse away from the desecration and rode back toward the herd. This would be the last of the cattle rounded up. It was time to leave.

But he wasn't foolish enough to think that it was over. He feared what would be waiting for them on the trip down. The county dirt road was about fifteen miles away. That's where Claude and his cohorts in crime had had the rented cattle trucks waiting to be loaded with the stolen beef nine years ago.

What would be waiting for him this time?

THE WIND TORE at her as Regina struggled up the hillside. She thought this was the direction she'd gone the day she'd found the cattle herd, the day she'd found J.T. She prayed she wasn't going in the wrong direction.

At the top of the hill, she let herself look back at the cabin. The flames had almost entirely consumed it. Smoke billowed up, the wind tugging at the rancid dark cloud, stretching it, distorting it.

She fought to catch her breath, taking the weight off her ankle for a moment, easing the pain, as she searched for any movement, any sign that whoever had started the fire was chasing after her.

The wind whipped her hair around her face. She brushed it back, holding it, her eyes watering from the wind and the smoke. She didn't see him. But that didn't mean he wasn't there, hiding in the pines.

Turning, she began to run again. Her lungs ached and she knew she wouldn't be able to go much farther on her ankle. She didn't dare look back, stopping only when she couldn't run any farther and only then to lean against the large trunk of a tree, hidden. She hoped.

Her chest ached from the smoke, the fear, the running. She fought to catch her breath, trying hard not to think about who was behind her or what he would do if he caught her.

Right now all she wanted was to see J.T.'s face. To hear him come riding up. To be safe in his arms.

She tried to quiet her breathing, the pounding of her pulse, so she could hear if someone was coming after her. A hawk cried overhead, making her jump.

She knew she couldn't stop for long. He was probably tracking her. She had to keep moving. She peered around the tree, saw no one, and turned, stumbling as she caught movement in a stand of the white-barked trees nearby. Her heart leaped to her throat in that instant before she saw that it was just the wind picking up the leaves, sending them sailing in a golden whirl.

She stared at the stand of trees. They looked familiar. If she was right, the ravine was just on the other side and beyond that the large meadow where the cattle were gathered.

Catching her breath, she stumbled toward the golden leafed trees, praying she was right. The wind whipped at her hair, the cold air biting her cheeks. She could see the dark clouds through the tops of the trees, feel the temperature dropping.

The first snowflakes seemed flung from the sky overhead as the black clouds snuffed out the sun. She slowed, the day suddenly darker and colder and more ominous. She stopped, that feeling that someone was watching her so strong—

Through the stark-white branches of the trees, something blue fluttered beyond the golden leaves. The wind whirled snowflakes and leaves around her, but she could see that what she'd seen was a piece of blue cloth. J.T.?

He'd been wearing a blue shirt today.

She couldn't run anymore. Her ankle felt as if it wouldn't hold her weight.

"McCall!" she called, the wind sucking the name away. "McCall?" Only the wind answered with a groan as it thrashed the limbs of the pines and sent the last of the aspen leaves hurling into the air.

What if it wasn't McCall?

The snow began to fall harder. Holding the gun in front of her, Regina inched forward, catching fleeting glimpses of the blue fabric through the trees as the wind whirled leaves and snowflakes around her.

Her fingers ached from the cold and holding the pistol so tightly, but she didn't dare lower it, didn't dare take her finger off the trigger.

What if it was a trap? She caught the sound of cows mooing on the wind. Her heart began to race. It had to be J.T.

But why wasn't he moving? She stumbled closer, suddenly afraid of what she would find.

J.T. REINED IN his horse as he neared the herd. The wind had picked up. He felt the cold on his face and knew even before he turned that Will Jarvis had been right. A storm had blown in.

The sky was almost black as the snow squall scudded across the treetops toward him. It came on so fast, that one moment the sun was out, the day mild, and the next snowflakes began to fall. He'd seen storms like this come in before, without warning, often the snow falling while the sun was still shining.

But today the dark clouds swept over the sun, extinguishing it and the light. The snow began to fall harder as the day darkened, the landscape quickly changing.

J.T. looked around for his men. He'd seen Roy earlier cutting some cows into the herd. Through the snow, he saw Will Jarvis dismount and bend down as if to check one of the horse's shoes. Nevada Black was nowhere in sight. But he'd been near just moments before J.T. had spotted the dead cow and ridden over to it.

As he lifted his face to the wind, he smelled the smoke. At first he thought it was coming from the dead cow but the wind was blowing the wrong direction. He caught a strong whiff of it, his gut tightening at the horrible memory of the scent of burned flesh.

In an instant, the snow obliterated everything. He called to the men, his voice swept away by the wind and the whirling snow. He lost sight of them, of the cattle herd below him. But he could smell the smoke now, even stronger than before.

He turned his horse back toward the cabin, riding as fast as he could with the visibility quickly dropping to nothing.

The snow whirled around him, huge smothering flakes of ice and cold that turned his world white, making him quickly lose his sense of direction.

He'd heard stories all his life about ranchers who'd gone out to feed the cows, got lost in their own pastures and froze to death.

Some ranchers had a rope that stretched from their barn to their house so they could get back that short distance in a blizzard.

Oftentimes the only thing that would save a man was his horse—if his horse could find his way home even in a blizzard. Many a cowboy credited his horse for saving his life in a freak snowstorm.

Lady Killer had gotten J.T. out of some tight spots over the years. He hoped to hell he did now as he gave the horse his rein. The smell of smoke teased him through the whirling snow. Not the smoke of a wood-stove or a campfire. This was the smell of destruction, of burned belongings, of destroyed lives.

He pulled the brim of his hat down against the storm and rode blindly toward what he hoped was the cabin—and Reggie.

THE SNOWFLAKES WERE so thick, Regina lost sight of the blue fabric through the trees for a moment.

She could hear the cows mooing on the wind, but something else, something closer. She stopped. Over the roar of her pulse, she heard a creaking sound. She waited, heard the creak again.

Just a branch creaking in the wind. She took a few more steps and caught another glimpse of the blue fabric again through the snowstorm. If she was right, this was where she'd seen Luke's horse when it had almost run her down. That image of the terrified horse burned itself into her mind, frightening her even more as if this spot held some evil. An evil a horse would sense. And a city girl would not.

"McCall!" She moved like a sleepwalker through the falling snow, the dead wet aspen leaves sticking to her boots, her gaze locked on the spot of blue, a prayer on her lips.

The aspens gave way to large old pines. She rounded one of the ponderosas and froze. She'd been right about the piece of blue cloth. It was a shirt. The same color as the one J.T. had worn this morning.

The cloth flapped in the wind. A sleeve. She stepped around the pine tree, her scream lost in the storm as she saw what was making the creaking sound. A rope bit into the bark of a wide limb. From the rope hung Luke Adams, his feet dangling just inches from the ground, the noose tied tight around his neck, the rope over the limb creaking as his body swayed in the wind.

Chapter Twelve

She came out of the snowstorm in a blur of red. Just moments before, the wind had seemed to shriek and suddenly there she was, the gun clutched in her hand.

J.T. drew his horse up short, but Reggie still stumbled into the two of them. He had to grab her to keep her from falling, swinging down from his horse to hold her upright and gently take the pistol from her ice-cold fingers.

Her eyes were wide with terror, her face as white as the snow and twisted in a mask of horror. She was crying and shaking, her words making no sense to him as they tumbled out all over each other.

"It's all right, Reggie," he said softly, pulling her into his arms. She slumped against him and he pressed his face into her wet hair. Her hair smelled of smoke. "What happened?"

She leaned into him, taking huge gulping breaths, her body jerking with each sob, her words incoherent and lost in the storm. He strained to see past her into the snow, fearing what might be coming after them.

Two words registered. "He's dead."

J.T. felt his skin crawl. "Who's dead, Reggie?"

She took a shuddering breath. "Luke. I saw him. He

was—" She choked on a sob. "The cabin. He burned it down."

"Luke burned down the cabin?"

She shook her head. "Someone burned down the cabin. I ran. I was looking for you when I found—" Her eyes teared up again, she bit her lower lip. "Luke. He's in a tree." She pointed behind her.

Luke in a tree?

Her blue eyes were wide with fear as she pulled back. "He had a rope around his neck and he was—" She started crying again. "His eyes were bulging and his tongue—"

"Okay." He drew her back into his arms. "I need you to show me where."

She nodded against his chest. He brushed the snow from her hair with his hand and took off his coat and put it on her. He had to get her out of the weather and if he'd understood her, someone had burned down the cabin. That would explain the smoke he'd smelled earlier, the same scent as in her hair.

She brushed away her tears with the heel of her palm. Her lower lip trembled. Snowflakes caught in her lashes. But she straightened and started limping back the way she'd come. He needed her to be strong now and was for once thankful that she was the kind of woman who didn't let anything stop her.

He caught her hand, turned her to face him and lifted her up into the saddle. She didn't protest. Adrenaline pumping, he slipped his rifle from the scabbard and led the horse. Reggie's tracks hadn't quite filled in. He followed them into the stand of aspens, the same area where Reggie said she had first seen Luke's horse the day before.

The wind wasn't as strong back here in the trees, but still the falling snow whirled around him as they walked through the stand of now nearly bare aspens. Reggie sat on the horse, gripping the pommel, her gaze riveted to a spot beyond the grove.

The wind had torn the last of the leaves from the limbs. The white branches were dark against the snow, looking sinister as if reaching out at them as they passed.

As the aspen grove gave way to the dense pines, he saw Reggie glance over her shoulder, shudder, then straighten, shoulders back, stilling the trembling in her lower lip as she bit down on it.

He stepped into the pines, the rifle in the crook of his arm, the reins in his other hand. It was darker in here, more protected from the storm. The snow fell silently. Cold shadows hunkered under the wide pine boughs. Past the quiet, he heard a creaking sound. Reggie must have heard it, too. She tensed, making the horse shudder beneath her.

Still following her tracks, he moved through the pines until he saw something through the branches. A blue shirt. His heart leaped to his throat. He'd been hoping that Reggie was mistaken, that in her fear she'd only imagined that it was Luke. That he would find a noose like he had earlier; a tree branch with nothing hanging from it but the rope.

That hope evaporated the moment he stepped around the last pine and saw Luke. He turned away, sick to his stomach. What monster would do something like this?

The rope creaked on the limb and he saw something on the body…. "Stay here," he said to Reggie and walked the few yards to where someone had thrown the rope over the limb and hung Luke Adams. As the body turned in the wind, J.T. saw that something had been written on the blue shirt.

Stepping closer, he squinted in the falling snow to read the scrawled word. The ink had run but he could still make out the word "Traitor."

A chill, colder than the day, rattled up his spine. He stepped back wanting to distance himself from this horror, from the mind that conceived this type of retribution. He wanted to cut Luke down, but he knew the body would be safer where it was. It was high enough off the ground that most animals wouldn't bother it. There was no cabin to take it to. Luke would have to remain here until he could get back with help.

He turned and hurried back to Reggie. She no longer looked terrified, just numb, eyes glazed. He handed her the rifle. She took it, blinking as if coming awake. He swung up behind her on the horse and retrieved the rifle and reins from her.

Even if someone had burned the cabin to the ground, the wall tents might still be standing. He had to get her into some dry clothing. He had some for both of them in his tent.

As he rode back toward camp, the wind died down. Snow fell around them in a cocoon of dense cold white, but the visibility was better. He knew where he was and where he was going. But still he wouldn't be able to see anyone come out of the storm until it was too late.

He tried not to think past getting to the camp. He couldn't even be sure the tents would be standing, but if they were, he and Reggie would get changed into some dry, warmer clothing. And then what?

He couldn't think that far ahead, afraid they wouldn't

even reach the camp. He expected a surprise attack, someone coming out of the storm. Whoever had killed Luke was out there somewhere. All of this was just leading up to something more horrible. He felt it as clearly as the cold. It was only a matter of time before he crossed paths with the killer. J.T. was sure of that.

And J.T. had several huge disadvantages. He had no way of knowing what the killer looked like. And he also had Reggie. J.T. had no doubt that the killer planned to use both against him.

The killer had to be either Will, Nevada or Roy. Or all three of them. He wouldn't know who was innocent or who was guilty until it was too late.

He smelled the smoke first, then what was left of the cabin took shape through the falling snow. Only the hulking dark shape of the old woodstove stood in the ashes of what had been the line shack.

The smell reminded him of another burned cabin nine years ago. Except there were no bodies in the ruins this time. At least he hoped not.

As he and Reggie neared the camp, no one appeared from out of the falling snow. Wisps of smoke spiraled up from the ruins of the cabin, disappearing into the falling snow.

Fortunately, no trees near the cabin had caught fire and burned. Through the pines he saw with relief that both wall tents were still standing.

As he rode into camp, he noted that the corrals were empty, the gate open, the extra horses gone. Someone had let them loose. Before setting the fire? Or after Reggie had taken off?

No sign of the men. No fresh tracks in the snow. He rode up to the tents, heard a horse whinny and raised the rifle. One of the extra horses came out of the snow toward him, head down, walking slowly.

He handed the rifle to Reggie and slipped off the back of his horse. Taking the lasso he kept on his saddle, he moved toward the horse.

It was a horse named Silver, the gentlest of the bunch. Silver eyed him, no doubt afraid after the cabin fire. J.T. got close enough that he could loop the end over the horse's neck. He spoke softly, rubbing the horse's neck to soothe it, then tied the end of the lasso to a limb of a nearby tree.

Going back to his own horse, he helped Reggie down. She stood hugging herself, fear back in her eyes. He handed her the pistol and motioned for her to wait by the horse as he took a look in the tents.

She nodded, her fingers closing over the grip.

He took the rifle and looked in the cowhands' tent first, expecting to find their gear gone and them as well. Their gear was still there. Someone was lying on a cot in the far corner, Nevada Black's cot, his back to the door.

"Nevada?" he called.

No answer.

He stepped closer, reached out to touch the man's shoulder and saw the knife buried to the hilt in the man's chest. One hand was over the knife handle as if he had tried to pull it out.

The skin on top of the hand was scarred from where it had been burned.

J.T. jerked back his own hand, his breath coming hard, as he stared down at Slim Walker.

What was Slim doing here? And where was Cotton? J.T. stumbled back toward the door, sure now that neither of them had reached the ranch. That meant his brother Cash wasn't on his way up here.

He and Reggie were on their own.

J.T. scrambled out of the tent, afraid he would find Reggie gone. But she stood next to the horse, still hugging herself, still looking scared.

"What is it?" she asked, obviously seeing how upset he was.

He didn't answer as he checked his own tent, afraid he would find another body inside it. The tent was empty except for the two cots and his and Buck's gear.

J.T. ducked back out to take Reggie's hand and pull her inside, out of the snow and cold. He took the pistol from her and laid it on the cot.

"McCall." Her eyes shone. "What did you find in the tent?"

He wanted to lie to her, to protect her, but she had a right to know how much danger they were in. He also needed her to be strong and not fall apart on him. Better now though than later when they could be in a worse situation. "I found Slim. He's dead. Someone stabbed him."

"Slim? But Slim left with Cotton…." Tears spilled down her cheeks. "Cotton?"

J.T. shook his head, and putting down the rifle, stepped to her. Gently, he thumbed away the tears on her cheeks, then pulled her to him, wrapping his arms around her. "We have to get dressed in dry, warm clothing. We have to get out of here, Reggie."

She nodded against his chest, then pulled back.

He gave her a reassuring smile. "That's my girl." He found some dry clothing, handed it to her, and turned his back so she could dress as he put on a dry shirt and a heavy coat of Buck's. He would give Reggie his winter coat, a heavier one than he'd been wearing earlier.

He could hear her behind him dressing quickly as he picked up the rifle. She put on the coat he handed her over the flannel shirt and long underwear and wool pants. All were huge on her, but at least she was warm and dry now.

"Here," he said, handing her a pair of lined boots. "They're Buck's. His feet are smaller than mine. I think with a couple pairs of socks…"

She pulled on the socks, then the boots. He noticed that her hands were steady. He knelt in front of her and laced them. Feeling her hand on his cheek, he looked up at her. He met her gaze. In that moment, he couldn't be sure what either of them might say. She had to know that the killer probably wasn't going to let them get out of these mountains. Not without a fight.

He'd die trying to save her. He figured if she knew anything about him, she'd know that. "I'll go saddle the other horse," he said quickly and stood. "I'll be right outside."

"No, I'm going with you."

He started to tell her that she would be warmer in the tent, not to mention drier, but he could see by her expression that she didn't want to stay alone any more than he wanted to leave her.

She got to her feet. The high boots seemed to help her ankle.

He picked up Luke's saddle and tack from where he'd put it in his tent last night. She followed him outside. The snow wasn't falling as hard now. The wind had died and the silence was heavy and close. He kept his rifle within reach as he saddled Silver for Reggie.

She swung up into the saddle and he handed her the reins. She winced as she put weight on her bad ankle in the stirrups but said nothing as she watched the forest and the falling snow. He didn't have to ask what she was looking for.

There was one thing he had to check before they started down the mountain, although he knew what he would find.

The snow stopped falling almost as quickly as it had begun. Low clouds hung over the tops of the trees. The air was cold and wet and stung his eyes.

As he topped a rise, the wide open meadow stretched below him. The snow had been trampled, the dirt kicked up.

The herd was gone, just as he knew it would be.

REGINA STARED DOWN at the meadow where hundreds of cattle had been yesterday. The only sign that they'd ever been there was the disturbed earth and trodden snow.

"Where are the cows?" she whispered as her horse edged up beside his.

"Headed for the black market, I would imagine," he said and looked over at her. "I guess that's what they've been after all along."

"They killed Luke and Slim for cows?" she asked.

"Half a million dollars worth," he said.

She blinked in surprise. "I had no idea—"

He nodded as if he suspected she didn't.

"You have to go after them and stop them," she said with a fierceness that surprised her.

It must have surprised him, too. He smiled. "The only thing I have to do is get you to the ranch where you will be safe."

"But if they have your property—" She saw by his expression that he feared whoever had stolen the cattle wanted more than the cattle and ultimately the money. "If I wasn't with you, you'd go after them, wouldn't you."

He laughed softly. "Probably and it would be the stupidest thing I could do. I don't even know how many of them there are. I'd probably get myself killed."

She doubted that. J. T. McCall was a man who could take care of himself.

"Come on." He spurred his horse and started back the way they'd come, then cut through the trees away from the trail where the cattle had gone.

Her horse followed without her having to do anything and she was grateful. Her ankle ached and she felt chilled from earlier. She stared at McCall's broad back, thankful that he was with her. Another man might have abandoned her to go after his cattle. Actually, most men she'd known. A half million was a lot of money. She doubted McCall could spare it and she feared she was at least partly responsible for its loss. If he hadn't had to take care of her...

The rocking motion of the horse put her to sleep.

She woke with a start, almost falling off the horse. McCall had stopped. She stared into the pines, surprised how dark it had gotten.

Her rump hurt from the saddle and her ankle felt as if it were ten sizes larger than normal, the boot too tight now and cutting into her flesh. She was tired and hungry, thirsty and her hair stunk of smoke, reminding her of the fire, her skin grimy.

But none of that mattered in an instant as she watched

McCall motion for her to keep silent as he dismounted and, raising the rifle, disappeared into the pines.

J.T. HAD BEEN following a trail through the snow for the last quarter mile. Now he caught a whiff of campfire smoke on the breeze. A moment later, he heard a horse whinny ahead of him.

He moved silently through the fallen snow with the rifle ready, stopping behind one of the pine trees to listen. A horse whinnied just beyond a small clearing.

The moment he stepped around the wide branches of the pine tree, he saw a figure crouched over a small fire in a heavy coat with a hood, a coat he didn't recognize.

J.T. edged silently up behind the man. Snowflakes danced in the air drifting restlessly on a slight breeze. The ground around the fire was dark with footprints but beyond it everything was covered in a blanket of icy white.

He pressed the barrel of the rifle to the back of the man's head. "Move and I will kill you."

The man froze.

Slowly, J.T. stepped to the side until he could see the man's face.

"Take it easy," Will Jarvis said. "This isn't what you think."

"You know what I'm thinking?" J.T. asked, shifting the rifle barrel to aim it at Will's chest, his finger on the trigger.

"I'm FBI," Will said his voice sounding a little strained. "You probably don't remember me but I was on the case nine years ago."

J.T. couldn't hide his surprise. Something about the man had been familiar, something that reminded him of the horror of that unforgettable cattle roundup. He couldn't remember any of the FBI agents, who'd been called in because of a federal warrant on one of the men, Leroy Johnson.

He didn't remember Will Jarvis, but that didn't really mean anything given the condition he'd been in after what had happened nine years ago. "You have some sort of ID?" He kept the rifle on him.

"If you'll let me reach into my coat pocket," Will said.

"I can pull the trigger on this rifle before you can pull a gun," J.T. warned.

"I'm no fool." He reached slowly into his coat pocket and brought out his identification. He flipped it open. FBI. William Robert Jarvis. Special agent.

"So it was your gun I found hidden in the tent."

Jarvis smiled. "We all know agents don't carry a 9 mm, but yes, it was one of several I had hidden around the camp. I like to have back ups, plus this." He pulled out a knife and met J.T.'s gaze. "As I recall, this was Claude Ryan's weapon of choice."

J.T. shuddered at the memory and lowered the rifle as Jarvis slid the knife back into a sheath under his pant leg. "What the hell is going on?" Out of the corner of his eye, he could see Reggie waiting in the darkness of the pines, watching. She had the pistol in her hands, her gaze on Jarvis's back.

"I think you know what's going on," Will said. "Someone's been killing off your cowhands, getting rid of them one by one. I would imagine your cattle are gone as well." He nodded, seeing that none of that was news to J.T. "I can tell you don't want to believe who's behind it. You don't even like saying his name, do you?"

"Claude Ryan is dead."

"Is he?" Will said and chuckled.

J.T. stared at Jarvis, surprised how much he wanted it to be true. "Are you telling me he's not?"

The FBI agent shrugged. "*Someone* from that cattle roundup is alive. He's left a trail of dead plastic surgeons across Mexico. I followed that trail to your cow camp."

J.T. was shaking his head. "A grizzly got Claude."

"Something got him all right," Will said. "I would imagine it was one of his gang."

"The other two were dead inside the cabin."

Jarvis smiled. "You think it was just the three of them in it together?" He shook his head. "There were five of them, maybe more. The ones I know about are Claude Ryan, Leroy Johnson, Billy Joe Brady, Slim Walker and Luke Adams."

J.T. had known the last two names were coming as sure as sunrise. "You're telling me that Claude killed Luke and Slim."

"I didn't know they were dead for sure, but I figured he'd get them," Will said. "Even though Slim risked his life to save Claude—got his hands burned—Claude considered them both traitors because they didn't kill you when they had the chance."

J.T. looked to the pines where he'd left Reggie. "How do you know all this?"

"Some of it I've figured out over the past nine years. That first night in camp I heard Luke leave the tent. Him and Slim. I followed them, overheard them talking about Claude, both scared."

J.T. studied Will, having trouble believing what he was hearing and not sure why. "Why would Slim and Luke agree to work for me after what happened up here?"

"I suspect Claude was behind it somehow. I heard Luke say he knew they shouldn't have come back up into the Bighorns. Said it wasn't worth what they were being paid. Don't think they were talking about cowhand wages, do you?"

"No," J.T. said and looked over at Reggie.

"Why don't you invite her over to the fire?" Will suggested and smiled. He hadn't turned around but he'd known she was back there.

"We're not staying," J.T. said. Reggie was safer in the shadow of the pines with the horses. "If Claude is alive, why wait so long to come back?"

Will picked up a stick and stirred the dying embers of the fire. "He was badly burned, horribly disfigured. Took years of surgeries, most of them unsuccessful."

"Are you telling me the last one was successful?"

Will looked up at him. "You didn't recognize him, did you."

J.T. felt something stir inside him as he thought of the six men who'd been in camp.

"It seems all these years he's been planning to come back here and steal your cattle—only make it work this time," Will said.

"You think that's all he wants?"

Will Jarvis shook his head. "I think not. The man obviously has a hell of a lot of patience. Nine years. That's a long time to hold a grudge."

"Not for Claude. It's an obsession with him," J.T. said. "He's sick. He's wasted his life hating me. He's a pathetic coward. Look how many people he's killed and for what?"

Will said nothing, just stared into the flames.

Something about Will Jarvis made him uneasy, had

from the beginning. "I would think if you hoped to catch him, you'd be following the herd."

Will smiled at that. "Then you don't know Claude very well. He's not interested in the herd." He looked up then, meeting J.T.'s eyes. Claude had gray eyes. None of the six cowhands had gray eyes, including Will Jarvis, but with today's colored contact lenses…

"He'll be following you," Will Jarvis said. "But first he'll come for me. I've been dogging him for years. He knows he has to kill me or I won't stop."

"So Claude will come down this way?" This was the shortest route to the ranch. Claude would know that, too. He knew these mountains maybe better than J.T. did because Claude was often unemployed, camping out all summer, living off the land and some of the Sundown Ranch herd, while J.T. was working.

"I followed a set of tracks down here yesterday," Will said. "Obviously he knows you, figured you would come down this way. He thinks he knows what you're going to do before you do it. If I wait right here, I'll see him."

J.T. shook his head. "You're a sitting duck."

Will smiled. "I've been waiting for this day for more years than I want to count. You and the woman had better get moving. You can still make the ranch before dark if you hurry."

J.T. studied Will Jarvis in the firelight. "Don't underestimate Claude Ryan. It will get you killed."

Will grunted and stirred the fire with the stick for a moment before throwing it into the flames. "You just worry about your own neck and your girlfriend's." He reached down to touch the knife in the sheath at his ankle. "And hope that Claude finds me before he does you."

Chapter Thirteen

J.T. turned and walked back to where Reggie waited in the trees. He should have been relieved that there was an FBI agent here.

"I don't trust him," Reggie said after they'd gotten out of earshot.

"Neither do I," J.T. said quietly. If Jarvis was right, Claude had ridden the shortcut the day before. For what reason? Looking for a place to attack? And when had Will Jarvis gotten away to follow him?

They could reach the ranch before dark if they continued down the mountain the way they were headed. But with the storm and the low clouds, they were losing light fast. They would be easy pickings. And if Will Jarvis was right, Claude had already anticipated that this was the way they would come.

Not to mention that Jarvis could be behind them right now, following them, tracking them.

Not too far down the mountain, they ran out of snow. In good light, J.T. knew they could still be tracked even without the snow. He was counting on it getting dark before anyone would find them. He couldn't risk going for the ranch as badly as he wanted to.

He rode along the side of the mountain, weaving

through the trees, keeping just below the snow line to hide their tracks before he turned toward the rock rim high above them.

REGINA LOOKED UP at the band of red rock and realized that was where they were headed. Not the ranch. She'd been turned around since she got to Montana. Without an ocean nearby or any distinguishing buildings, she couldn't tell east from west.

But she was smart enough to know they weren't headed for the ranch. The ranch was down the mountain and they were headed up.

As J.T. dismounted at the foot of the wall of rock, she lost all hope of a hot bath and a real bed.

"We aren't going to the ranch," Reggie said as he lifted her down. "Sorry. Too dangerous. We'll leave before it gets light. Don't worry, by tomorrow morning you'll see civilization again."

She nodded. She ached all over and realized she could sleep anywhere. As long as she didn't have to ride a horse anymore today.

"Come on." He led her and the horses along the edge of the rock face.

The boots were too large and she stumbled several times and almost fell. Her ankle ached and she was limping badly.

"Here, take my hand," he said, removing her glove and enclosing her hand in his large one. His hand was warm and strong and she wished he would do the same with her entire body. She felt cold and so tired that picking up her feet took every ounce of her energy.

Finally, he stopped. In the last of the light, she could see that they were high above the valley. Lights glittered in the far distance. Her chest ached from the climb and sudden longing to be down there away from the cold and horses and killers.

"This way," McCall said, as if sensing her yearning for the city and everything she'd left behind. He led her and the horses through a narrow slit in the rocks. The space opened, a tree towering over their heads. J.T. shoved one of the branches aside, and leaving the horses, pulled her into what she realized was a cave.

Once through the small opening, he snapped on a flashlight and she saw that she could stand up. It was cold and dark in here but the floor was dirt and soft.

"Here," he said handing her the flashlight. "I'll tend to the horses and be right back."

He was good to his word. He returned with firewood and built a small fire in a corner near a crack in the rock. The smoke rose and disappeared out through the crack.

"Still cold?" he asked as she curled around the fire, unable to keep her eyes open.

"A little." The side of her body exposed to the fire was warm but her other side was cold. She kept turning like a chicken on a rotisserie but still couldn't get everything warmed.

"Here, lie down," he said.

She curled around the fire and felt him lie down behind her, curling his warm body around hers.

"Better?"

"Hmmm," she said and closed her eyes, the fire flickering on her face, the crackling of the flames lulling her.

"You did really well today," he whispered. "You're okay, Regina Holland."

She opened her eyes and smiled to herself before

closing them again and falling into a deep sleep. She didn't hear the scream that awakened J.T.

J.T. GOT UP, careful not to wake Reggie and, picking up the rifle, went out of the cave to the edge of the cliff.

The night was cold and clear. He wished to hell he was at the ranch and that Reggie was upstairs asleep in the guest bedroom, safe. But he knew he'd made the right decision to wait.

He let his gaze travel down the mountainside to where Will Jarvis had camped, not sure what he thought he might be able to see. Maybe the trees around the clearing on fire.

There was nothing but darkness. Nor did he hear another sound. He told himself that the scream he'd heard could have been a mountain lion. Men didn't usually scream like that. Unless they were in a lot of pain.

He shivered, thinking of Claude Ryan. If Will Jarvis was right, Claude would kill as many people as it took to get to him.

Back inside the cave, the fire had burned down to coals. He covered Reggie with his coat, then went to sit in the shadows at the cave entrance to wait. They would ride out at first light, going down a way that Claude would least expect—straight down to the county road.

A DARK SHADOW moved over her. Startled, Regina jerked back.

"It's just me," McCall whispered. "Sorry to scare you."

She blinked, trying to wake up, the dream still with her, a dark weight that pulled at her. "I was having this horrible dream...."

"It was just a dream," he said and sat down across from her, the fire between them.

She sat up, letting herself drift as she stared into the flames of the fire and soaked up the heat. She could tell it was the middle of the night, still dark outside.

"Wishing you had just gone with a model?"

She looked up at him over the top of the fire and shook her head.

He chuckled softly. "You still haven't given up."

"Have you given up getting back to the ranch, getting away from this madman?"

He shook his head, licked his thumb and reached across the fire to wipe a smudge of dirt from her cheek.

She froze, her gaze locking with his. He seemed to hold his breath. The fire popped softly. He drew back his hand to rest it on his thigh.

She reached out to touch his fingers. Her hand was cool on his but it sent a shaft of heat through him.

He shook his head. "You don't want to do this, Reggie."

She smiled a little at that. "I'm a big girl, McCall. I know what I want." Tears shone in her eyes. "Hold me?"

He moved around the fire to her. She melted into his arms. The flames flared, sparks rising into the darkness of the cave.

She felt soft and warm and he wanted to envelop himself in her, to feel the pounding of her pulse, to hear the drum of her heart, to assure himself that she was alive. That he was alive as well.

He tried to think of tomorrow, how they would both feel if he did the one thing he wanted, make love to her. But right now it didn't feel as if there would be a tomorrow. There was only now. The two of them in this cave. A crazy homicidal maniac or two out in the darkness.

Her kiss was soft, a gentle kiss, tentative, questioning.

His answering kiss was fire and heat, all consuming. She had known that it would be all or nothing with him. Like the first kiss, McCall didn't do anything halfway. He wrapped her in his arms, in his kiss.

Her pulse jumped at his gentle touch, his big hands stroking her body until she was the fire, burning hot inside the cave. His mouth moved over her, warm and wet, sparking fissures of pleasure, stripping her bare beneath her clothing until he possessed every inch of her body.

Wrapped in his arms, he took her as she cried out in pleasure and release, her body pressed hot against his damp flesh, his mouth stealing her cries as the fire flamed, shadows flickering on the cave walls.

"IT'S TIME."

Regina opened her eyes. He still held her, his face inches from her own, their bodies melded together, clothes pushed aside, sleeping bare skin to bare skin.

She didn't want to move. Didn't want to leave this cave. Or his arms. But she feared they couldn't stay here for long. Just as she feared what waited for them outside.

He moved away from her, getting up to dress. Cold air skittered over her exposed flesh. She could feel his eyes on her as she sat up and covered herself.

When she read his expression, she saw that he wanted to make love to her again almost as badly as she wanted him to. But faint light bled into the cave. They had to leave, had to try to get to the ranch. She tried not to think about all the miles. Or the darkness of the trees. The shadows that could be death.

She rose and stumbled ahead of him to the cave entrance, her ankle aching along with the rest of her muscles. She clung to their lovemaking, to the memory of McCall's gentle hands, and tried not to look into the shadows as she stepped outside.

A slice of moon still hung in the dark sky high over the valley, a few stars, a shimmer of light low on the horizon the only hint of the coming day.

Regina shivered in spite of herself. The horses were saddled. McCall must have slipped away to do that, then returned to lie next to her. She couldn't remember ever being this tired. Her whole body ached and she felt cold all the way to her bones.

Just the thought of getting back in the saddle made her want to cry. He helped her up onto the horse as if sensing her resistance.

He walked the horses down the mountainside. She had to lean way back to keep from going over the horse's head, the terrain was so steep. Finally they reached flatter ground and he stepped into his saddle, motioning for her to keep quiet.

She nodded. It wasn't like she had anything to say this time of the day anyway. It was too late to be out on the town, even in L.A., and too early to be getting up. She would have been sleeping in her warm bed, worrying about work, not worrying about dying.

The dream she'd had earlier in the night came back to her. She could feel it around her, hanging over her like a dense awful shroud. She couldn't remember a lot of it, just that horrible feeling of being grabbed by the man. She never even saw his face. He'd come at her from behind, covering her mouth, then her eyes, then binding her so she couldn't move, couldn't scream.

She shuddered at the memory and let the horse lull her, drifting in and out of sleep, her mind like thick fog.

Regina heard the sound first, a noise off to her right. She opened her eyes, startled as she caught movement coming at her from the side.

The man came out of a thick stand of pines, running low, reaching for her, one bloody hand outstretched, the other clutching a knife. The blade glistened in the dull light of the day where the blood hadn't completely dried.

She screamed and tried to get off the horse, but her boot was stuck in the stirrup. Riding in front of her, McCall spun his horse around and was already leaping down as the man grabbed her calf with his free hand.

McCall lunged at the man, knocking him to the ground with the butt of the rifle.

Regina's horse reared and suddenly she was falling through the air. She landed on the ground hard, all the air knocked from her lungs.

When she looked up she saw McCall standing over Will Jarvis, the rifle pointed at the man's head.

"Are you all right?" McCall cried, moving to her side, while keeping the rifle aimed at Jarvis.

She could only nod.

"Can you move?"

She nodded again. But she didn't want to move. She wanted to lie there. She promised herself she would never get back on a horse.

"Help me," Jarvis whispered.

She could see the blood across the front of his coat, on his hands and the knife, and realized it was his blood he had all over him.

He released the knife, dropping it as his fingers opened and his eyes closed.

She heard another noise. McCall turned to listen. It sounded like a vehicle coming slowly up the mountain. As she turned her head, she thought she saw what looked like a dirt track down the hillside through the trees. A road?

J.T. motioned her to silence as a truck came around a bend in the road below them.

She saw the Sundown Ranch logo on the side and began to cry. There was no way the driver would be able to see them up here on the hillside. He would drive right past.

McCall raised the rifle, the barrel pointed to the sky and fired three shots. They boomed in the morning air.

The driver of the truck hit his brakes. Dust boiled up. McCall fired another three shots and the driver was out of the car, looking up the hillside.

Regina closed her eyes, tears spilling down her cheeks. When she opened them, two men with blond hair and blue eyes were looking at her in something close to disbelief. One of the brothers, the one J.T. was calling Cash, had on a sheriff's uniform.

Vaguely she remembered McCall lifting her from the ground, touching her forehead, his palm ice-cold and him saying, "My God, she's burning up."

He'd carried her down to the truck. She remembered leaning against him, her face buried in his chest, his arm around her, shivering, trying to say something but her lips felt so dry and her mind so filled with fog.... She thought she recalled McCall's lips against her hair whispering, "You're going to be all right, Reggie" as the truck bumped down the mountainside.

Chapter Fourteen

"Who is this woman, James Thomas?" Shelby McCall
demanded of her son as she drew him aside into the
empty den and motioned for him to take a seat.

J.T. was too tired to argue. He sat and scrubbed a
hand over his face. He hadn't slept last night, instead
spending the hours beside Reggie's bed after the doctor had left. "It's a long story."

He was anxious to hear from Cash, to find out if
they'd found Claude Ryan. If Claude really was alive.

After the pickup ride down the mountain with J.T.
and Reggie, FBI agent Will Jarvis had been taken to
the hospital where he had been flown to Billings for
immediate surgery. The last time J.T. had checked, he
was still in surgery for knife wounds.

But before Cash had got him out by helicopter from
the ranch, Jarvis had said he'd wounded Claude badly
and that they should look for his body on the mountain.

Unfortunately, Claude had also wounded the agent.
Will Jarvis was lucky to be alive. If he hadn't headed for
the county road and stumbled across J.T. and Reggie...

"James Thomas?" His mother had her arms folded
in front of her, waiting for his answer as if she had all
the time in the world. She did.

"I'd rather hear about what's going on with you and the old man," he said. He'd seen his mother and father with their heads together earlier, then Asa had left, taking Brandon and Dusty with him to try to find the missing cattle.

Cash had gotten a call from a bow hunter who'd seen a bunch of cattle with the Sundown Ranch brand on national forest land in the Bighorns south of the cow camp.

"Looks like your killer wasn't after the cattle," Cash had said before leaving with the state investigators.

"You and the old man seemed to be arguing about something," J.T. said, watching his mother. She had never told any of them why she'd come back here after pretending to be dead for so long.

She gave him a look that only a mother can pull off even though she hadn't been in their lives for over thirty years. "Don't call your father 'the old man.'" Were those tears in her eyes? She really did seem to love the old man. "About this woman…"

J.T. shook his head, raked a hand through his hair and sighed. "I met her on the highway. She had a flat. I fixed it. She works for a blue jeans company and she was in Montana looking for a cowboy to do a commercial." He glanced at his mother. She was still waiting. "Reggie got the idea that I was that cowboy. I told her I wasn't interested but as determined and foolhardy as she is, she conned Buck into giving her a job as our camp cook."

Shelby lifted a brow.

J.T. nodded. "You know the rest of it, at least as much as I do." He'd barely reached the ranch when the call had come in from a neighboring rancher that they'd found Buck and taken him to the hospital. He had a mild concussion and some abrasions, couldn't remember what had happened to him. He thought he'd been bucked from his horse. But he was doing well and was expected to be released by the end of the week.

J.T. wanted to go see him, but couldn't leave Reggie. Nor could he leave the ranch until he heard from Cash.

"This Reggie sounds like quite the woman," his mother commented.

J.T. smiled. "She is something, all right."

Shelby was eyeing him intently. He still couldn't call her mother. "You obviously care about her."

"I'm just worried that she's going to be all right," he said, wanting this conversation over. The doctor had said Reggie needed bed rest. She was suffering from exhaustion and a low-grade infection from a cut on her leg.

He'd noticed the cut on her calf last night when they'd made love in the cave. She'd said she didn't remember when she'd gotten it. The past few days had been so crazy....

"It's all my fault," he said.

"Oh, stop looking so down in the mouth," his mother said. "She's going to be fine. She can stay here as long as she needs to. But what about this commercial?"

"I refused to do it."

Shelby gave him that mother look again, making him think of all the years he'd been spared it.

He got to his feet. "I need to go check on her."

"No, let me." She rose, daring him to argue. "Get that old wheelchair out of the barn. We don't want her walking on that ankle once she's up and around."

He nodded, anxious for Cash to return with news. He hoped that herd in the Bighorns really was the Sundown Ranch's missing cattle. But this wouldn't be over until

Claude Ryan was found. If it really was Claude who FBI agent Will Jarvis had wounded on the mountain.

"I think you should do the commercial," his mother said, her look speaking volumes. She thought he owed Reggie. He thought so, too. But it was more complicated than a simple debt, he thought, remembering their love-making in the cave.

As he headed for the barn, he saw the sheriff's four-wheel-drive SUV coming up the road. He walked out to meet his brother, afraid to hear what Cash had found up on the mountainside.

REGINA WOKE TO sunshine streaming in the window. She blinked, afraid she was only dreaming. She was lying in a nice soft bed with warm covers over her. Her hair beside her head on the pillow smelled clean and fresh as the sheets.

She heard a sound at the open doorway and looked up. A beautiful blond woman stood there, her eyes the same color as J.T.'s.

"You're awake," the woman said, coming into the room. "How are you feeling?"

"Better," Regina managed.

The woman sat down on the edge of the bed and smoothed the covers as she smiled at Regina. "I'm Shelby McCall, James Thomas's mother."

James Thomas. She'd wondered what the J.T. stood for. "Regina Holland."

Shelby's smile broadened. "Oh, I've heard all about you."

"Really?" She wondered what J.T. had told her. Her face flushed at the knowing look in the pale blue eyes.

"You must be starved," Shelby said.

Regina's stomach growled on cue. She laughed. "I guess I am."

"Good, there is nothing wrong with a healthy appetite," J.T.'s mother said, her gaze intent on Regina. "I have Cook making you some breakfast. We can visit while you eat."

The phone rang. Shelby McCall picked it up. She was beautiful. Regina could see where J.T. got his looks.

"It's for you," Shelby said, her look saying, *It's a man.*

Regina didn't reach for the phone. "No one knows I'm here."

"He says his name is Anthony Grand?" Shelby said.

Anthony. Regina had completely forgotten about him, about the jeans company, the commercial, her life in Los Angeles. How was that possible?

She felt completely off-kilter. After everything that had happened, all the things that had been a matter of life or death in Los Angeles seemed silly. She really had been in a life-and-death situation.

But she knew that wasn't what had changed her priorities. It was J. T. McCall.

She took the phone. "Anthony?" She saw Shelby lift a brow and motion that she would leave. Regina nodded and smiled and waited until she disappeared before saying, "How did you find me?"

"It wasn't easy. I heard the most amazing story about you being a cow camp cook and then almost getting killed by some homicidal maniac?"

"A lot has happened," she agreed. "I got thrown from a horse."

"Oh, darling, what in heaven's name were you doing on such a beast?"

"It's a long story, but I'm fine. I just have to stay off

my sprained ankle for a while." She heard a squeak in the hall.

"A while? Sweetie, you haven't got a while. We need to go into production ASAP. You have the contract, right?"

She took a breath, glancing toward the doorway. J.T. was framed in it. "I'm going to have to get back to you."

"I don't like what I hear in your voice. Your cowboy did sign the contract, right?"

"I'll call you later." She hung up before he could pressure her for more details. "A friend," she said to McCall.

He nodded, looking more than skeptical that it was a "girl" friend. He rolled an antique wheelchair into the room. "The doctor said you were not to walk on your ankle. Is everything all right?" McCall asked.

"Fine." She gave him a smile but she could see he wasn't buying it.

"How are you feeling?"

"Better."

He pushed the wheelchair over by her bed. "You want to have breakfast in bed?"

"Would you mind if I tried the chair?" She wanted to see the house. She felt like an invalid lying in the bed and she had so much she wanted to ask McCall. "So the J.T. stands for James Thomas?" Regina asked, smiling at him after he slipped his arms under her and lifted her effortlessly into the wheelchair.

"I'm named after my mother's grandfather."

She looked down and saw that she was wearing a beautiful cotton nightgown.

"My sister Dusty lent you a few clothes until I can go to town for some," McCall said, seeing her surprise. "The two of you are about the same size fortunately."

Regina vaguely remembered being in a bathtub filled with warm water and lots of bubbles and McCall washing her hair. The memory swept over her like the warm water and McCall's soapy hands. She felt her cheeks heat. "Thank you."

He snorted. "For what?"

She touched her hair and met his gaze. "Everything."

He looked away. "I almost got you killed."

"You heard something from your brother about what happened back on the mountain," she said.

J.T. nodded and told her everything that Cash had told him. "It looks like Claude Ryan is dead. They found another body not far from where FBI agent Will Jarvis said he wounded the man who attacked him, the man he said was Claude Ryan. It was Roy. Roy Shields. He was dead."

She looked surprised. "Roy. The quiet cowboy who never said two words. And you're sure Will Jarvis is an FBI agent?"

"Cash called. Agent Will Jarvis has been working with the Mexican government on the killings of the plastic surgeons and the possible connection to Claude Ryan," he said.

She seemed to breathe a sigh of relief. "What about the others?"

He shook his head. "They found the bodies of Slim Walker, Luke Adams and Nevada Black. Cotton's body was found part way down the mountain. He'd been shot in the back of the head."

Her eyes filled with tears.

He covered her hand, still feeling sick. "It's over. Claude Ryan is dead. He won't be hurting anyone else."

She nodded and turned his hand, pressing it to her lips. He could feel her breath against his palm, warm and moist, and he thanked God that she was alive and safe. He didn't know what he would have done if Claude had gotten her.

She looked up into his eyes and he felt desire spark and begin to burn through him. Desire and something deeper, something that made him ache to take her in his arms.

"I've decided to do your commercial."

She looked so surprised, he wanted to laugh.

She shook her head. "No, you don't have to do that. I don't want you doing it because—"

"I'm not." He wasn't sure what she'd been about to say. He didn't want her thinking he was doing this because of what they'd shared in the cave. "Make the arrangements. The sooner the better."

He just wanted to get it over with. He didn't want to delve into his reasons for agreeing after swearing that nothing could change his mind. He'd been wrong about that, wrong about a lot of things.

"This isn't the way I wanted it," she said, and he thought she might cry.

"I thought you would take it any way you got it," he said, unable to hide his surprise. "You said it meant *everything* to you."

She shook her head and said nothing. He wheeled her down the hallway to the kitchen where his mother was waiting. She waved him away, saying she and Regina were going to get acquainted. He hated to think.

But as he looked out the window, he saw almost six hundred head of cattle coming across the valley toward the ranch. "I'm going to go help bring in the cattle," he said.

Neither woman seemed to notice.

As he left, he told himself he'd made the right decision about the commercial. A few years of grief over his backside was nothing. He couldn't let Reggie lose everything. He felt responsible, no matter what he said.

He tried not to think past that because he knew once the commercial was over and Reggie's ankle was healed, she'd probably be eager to get back to Los Angeles and her life there.

And that was just what he wanted too, he told himself as he went out to saddle his horse and go meet the herd.

SHELBY QUIZZED REGINA over a breakfast of steak, eggs, biscuits with butter and honey, fresh fruit and juice.

Regina was surprised how hungry she was. A woman who'd never eaten breakfast in her life and she was eating like a truck driver.

"You really need to tell him," Shelby said when Regina had finished eating.

Regina looked up in surprise. "Tell who what?"

"My son James Thomas," she said. "You need to tell him how you feel about him."

Regina opened her mouth, closed it and opened it again. "I… I don't think that's a good idea. He already feels guilty enough about everything that's happened."

Shelby just smiled sadly. "He might be a little confused right now. He *is* a man. They're easily confused. He's doing the commercial, isn't he?"

Regina nodded, a little confused herself. What was it his mother thought she should tell him?

Shelby looked thoughtful for a moment. "Maybe it would be better to wait. At least until after the commercial." She got up. "Let me take you back to your room. You look as if you might fall asleep right there in that chair."

After Shelby helped her back into bed, Regina picked up the phone and dialed Anthony's number at Way Out West Jeans. "It's me."

"You don't sound good, sweetie."

"The commercial is a go. Get everyone up here."

"Your cowboy agreed to do it? Oh I knew you could pull this off." She wanted to tell him not to call McCall her cowboy. "Sweetie, why aren't you jumping up and down for joy? You did it!"

Yes, she thought. She'd done it. Unfortunately, it was a hollow victory. Her driving ambitions had changed over the past few days. Changed since she'd met J. T. McCall. But she wasn't about to tell Anthony that any more than she was McCall himself. She knew how he felt about city girls. Especially this city girl.

He'd only agreed to the commercial because he felt responsible for what had happened at the cow camp and the cave and he wanted to get rid of her. By the time the commercial was shot, her ankle would be strong enough for her to leave.

"I can have the crew there within days," Anthony was saying. "This is such great news for everyone here. You're going to pull this off, darling, so be happy."

"Yes," she said, finding herself close to tears. She'd forgotten that she wasn't the only one who was counting on this commercial's success. She had everyone at the jeans company to consider. She was doing the right thing. So why didn't it feel like it?

Because she knew the only reason McCall was doing the commercial was because he felt like he was to blame for everything that had happened.

She hung up, feeling miserable.

Chapter Fifteen

Regina watched the filming from the bedroom window. Since she couldn't see it from the wheelchair, she stood, hiding at the edge of the drapes, not wanting to be seen.

She knew McCall must be hating every moment of it. She had been getting better every day and knew there was nothing to keep her here after today. The commercial shoot would be over, the crew would leave and she would have no choice but to go back to Los Angeles.

The problem was she didn't want to leave. She'd fallen in love with McCall. She wasn't sure when it had happened exactly but the thought of leaving here, of never seeing him again, broke her heart.

She'd also fallen in love with his family. Crusty old Asa was a sweetheart under that rough exterior. He reminded her of Buck but more cantankerous. Buck was out of the hospital and convalescing in the other guest room. Shelby was an amazing woman, very perceptive and loving.

Regina had come to know eighteen-year-old Dusty McCall. Dusty had been reserved at first but now came up to talk about boys with her. Regina smiled at the memory of their "talks."

Rourke was still on his honeymoon, but she felt as if she knew him from everything she'd heard about him.

Brandon was quiet around her, almost shy. Something was going on with him. He'd been sneaking out at night and meeting some woman. At least that was the family scuttlebutt. Everyone wanted to know who Brandon's secret woman was, but he wasn't talking.

She'd only seen Cash a few times. He seemed the most serious of the McCalls. Dusty had filled her in on Cash's lost love from college. Jasmine Wolfe had been on her way to Antelope Flats to meet his parents so the two could announce their engagement. But Jasmine never made it. She disappeared and was never found. Brokenhearted, Cash had stayed single all these years, pining away for her.

The McCalls were full of stories. The only McCall she hadn't seen much of was J.T. He seemed to be keeping his distance making it clear he just wanted the jeans commercial over with so the ranch could get back to normal.

Tears burned her eyes. She brushed at them, angry with herself. She'd never been a woman who cried at the drop of a hat. Until recently. She blamed the horror of what she'd been through, but knew it had more to do with her feelings for McCall. The dire situation at Way Out West Jeans. Her conflict of interests.

Through the window, she watched the film crew set up the next shot, the director signaling J.T. to ride through the scene. She hated the way the commercial romanticized his life, almost devaluing the man and his rugged, hard-earned lifestyle, which she had come to admire.

"It's just a commercial," she said to herself in the empty room. But it wasn't. This commercial would make millions of dollars for Way Out West Jeans. Hadn't that been the plan? It would launch the line, take the company national—public—and change her life.

She just hadn't figured on it changing her life this much. The contrast between her world and McCall's was so extreme...and suddenly she didn't feel like she belonged in either. She'd changed and in ways she couldn't even comprehend yet.

She looked out across the land and felt an ache for all this space—and for that man down there on the horse. She didn't want to leave this ranch—or McCall.

J.T. COULDN'T BELIEVE Reggie had gone to all this trouble for a stupid television commercial. It wasn't bad enough that she'd almost gotten herself killed, she'd turned his ranch into a circus.

This commercial didn't reflect his life in the least. She could have gotten herself some L.A. model and saved herself a lot of money, time and trouble. Not to mention save him a lot of grief.

He knew why he was in such a bad mood. This was the last shoot. Then it was over. The commercial and Reggie. He wondered how long she'd stay once the commercial was shot. She was probably packing at this moment. He swore at the thought.

As he rode across the set, he told himself that this was how Reggie saw him and his lifestyle. As a fantasy western life straight out of the movies. She didn't want the reality in her commercial any more than she wanted it in her life.

He swore under his breath as he heard the director yell, "Cut! Let's try that one more time."

J.T. trotted back to the man. Anthony Grant. Reggie's friend. He seemed like a nice enough man but after fourteen "takes," J.T. had had it.

He rode up to him and leaned down so only Anthony

could hear. "I think you meant to say, 'That's a wrap,'"
J.T. said, meeting the man's gaze.

Anthony squirmed under J.T.'s intent stare. "Yes,"
he said. "I see your point. I think that last one was perfect." He raised his voice. "That's a wrap."

"Thank you." J.T. rode toward the barn. He couldn't
wait to get these clothes off, couldn't wait to get these
people off the ranch, couldn't wait for things to get
back to normal.

Normal meant Reggie leaving, he reminded himself.
He couldn't believe the way his family had taken to
her. But then she could be quite adorable. The thought
made him ache.

He'd done his level best to keep her at a distance. At
night though, he would weaken and think about going to
her, holding her, making love to her, begging her not to go.

And that is exactly why he hadn't gone to her.

She couldn't stay even if she had wanted to. It was
perfectly clear how much all of this meant to her. He'd
seen how responsible she felt for the crew and knew she
was banking on this commercial selling a lot of jeans.
And that was her life. L.A. and blue jeans. Not the Sundown Ranch and cows.

He swung off his horse and kicked at a dirt clod,
angry with himself for letting the woman get to him.
Well, she had what she wanted. There wouldn't be anything keeping her on the ranch now that the commercial
was done. Her career meant everything to her. Everything, she'd said.

Even if she'd had a change of heart—which she
hadn't or she wouldn't have let him do the commercial—
she would never fit in here on the ranch. The woman
couldn't cook anything but pancakes! And he had no

intentions of living in the main ranch house with a hired cook and housekeeper. He'd always wanted to build a place a few miles from here. There was a perfect spot in the foothills.

But he wanted it to be just the two of them. Until the kids came along. Although, knowing Reggie she could get the hang of being a ranchwoman—if she set her mind to it.

He shook himself, amazed where his mind had taken him. But damned if for a moment he hadn't imagined that log house with Reggie and a houseful of little Mc-Calls running around in cowboy boots.

"Damn," he said under his breath. The last thing he wanted was for Reggie to go back to L.A. and that scared the hell out of him.

He thought of his own parents. All those years apart because as much chemistry as they'd had between them, they couldn't live together.

He realized that could be him and Reggie.

J.T. looked up and saw Cash driving up in his patrol car. He'd already had Brandon giving him a hard time, saying things like "nice duds" and "nice ass." He didn't need Cash getting his two cents in. J.T. was just thankful that Rourke wasn't around. That would be the last straw.

He'd managed to keep the filming of the commercial quiet. He'd take the storm once the commercial hit national television.

Cash got out, glanced at the fake western set, and shook his head.

"Don't ask," J.T. said. "What are you doing here?"

"You agreed to do the commercial?" Cash sounded more than a little surprised as he glanced from J.T. to the set, looking as if he'd suddenly been dropped into Hollywood. His speculative gaze came back to his brother. "I don't believe it. Why would you do that?"

"Don't read anything into it," J.T. snapped. "She was going to lose her job. She almost got killed up at the line shack. I owed her."

"Uh-huh," Cash said nodding.

"What?" J.T. demanded, scowling at his brother.

"I ran a check on her." He held up his hands and stepped back as if he thought J.T. would take a swing at him. "I ran a check on everyone at that line shack. It's my job, J.T. She wasn't about to lose her job. She *owns* the company."

He could only stare at Cash. Reggie owned Way Out West Jeans?

"But that's not what I came out to talk to you about," Cash said. "Can we talk in the barn for a minute?"

J.T. didn't like the sound of this. He followed his brother over to the barn, still trying to digest what Cash had told him. How was it possible that Reggie owned the company? She'd made it sound as if her career was riding on this commercial. Was it possible the woman had conned him? He almost laughed.

Reggie had won. He'd done the commercial. She must be gloating in her room at the back of the house. His mother had given her the first-floor guest room so she could get around in the wheelchair until her ankle was better. There was no doubt that she'd played on the sympathy of his family—and him as well. She knew he felt responsible for everything that had happened to her.

Well now that the commercial was in the can, her ankle would be miraculously better and she'd be on the next plane to L.A.

"I have some bad news," Cash said without preamble once inside the barn. "We just got a positive ID on the man you called Roy Shields. His real name is Roy Sanders. He's with the FBI."

J.T. felt all the air rush out of him, knowing what was coming.

"Roy Sanders was working on a case with Mexico involving the deaths of three plastic surgeons."

"If Roy was the FBI agent, then Will Jarvis—"

"An FBI agent by the name of Will Jarvis was also on the case," Cash said. "I got a photo of Will Jarvis the FBI agent faxed to me. No resemblance to the wounded man you knew as Jarvis. Sheridan, Wyoming, had Claude Ryan's DNA from a rape charge when he was about nineteen. The hospital had a blood sample of the man who called himself Will Jarvis. The DNA samples matched. The man you know as Will Jarvis is really Claude Ryan."

J.T. knew what was coming. "He isn't in the hospital in Billings anymore, is he."

Cash shook his head. "He survived surgery and had been moved to a private room to recover. After I got the news about Roy, I had the DNA samples checked and sent police to the hospital to detain Claude Ryan, but he was gone. The others found one of the doctors dead in the hospital room closet, naked. Claude had stolen the man's clothing. The doctor's car is also missing."

J.T. thought about the talk he'd had with Will Jarvis around his campfire. He hadn't been waiting for Claude Ryan to come to kill him. He'd been waiting for the FBI agent Roy Sanders. Claude had just been playing with him. He could have killed him then. So why didn't he?

"When we went back up to the line shack nine years

ago, we found drag marks and grizzly tracks. We also found boot prints but with everyone tromping around up there searching... We'd been so sure the grizzly had gotten him," Cash said.

"He had help getting away," J.T. replied, the pieces starting to fall together as he thought about what Will Jarvis had said about the burn scars on Slim's hands. J.T. remembered the fear he'd seen in Slim's eyes. Slim had known that one of the men in camp was Claude Ryan. But like J.T., he wouldn't have recognized the man's face because of all the plastic surgery Claude had been through. The only people who had seen Claude after the surgeries were the doctors and they were all dead.

J.T. felt his heart take off as he looked toward the ranch house. "Claude is alive." And he wasn't finished. He'd somehow gotten Slim and Luke to the line shack to kill them.

"I have the state police on their way down here to make sure the ranch is safe—"

But J.T. wasn't listening, he was already running toward the ranch house, afraid he was too late.

REGINA HEARD THE bedroom door open behind her. She'd been so intent on her thoughts that she hadn't realized that the shooting of the commercial was over, everyone packing it in. She didn't see J.T. anywhere. Time had run out.

She turned, realizing she couldn't leave here without telling J.T. the truth. She'd fallen in love with him.

But it wasn't J.T. standing in the doorway. She stared at the man, at first too shocked to react. And then it was too late. Before she could scream or move, Will Jarvis grabbed her, pressing the tip of the knife blade into her side, the blade biting through her shirt to her skin, his hand covering her mouth as he whispered next to her ear, "Make a sound and I'll kill you."

Her mind raced. This man wasn't an FBI agent. Oh God, he was Claude Ryan. He dragged her out the back door, the same way he'd come in. She'd been given this room because it was on the first floor at the back and had easy wheelchair access.

With all the commotion of the commercial, no one noticed as he dragged her across a small patch of lawn then through the trees toward what appeared to be an old shed.

The lock on the shed door had been broken, she noticed as he pulled her inside and shoved her hard against the wall.

The shed was long and narrow, dark except for a little light sifting in through a small dirty window. It took a moment for her eyes to adjust.

He smiled, looking her over. "I saw the number you did on J.T." He laughed. "You had him where he didn't know if he was coming or going. What the hell was he thinking hiring someone like you to cook at a cow camp?"

"He didn't hire me. Buck did," she said, lifting her chin, determined not to let him see her fear. Men like him fed off fear. She seemed to know that instinctively. Just as she had never trusted him.

He drew back a little in surprise and smiled. "You're a feisty one, you are. I still can't believe you got out of the cabin before it burned to the ground."

She took a breath and tried to calm her pounding pulse as her eyes adjusted to the semidarkness inside the shed and objects began to take shape. An old stool, some garden tools against the far wall, several old wooden buckets, a few old doors leaning against the wall next to her, lots of cobwebs and dust.

She shivered at the thought of spiders and realized how ridiculous that fear was right now. She was in an old shed with a crazy man with a gun and a penchant for killing.

One thing was for certain. She didn't want to die in this shed. Not before she told McCall how she felt about him. A week ago she couldn't have imagined herself in this predicament, not in a thousand years. Not only had she never been in love, but she'd also certainly never been through what she had the past few days.

But because of both, she felt stronger, more capable and she had every reason to want to live. She took in the junk in the shed, decided what would make the best weapon. This man wasn't going to kill her without her putting up a fight.

"You tried to burn me up in the cabin?" Her voice broke, betraying her a little. "Why are you doing this?"

Meanness shone like insanity in his eyes. "You have no idea what it's like to feel your flesh on fire, to feel it melting off your face." He put the gun into his pocket and took out a knife, rotating it back and forth so the blade caught the dim light. He stared at the blade as if hypnotized by the flicker of light and dark. "I have been under the knife so many times I lost count. I knew I couldn't come back until I had a new face, one that showed no sign of the scarring."

"You wanted a new face just so you could get revenge?" she asked, unable to hide her astonishment.

He glared at her as he put the knife away and pulled a length of cord from his pocket, advancing on her. "I survived only to get my revenge. So many times I wanted to die, but then I would think about J. T. McCall, back here on his big ranch."

"What a waste of your life, revenge," she said, almost feeling sorry for the man. She couldn't imagine what demons motivated him, only that he was a tormented man, obsessed with J. T. McCall.

"Shut up," he snapped and moved toward her, just as she knew he would, anger and hate in his eyes. "I am going to set this shed on fire and watch it burn from the hills just beyond here. I will hear your cries when your flesh melts like mine did. J.T. will hear your cries but he won't be able to save you. He won't be able to save himself. I will kill you both slowly. With J.T., an inch at a time, taking from him everything, just as he did me."

He was close enough now. She grabbed the edge of the doors and pushed with all her strength as she dodged to the side. The old heavy doors toppled over, hitting him in the shoulder, making him shriek in pain just before the stack thundered to the shed floor in a cloud of dust.

She ran for the shed door but he was on her before she could reach it. She let out a scream and he slapped her, knocking her to the floor. That's when she saw the gas cans in the corner. New cans and she knew that's how he intended to burn down the shed—with her in it.

"WHAT IS IT?" his mother cried as J.T. ran through the house to the back guest room and threw open the door to Reggie's room. She was gone!

"Have you seen Reggie?" he demanded, not surprised to find his mother and sister behind him. They both shook their heads.

"She was in here packing, planning to leave as soon as the commercial was over," Shelby said, accusingly. "She was upset."

He glanced around the room. Her suitcase was open on the bed, packed, ready to leave. But he'd seen her little red rental sports car on his way into the house. It was parked out front.

"See if she is outside with the crew," he said, glancing toward the back door. "I'm going to check out back. If you find her, keep her with you."

"James Thomas, what is going on?" his mother demanded.

"The killer could have her." And then he was gone out the back door. He hadn't gone but a few feet into the trees when he saw the fresh tracks.

His mother had insisted on an area of lawn behind the house and Asa had had sod put in and a sprinkler system that came on every few hours during the summer.

The grass was wet now from early frost. So was the ground at the edge of the lawn. Boot tracks. And another track where someone had been dragged, heels digging into the wet earth.

He looked up and saw the old shed in the distance and began to run toward it. He hadn't gone far when he heard something heavy crash to the floor and then a scream.

REGINA TRIED TO fight Claude off but he was too strong for her. He held her down while he began to bind her wrists in front of her with the cord.

She kicked and screamed until he hit her again, making her see stars. He bound her ankles, holding her down where she couldn't kick out at him. The shed floor was rough against her back as he pressed her into the wood and dust. She struggled to breathe, the pressure of his body on her heavy and painful. And then he released her.

She futilely fought the cords he'd put around her wrists and ankles, as she heard the splash of liquid against the walls and smelled the gasoline.

J.T. HIT THE shed door, bursting into the shed in time to see Claude Ryan dumping gasoline on the floor of the shed.

Claude stopped when he saw J.T., dropping the can to pull the knife. He smiled. "You're a little early. The party hasn't started." Claude had a lighter in his other hand, his thumb poised over it, ready to flick the flame to life.

J.T. saw Reggie on the floor behind Claude. She was bound, eyes wide in the dim darkness. If Claude ignited the shed from where he stood, he wouldn't be able to get out. But then neither would J.T. be able to get to Reggie in time.

"You do that and you will burn up in this shed," J.T. said, looking at the lighter. He thought about rushing the man but knew Claude would set the shed on fire if he did. "I'm not letting you past me. I'll die first."

Claude Ryan laughed. "You'll die first all right." His expression turned mean. "Do you know how long I've waited for this day, J. T. McCall?" He glanced over his shoulder for just an instant at Reggie. "I have something you want for a change and there is nothing you can do about it."

"You would burn up in this shed to even some score

between us?" J.T. saw the insanity in Claude's gaze, knew this had never really been about him. It was something inside of Claude Ryan, something sick that had only gotten more malignant over the years.

Behind Claude, J.T. saw Reggie. She had pushed herself against the wall and managed to get to her feet. Balancing precariously, ankles and wrists still bound, she worked her way over to the shovels leaning against the wall. Did she hope to cut the cord on the dull blade of the shovel? He knew it was futile. No way was Claude going to give either of them that much time.

"I know you," Claude said smiling again. "You won't be able to live with yourself if you can't save the damsel in distress." He flicked on the lighter. The flame flared, catching a light in Claude Ryan's eyes that chilled J.T. to his soul. Claude tossed the lighter toward the wall he'd just soaked with gasoline.

But only an instant before, Reggie had gripped the shovel handle and throwing her body into it, managed to swing the shovel as she fell.

The shovel blade caught Claude in the center of the back. Off balance and not expecting the attack from behind, Claude was knocked against the wall as the lighter dropped, the flame licking at the gasoline and the air suddenly whooshed in a bright loud boom— Claude right at the center.

Flames leapt on him, setting his clothing on fire in an instant. He shrieked, arms and legs flailing in a dance of horror as his body went up in a blaze.

J.T. dove for Reggie, sweeping her up in his arms and lunging out the door of the shed an instant before it exploded.

Epilogue

J.T. came out of the barn, swearing under his breath as he looked toward the ranch house. Christmas lights blinked through the falling snow. His mother's doing. She had announced that they were going to have an old-fashioned Christmas this year.

He'd caught her crying just this morning as she was wrapping presents.

"I'm just feeling a little sentimental," she'd said when he asked her if something was wrong. "This is my first Christmas with all of you."

He hadn't pointed out that it had been her choice—and his father's. He'd just nodded and left the room, running into Rourke and Cassidy. They'd come back from their honeymoon and had taken over one wing of the house until they could break ground on their place in the spring.

He'd never seen Rourke so content or happy. Even Dusty was getting along better with Shelby, although like the rest of them she wasn't calling her Mother yet. Brandon was obviously still seeing his mystery girl-friend and actually seemed to be enjoying working on the ranch. He was to start law school next fall.

Cash had come out to help their mother decorate

and put up strings and strings of lights. Asa had insisted on getting the Christmas tree, riding up into the hills to bring back a huge tree that was now glittering in the living room.

It was as if his entire family had been transformed into a Christmas special. Everyone seemed to be in good spirits except him.

He still had nightmares about fires. Only this time Claude died in the shed fire. Cash and the state investigators found his body and made a positive identification based on the DNA samples. Claude Ryan was dead. J.T. paid to have him buried at the local cemetery. He'd even bought him a stone that read May He Rest In Peace under his name and dates.

He and Reggie had talked before she left for Los Angeles. She'd admitted that she owned the jeans company. It had been passed down to her by her mother and grandmother, but it was in trouble financially. She had to make one last-ditch attempt to change the company's image. Her mother and grandmother were depending on her.

She'd never wanted the company, never wanted that life to be hers but hadn't known anything different because she'd been raised in the garment industry.

But neither her mother or grandmother had realized the need to change the company's image until it was too late. Both were broke. It had been left up to Reggie to save the company and take care of her mother and grandmother.

She was sure this new commercial promotion would do it. Then she had intended to take the company public, set up a trust fund for her mother and grandmother and finally get a chance to decide what she wanted out of life.

J.T. had listened to how she had to return to Los Angeles to finish what she'd started.

"I want to come back," she'd said. "Back here, that is if…"

He'd been so surprised he hadn't said anything for a moment. And he certainly hadn't said what was in his heart. He believed that once she got back to Los Angeles, she would never want to return to Montana. Not to a ranch in the middle of nowhere. Not to this life. Once she'd gotten the jeans company back on its feet and sold it, she'd have enough money to do whatever she wanted. He couldn't imagine she would want Montana ranch life or him.

"You know you're always welcome here," he'd said.

She nodded, biting down on her lower lip, tears in her eyes. "I'm sorry I didn't tell you everything from the beginning."

"It wouldn't have made any difference," he said. The commercial had come out. He was now known as Hollywood McCall in town. It hadn't been as bad as he'd thought it would be. He tried not to catch the commercial when it came on TV. It only reminded him of Reggie. He just hoped the promotion turned her jeans company around and that she was happy.

As he walked through the snowstorm toward the house, he realized he would do the commercial over in a heartbeat just to have Reggie back here. His whole family had missed her after she'd left but not half as much as he did.

Hell, he'd fallen for her against every ounce of common sense he'd ever had. And his heart broke to think that he would probably never see her again.

As he neared the house, he heard laughter over the sound of Christmas music and started to turn around and go back to the barn. He had no Christmas spirit this year, wasn't sure he would ever again.

"McCall?"

He looked up at the sound of her voice, caught half-turning back toward the barn.

She was standing at the end of the porch, her dark hair floating around her shoulders. She had on a sheep-skin coat, jeans and boots and she looked so right standing next to the ranch house that his heart just stopped.

"Reggie?" He thought he must be seeing things.

"I told you I'd be back." The snow fell around her as she stepped off the porch and came toward him. "The commercial promotion worked. I don't have to worry about my mother and grandmother anymore. I'm free."

He just stared at her. Was she saying what he hoped she was?

"I love you, James Thomas McCall. I had to come back and tell you."

"Reggie." His voice broke and his feet were moving and she was smiling at him, crying, running toward him now. He threw his arms around her. Nothing had felt more right than holding her.

Snowflakes drifted down around them. She snuggled against him. "Merry Christmas, McCall."

He pulled back to look down into her face. "Oh Reggie, I love *you*. Merry Christmas." He kissed her, lifting her into his arms. He would have carried her away but the Christmas music seemed to grow louder and when he raised his lips from hers, he saw his entire family on the porch. They began to applaud.

And he realized how much he loved them and needed them. This was going to be the best Christmas he'd ever had. But it was only the first of many. He put his arm around Reggie and they walked back toward the ranch house and his family.

* * * * *

HARLEQUIN
PLUS

Try the best multimedia
subscription service for romance
readers like you!

Read, Watch and Play.

Experience the easiest way to get
the romance content you crave.

Start your **FREE TRIAL** at
<u>www.harlequinplus.com/freetrial</u>.